THE LACE WEAVER

By Lauren Chater

The Lace Weaver

The Winter Dress

THE LACE WEAVER

LAUREN CHATER

Allison & Busby Limited
11 Wardour Mews
London W1F 8AN
allisonandbusby.com

First published in Great Britain by Allison & Busby in 2023.

A CIP catalogue record for this book is available from
the British Library.

First Edition

ISBN 978-0-7490-2920-3

Typeset in 10.5/15.5 pt Sabon LTD Pro by
Allison & Busby Ltd

FSC
www.fsc.org
MIX
Paper | Supporting
responsible forestry
FSC® C171272

The paper used for this Allison & Busby publication
has been produced from trees that have been legally sourced
from well-managed and credibly certified forests.

Printed and bound by
CPI Group (UK) Ltd, Croydon, CR0 4YY

For the knitters of Estonia, wherever they are scattered

Each lace shawl begins and ends the same way – with a circle. Just like the stories we tell to keep ourselves warm. Everything is connected with a thread as fine as gossamer, each life affected by what has come before it and what will come after.

Sometimes a shawl is not just a shawl.

It is a voice, a force, a way of remembering. And every shawl we have made is precious, delicate enough to pass through a shining gold wedding ring.

This is our story.

Prologue

Elina
December 1939

THEY SAY ESTONIA HAS FIVE SEASONS.

Bitter winter. Pale spring. Autumn, when the forests are carpeted with mushrooms. Summer, with its blue cloudless skies and rich harvest of fruit. Lastly, my favourite: the thaw. That month of watery deluge when the ice floes break up to flood the land. In those weeks, it is impossible to get from place to place in the forest without a canoe or bog shoes to skim the marsh. The tide makes food scarce. One learns to get by on what exists in the pantry: lingonberry, gooseberry, juniper jam spread on thick slices of *must leib* – the black bread so prized by our people that a loaf, clumsily spilt, must be kissed to restore favour.

The pantry grows barer as the flood levels rise. The damp creeps into everything. And yet, I have always loved it. The isolation. I know that my granddaughter, Kati, feels the same. Forced inside, with the animals penned safely away and the outside chores impossible to complete, there is more time to be spared for the knitting of lacy shawls.

It is almost like winter, when the days are so dark the sun struggles to shine in the sky for an hour or two before fading away; but the thaw has none of winter's cruel bite. Even now, closeted in my daughter's house with the fire burning nearby, my hands are too stiff to take up the needles. The best I can do is hold the wool between arthritic fingers and let the spinning wheel do the work. Spinning wool is all I can be trusted with now, a job given to the infirm or the very old, and since I am both, this seems to be my fate.

The treadle beats softly on the floorboards in time with my heart.

What a pity I will not be here to see the thaw arrive this spring.

'Grandmother?'

I look up. Kati is frowning, brows drawn down over eyes which are the crisp yellow-green of windfall apples. The knitting needles are held loosely in her hands, the wool a thin curtain of lace between them. I find a moment to be satisfied, to be proud, before her expression makes me frown in return.

What were we speaking of?

It's so hard for me to follow a thought, a memory, these days. I'm never certain where it starts or where it will end. It might begin with the National Awakening; with the writer Carl Robert Jacobson and his rival Jakob Hurt, that collector of tales who set out in 1872 to record and preserve Estonia's folk history. I might move on to the expulsion of the Baltic German nobles from their lands in the 1890s and then to the declaration of Estonia's independence in 1918, the war with the Russians that followed, the victory and years of peace since. And of course there is my own history, less solid perhaps, the dates open to interpretation. A childhood in Haapsalu, a little seaside town on Estonia's western coast. Warm days on the promenade sitting knee to knee with Mama, knitting shawls to sell to the tourists who poured in by ship or train beguiled by the promises of the local mud's restorative properties. Folk songs at choir practice. Tales by the fireside.

Dances at the local hall, where I met the man I would marry; the man who would convince me to trade the narrow streets and brightly coloured timber houses of my youth for a farmer's life among apple orchards at the edge of the university city of Tartu.

'You were talking about the War of Independence,' my granddaughter prompts.

'I was?'

'Yes.' A pause while she tucks away wisps of fair hair which have worked their way loose from her plaits. 'And about Grandfather.' Picking up her needles, she shakes them. The yarn is coiled in her lap, starkly white against the dark blue wool of her skirt. I recognise the skirt as a discard from her cousin Etti. Marta has lengthened it by adding a panel at the waist, so the hemline falls to brush Kati's shins. The result is not fashionable. I may not see well, but it's hard to miss the way girls get about in Tartu these days in skirts which barely graze the knees, displaying lengths of calf as smooth as buttermilk, even in winter. I don't fancy Kati minds so much. Hasn't she, after all, tasted the very thing those girls crave; the sweetness of a friendship which has blossomed into love?

I knew at once, of course. She didn't even have to tell me. One look at the flush in her cheeks when she says her sweetheart's name brings memories of my own courtship flooding back. The sweet smell of floor wax mixed with kerosene from oil lamps strung up around the hall. Eduard's palm resting against my back as he guided me through the polka steps.

I let my foot pause upon the treadle. The yarn slackens in my hand. From outside the window comes the rhythmic thump of snow falling from the eaves. I let its meter dictate my words, thinking of my husband's fate. It's a story I've not told often and I wonder at my choosing it. 'He was part of the Tartumaa Partisan Battalion.' I pause. 'He was killed in the Battle of Paju.'

We sit in silence. There is pain in talking about such things, but it will not be long, I suppose, before I join him. The ache in my bones is worse now. At times I find it difficult to move from my bed. On the coldest days, not even the tempting smell of Marta's rye bread can shift me. Of course, I don't complain. Estonian women are not given to moaning about their lot. My own mother was up and scrubbing linen mere hours after I was born; a story she used to tell with a shrug of her broad shoulders, as if such feats of female accomplishment were not worthy of admiration. They were simply facts, as certain as the seasons, as unchanging as the slaughter of sheep in spring or the harvest of hay in June.

Sometimes, it is as if I can already sense my husband; I might turn and find him sitting in his favourite chair, watching me with eyes the deep mirror blue of the Haapsalu tide. At such times, I am seized by questions. Am I ready to let go? My family still needs me. I still have so much to say. Who else will listen to the knowledge I have to pass on? Who else but Kati will care to remember that the finest yarn for knitting can be found on the back of a lamb in the soft depression at the base of the neck, or that the best needles are lilac wood, oiled with sheep's fleece? And what of war? For the past months, there has been restlessness in the town. Rumours fly about like wayward flags snapping in a cold breeze. There are military demonstrations on the Russian border that suggest a time may soon come when the fragile peace in our land will be broken. I have seen the invasion in my dreams a dozen times; heard the rumble of tanks, tasted the gunpowder on the air. How will my family survive, my friends in the knitting circle? It will be as things were before the

War of Independence. Estonian language outlawed. Old tales reinterpreted until they reflect a Russian taste. Who will keep our stories? Who will guard our history until it is safe to tell?

I sense Kati watching me, although she pretends to concentrate on slipping her stitches onto the next row. Her fingers dance around the needles, barely touching the fine yarn. She holds her hands slightly bent, thumbs flat, the way I taught her. In the lace already knitted I see my favourite shape leap out: wolf's paw, a pattern I designed many years ago as a child, long before we moved into this farmhouse nestled among the firs.

Why a wolf?

In Haapsalu, we did not see wolves. The coastal air was too laden with salt for their taste. Such creatures prefer the scent of balsam. It was foxes who came to our doors and windows. Foxes who rummaged in the kitchen peelings for scraps and riled up the chickens, melting away through broken fence palings when we shouted at them from the window.

It was not foxes I dreamt of as a girl, though. It was wolves, travelling fleet-footed through the snow, dancing across the marshes, skirting farmhouses on their way into the deep forest. I've always wanted to see one but it has never occurred. Perhaps I knitted my desire into my work. I wonder if Kati, too, dreams of wolves or if she, in reverse, dreams of the sea. She travelled outside Tartu but once as a child and so can only imagine Haapsalu from my descriptions – the sweeping promenade, the lap of the tide, the narrow streets which all lead down to the sea.

It comes as if I have conjured it; a howl that pervades the room, a lone animal cry from the darkness beyond the window. I'm not surprised. Winter is wolf season. Best check the bolts and count the ewes, my husband would say. Yet I can't help but think that the sound is symbolic, a portent meant for my ears.

Kati begins to rise to her feet, unnerved, but I shush her with a gesture and take up the yarn again. The wool unspools in my hands, the fibres separating briefly before the spindle draws them in, twisting them together in a soft rope. 'When I'm gone,' I tell her, 'I will send you a sign. You will know it's me. I will wear the pelt of a wolf.'

She makes a small noise of disbelief.

'There will be no need to fear,' I continue. 'I will travel alone. Everyone knows a lone wolf is kind.'

'You're dreaming,' she says softly. After a moment, her needles begin to click again. 'You're tired.'

I smile to myself. Let her think she is right.

In my mind, I turn away from my husband's ghost. His face is full of sorrow, and for that I am contrite. He reaches out a hand to touch me, but his fingers find only mist. One day, I tell him, we will be together again. But not now. When he begins to fade, his eyes are last to disappear.

'Grandmother,' I hear Kati say again, but it is as if we are speaking from opposite ends of the forest. The trees form a barrier between us. The air is sharp with sap and silt. My limbs no longer ache. They pound the ground and blood thrums in my veins. Old songs and stories cry out from each twig and leaf. My breath is a plume of white mist.

It would be easy to lose myself in the intoxicating sense of freedom, but I hear Kati's cries drawing me back. A weight settles over me like a mantle of snow. There are shadows up ahead. Horrors nobody else has foreseen.

I have made a promise I intend to keep.

Wolf's Paw

Katarina
June 1941

I saw my wolf again tonight.

She appeared at dusk, a shadow among shadows, slipping down the slopes on spindly legs to the edge of the forest where the trees begin to thin. The dying sun made a golden silhouette of her pointed ears and muscled flanks, her long whiskered snout.

I say 'my' but she no more belongs to me than does the wind that rattles through the ash trees or the soggy fields surrounding our house where people buried their belongings in haste before they fled the Soviet invasion. Tarnished cutlery, a child's soiled leather shoes, a bound journal of spotty, dog-eared photographs. The churned earth spits up their treasures after a heavy rain as if to say, *You see? Nothing stays buried forever.*

In the room behind, Papa tapped his pipe against his hand, a familiar *thwack-thwack.*

Mama clattered the bowls into place on the table, humming a song beneath her breath. The rhythm of it rose and fell: an old folk song about the baking of bread. I knew the words. I longed to hear them. But I knew also that Mama would not sing them aloud.

I pressed my ribs against the sill, searching in the semi-darkness with my hand until I found the hard edge of the planter box on the other side where our herbs were kept, far away from the greedy maws of sheep. The sprigs of dill tickled my palm.

The soup was spluttering on the stove. Sprinkling the herbs over the broth, I let my mind wander to the sheep, already penned in the barn below us, the ewes separated from the ram by a thin timber wall.

Should I warn Papa about the wolf? Some said that to slaughter a wolf was to bring misfortune down upon your herd. There were better ways to deal with such things; smearing birch tar upon the sheep's fleece to mask its scent. Scattering a sacrifice of bones into the forest when the first frosts came. In my great-grandparents' time, perhaps a spell. My grandfather once told me of a wolf that had wandered so far from the forest that he became lost in the village, and my great-grandfather along with the other local men had driven him back, arms raised, calling at him: 'Be gone, old grey streak eye, billygoat of the forest! Go back to the bogs, go rove in forests, scratch the trees, tear at stones.'

Yet none of those men had dared raise his gun at the creature for fear of the bad luck it might bring.

Throwing caution to the wind, I glanced back at the window and the gathering darkness filling the yard.

My wolf was gone.

I breathed again. Despite his reluctance, there was no doubt Papa would be obliged to take up his gun. While other farms were forced to hand over all their goods and livestock to the state when the Soviets first arrived last year, we were, by some fortune, permitted to stay. As long as the sheep were kept safe and the apple trees in our orchards continued to bear fruit, we were allowed to continue living as if our lives were not pieces on a chessboard, able to be scattered at will by the local Partorg, the Communist Party Organiser, whose job it was to ensure that the state's property was in good hands. My father often said that the sheep were our angels and I their guardian.

If I was of good humour – if the weather had been mild, if I found a moment to add some stitches to my shawls and there was the prospect of meat or tender vegetables to line my belly, I would grit my teeth in a smile. But most of the time, I didn't. Each bleat and baa echoing up through the floorboards was a reminder of how the stupid creatures were fed the best of each harvest, while we boiled chicken bones until they were bleached of every marrow scrap. Each snuffle and scrape of their horns, a reminder that they were worth more than we were. The only thing they were good for, the only thing that made me bless their 'angel' heads, was the fleece we sheared from their backs each spring. Sometimes in my dreams I saw blankets of fleece laid out upon the threshing-room floor, ready to be sorted and fed through the spindle to create the yarn we send to factories, after I have saved some for the knitting of shawls. In dreams, there was an endless supply, a bounty; as soon as the wool was spun, more fleece appeared to take its place. Even asleep, I was aware of this blessing. It meant our knitting circle would never falter. It meant my promise to my grandmother would not be broken.

Mama cleared her throat. 'Katarina?'

'What is it?'

'Your sleeve is in the soup.'

I cursed and stepped back from the pot, flicking

droplets of broth onto the floor. Mama sighed and nudged me away. 'Here. Let me serve. You've got your head in the clouds again. What were you thinking of?'

She took the soup pot off the stove, sliding it onto the rough-hewn table that bore the scars of the childhood I shared with my older brother Jakob, who now lived ten miles away at the university dormitories in Tartu. Here was the deep groove where my sewing scissors had slipped. Here were the runes where my pencil had worn through my exercise books and left an impression upon the grain. I ran my finger along a chip in the timber. Literature and history. Subjects for which I would drag myself across snowy fields and the bog marshes to our little parish school, eager to learn more while Jakob dawdled behind, carving symbols into the trees with his knife. That was before everything changed. Before Grandmother passed, before the Russians marched in to seize the lands, before Oskar disappeared. Before Papa put me in charge of minding the sheep, and my dreams of studying stories and folklore at the university were extinguished.

I heard Papa's voice, as clear as if he had spoken, although his pipe was clamped between his lips now and he was staring silently at the soup my mother had set before him. The words I remembered were an exchange between my parents from years ago, overheard one night as I sat up late reading.

'You cannot allow them both to continue their schooling, Erich,' my mother said. 'We can't manage the farm alone.'

The bed squeaked as Papa turned over. 'There'll be workers in June to help.'

A pause. I imagined my mother frowning.

'One of them may go and one of them may stay to help,' he

said. 'We can only afford to send one to the university anyway.'

How naïve I had been to think that one would be me.

The oak table was warm beneath my hand, as if it too could remember a time when life seemed full of potential. I slid into my chair and took a quick slurp of broth, forgetting to cool it first. The spoon clattered to the table as tears stung my eyes. Mama clucked under her tongue and thrust a cup of water before me. I gulped at the cool liquid until the burning in my throat eased.

Mama shook her head. 'Really, Kati. You are nineteen. This daydreaming has to stop.'

She glanced across at my father, who slurped at his soup but did not look up.

'Erich?' my mother prompted. 'Don't you agree?'

'Perhaps,' he said. He set down his spoon. 'Or perhaps it was Kati's polite way of saying that the broth is not very good.'

Mama looked from me to Papa, lost for words. He picked up his spoon again and took a long, lazy slurp.

Finally, she said, 'Well, it would not be so bad, Erich, if I had something other than old chicken bones and rancid turnips to cook with.'

Papa glanced at me and wiggled his thick eyebrows. Suddenly, the whole situation seemed humorous.

'I just so happen to like turnips,' he said. 'But this tastes less like fresh turnips. More like water into which a turnip has been dangled and then snatched away.'

Mama's shoulders relaxed. She smoothed back her hair and adjusted the shawl around her neck which had slipped a little as she moved about serving the food. The snowy white lace made even her threadbare dress, with its faded pattern of roses, seem almost elegant. Although she was thinner than last year, she was still beautiful with high cheekbones and an elegant nose which both Jakob and I had not inherited. We both had the Rebane nose; short and wide, with a sloped tip.

'You are welcome to suggest something better, Erich,' Mama said, her pointed chin lifted.

'Perhaps tomorrow we could have turnip pie,' he said, the corners of his mouth creasing. 'And with it, a turnip salad?'

'And . . . turnip ice cream,' I supplied, my heart lifting.

'Well,' my mother conceded, 'I could do better than turnip soup, if you would only allow me to buy a few of those black-market potatoes.'

'Oh yes!' I said, stirring my spoon round and round through the weak soup, allowing myself to dream, along with my mother. 'Those fat, creamy potatoes . . . or thick, buttery carrots.'

It was the wrong thing to say.

Papa snatched up his spoon again, gripping it in his fist. 'Put it out of your mind, both of you. I've told you; those items are banned. Do you want to go to prison? We can't afford to be arrested.'

Arrested.

The word hung between us.

Below, the ewes bleated, the sound drifting up through the floorboards like laughter. Papa sipped his soup, but his smile was gone.

If Jakob were here, I thought, he would know what to do. He would tell a joke, a slightly inappropriate one that would make my mother exclaim, *Jakob!* and would make Papa's lips curve in a secret, knowing smile. But I am not Jakob. I am Katarina, a girl considered not worth sending to the university to further her studies, a girl who must endure day after day of the same monotonous tasks, shackled to the responsibility of keeping a flock of guileless sheep safe from harm. A girl whose only pleasure comes from knitting and from remembering the stories her grandmother left behind.

Perhaps even Jakob could not make light of the way the Russians terrorised those of us who remained behind when the occupation started. There was nothing funny about the way our leaders had been arrested and parliament dissolved, or the seizing of radio stations so that the Russian occupiers could assure us all our government had been the enemy. There was nothing playful about the way their soldiers commandeered vehicles and houses, throwing Estonians and their children out of their homes and deporting anyone they suspected of holding 'capitalist sympathies'. My grandmother would have wept to see Tartu now; all the lively cafés gone and Estonian businesses boarded up. Patrols of young Russian soldiers roaming the streets in packs, looking for any excuse to refer people to the NKVD Secret Police at the Grey House on Põder Street, the place where one could be tried and shot before their family even noticed they were gone.

This was the reality of our lives now. Everywhere I went and every action which took place outside the privacy of home was accompanied by an undercurrent of fear. Each stranger I spoke to could report me as a spy. Each knock at the door could be an agent with a warrant to search our house. There were no safe places left except the arms of my family and my private thoughts. There was no way of resisting except to stay alive and to fulfil the promise I had made my grandmother; to maintain our culture through the knitting circle, to keep sharing our stories and continue the tradition of making shawls.

I sighed and drained the last of my soup, stomach still tight with hunger, then I stood to help Mama clear away the things.

Papa shifted in his seat. He cleared his throat.

'Katarina . . . I need to speak to you.'

I froze, the empty soup bowl suddenly heavy in my hand. 'It's not . . .' I could not make my lips form my brother's name.

'No,' my father said quickly. 'Jakob is safe.'

Relief was instant. Demonstrations. Deportation. Death. It was hard not to let my mind wander to the worst, especially with Jakob staying away for months on end, avoiding trips home, spending all his time in the dorms with his friends. Mama had threatened to go to town herself but Papa dissuaded her.

'Then who?' I continued.

In my mind, I was flicking through the faces of the people I knew. Which one of them had been punished this time, or worse, had vanished without warning? Not Aunt Juudit, I prayed, thinking of her wide-set green eyes, so like Papa's and my own. Not gentle Etti, her husband taken and killed at the hands of the Soviets while she remained, big with child, unable to push herself off the lounge unassisted. How could she run?

Papa, watching me, summoned up a weary smile. 'Nobody has been hurt, Kati. Yet.'

I wanted to sink into my chair, but I continued to stand. My father had more to say. I could see him measuring the words carefully in his head, thinking of how best to frame them. His pipe was clutched in one hand, the embers turning to ash.

Whatever was coming, it was something he knew I wouldn't want to hear.

'Kati, the Partorg's men were here earlier.'

I forced myself to remain standing. 'What did they want?'

My father scratched at his whiskers. 'I'm afraid there will be no wool for shawls this winter.'

I stared at him. 'No wool?'

'I'm sorry. The Partorg has increased our wool quota for the coming year. The only way we can meet it is to give up the fleece we use for your yarn.'

I blinked. 'No wool,' I repeated. I waited for the words to bring relief with them. Nobody was injured. Instead, an empty, hollow feeling opened up inside me.

No more wool meant no more shawls.

'There must be a mistake.' I glanced across at my mother, willing her to smile, to slap my father on the arm the way she had done earlier in that brief shining moment of camaraderie. But my mother's face was pinched.

'No mistake,' Papa said. 'I wrote the figures down myself.' He reached into his pocket and drew out the small book in which he kept all the details of our farm. The tools, the position of the apple trees, the demarcations that divided our land. He had bought the book last year, when the Soviets first seized power.

'We will not resist,' Papa had warned us. 'We will be model Soviets.'

Now the pages of that little book were black with soil and well thumbed, the green cover creased. My father flicked it open in the middle, holding the pages out for me to see.

I did not lean forward to confirm my loss. I couldn't.

'What about the reserve?' I said, thinking fast, calculating how much wool was needed for one row of stitches, how much yarn could be stretched to piece together a shawl. 'We still have the bales left over from last year.'

My father was shaking his head. 'They already suspect us.' He heaved a sigh. 'They are questioning the sale of your shawls at the flea market. Claiming that what I've been handing over is too little.'

'Ridiculous. We earned that money!' It was hard for me to keep the righteous anger from my voice. Although there was a flea market in almost every village, and they were quite often raided, the Russians had not yet banned the sale of handicrafts, which were considered worthless, therefore less of a threat than foodstuffs and clothing, goods which were controlled and distributed by state-sanctioned factories. The Partorg had allowed us to continue operating our little market stall once a month provided most of the profits were handed over along with Papa's quota of apples for the month. What we made was hardly enough to cover the cost of the wool. It certainly did not cover the time I spent dreaming up designs and the effort we all made to knit the shawls, but money had never been our motivation. When I stood at the stall, my head held high, and watched the Russian professors stop to admire the neat stitches in my shawls, I imagined a tiny bit of power kindling in my chest. When I took their roubles and placed them in the jar below the table, a warm feeling spread through my hand, knowing that we were, in a small way, defying the Russian government's attempts to stamp out our past. I always smiled as I passed over the neatly-wrapped shawl and sent out a little wish as I watched the buyer's departing back, hoping that the shawl would be cherished and admired, perhaps passed down through the family so that its link to Estonia was forever strengthened.

'I know, Kati.' My father sounded weary. 'I know you did. And I was willing to overlook it. But they know us and they know the farm. Every last bit of it, every last blade of grass.' He frowned at the little book. 'Perhaps I should not have been so hasty in writing it all down.'

My mother patted his arm. 'You are the reason we are still here, Erich. Without you, the farm would not have survived. We would not have survived. Kati understands, don't you?' She flicked a warning look at me. 'They are just shawls. Just bits of cloth. Shawls are a luxury these days. Nobody can afford to buy them anyway – or sell them, it seems.'

I stared at her, but my mother shifted her gaze, still patting my father's shoulder in a comforting manner. A slow burning heat spread across my skin. *Just bits of cloth?*

My grandmother had been right. Mama had never loved knitting the way we did. She was born of a generation where freedom cost dearly; her own father and brothers were killed trying to drive out the Red Army and the Baltic Germans during the War of Independence. We were but a tiny country, a stone cast between the Gulf of Finland and the vast landmass of Russia. Even with the aid of our Baltic neighbours, the Latvians and Lithuanians, we did not have enough people to defend our borders from attack. We'd been lucky to defeat the Red Army back in 1920 and, although many would not say so, it was likely that such a victory would never have taken place if the rest of Europe had not been preoccupied with their own struggles. At the mercy now of the great Soviet powers, how could Estonia hope to remain free? All we had was ourselves, our history, our stories of the land. Papa had told us when the Soviets arrived that our survival depended on our compliance. He could remember a time when resistance was met with the end of a bayonet. Better to sign away some of your rights than to lose your life, he had said. Better to stay and try to make it work than to flee to unknown shores, leaving behind your family and your friends, everything you had worked so hard to gain.

I tried to imagine what my life would be like without shawl-making. Sometimes it seemed as if shawl-making was all I had left. It was my lineage, my passion. It anchored me not only to the knitting circle but to my grandmother. Widely acknowledged as a master knitter, she had started the circle when she moved from Haapsalu, gathering women first to our little croft and when that became too small, convincing Aunt Juudit to host the group at her apartment in Tartu. I'd been accompanying her to their gatherings since I was five years old and had successfully knitted my first lace shawl; a miniature version of the pasque-flower design for Maimu, my doll. With endless patience, my grandmother had teased out the latent talents of her friends, restoring confidence when required or providing challenges whenever the knitter seemed ready to move on to a more difficult stitch. Since her passing, I had done my best to live up to the legacy she left behind. I missed her most when I had a question about how she achieved a particular effect in one of her prized lace shawls. How she was able to keep the tension in her yarn as she sewed on the lace *nupps,* the small lacy bobbles that told a buyer that a shawl had been sewn by hand. How she could join two pieces of lace as if they had always been one.

If she had not passed away, she would still be organising the production and sale of the shawls for the knitting circle. Instead, she had appointed me to distribute the yarn for carding and spinning, to assign the various designs to each woman depending on what I thought would sell.

Although it had not been easy to step into her shoes, I knew she would not wish the circle disbanded. How could we give up knitting now, at this crucial point in Estonia's history, when the Soviets wanted to wipe our culture clean as if it never was? Even the usual forms of communications were forbidden now. Radios had been confiscated, type-writers banned. With no way to contact the outside world, the Soviets imagined we had no choice but to comply, that we would forget the glorious freedom of expressing ourselves. I could almost hear her voice, creaky with age, whispering encouragement into my ears. *Every shawl we make will be laced with defiance. Every stitch will carry a message out into the world.*

Now that would be lost too.

Bitterness churned within me. 'We should have gone,' I said, banging the bowls together. 'We should have left here like the others while we still had a chance.'

'Kati!' My mother blinked hard. 'Don't say such things! What about Jakob?'

'You could have called him back.' I glared at her. 'Where has it got us? We have done everything they asked and still, it's not enough. What about Oskar? What happened to him? What happened to Imbi Mägi? To Aime?' My parents were silent, but I noticed my mother's eyes glimmer with sudden moisture. I snatched up Papa's bowl, unwilling to relent, unable to hold back the flood of anger that had grown inside me since the Partorg's men had first set foot on our property. 'This year it's wool. Next year it will be apples.'

I waited for them to argue, but nobody spoke.

'Aunt Juudit will expect me tomorrow.' Disappointment dulled my voice. 'At least let me go and explain to the knitting circle in person.'

My father spread his hands on the table, gripping the edges with his thumbs. 'Fine. But you will go there and tell them and come straight home. No dallying. No sitting around until dusk wagging your tongue.'

'But—'

'Enough!' Papa slammed the book down on the table. 'Kati, I'm not asking for your opinion. I'm telling you the way it is. Do you understand?' His chair screeched as he scraped it back.

Words died in my throat and I lowered my gaze. Somebody, my grandmother perhaps, had dropped something hot on the floorboards some years before and the burn had penetrated the thick hardwood, leaving a charred, black ring to stain the varnish.

'Kati? I am waiting for an answer.'

Although my cheeks burnt, I forced myself to nod.

'Good.'

The wooden floor creaked beneath Papa's feet as he moved away, lurching towards the worn couch where he would sit for the next half-hour, going over the inventory of the farm in his book, before exhaustion overcame him and he retired to the bedroom. I was left facing Mama, who could not meet my eyes. Instead, she grasped the remaining cutlery and turned away, hunching her back against me in disapproval.

Cutlery splashed and sank in the tepid grey suds that

filled the sink. The only other sound came from the wind that sounded against the windows, rattling them in their panes.

Knock, knock.

The sound came again.

Knock, knock, knock.

A knife slipped from my mother's hand and clattered to the floor.

'Stay here.' Papa's voice was sharp. We listened to his feet pound down the stairs, the groan of the barn doors being opened. My heart bumped painfully against my ribs.

Muffled voices echoed in the stairwell below, then silence.

Moments later came the sound of footsteps, slowly ascending the staircase that led into the living space. Mama reached out and squeezed my hand, her palm unsteady.

When at last Papa emerged at the top of the stairs, a thin sheen dampened his pale skin and his eyes were drawn. It was the same look he had worn the night we heard the Soviets arriving, when the sound of tanks and shouts echoed across to us from the main road that ran alongside the farm, when the truth of the rumours flying around Tartu had finally hit home with staggering force.

I closed my hand around Mama's, a child again, seeking a path out of the unending nightmare that was the Soviet occupation. Would it never come?

A figure stepped out from the shadows behind Papa. The golden lamplight streamed over his features so that he seemed to glow at the edges, a figure conjured from a dream. Hope and longing collided in my chest.

Oskar. He was back.

Apple Pattern

'OSKAR MÄGI . . . CAN IT REALLY BE YOU?'

In the living room of our farmhouse, Mama dropped my hand and took a hesitant step forward, her gaze fixed on the visitor before us as if she expected him to disappear the moment she looked away. 'I can't quite believe it.' Her voice was quiet, equal parts fear and joy. 'I feel like I'm staring at a ghost.'

Oskar's face remained impassive but he lifted his chin. '*Ma ei ole kummitus*,' he said, in Estonian: not a ghost.

I heard my mother's indrawn breath and knew that she too felt the fluttery strangeness of hearing our language spoken again. The long Uralic vowels, the rhythm like a song. Hearing it awakened an unexpected longing in me. We had spoken only Russian since the Soviets arrived, even at home; it was safer that way. It was only now I realised how much I had missed it. How bleak and empty the world seemed without the comfort of those familiar sounds.

'It's good to see you, Marta,' he said, still in Estonian. The realisation that he refused to speak Russian made my skin tingle, made the memories flood back.

The light from the oil lamps glinted on his face. Half-hidden behind Mama, I was able to study him.

His face had lengthened, the angled cheekbones more pronounced, although we all looked thinner. He wore a uniform of mushroom brown in a style and texture I had not seen before. It was wool; I could tell from the way the material absorbed the light, muting it so that if he stepped away, into the shadows, he might disappear altogether. His hands were encased in gloves. Crimson yarn, woven through with a pattern of white winter berries.

Somewhere in my body, an invisible, familiar drum began to beat, its steady rhythm pulsing outwards until I could no longer hear the snuffling sheep below us, nor taste the greasy residue of my mother's turnip broth. There was nothing else.

I put out a hand and gripped the back of the nearest chair. The oak beam was solid, but a loose chair leg wobbled beneath the weight and squeaked. The sound made Oskar turn his head.

'Kati.'

Our gazes connected, and a wave of memory caught me up.

Burnt sugar. The mournful lowing of cows waiting to be milked. A band of golden sunlight illuminating the varnished floor. And blood.

I turned away as nausea filled my stomach.

Swallow. Breathe.

Oskar's mouth twisted. He took a step towards me but Papa coughed and he froze.

'The Russians say you killed your mother and sister.' Papa's voice was heavy.

My mother flinched and glanced away. I too, wanted to turn my head, but could not bring myself to do so in case Oskar thought I believed what the Russians said. In the awkward silence that stretched on, I heard again the voices of the soldiers in my mind when they came to see us the day of Imbi and Aime's deaths. The harsh guttural sound of their

31

words. *Murderer. Outlaw. Criminal.* I remembered their faces as they spun us their version of what had happened, telling us that Oskar must have killed his family after arguing with them about resisting the order to hand over all weapons. It was not so surprising, they'd said, considering his socialist sympathies. Some passing soldiers heard what was happening and chased after him, but it was too late; he had already run into the forest so they went back into Tartu to alert their superiors. Those socialists would kill their own grandmothers given half a chance, one soldier had told us. If anyone from town was caught helping him, they would be arrested and tried at once.

All through their speech, I had wrestled with my desire to shout that they were wrong, to defend Oskar's innocence but Papa's hand on my arm was firm and so I kept my own thoughts locked away. But in my heart I was grieving, not just for Imbi and Aime, but for Oskar, too. They had covered up their own crimes by pinning the murders on him. They might as well have shot him.

'I didn't kill them,' Oskar said softly now. His gaze darted to Mama. 'Please, Marta. You must believe me.' Beneath the hard lines in his face, I caught a glimpse of the old Oskar, the one who had played Vikings and built castles with me in the rambling orchard beyond his house and walked me home each day after school. The boy who turned his face away at choir practice so the other children would not see how the music moved him. The boy who had endured the teasing of my brother and his friends without ever raising his fist in retaliation. The boy who always brought his mother the first sprays of wildflowers when they appeared in Spring and gave his sister half his roll at lunchtime to ensure she had enough to eat.

Mama could remember that boy too. Her eyes were wet with tears. She brushed them away. 'Of course we believe you,' she said softly, ignoring Papa's warning look. 'Erich and I discussed it, once the soldiers were gone. Poor Imbi. And little Aime. She was too young.' Her eyes filled again. Averting her face, she scurried to the cabinet and snatched up a mug. Filling it with water, she thrust it into his hand.

'Thank you,' Oskar said. He looked down at the mug, as if surprised by this sudden kindness. 'I heard that you found them, Erich,' he said. 'I'm sorry. I wish I could have done something to spare you the shock.'

Papa shook his head. 'It wasn't me, Oskar,' he said. 'It was Kati.'

Oskar's eyes widened. 'Kati? Is that true?'

I dropped my gaze, afraid to look up and see the suffering this news might cause him. It was hard enough to face the memories I had to endure alone.

It had been spring when I found them, warmer than the one we were now experiencing. The wildflowers had bloomed early. Their spiciness mingled with the green scent of the rain that had left the river swollen and washed the sky a clear, cloudless blue. As I'd trudged the forest track that led between Oskar's house and our own, I had brushed my hands along the edges of the fir trees. Their trunks soared above my head. They had set down their roots long ago, before the first settlers arrived, when Estonia was just a belt of wild forest filled with beasts. That Estonia was the one of Vikings and of the sagas of Iceland, her coasts a harbour to shelter in on the way to hunting waters, her islands stepping stones among the tides. It was the Estonia of men with the strength of ten plough horses and women who foretold their own destiny in dreams.

In the quiet of the forest, it was possible to imagine not much had changed at all.

The scent of fir needles lifted into the air, engulfing me as I walked the track I knew as intimately as the pattern of my grandmother's lace. There was no chance I would linger idly, enjoying the breeze as it wafted through the trees. Oskar was waiting.

I could picture him pacing the small porch that wrapped around the farmhouse, eager to escape his chores, perhaps rubbing his toe against a loose board, eyes searching the track. His mother too would be awaiting my arrival. She'd always been fond of me, but lately she had been nervous. The presence of the Russians in Tartu disturbed everyone. She would grab my arm when I arrived and pull me indoors, her worried expression clearing until her round face was again as smooth as the dough resting in its bowl in the sun.

The dozen apples in my knapsack jostled and bumped against the small of my back. Mama had sent them for Oskar's mother, a gift. In exchange, Imbi would send back the berries that she and her daughter Aime had picked. Thinking of Aime always brought a smile to my face. Although there were six years between us, I'd known her so long I sometimes felt she was my little sister, too. Once during the autumn holidays, Oskar had fallen ill with the measles and Aime had come to stay with us. She shared my bed and risen early to help me prepare breakfast and unpen the sheep. Although she found knitting difficult because of the long hours of sitting, it was a pleasure for her to tramp into the forest to harvest fruit. She delighted in showing me how to peel back the moss to reveal a clutch of fenberries hidden beneath. Imbi had taught her which berries were safe to eat and which must be left behind. Cloudberries, small orbs of shiny copper with a lingering honey flavour, were the most prized, for each plant only grew one stalk.

'You should make a cloudberry shawl,' Aime had once advised, her eyes sparkling as she dropped one of the precious globes into my hand and tucked the rest away in a soft sack for her mother to preserve.

Imbi was the queen of preserves. My mouth was already watering in anticipation of the sweet seeded strawberries she soaked in elderflower wine and served with thick slices of malty brown bread. She was my champion, always encouraging Oskar to invite me over, pressing jars of pickled blueberries into my hands. I had given her a knitted scarf for her last birthday, covered with *vikkel*, travelling stitch, the edges woven through with braided ribbon. I could tell Oskar was pleased, although he would have preferred for us to meet in the wild, overrun orchard beyond the house or in the paddock where they kept a few straggly cows. Imbi was not one to be argued with, though, and she liked my company so the farmhouse was where we spent most of our time, telling stories or helping Aime with her schoolwork while Imbi plied us with small battered cakes she had fried on the griddle and doused in her own special syrup; an assortment of berries steeped in the honey of wild forest bees. It was only in the midst of preserving that Imbi seemed to forget we were there, too busy preparing the sugar-water and instructing Aime on how to steep the fruit to notice the sound of our footsteps and the squeak of the door as Oskar and I slipped into the forest to be alone.

Once there, we could sink down among the mossy tussocks

and watch the clouds race by, imagining how our lives might be, if nothing stood in our way. Although I couldn't go to university, I wondered aloud if I could one day write a book, a collection of all the stories my grandmother had told me. I would still have to mind the sheep, of course, and help my parents with the farmwork, but in my spare time, I would run the knitting circle and perhaps even take trips outside of Estonia to see the world. Oskar would be a carpenter like his father had been before he grew ill and died, leaving Imbi to raise their children alone. Imbi had been forced to sell Oskar's father's tools at the flea market to make ends meet but that did not dampen Oskar's plans to one day rebuild his mother's cottage from the finest oak, with heart-shaped windows and a grand kitchen where Imbi could spend her days preserving without worrying about milking the cows and churning butter until her hands ached. There would be a shelf in the parlour so Aime's dolls could watch over her as she studied and a room with large windows facing the garden which let in plenty of light so I could knit in comfort, without ever having to squint down to check that my stitches were even. It was a dream-house, a fantasy built from years of refinement and the countless hours Oskar and I had spent lying side by side, lost in our thoughts beneath the peace of the clouds.

In all our dreaming, we always spoke of our future as if we intended to live it together. Our pairing felt as natural as the shifting of seasons. My parents, I hoped, would not deny the match. Imbi, I felt sure, would be overjoyed.

A grin spread over my face. A twig snapped beneath my boots, pulling me out of my daydream.

And then I heard the cows.

The sound echoed across the forest, slipping in between

the trees, filling the space and freezing me in my tracks. Their cries were loud, desperate.

I paused at the edge of the clearing that held Oskar's farmhouse. From where I stood, it looked unchanged. The funny crooked windows, the small barn tacked on to the side, the fragrant herb beds nestled against the path that led up to the front door. But then that sound came again, loud and shrill, full of pain. The cows were trapped in their barn. There was nobody to milk them or set them free.

My feet seemed to move of their own accord, propelling me towards the house. My breath came in short, sharp bursts. When I reached the door, it swung open.

I bent my head, listening. I wanted to call out. I wanted to hear anything but those pitiful cries from the barn. But my voice was trapped in my throat.

I stepped inside. Sunlight slanted across the floor, illuminating the dust on the old floorboards, carving up the room into light and shade. I squinted, waiting for my eyes to adjust. That was when the smell reached my nostrils, the cloying scent of burnt sugar. Something had been left bubbling on the stove, now nothing more than a blackened sugar crust.

I moved towards it, intending to lift the pan but as I skirted the table, my boots met something soft. I looked down.

Imbi lay on her back. Her face was frozen, eyes staring up as if she could see through the roof to the sky. Bullets had torn holes in her dress and there was a wound near her forehead. Her arms were flung out in warning or surprise. In contrast, Aime was curled on her side, arms wrapped around her middle. Her eyes were closed, the skin on her eyelids a pale crinkled blue like the crushed fabric of her doll's dress. The sun streaming in caught the rosy highlights of her hair. She might have been sleeping.

I squatted down and reached out my hand to touch her shoulder. It was stiff and unyielding. Understanding struck and I shot to my feet, gagging.

Oskar, where was Oskar?

My face was hot. I forced myself to lurch towards his room. It was empty. Relief was quickly followed by terror. I needed to find him, but I could not do it alone. My hands shook so hard I could barely turn the door handle to fling myself outside.

I stumbled home in a fog of panic.

My father was inspecting fruit in the apple orchard. One look at my face and he ordered me to go into the house and find Mama and wait for him to return. Mama was in the laundry shed behind the house, plunging Papa's soiled shirts into a bucket of grimy water. She looked up in surprise as I ran towards her. The shirt fell from her hands and splashed back into the bucket.

'Kati! We weren't expecting you back till tea time.' She wiped her hands on her apron and came towards me. 'What's wrong?'

I tried to speak. My teeth chattered. Nausea churned from the base of my stomach up to my mouth. The words finally came in gurgles and gasps, like water running from a broken tap. I watched Mama's face grow ashen and then her cold hands wound around me and she held me as if I was a child, smoothing back my hair with fingers which smelt of soap and tea.

'Oskar,' I managed to say. 'Papa must find him!'

We went together into the house and I stood at the window at the back, my gaze fixed on the far paddock where the path which led to Oskar's farmhouse began.

It was less than an hour before Papa returned, but it felt like so much more. Every moment he was gone had shown me Imbi and Aime's bodies on the farmhouse floor interspersed with visions of Oskar lying bleeding somewhere in the forest. Even the warm milk Mama pressed into my hands could not melt the chill that spread through my body. I couldn't imagine my life without him.

At last, I saw Papa emerge from the forest and cross the fields towards the house. His movements were slow, his body bent inwards as if he was walking into a strong wind. We hurried down the steps to meet him.

'Well? Did you see them?' Mama said when he reached the farmhouse. 'It can't be true. They're not—'

She stopped, caught herself. Papa's skin was the colour of oatmeal. 'It's true.'

Mama began to cry. A wave of dizziness made my head spin and I clutched at Mama's hand to steady myself.

'Did you find Oskar?' I said.

Papa's gaze swivelled towards me. There was a strange look in his eyes. 'No,' he said. 'No, I did not.' He said the words carefully, sounding each one out as if he was speaking for someone else's benefit. 'When I got to the farmhouse, there were NKVD agents already inside. They are coming to speak with us later.'

'Perhaps they will find him.' I hugged myself. 'They will look for whoever killed Imbi and Aime, start an investigation.'

My parents exchanged a look.

'We don't have long,' Papa said to Mama. 'Let's bring the sheep in. The cars might startle them.'

Something about his tone made me search his face. 'Papa?'

He was already turning away. He looked back and his

shoulders slumped. 'Kati, there won't be an investigation.' I stared at him blankly. His mouth twisted. 'Think; there can only be one group of people who hate Estonians enough to slaughter innocent women and children.'

I felt sick. A curl of anger twisted inside me.

'We must be prepared for the worst,' he continued. 'Oskar is gone. We may never know what happened to him.'

'But what reason would anyone have to hurt him? To hurt Imbi and Aime?'

Papa's face darkened. 'I ran into Johannes Tamm this morning. Did Oskar tell you that he whistled an Estonian song as the Russians marched past the market in Tartu last week? The soldiers did not hear but Tamm's Russian neighbour did and he recognised Oskar and reported him. Tamm told me so himself.'

'No.' I tried to conceal the surprise and hurt in my face. Oksar had voiced his disapproval of the Russians to Imbi and me in private but I had not thought him so foolish as to publicly endanger his family. I could only guess that he'd thought the Russians would not hear him. If he considered himself in trouble, he would surely have told me. We had promised we would not keep secrets from each other. 'He didn't say a word.'

Papa looked towards the road, as if he heard the crunch of tyres. 'When the soldiers arrive, we must say nothing to incriminate ourselves. You understand? You saw what happened to Oskar's family. That is what happens to anyone who opposes them. Or worse. Think of your mother.' I flinched. His voice gentled. 'You must forget that boy, Kati, and hope for his sake and ours that he never returns.'

He wrapped me in a tight embrace. I wanted to hug him back, but I could not force my hands, my limbs stiff with shock and fear, to move.

Now, a year later, here was Oskar standing before me. How many nights had I dreamt of him, willed him back? But I had never imagined it like this; my parents standing silent, my father's wary gaze. So much was different. So much had been altered by the continuing Soviet influx. Estonian families exiled or deported, their properties broken up into collective farms. Others ordered to leave their office jobs to work in the fields or consigned to the darkness of the mines. Villagers had been encouraged to join the Communist Party; anyone who didn't was viewed with suspicion. Cars and horses, even bicycles, were confiscated. Families came home to find their belongings flung out into the street and strangers sleeping in their beds. Whatever the Russians needed, they took for themselves. Anyone who resisted was beaten violently or taken to the NKVD headquarters for interrogation. Papa was right; it was best to try to forget. If only it was so simple.

'I'm sorry,' Oskar said. 'I'm so sorry, Kati. I didn't realise.' His voice was low, edged with pain.

I glanced up and our eyes met again.

I'd forgotten the paleness of Oskar's blue eyes. In the lamplight, they were almost grey, a stream reflecting an autumn sky. They were the eyes of the man who knew me best. They could see past the thin barriers I had built to protect myself. Once, I had been able to read Oskar too. Now there was a veil drawn between us, a darkness that clouded my judgement. I had no way of knowing; had he missed me as desperately as I'd missed him?

41

Papa spoke suddenly. 'Why are you here, Oskar? It's late. We are tired. You've risked our lives by coming back. Tell us what you want and then leave. If it's money, we have none.'

'It isn't money,' Oskar said. He stole another glance at me before turning back to Papa. 'Change is coming, Erich. It affects us all, but it will affect, most especially, your family. I have come to warn you that the war is coming to Estonia.'

'Ridiculous,' my father replied.

'It's true.' Oskar hadn't sipped the water. He stared down into it, as if looking for answers written in the mug. 'It has already started.'

'The war between Britain and Germany has nothing to do with us,' my father said. 'Stalin and Hitler have signed a pact of non-aggression. We read about it in *Postimees* last year.'

Papa had shown me the clipping, complete with a picture of Hitler's agent, Molotov, signing the treaty while Stalin looked on, smiling. The treaty had stated, in simple terminology, that if either party went to war against a third power, the other party was required to remain neutral. Papa had explained to us quietly that it essentially absolved Russia of any responsibility if the Germans invaded other countries. It was Russia's way of keeping out of the way, and giving Germany free rein to dominate Europe.

'The pact will not hold,' Oskar said.

Papa's face darkened. 'I don't believe you.' He waved a hand. 'You know nothing about what's happening out there. How can you? Where have you been, all this time, to know things like that? I assumed you fled to Finland, like so many others. I hoped you had. It would have been best for you. For us.'

Oskar's fingers tightened around the cup. 'No,' he said,

his jaw flexing. 'That's not what happened.' He paused. 'I've been living in the forest.'

Mama drew in a loud breath. 'All alone?'

Oskar nodded. 'At first, yes. I had no friends to help me. I couldn't ask you.' He shot me a quick, apologetic glance. 'I couldn't risk telling you I was still out there. I knew you would feel obliged to help me. The authorities would arrest you if they knew.'

My father grunted his approval. 'At least you had the sense not to come here.'

'Just so.' Oskar swirled the water in the cup. 'I made the best of it. I lived on mushrooms and berries. I slept under the stars. Eventually, more people fled into the forest. You remember what it was like, the first weeks of the occupation?'

Papa said nothing. Did he? Was he thinking of the information he had passed on to the Partorg? When they asked him to value the farms around us, my father had complied. At the time, he had told us he had no idea they would use the information to make arrests. Now I wasn't so sure. My heart gave a sharp, painful tug.

Although the bodies of Imbi and Aime haunted my nightmares, those memories had partially dimmed. The invasion was different. Every day, there were reminders. People starving on the streets. Young women harassed by soldiers and men beaten for jumping to their defence. I remembered the rumble of tanks on the road nearby. The day after the invasion began, we had gone into Tartu to check on Aunt Juudit. Cattle cars were lined up in the station, and families were being herded inside, men separated from the women and children. I recognised some people from our village. Councillor Karro and his wife, along with their twin girls, all wearing woollen jackets though the sun blazed overhead. Elsa Hamit, who taught handicraft at the local tech. I watched my old school teacher, Josef Tavert, help his father, a frail, limping man, up into the railroad car beside him. When he finally succeeded in clambering up, he leant heavily against Mr Tavert, wheezing. I wanted to call out but before I had a chance, the door was slammed shut.

We watched from a safe distance, standing in the car park of the station with a knot of other people. Those who were braver fought against the crowd until they reached the cattle cars, pushing notes to their families between the bars or parcels of food for the long journey ahead. When the Russian soldiers noticed, they started shouting. One man fired his weapon into the air, causing people to scatter away from the cattle car towards the safety of the car park. The women trapped inside the train drew their children closer, shielding them with their hands and bodies. The men separated in their cattle cars could do nothing but cry out, hoping to hear the voices of their families reassuring them they were safe.

Papa's face had been unreadable as the chaos unfolded.

'They take the educated ones first,' an old woman had said beside my elbow. I knew she was right. My grandmother had predicted the same thing before she died. First the government would be replaced by a puppet one, she said. Then they would arrest and deport the people who were thinkers, those who could educate or warn others about the regime to come. With that class gone, they would turn to the workers and landowners; men like my father. Communist pamphlets had already been distributed, warning us about the *kulaks*. The *kulaks* had been the richest farmers in the village. They had kept all their wealth to themselves, while those below them starved. Now their goods would be distributed to those who needed it most. Although the propaganda was always carefully worded, it was not hard to see through it when life revealed so starkly that the truth was quite the opposite. Estonia and the other Baltic countries with their rich bounty of farmland and minerals would help pay the price for the spread of Communism across the world.

'Where?' I said. 'Where will they take them?'

The woman had not answered. Perhaps she thought no answer was necessary. There was only one place those cattle cars were going: out east to the inhospitable *Oblasts*, to Siberia and the farthest reaches of the Soviet empire, frozen tundras where nothing survived. I knew, from what my grandmother had told me about Estonia's years under the Tsar, that people did not come back from there.

I looked to Papa, waiting for him to move, to speak out. Instead, he seized my shoulder roughly and marched me back to the lorry where Mama and Jakob were waiting.

'Did you see Professor Kärner?' Jakob's skin was grey, his mouth pinched. He'd refused to leave the safety of the vehicle and Papa would not have allowed him to, anyway. The only reason Papa had taken the risk of stopping at all was to see if any of his friends were among the deportees. Jakob was lucky he was only a poor student in his first year of university and so clearly not considered enough of a threat. He wiped his hand across his pale brow. 'And the Jurvetsons? They were marched out of class this morning.'

The door of the lorry squeaked as Papa climbed in. I opened my mouth to reply but Papa silenced me with a glare. I watched the train recede in the rear mirror as Papa drove the lorry out of the carpark. A terrible weight sat heavily on my chest. I had seen Jakob's math professor being herded towards the train and driven inside. The Jürvetson boys, blond twins who had been in Jakob's school year and now studied with him at the university, had been separated and pushed into different cars. I'd seen the anguished expressions on their faces before the doors closed. They did everything together. I could not remember ever seeing them apart. Now they would be trapped alone, in the comfortless dark, without each other's company. It seemed so cruel and spiteful but there was nothing they could do or say to resist. They were as helpless as the children whose cries squalled over the heads of the waiting crowd.

I would rather run than be caged, I decided then. If the Soviets came for us, I would convince my family to take our chances in the forest. I did not want to die in some unknown place, hearing Russian voices all about me.

I knew now that Oskar had felt the same.

He was still staring down into his mug of water. 'So many people came to live in the forest that groups formed. People began to help each other, building shelters, finding food. Some of us, the bravest I suppose, or the stupidest, the ones with nothing left to lose, suggested we should take up arms. Some people had pistols they brought with them. Others stole rifles. That was when the Soviets sent in their first patrols.' His hands curled around the cup. 'Women. Infants. Young boys and girls. Nobody was spared. What crime did they commit? What offence would you assign them, Erich, knowing they had no choice except to submit to arrest and deportation or scrape a life together in the wilderness?' His jaw tightened.

'What did you do, Oskar?' It was the first time I had spoken.

Oskar turned his head slowly. Something soft and wordless passed between us. I wondered if Oskar had missed my voice, as I had missed his. A beat passed before he shook himself. 'Some of us managed to escape. We hid in a cave, waiting for the screams to stop. Eventually, they did. But the anger; that was not gone. The defiance, too. It was stronger. It was a living, breathing force now. Those of us who were left behind took a vow that we would not forget. We would honour the memory of those who were slaughtered – by killing as many Soviet pigs as we could lay our hands on.'

'Oskar.' My father's voice carried a thin note of warning.

Oskar's shoulders drooped. He looked tired suddenly. There were dark bruises beneath his eyes. I wondered how he dared even to sleep, knowing the authorities could catch him at any moment. He was an outlaw now, a criminal. According to the Russian authorities, he had murdered his mother and sister in cold blood. The penalties for such transgressions were swift and fatal. No wonder he had not sent word to us that he was still alive. The things we took for granted – food, shelter, a mattress – were things Oskar and others like him had to fight for. The burden of it might be enough to crush an older man and yet here he sat, in our kitchen. Where were all those other boys and men now, people like Josef Tavert and his old father? If they had survived the journey to Siberia, would they have fought? Would they have had the strength to run if such an opportunity came? I could not imagine Jakob, sleeping comfortably in the student dorms and eating in the cafeteria, finding the resilience to go without food for days at a time, to lie down on a bed of pine needles with only an old blanket for warmth against the bitter cold.

At nineteen, Oskar had achieved what most had found impossible after the Soviet invasion: he had survived.

'I'm not telling you this because I want to worry your family, Erich,' Oskar said. His head tilted slightly towards me. I caught the flicker of memory in his eyes; the promise we had made to each other to always tell the truth, no matter how painful it might be. 'I'm telling you because the time has come for you to make a choice.' He paused. I watched his throat ripple as he swallowed, draining the mug.

'We've had help from other farmers. They were scared, at first. Of course. But they have slowly come around. There are many here who are too scared to fight openly, but they've been supplying us with food, some with rifles. Sometimes they pass messages for us, or provide safe houses for people who know their names are on the list. Just a bed for the night, until they can find a way to let us know we have another soldier ready to join us, or a sister who can help prepare meals and keep the camps clean. Resistance is growing. It's up to us to fight for them.'

'This is your war?' Papa finally said. His eyes were narrowed. 'A war between the many millions of Soviets and a bunch of rag-tag forest boys? This is what you would risk our lives for?'

Oskar recoiled at his words, but recovered swiftly. 'After that first slaughter, there were fifteen of us,' he said. His eyes had lost their soft look. 'Fifteen left out of a hundred. Do you know how many fighters we have now, Erich?' He paused. 'Five hundred. More spread out across the forests. It's not just the forest soldiers the Soviets should be worried about, either. We have support from a power far greater than that, a nation that has helped Estonia in the past. Now she is coming to our aid again.'

My father's face was mottled pink and white as he struggled to contain his shock. 'The pact,' he said. His voice was less certain now. 'The treaty. Stalin and Hitler will not abandon it. They cannot.'

'It's worth less than the parchment they signed it on.' Oskar shook his head. 'The Germans are already here, Erich.' I heard Mama's indrawn breath. 'We've been helping them and now they are helping us, training our soldiers. Giving us weapons. Germany will march on Russia. I swear it. You're an Estonian,' he said. 'That should count for something. I'm not asking you to fight. Just to turn a blind eye. To lend us your barn as a safe place for German parachuters to land when war comes. A field or three. You have a choice, Erich. You didn't last year; none of us did. But now you do. And, with the help of the Germans, we have a chance. Will you help us? Will you choose to free Estonia from Soviet bondage?'

I looked eagerly at Mama and Papa. Had they heard the passion in Oskar's voice? Had they been stirred by Oskar's words?

My parents were frozen like figures in a tableau. Mama's head was bowed, hands clasped before her. Papa stood as immovable as an ancient apple tree, hands knotted by his sides. Only his face revealed any emotion, his eyebrows drawing together until a large crease formed in the centre of his forehead. For a moment, I caught a glimpse of the young man he had been. The boy who dreamt of nothing but blankets of warm fleece and apple trees as far as the eye could see. A man whose parents had fought to emancipate

49

themselves from the grip of Russia and the Baltic Germans. My paternal grandmother had spoken with great pride of the liberation; of how she and my grandfather, like so many others, had adopted new names for themselves in the wake of Estonia's independence. They'd chosen surnames that reflected the natural world, a world free of human violence and greed.

My grandparents had become *Rebane*; the fox, a creature of great beauty and stealth, who knew how to use both cunning and wits to survive. They had struggled to survive in a world which had ignored them. Nobody had come to their aid when they fought for their independence. No allies. Those days were over. I knew Papa had made up his mind before he even opened his mouth. 'It's time for you to leave now, Oskar.'

Oskar didn't move.

'Didn't you hear me?' Papa's voice trembled. 'Please, leave now. You shouldn't have come back here, bringing trouble to my door. You've put us all in danger. Me and Marta. Kati. I am the head of this family. It's my duty to protect them. Nobody can win against the Russian army. Everyone knows that. If you had any sense, you'd leave now. Run off to Finland, as you should have done before.' He mopped his forehead with his sleeve. 'Go on. Go now.'

I closed my eyes.

After a moment, I heard footsteps, creaking floorboards, the sheep bleating nervously below in their pens. When I opened my eyes, Papa was still standing there, hands by his sides. Mama had raised her face. She looked stricken.

Oskar was gone.

Winter Berries

'I'M GOING TO BED.'

The floorboards groaned beneath Papa's feet. Moments later, the bedroom door in the hallway slammed closed. Almost at once, my mother began to move, throwing the remaining cutlery into the sink, snatching up Oskar's empty mug from the table and scrubbing it so vigorously with the dishcloth I thought it would crack.

I watched her with a strange detachment.

Mama set the upended mug on the counter to dry and took up the wet rag, scrubbing at the faint ring it had left on the surface of the table until every trace of our visitor was wiped away. She was silent, too unsettled even to hum.

As I stood watching her rag slap against the table, I heard it; a sound so much like the wind it could hardly be distinguished. A lonely bay. An animal voice crying out in the dark.

Elina. Still out there, still waiting.

The chicken bones on the table were already cold; a little gristle clung to them. I threw them into a dishcloth and folded the corners to make a parcel. The wind had come up. I heard it whistling through the roof where the thatch was thinning. My grandmother's shawl was draped on the hallstand. I wound it around my neck, tucking it into my blouse.

I waited until Mama's back was turned before slipping

down the stairs. She hadn't heard the wolf; all she had heard was the wind knocking against the windows like a child begging to be let in.

The ram grunted when he heard me, shifting restlessly among the hay as he prepared to bed down.

'Elina?' I whispered, peering out. 'Are you out here?'

'Kati.' Oskar was leaning against a birch, standing so still I had to wait for my eyes to adjust to discern his features. The tar scent of his cigarette reached me, sharp and sweet. As he threw it aside, the embers scattered on the ground in one final burst of orange and red.

He took a step towards me. 'Wasn't Elina your grandmother's name? Why are you calling to her in the dark?'

I tucked my hands under my arms and cast about with my eyes. The yard was empty. Moonlight glimmered on the stones.

'You must have misheard.' I paused for a moment. 'I was looking for you.'

'For me?'

'Yes.' I could feel my hands trembling. 'I wanted to speak to you. To explain.'

'Does Erich know you're out here? Your mother?'

I shook my head.

'You've changed your hair,' he observed. 'Just one plait now, is it?'

I lifted my hand automatically to feel the braid. The weave I'd made of it this morning was still in place, but the ends were straggly, uneven. 'Jakob said two braids made me look fifteen.'

Another step.

'Since when did you take Jakob's advice?' He was so close I could smell the forest on him. Sun-warmed earth. Mushroom dankness. And something else; something chemical. The scent of paraffin. Of danger and resistance.

Goosebumps rose on my skin.

'Kati . . .'

My name, when he said it, was intoxicating. An island, a stepping stone in a deep river. If I let it, that word would lead to more words, words I would not be able to unsay.

With an effort, I moved away. 'You shouldn't have come back.'

Oskar stiffened. He dropped his hands to his sides, shoving them into his pockets.

That's it, I thought, reminding myself to breathe, to ignore the prickle of tears that threatened at the back of my eyes. *Let him go.*

'Do you remember these?'

I forced myself to stare at the objects Oskar was holding out in his open palms. The gloves, one in each hand. Red wool, threaded through with a white pattern of winter berries.

'Yes.'

They were the last things I had knitted for Oskar before Imbi and Aime were murdered and he disappeared. An early birthday gift. I'd left them on the doorstep of the farmhouse on my way into Tartu, knowing Oskar would find them and divine they were from me.

Oskar closed his hands around them and I watched them disappear back into his pockets.

'I take them with me everywhere. Even when it's too warm to wear them. They're my good luck charm.' I could not raise my head to look at him. 'I thought you would be glad to see me, Kati,' he said softly.

I brought my head up sharply. 'I am. I never believed those rumours. But we couldn't say anything. It wasn't safe. Papa said they would come for us.'

'Then he's not as foolish as he appears.'

'Papa is no fool.'

Oskar grunted. 'He thinks he doesn't have to choose sides. That he can go on pretending nothing has changed.'

I watched him plunge his hand into his pocket and bring out another cigarette. He let it rest between his lips as he struck a match and lit it with steady hands. The cigarette flared in the darkness, splashing light across his face.

I was suddenly aware of how old he seemed. How changed. He had never smoked before. Imbi Mägi would have switched his backside as soon as she caught a whiff of tobacco on his clothes. I was alone, in the dark, with a stranger who wore the familiar features of my childhood friend. My heart still yearned for him, as if it could remember the time he had once dived into the freezing river to retrieve Maimu when I dropped her in the river. The time he had shown me how to freeze milk into discs and hang them up so they would last all winter long. The time we had danced together at Raimo Vagula's barn-dance when we were fifteen and he held me close, one arm cradling my back, until I felt the tingling burn of desire creep up my body and excused myself, afraid of the depth of my feelings, the need to hold back when all I wanted was to give in.

I shook my head when he held out the cigarette, drawing my shawl close around my shoulders. He merely shrugged, flicking the match with his fingers until the flame was extinguished. 'You know, you could come with me,' he said.

'And live in the forest?' I wanted to laugh, but the sound caught and died in my throat. 'You know I can't.' I turned away. The scent of the cigarette was unsettling. 'I'll speak to Papa. About your proposal.'

'He won't change his mind.'

'You don't know that.'

'And you're still the same. Still your father's girl. Too afraid to say no.'

'I'm not afraid!'

Oskar scoffed. 'Did you even protest when they decided Jakob should be the one to go to the university?'

'Of course I did.' My voice was as dry as skeleton leaves.

Oskar's hand found mine suddenly in the darkness. It was so startling I drew in a breath. His palm was rough and warm. Familiar and yet different, the bumps and creases a roadmap of our youth. 'We promised never to lie to each other.'

Carefully, I drew my hand back. I thought I heard him sigh, but it might have been the wind in the trees. The pale light brightened as the clouds shifted above, revealing the thin wedge of the moon, circled by stars.

Oskar moved away from me, his shoulders stiff, a stranger again. 'Speak to your Papa, then,' he said coolly. 'If he waits too long, decisions will be made for him.'

A cold leaf, shaken free from the birch above, plastered itself on the bare spot at the back of my neck. I reached up to pluck it off, but the cold remained, worming down through my skin and into my bones.

I was suddenly afraid. 'Are you threatening us?'

Oskar dragged on the cigarette and then exhaled, issuing a plume of smoke that curled in the air between us. 'I would never let them hurt you, Kati. But the Germans are determined. They want to succeed. At any price.'

A pulse beat faster in my neck. 'I should warn him.'

'Why do you think I came back?'

Our eyes met. *For me.*

But I didn't dare speak my hopes aloud. I watched Oskar take a last puff and grind the cigarette out beneath the heel of his boot. He straightened up and gave me a curt nod. I felt the distance gape between us, stretching like a frayed shawl. Whatever was left of what we had once felt was not enough.

'Take care, Kati.'

I tried to make my mouth form the word. *Goodbye.*

Something soft pressed into my hands and I looked down. The gloves were still warm. I balled them up and tucked them in my pocket.

Then Oskar turned and drifted away into the trees. I watched him go, my stomach aching as if I had not eaten all day, that old familiar feeling of hunger, of gaining something but never being satisfied.

I'd lost him again. We'd not even spoken about his mother, or Aime and the violence which had ripped them from both our lives. But there was no more time to linger here with ghosts; I needed to catch what little rest I could.

I turned in time to see her emerge from the shadows at the end of the stone-strewn drive. Elina. My wolf.

Her eyes caught the light in silver crescents. We stared at each other, unblinking. Her yellow irises had become milky, and the sleek dark grey of her wolf coat was patchy, peppered with white hairs. When I had first seen her the day after my grandmother's funeral, her coat had bristled with shiny fur that glowed a dusky red against the patina of moss-covered boulders at her back and the curtain of willow submerged into the river's depths beside the bank. Her presence had been startling. When I heard her footsteps, I assumed Jakob had followed me, thwarting my desire to flee into the forest to be alone.

At that time, I had not wanted to believe the truth; that my beloved grandmother had finally gone. Nothing would be the same again and I wanted to join her, in the deep, damp earth.

My cheeks were flushed from running. I had followed a twisted path all the way to the river, where the rushing of water over stones would drown out my sobs. When at last I looked up, I had seen the wolf watching me from only a few yards away. Her eyes were a brilliant yellow–green, the same colour as the leaves that wavered and danced in the wind. For a moment, we were frozen in time. I was aware of her body, the taut muscles below the flesh, her warm heart beating within its bower of bones. But I was not afraid. Hadn't my grandmother warned me she would return?

After some moments, the wolf turned and disappeared into the trees, and the colours of the world seemed to bleed back in. She did not return. Since then, I had seen her a handful of times – always at a distance. Once, picking her way along the ridge of trees at the edge of our field. Another time, during winter, shaking the powdered snow from her coat as she followed the frozen path of the river into the forest. But she had never come so close again.

'Here.' I opened my parcel and scattered the bones at her feet. She fell on them, her eyes never leaving mine. As we stood taking the measure of each other the wind died down, falling away until there was only empty silence and the crunch and snap of her jaws grinding up the bones.

Fear gripped me. What would happen if my wolf perished, too? I would be all alone. The knowledge that she was out there had always comforted me, her appearance so soon after my grandmother's death too coincidental to be anything but *saatus*: fate. Yet here she was before me. Not a spirit: flesh and blood. She was as real as I, as fragile and fallible as the heroes of old tales.

Suddenly, there was a rustle and a frightened squeak in the hedge bordering the path, followed by a desperate thrashing. An animal – probably a rat – had caught itself up between the gnarled tangle of twigs. In one fluid movement, my wolf launched herself across the path towards the sound with the grace and agility of a much younger animal. I watched her streak into the darkness, heard the scuffle of battle and then a satisfied crunch.

I waited a few moments longer, but she did not emerge again. The barn doors were heavy, the hinges rusted with age. I braced my shoulder against the timber, grunting with the effort. Slowly, the doors heaved closed.

'Farewell, Elina.'

Mystery Stitch

Lydia
June 1941

I STOOD INSIDE THE ENTRANCE OF THE VOLGA CINEMA, waiting for Joachim. The wallpaper of the lobby was dull, the ceiling stained yellow like the ivory piano keys in the Kremlin's musicians gallery. Faded posters plastered the walls, showing advertisements for films released a few years before: *Volga Volga* and *Alexander Nevsky*. *The Shining Path*, one of my favourite films, a Cinderella story about a humble servant girl who astounded her superiors with clever cleaning methods and rose through the ranks to become head of the factory.

A few patrons milled about, slurping ice-cream cones or flicking through the latest edition of *Pravda*. None of them glanced my way. Beneath the glass doors, the sounds of the street trickled in: the chime of trolley-car bells, the hum of traffic from Stalinskaya Parade.

The lobby looked exactly the way it should; a little shabby and careworn from its former life as a theatre for Bolshevik stage plays. It was neither the grandest nor the most popular cinema in the city; instead of the latest films, it showed re-runs of old favourites, which was why we had chosen it.

Nothing was odd or out of place. There was no reason to be afraid. I was just a young woman waiting for her beau on a typical spring day in Moscow. So, why could I not shake off the sensation that something was wrong?

Mamochka, I whispered. *Are you there?*

Nothing. I squeezed my gloves hard in my hand. Some might think it odd to speak to one's dead mother, but I liked to imagine she was still with me. It seemed as if everyone else had forgotten her, apart from Olga, my once-nursemaid and now companion in the strange existence I occupied as a ward under my uncle's care. It was a dull life enlivened rarely by official party functions and visits to State-sanctioned entertainments on my uncle's behalf like the ballet or the theatre. I was not only my father's representative in Moscow but my uncle's. It had been pressed on me since I was a child that it was my duty to fulfil the role my mother had once occupied. To smile and feign interest, to amuse visiting dignitaries with poems and songs I had learnt by heart; those of Pushkin and the great speeches of Lenin. To be winsome and charming. Although I did my best, I was not sure that I always succeeded. I was too shy. I did not have a sparkling wit or a quick sense of humour. Mama had been a wonderful entertainer, Olga said, with an uncanny ability to make her guests feel comfortable. Strange, then, that nobody ever mentioned her name now, especially in my uncle's presence.

Was it the talk of war that made my stomach clench? War was on everybody's lips these days. It was impossible to sit in the trolley car without overhearing somebody mention it. 'Did you hear about what happened in Greece?' The old woman in front of me had said to her friend as I took the tram earlier that morning from Red Square. 'Yes,' her friend had replied. 'A whole factory destroyed by the Germans in under an hour!' War was the flavour of the month and had been for some time. People wondered aloud if the treaty between Russia and Germany would hold. And yet despite these musings, things were not as terrible as one might fear. People went about their lives. There were some shortages. That was to be expected. It was more difficult, according to Joachim, to find matches and salt. The queues for shoes were always lengthy. Joachim complained about having to line up for hours to buy tinned peaches only to find when he reached the front that the shop was selling caviar he could not afford.

Everyone knew that if war did come, it would end swiftly. I, along with many people, still remembered the film *If War Comes Tomorrow*, released four years ago but quietly shelved since the signing in 1939 of the non-aggression pact. Its depiction of the Red Army driving back Germany's troops, of German peasants rising up to greet the victorious Soviet soldiers as their saviours had stayed with us. There was no reason to think that life would change so much. War meant sacrifice. It might mean wearing the same evening dress half a dozen times or arriving a little late at functions because there were not enough workers to drive the State's fleet of cars. It might mean doing my hair myself, instead of going to the salon to let them style it for me.

I'd already begun practising in secret, with mixed results, trying to coax it to resemble the glossy waves modelled by my favourite American film star, Greta Garbo. Olga insisted my hair was deep brown, almost black, but I liked to think it was more of a dark red, the same shade as the amber liquor she sometimes slipped into her coffee after meals. It was so long and thick it took an hour to separate and a dozen attempts to smooth down each section and clamp it to the curling spring.

Beauty treatments aside, things would get much worse if the war playing out across Europe drew in the Soviet State. But the Russian people were strong. Endurance was in our blood. If it was war Germany wanted, Russia would comply but there was no doubt at all that the Soviets would triumph.

My uncle had told me so himself.

A sudden flood of warmth fanned the air as one of the cinema lobby doors was pulled back and Joachim sauntered in.

I watched the smile fade a little on his face as he scoured the room, a frown forming between his dark brows. He was dressed in a white shirt and grey suit, a tie knotted loosely at his throat; the same outfit he'd been wearing when we met in the courtyard of the Café Stolovaya months ago. The suit had been his father's; a gift from the film institute to congratulate him on the release of his third film. Sorkin Snr had worn it to the film premiere and then passed it on to his son. If it hung a little loose on Joachim's thin shoulders, what did that really matter? His pleasing features more than made up for his lack of muscles. Dimpled cheeks. A slightly crooked nose. A dazzling smile with just a hint of sardonic humour lurking behind it. My breath shortened. Pins and needles spread in a tingling arc down my back and made me shiver. Seeing him always evoked the same reaction; a mixture of excitement and pleasure, underscored by guilt.

A twist of hair fell over one eye; he smoothed it back, his gaze lingering for half a second on two girls about my age giggling and flirting with a soldier nearby while their ice cream cones dripped unnoticed onto the carpet. One of the girls leant forward boldly and kissed the soldier on the mouth, which led to more giggling. I saw Joachim's lips compress and knew exactly what he was thinking.

Young fools.

With the possibility of war threatening like storm clouds on the horizon, could anyone really afford to make attachments they did not intend to keep? Love was a dangerous game. It was not for the faint-hearted. Only the strongest relationships would survive something as ugly as the separation of war. It was lucky, then, that what Joachim and I felt for each other was more than just a passing attraction. The very moment our eyes had met as he introduced himself in the café, it was as if a rebellious longing had roared to life inside me. Until that moment I'd been sitting alone in the café's courtyard, waiting for an old school friend who had not shown up; not altogether surprising, considering my past history. As my uncle's ward, I was used to people getting cold feet or staying away because they were afraid I would feed information back to him. Often, they would cancel at the last second or make up stories about traffic delays. I knew what I would find when I returned home; a note in a cream envelope, hurried lines of apology. It was nothing new at all but it did not stop the disappointment from blossoming as I drained the bitter coffee in my cup and prepared to leave. That was when I noticed him walking towards me, the first moment I felt the spread of pins and needles down my back.

He'd paused beside the table and asked if he could sit down.

When I told him my name, who I was, his eyes had widened just for a moment, and I felt my muscles tense as I waited for him to make excuses and leave. When he stood up, I stayed sitting, determined to preserve the little dignity I still possessed. Instead of walking off, he threw down some roubles and asked if I would stroll with him to the Tretyakov Gallery on Lavrushinsky Lane. In a blissful dream, we spent the afternoon chatting until the ring of the guard's bell alerted us that the gallery was closing. We'd parted after agreeing to meet for coffee and a movie the following week and I had taken the trolley home in a daze, unable to remember any of the paintings we'd seen, my thoughts too preoccupied by the handsome, mysterious young man I'd just met, who did not care at all who my uncle was or how he could benefit by association.

Three months had passed since that day. I knew now that he was not only handsome but principled, too, and interesting with a dry sense of humour. What I liked most about him was that he was living his own life the way he wanted, shunning his parents' comfortable apartment in favour of a communal flat. He wanted to live the same way ordinary people did, without the comforts awarded to the privileged few. It made him more attractive, in my eyes. I wanted nothing so much as to be normal. Being with Joachim made me feel as if such a thing might one day happen; as if it were not such an impossible dream.

'There you are!' He crossed the room quickly, his cheek grazing mine. He leant back to admire me. I felt a blush creeping up my neck. I'd chosen my outfit carefully. It was a sweet cotton dress with a pleated skirt that fell to my knees and a frill of Ukrainian lace at the collar. None of my clothes came from the Main Universal Store. They were all specially made by a tailor in Pokrovka Street; a favourite of my uncle's. At least I'd been allowed to pick the colour; a bright cornflower blue which matched my eyes. I'd matched it with a pair of flat sandals, instead of my usual heels, thinking wisely of the walk to the trolley car stop. It was the perfect outfit for meeting my girlfriend Sveta for coffee in the warm weather. But of course, I was not meeting Sveta. Although my hair was not as smooth as I'd hoped, I was pleased to see Joachim's eyes darken with desire. 'You were hiding from me,' he said. 'Where is Kirvenko?'

'Waiting outside.'

'Funny. I didn't see him.'

'That is sort of the point,' I said. 'But, then, he didn't pass his final exams in shadowing. Remember?' I waited for Joachim to laugh. It was a joke between us, my bodyguard's failings. He had been assigned to me two years ago, handpicked by General Nikolai Vlasik, my uncle's personal head of security. And despite our mocking, Kirvenko was in fact perfectly capable; an older man with hard grey eyes like pebbles who always wore a suit no matter what the weather. But despite his appearance, he was soft. Joachim and I had discovered this when our trysts began. It had only taken one pleading word from me for him to agree not to say a word to Olga. Perhaps he felt sorry for us. He likely thought our romance the stuff of children; harmless. It would blow over soon enough. Now when we met, Kirvenko made himself invisible, staying out of sight although I knew he would come running if I called him. I'd only had to shout for him once, when one of my uncle's drunken friends cornered me one night in the pool-room of the *dacha*. The speed of his response as he grasped the man by his shirt and sent him sprawling into the hallway had surprised me. For all that we teased him about being dull-witted, it was clear Kirvenko could move swiftly if required.

'I thought you might not come.' Joachim's smile did not reach his eyes. 'Changed your mind.'

'No, no,' I said. I caught up his hand. His pulse beat, as steady as a metronome, through his palm. 'Why would I do that?'

He opened his mouth to speak but seemed to change his mind. His gaze travelled down my blouse to linger on my waist. 'Let's talk afterwards.'

I watched him hurry to the ticket booth, a spill of dark curls falling across his face as he spoke rapidly to the female attendant. When he glanced back at me, he grinned, causing a swell of happiness to crest inside me. We'd been meeting here for weeks now. The last time, I had allowed him to kiss me in the shadows of the cinema while the strains of Prokofiev's music soared around us. For hours afterwards, I could still feel the warm spots on my neck where his fingers had stroked my skin. Back in my apartment at the House on the Embankment, the grand building designed to house the families of Moscow's elite, I hugged the memory of that encounter close. If Olga knew of my deception, she would be horrified. Although school had finished last year, Uncle had forbidden me to go anywhere other than to the *dacha* in Zubolovo during summer or the State-sanctioned dinners and functions I attended on his behalf. I would certainly not be allowed a boyfriend, Jewish or otherwise. I did not even dare to ask. But although I had found the courage to lie to Olga, to tell her that I was meeting an old girlfriend for lunch, not the son of a Jewish film director, I was never brave enough to forget myself entirely. There would be nothing beyond kisses, and I did not allow myself to imagine further. After all, I was Lydia Volkova, daughter of Piotr Volkov, Chief of Security, and though he was currently stationed in Estonia in a city called Tartu, I was under close scrutiny in my home city of Moscow. And as if that were not enough, I had been placed as a child in the hands of one of the most powerful men in the world. I called him 'Uncle' but in fact he was my father's employer. They had fought together in the Revolution as young men and spent some time wrongly imprisoned for treason against the Tsar. It was my 'uncle' who had overseen my schooling after Mama's sudden death from appendicitis when I was eleven. Uncle who even now controlled what I ate and where I went and whom I saw. I imagined it was my uncle who would be most displeased to know I was stepping out with a Jewish boy, but I hoped that in time he would come around to my way of thinking, that he would begin to see me not as a child, but as a girl on the verge of womanhood. Until then, I would have to keep my rebellion a secret.

Inside the warm fug of the cinema, Joachim's hands were busy as soon as the lights dimmed. I felt his fingers caress my neck, his mouth moving to cover mine. He tasted of cinnamon pastry and cigarettes. I tried my best to kiss him with matching fervour, although the arm of the seat dug into my leg and my back ached from being twisted about. *Relax*, I scolded. *This is what you wanted, isn't it? To be ordinary. Not a princess locked in a tower. A normal girl with normal desires and dreams.*

On the screen, Greta Garbo lifted a hand to her heavily pencilled brow, her mouth an O of pain. 'I have grown up in a great man's shadow,' she cried. 'I long to escape my destiny!'

I stiffened. Although the film marched on, the words lodged inside my brain.

Joachim pulled away. He was breathing heavily. I felt my cheeks burn and was glad of the darkness. 'Lida?' he whispered.

'What's wrong?' A loose spiral of my hair had escaped its pins. He tucked it back, his fingers lingering on my earlobe.

I tried to answer but my mouth was dry. What was wrong with me? Greta Garbo continued to agonise as Queen Christina, the seventeenth-century monarch of Sweden. The movie was a re-run; the first time we saw it we had laughed about it, Joachim joking that he was the lovesick peasant and I the rebellious princess who conspired to change her fate. Yet today the words seemed laden with special meaning. Perhaps I was simply unprepared for the way our relationship had moved so quickly into the physical realm. Meeting for conversation and coffee seemed far less dangerous than what we were doing now. Kissing boys in the back of a theatre was not the sort of arrangement made by daughters of the elite.

Breathing deeply, I shook my head. 'Nothing.' I was angry with myself for spoiling my few brief hours of freedom. Soon enough, the lights would come up and life would return to its usual monotony. I would take the tram back to the apartment, Kirvenko trundling behind. Olga would, of course, be waiting. Sometimes I would be allowed to visit our cook Zoya in the kitchen while she prepared our meals, listening while she prattled on about those who had been recently arrested for being enemies of the people or encouraging anti-Soviet sentiments.

'They are parasites!' she would cry as her fists pummelled the dough for our bread. 'They should be burnt alive for their wicked deeds!'

I would nod and sip my tea, waiting for her to grow bored and perhaps tell me instead about what life was like outside my sheltered existence, about the things she had done and seen before she came to live with us. Everyone agreed that anti-Communists should be punished. At least there were fewer arrests these days. Five years ago, it had not been surprising for me to come home from school to find our neighbours gone, taken off for questioning. Although everyone expressed surprise and shock, there was no question that they deserved whatever fate awaited them. There were occasional mix-ups, of course; that was unavoidable when so many dangerous elements were conspiring to ensure the downfall of Communism. Sometimes even Uncle and his advisors could not unravel the complex plots being woven around us. But there was no disputing that anyone truly innocent need be worried; the NKVD did not make mistakes, as my uncle often said himself.

At dinnertime, Olga would coordinate supper and help Zoya bring out the slices of thick bread and soft cheese, caviar and pickled herrings swimming in oil. At night, she would tuck me into bed, a glass of warm *kakavella* – cocoa beans roasted with milk – clutched in her hand and a story on her lips, just as she had when I was a child.

Shaking off caution, I leant forward and pressed my lips against Joachim's mouth. I felt his breath catch with surprise before he responded, his hands moving hesitantly up my stomach to cup my breasts. A thrill arced up my body, electrifying my limbs. I was not some captive; I was in charge of my own destiny.

The lobby was warm and bright when we at last emerged. I knew my cheeks were flushed. I wanted to splash water on my face but Joachim's arm was around my shoulders, heavy and languid. He was wearing a smile and kept shooting puzzled glances my way, as if he was surprised to find it was me he had spent the past hour kissing, not someone else.

'What's the matter?' I said as we strolled towards the exit.

'Nothing.' He paused near the door, forcing me to stop too, and bent forward to nuzzle my ear. A long art-deco mirror, speckled with age, hung over a potted plant near the doors. I caught a glimpse of my reflection; thick strands of dark ginger hair coming loose. A slim face with a strong jawline which angled down to terminate on a decidedly pointed chin. My freckles stood out vividly; a constellation of tiny marks swirling across cheeks made crimson by our activities inside the cinema.

I looked wild and dishevelled. Even my eyes had a shifty look, the pupils dilated to pinpricks so the rich blue of them seemed to dominate, lids half-lowered beneath eyebrows the colour of strong tea.

Joachim's warm mouth tickled my skin. I pushed him gently, angling my body so he had no choice but to move away.

'We should be more careful,' I told him. Other patrons pushed past us, eager to reach the tram stop before the next service arrived.

'Why?' He shrugged a shoulder. 'Your uncle knows.'

'What?' I whirled to face him. 'What did you say?'

'Don't worry. I think he got the message.' Joachim smirked. He tried to catch my hand but it eluded his grasp, as slippery as a fish.

'What do you mean, he knows? Did you speak to him?' My voice had risen. I could feel people staring at us. Pulling him roughly by the shoulder, I dragged him outside. It was warm on the boulevard. The sun peeped through the cinema's curled iron awning, casting lace shadows upon the road.

Joachim put up his hands. 'Listen. Calm down.' He straightened his jacket, smoothing out the rumples where I had grasped his sleeve. 'You're overreacting. I didn't speak to your uncle but I took a call from a Colonel Rumyanstev. Last week.'

I tried to swallow but couldn't. Colonel Rumyanstev was the second in command of my uncle's security detail. I had met him once at a dinner and could still recall the way his small eyes roved about the room, never resting, even as he chatted with my uncle about politics in the Baltics and the backlash against the revolting *kulaks* in Belarus.

'They cannot keep fighting us forever.' Ice had clinked in his glass as he swallowed. 'We know they are hoarding grain and meat for the winter. Some of them have started circulating pamphlets to encourage resistance. It's time to shut down the black markets permanently. Even the flea markets. Nothing can be spared. Wool, grain, timber. Everyone must sacrifice, for the greater good. Look at this. There's more ice in this glass than spirits. You see? We too must be prepared to set an example and forgo.'

A tram going the other direction dinged to a halt not far away. I wanted to push Joachim onto it and tell him to run, to jump aboard and ride it all the way to the end of the line. But I had to know what had happened. 'What did he say?'

'He told me the security detail knows everything; they've been tracking us for weeks. He said I was to leave Moscow. Immediately.' Joachim rolled his eyes. 'I asked him if he knew my father. He said he did.'

'And then?'

Joachim folded his arms. 'Then, nothing. I'm still here, aren't I?'

'But you won't stay here.' I raised my thumb to my mouth, tearing wildly at the nail, ignoring the sharp sting as my teeth raked the nail bed. 'You'll ask your father to send you somewhere. Anywhere. Didn't you say he has friends in Hollywood?'

'Like hell.' Joachim's face darkened. 'You see? I knew you'd be like this. You see now why I didn't want to tell you. Look . . .' His face softened. He plucked my hand away from my mouth, capturing it between his own. 'I will talk to my father, if it makes you feel better. But I'm not going anywhere. That's what I told them. I haven't done anything wrong.'

'But my uncle . . .' I glanced around. My chest was tight. 'He will kill you! You must tell your father now.' I pulled my hand free of his grasp. 'You must go to his apartment at once. You mustn't go home.'

'Why not?'

Joachim seemed genuinely surprised. His mouth opened and shut, and in that moment I realised he was just a boy. He had no idea about the things that had gone on before. It had started when I was sixteen, when my uncle first began to criticise the clothes I wore, commenting that my skirts were too short, my blouses too revealing. To Olga, he had made pointed remarks about my 'desperation' in wanting to attract the notice of men. At the time, I'd been so embarrassed I asked Olga to let my school skirt down until it brushed past my knees. But the comments had grown worse as time wore on. The last time I visited him with Olga, six months ago, he had flown into a rage, accusing me of seeing men when I'd been expressly forbidden from having lovers. The possessive rage on his face had frightened me, but it had also strengthened my resolve when the opportunity came to rebel. If I was already accused of such misdemeanours, why should I not taste for myself the forbidden fruit?

'They will be trailing you,' I told Joachim. 'Surely you must know they will still be watching us. How could you be so naïve?' Through my rising panic I saw a trolley car approaching, its vague outline growing closer.

I tried to push Joachim towards it, but he resisted, digging in his heels.

'Don't call me,' I said. The liberating sense of freedom – how had I ever thought that kissing a boy in a darkened cinema would be allowed – evaporated into the blue sky. 'It's not safe.'

Mamochka, please, I thought, picturing my mother's face. *Just allow me time to speak to Uncle first. To explain.*

A word floated back to me, suffused with the faintest hint of night-blooming jasmine; my mother's favourite scent. I felt her voice calling to me, the word growing clearer until it filled my head with a sound like breaking glass.

Run!

Tyres squealed behind us. I spun around. A car – sleek, black; a Packard – juddered to a halt at the kerb. The chatter of people's voices around us fell away. A man emerged from the passenger side and walked straight towards us, his shoes clipping the pavement.

'Joachim Sorkin?' The agent did not wait for Joachim to speak. 'I have a warrant for your arrest. You must come with me.' He seized Joachim by the arm and pulled him towards the car.

Desperately, his courage fleeing, Joachim looked back.

Help me, he mouthed, his chin trembling.

His black dress shoes squeaked, slipping against the concrete.

I wanted to move, to do something but my legs were locked into place. 'Where are you taking him?' I said.

The agent pulled the door back. 'To the Lubyanka. Go back to your apartment. You have visitors.' Turning back to his work, he shoved Joachim roughly into the car's interior. The car door slammed, a thunderclap in the silent street.

I staggered back, my head pounding. Lubyanka: the prison where spies and those accused of anti-Communist behaviour were held before they were executed. And waiting for me at my apartment, Uncle's cronies, ready to scold or excoriate me, to mete out whatever punishment he had devised.

Olga was waiting for me in the hallway of our apartment block, pacing back and forth. When I stepped onto the landing, she shrieked then rushed towards me, her thick fingers twisted together.

Wisps of white hair escaped her bun as if she'd been sitting in a sauna. A house dress of pale blue crepe dotted with daisies clung to her plump body, the fabric slightly crushed. I remembered with a guilty start that today was the second Thursday of the month, the day she often wandered downstairs to the beauty salon to have her round face scrubbed until it was tight and shiny and her nails trimmed. With a sick feeling, I wondered if Uncle's men had dragged her out of the salon to question her; whether my own selfishness had been responsible for this added humiliation. I waited for her to rap my fingers and yell at me as she had done when I was a child. Instead she flung her arms around my waist and squeezed me tightly to her chest. When she drew back, her hazel eyes were reproachful. 'You are a wicked girl, Lydochka. Why did you lie? You told me you were meeting with Sveta for coffee. Now I find out it was a young man!' She shook her head, her nest of hair trembling.

'I'm sorry,' I said. 'I should have told you the truth.' I pressed the heels of my palms into my aching eyes; I had not been able to hold back my tears on the trolley car home. Joachim was gone. Who knew what they were doing to him? In my wretched state, I had only barely registered the man following me, shadowing my footsteps. Not Kirvenko. A stranger. A new bodyguard. Had Kirvenko betrayed me? It didn't matter now.

Something creaked behind me; I turned, heart thumping, wondering if the guards I had passed at the entrance downstairs had followed me up. But there was only the silver mirror in the hallway throwing my own dishevelled image back.

Olga was still staring at me, her lips puckered in disapproval. Then her face relented a little, and I saw fear creep in, replacing the hurt. She tugged me towards the door.

'Your uncle is waiting to speak to you,' she said. She lowered her voice. 'Lydochka, I've never seen him so angry.'

'He came himself?' I tried to swallow the burning lump in my throat. Surely he was too busy to bother with me. He had any number of people to do his bidding. Was the crime

I had committed so terrible? Why had he not sent Colonel Rumyanstev to punish me?

There could be only one good thing to come from his being here: the possibility that I could beg him for Joachim's release. Perhaps, if I apologised, I could convince him to grant Joachim a pardon, or at least have him placed under house arrest. His parents might be able to smuggle him out. It all hinged on how Uncle took my apology. What could I say to soften him, to make him laugh? When I was a child, playing about his feet when we visited him, I had always managed to bring him out of his rage by flinging myself around his boot.

'Dear boot,' I would say, stroking its polished surface. 'How angry you are. Why do you shout so? You must rest. You must be calm. Shall I sing you a song? Shall I tell you the story of Brave Vasilisa?' Then I would feel the boot shake with laughter, the adult voices growing calmer, my father's rational words easing the tension from the room.

But I was no longer that child, and he was no longer just my uncle. Now he was the State. As his power had increased, so had his temper, his intolerance for little things.

Olga prodded me forward into the parlour where we took our tea each afternoon, the *samovar* filling the room with clouds of steam. He stood beside the window looking out over the River Moskva, hands gripped behind his waist, a short man in a grey suit.

His hair was combed back, streaked with silver–grey. His uniformed guards stood at attention, their faces expressionless. They looked strangely incongruous standing against the fine wallpaper and wood panelling of the apartment walls. My legs wanted to turn and run, dragging me with them, but I forced them to be still. *Think of Joachim's face*, I told myself. *Imagine his fine nose, his dimples. His grin. Think of the books he gave you, the records smuggled in from America beneath his sweater. You must help him!* I willed my feet to shuffle forward but I could not stop my hands shaking.

'Uncle.' He turned slowly towards me, his eyebrows lifted in surprise, as if he did not expect to see me standing in my own apartment. Perhaps he had thought I would run, leaving Joachim to his fate. Well, he was wrong. Still, I hesitated, my sandals touching the edge of the intricately patterned Turkish rug in the middle of the room.

I knew I should lower my eyes – everybody did so in his presence – but some part of me, some reckless part, made me hold his gaze. His eyebrows drew together, his bottom lip pushing out like a child's. Then he began to laugh. The sound bounced off the walls, filling the room all the way to the high ceiling.

His body shook with laughter, his stomach wobbling beneath the grey fabric strained across it. I stood straight-spined, waiting for him to finish, uncertain what to do. Wiping tears from his eyes, he strode across the rug and embraced me. He had to raise up slightly on his heels to plant a kiss on my cheek. Although I had not inherited my mother's creamy skin and pale hair, I had been blessed, or cursed, with her height.

'Little Lyolka,' he said, using the pet name he had invented for me as a child. His eyes shone. They were crinkled at the edges, his face more lined than I remembered from six months ago. 'You are almost the image of your mother, do you know?

77

Except for her hair. Your freckles, your nose . . . everything. Even down to that *look*, the one she used to give me when I had kept your Papa working too late. I would bring him back here the next day – perhaps carried is a better word – and she would be standing here, just as you are, glaring at me, that same rebelliousness, those eyes . . .'

He leant forward, his breath in my face, smelling of wine and meat. His fingernails dug into my arms, sharp pincers in my skin. I whimpered. I wanted to pull away, but I was caught, ensnared.

Without warning, he released me. I stumbled back, my heel catching on the edge of the rug. My ankle twisted one way, my foot another. The room spun as I crashed backwards, landing heavily on my backside, the wind knocked from my lungs.

My uncle looked away, his mouth a moue of distaste. He didn't offer to help me to my feet. I had to roll onto my knees and push myself up.

'You have been busy, I understand,' he said, his tone sharp. 'You have a boyfriend.'

I shook my head. My mouth tasted of iron; I had bitten my cheek when I fell. 'No,' I said. 'Just a friend.'

My uncle snorted. 'A friend,' he mimicked. Sweat had broken out across his skin. Reaching into his pocket, he drew out a handkerchief, dabbing at his hairline. 'Your mother had lots of friends. Did you know? She was most popular. One of my favourites. If she had not married your father, I might have asked her myself.'

'Joachim,' I said, pushing away the revulsion I felt at the possibility of my mother entertaining my uncle's advances.

'Please, Uncle. Is there nothing you can do for him? He has done nothing wrong. It was me. I was lonely. You know how I have tried to lead a quiet life, always observing your teachings, listening to those wiser than myself. I'm an adult now but I still make mistakes. I should have written to you first, asked permission. I . . .' I swallowed. 'I am begging you. Please, help him.'

His hand shot up so quickly I failed to see it, but I felt heat blossom in my cheek. He raised his hand again. This time I heard the smack of his palm against my skin as if it came from far away.

'Help him? *Help* him?' he screamed as my vision swam. 'Your boyfriend is a Western spy! The Germans are threatening war and all you care about is *fucking*?'

The apartment was silent except for my breath, ragged and shallow. Tears forced themselves from my eyes and dropped onto the rug below, dotting the floral patterns.

My uncle watched me, his lip curled in disgust. His breathing had returned to normal. The only evidence that the exchange had cost him anything was the colour of his face, the skin mottled red.

'Your boyfriend will be tried today,' he said. 'If he is found guilty of his crimes, Colonel Rumyanstev will have him sent to a labour camp up north.' He smiled. Goading me. Waiting for me to beg again.

I turned away. I should argue, protest. Inside, I was screaming. But I knew it was too late to save Joachim. Nothing I said would make any difference now.

I felt the air stir against my scorched cheek as he huffed through his nose and strode past me. The guards moved away from the walls, their boots squeaking against the polished wood floors.

My knees trembled. Any moment, they would give way.

Beyond the window, the river moved slowly, the currents eddying past, leaves dancing on the surface. Sunlight sparkled on the Bolshoy Bridge, a dazzling steel construction erected only three years ago by one of Uncle's favourite engineers. Although everyone had marvelled at its modern elements, I privately preferred the old stone bridge it had replaced. *What have those stones witnessed*, Olga would say to me as we strode along beside the horses with their carts that were always backed up across the embankments, their wheels interlocked when they tried to pass each other. *What stories of old Russia would those mossy stones tell?*

'Lydia.' I turned my head. My uncle had paused in the entrance to the hallway, flanked by his guards. 'Your mother. You should know: she killed herself.' His voice soared, an arrow shooting across the room. I felt the shaft of it burrow under my skin. He shook his head. 'I am very sorry to be the one to tell you. She poisoned herself.' He drew in a breath. He did not sound sorry. 'But . . . you are an adult now, as you say. It's time you knew.'

I stared at him.

It could not be true.

Whispers flew around in my head. Snatches of servants' gossip. The world around me grew light and then dark, the furniture shrinking then swelling as if seen through a telescope. I remembered my mother's corpse, her face surrounded by white roses. Her skin was unblemished, creamy and waxen beneath the light from the candles. I bent forward to kiss her farewell, her cheek soft beneath my lips, my nose filling with bitter almonds. Later, I had supposed I imagined it.

A sob escaped my mouth.

Satisfied at last, he left, his footsteps dying away, until I heard the door of the apartment close with a bang.

'Don't cry now, dear one. Think of Brave Vasilisa, the little cloth-maker's girl who defeated the witch and defied the odds to marry the Tsar.'

Olga's words floated down to me like feathers skating on the wind. I was lying on my stomach on the bed, my head in her lap, her fingers raking my hair. It was night time – I knew because the lamp on the table was lit – but I did not know the hour. It did not matter.

Night or day, Joachim was imprisoned. Tomorrow, he might be thrown onto a train, bound for a labour camp in the North. I would never see him again.

My mother was dead and those who knew the truth of her final moments had lied to me. My uncle was a tyrant. My face burnt where he had struck me.

Olga's fingers paused. I felt gentle tugging as she pulled apart a knot, untangling my hair with practiced ease. A dozen toys watched us from the shelves lining my room, reminders of the childhood I seemed unable to leave behind. Stuffed bears whose arms had once held chocolate boxes from the Lenin Chocolate Factory. A yellow puppy, watching me with mournful eyes, its fabric skin threadbare, stitches loosened from repeated embrace. My red Pioneers scarf was looped about its neck, along with my badge on which the cheerful words 'always ready!' were emblazoned. Beside the toys sat trophies from my school days: awards for gymnastics, for singing, for writing letters to 'our Father, our leader, the great Chieftain' who would unite the Soviet countries to the same cause. On the wall near my picture of Lenin was a childish sketch I had done of Papa, what I could remember of him, and a large framed photograph of my Uncle Stalin, his face wreathed in a gentle, beatific smile. It was the same one issued to each student of Model School No. 25 at the graduation ceremony. The glass sparkled brightly in its wooden frame. Our maid cleaned it every day, polishing it to keep off the dust and coming in each afternoon to draw the shades so the sun would not fade the colour print.

I jerked my head sharply, turning away from it towards the bare wall. Olga's fingers were still tangled in my hair, and I felt a few strands tear away, twisted from the roots. My scalp burnt. *Good.*

Olga gasped. Her hand fluttered over my back, hovering like a bird afraid to land.

'Why didn't you tell me?' My voice was muffled by her dress. 'Why did you lie?'

There was silence. *She's thinking*, I thought. *Imagining how to phrase her lies so they are tastier, so I will swallow them like medicine.* 'Oh, my little Vasilisa . . .' she said at last, her hand cupping the back of my head.

'No.' I sat up, shaking myself free from her grasp. 'Don't call me that.'

Olga's face fell. She looked suddenly old in the lamplight, her skin like crinkled linen, her eyes dull buttons aged by time. A surge of pity and love rose up inside me. Along with my mother, this woman had raised me. Her stories were woven into every memory, her funny sayings and proverbs always in the back of my mind. My mother had hired her before I was born. Before she came to work as Mama's trusted companion and confidante, Olga was married to a chef employed at the world-famous Hotel Metropol on Theatre Square. In the years before the Revolution, the Metropol had been the glamorous epicentre of life in Moscow, with film stars attended by uniformed bellhops, a restaurant with full silver service and a bar that played American jazz every night of the week. During the battle with the Tsar's loyalists, Bolsheviks had shot out every window in the hotel's expensive façade. The White Army had responded with force, peppering the streets with bullets. Some of the fleeing staff had been killed, including Olga's husband. Bereft, Olga had taken up work as a cleaner at the House on the Embankment, and it was here that my mother met her. Each day, Olga would clean Mamochka's rooms and tell her stories. Eventually, Mama gave her a job as her companion and her own room in our apartments. She could not bear to be without Olga and her stories, and when I was born, she had entrusted me to Olga's care while she attended Party meetings and tried to improve her education with courses at the Industrial Academy. Olga was the closest thing I had to a mother. Hurting her was like sticking a needle beneath my own fingernail.

Sitting up, I took her hand and held it in my lap.

She sniffed. 'I should have told you,' she said with a sigh. 'But it was not my decision to make, and your uncle, he made us all promise, swear, that we would keep it a secret from you. He said it was for your own good, that your mother's memory should not be tainted by scandal. It was to protect you.' Her mouth hardened. 'Now I see he was saving it, to use it against you himself. How could he hurt you this way?'

Her voice made me look up sharply. Much worse had happened during the past few years. So many people had been arrested. Many of the ground floor apartments in our building were still empty, the residences sitting bare, their occupants held in Lubyanka accused of spying and feeding intelligence to the West. A sudden coldness crept over my skin.

I found myself thinking of Alyona Petrova; a quiet girl I had met four years ago at the Model School. Alyona and her parents had moved to Moscow so her father could pursue his work as a State Publisher. One morning she had simply failed to return to class. Rumours circulated that her father had been exposed for printing anti-Soviet pamphlets. And then there was the Vasiliev family from apartment 120. Every one of them – three daughters, two sons, wife and husband – had disappeared one cold winter night last year. Zoya told us that they'd been reported for criticising the Soviet regime and spreading rumours about Lavrentiy Beria, the powerful head of the NKVD. They had fled before they could be captured.

A new thought struck me. What if people like Alyona's father and the Vasiliev family had been innocent, as Joachim was? Joachim was no spy and yet he had been accused. I knew now that he would be convicted, no matter the truth. Had Olga and I so blindly believed everything I was told that we had cut those neighbours from our lives and thoughts, ignoring the evidence before us? What if their crimes had not been crimes at all, but slights against my uncle and his friends? What if their imprisonment was nothing more than the will of a madman, bent on revenge? I felt sick with regret.

'He must hate me,' I said. 'That's why he keeps me here in this place. To control me.'

Olga said nothing. She tried to tug her hand away, but I held it fast.

'Is that why Papa left?' I said.

Olga's eyebrows drew down. 'Your father . . .' She paused, her fingers plucking at her skirt. I knew she did not want to discuss it; it was something we did not speak of often, the way Papa had virtually disappeared after Mamochka's death, leaving Olga and me to deal with the aftermath, travelling instead to the furthest reaches of Russia's empire to carry out his duty. Now I wondered if there wasn't another reason for his sudden absence. What if he had been sent away against his will?

I knew Papa still cared for me; he wrote a few times a year to tell me where he was stationed, what his life was like. My situation was not unusual for the daughters of bureaucrats. I knew one girl, Natalya Kruglova from apartment 280 in the ninth entrance, whose mother had died in childbirth. She had been raised entirely by her nanny and an army of servants while her father, a General, moved on to remarry and spend time with his new family in the Ukraine. At least my father had not left me completely behind. At least he had kept me informed of his whereabouts and sometimes responded to my questions about life outside of Moscow.

The last letter he'd sent had been postmarked Tartu. I'd been excited to receive it, aware of my mother's connection to Estonia, wondering if my father recalled the warm memories Mamochka had shared about her birthplace or if he'd had time to visit the coastal town of Haapsalu where she had lived until my grandparents brought her here. I had filed the letter in my desk, wedged between two books, the paper creased over many times. It had, sadly, not contained any stories about Mamochka or about Haapsalu, but perhaps those memories were too painful for him to speak about. Instead, he had described his work as Partorg of the area and the surrounding parishes, detailing the poor conditions in which the Estonians had lived before the Soviets arrived; their farms bare, empty of workers to maintain them and harvest produce; the local government full of corrupt officials skimming money from funds that should be used to educate the less fortunate. In return, I had sent him a clipping from *Pravda* about the way the Baltic populations had welcomed the Soviets with open arms, praising Stalin and sending him good wishes in the form of poems and stories. Although Papa had been too busy to respond, I liked to imagine him smiling as he received my package, perhaps reading my letter over breakfast before he put on his uniform and climbed into the car waiting to take him to his office. We might not be physically close, but I was convinced there was a tenderness in his letters that remained unchanged all through the years. He still signed his letters, *Your loving Papochka.*

'I don't know,' Olga said at last. 'Your papa thought you would be safer here. It's not easy, the life of a police captain. Moving about wherever you are sent. Your papa does love you, that I do know. Sometimes love is complicated, though. When you were younger, you would host parties in his honour and all your toys would be police captains and lieutenants. Do you recall?'

I did. I remembered making my toys drink cups of milk

while I watched my parents dance from beneath a table during a garden party my uncle was hosting in the Kremlin's gardens. My uncle had asked my mother to dance. I could still see her fine pale hair caught up in an elegant chignon on the top of her head and hear the bell-like notes of her laughter as Uncle swirled her around, the flash of her teeth as they caught the dazzling light from the nearby fountain.

My vision swam with unshed tears.

'You should rest,' Olga said, heaving herself off the bed. 'Your face will be sore tomorrow, I expect. Worse. I will send Zoya for some cold cuts to reduce the swelling.' Gently cupping my chin, she inspected me. She ran her thumb lightly beneath my half-swollen eye but I still winced. Olga clicked her tongue. 'Such a man it is who beats young girls. Ah. But to say such things is not wise. Even the walls in this place have ears.' She turned to go but stopped with one hand on the door. 'Don't think too harshly of your papa or your mother,' she said. 'She was a beautiful woman but she was sad. Always homesick. You remember the stories she used to tell you, her Estonian tales. She always had to hide such things from your uncle. She did not dare remind him of her Baltic heritage. It was a sore point, with your uncle; the lost countries.' Olga tilted her head, her eyes thoughtful. 'Now that the Baltics belong to Russia again, I suppose he would not care.'

She let the door fall closed with a click.

I lay back on my bed, thinking about Joachim in Lubyanka, wondering if even now he was shivering on the concrete floor of his cell or whether he was already in a smelly boxcar travelling north to one of the barren oblasts. Wherever Joachim was, it was my fault. I squeezed my eyes closed, trying to shut out the images of his arrest that kept repeating themselves over and over. I knew I should sleep but what point was there? When I woke up Joachim would still be missing – I knew that not only would I never see him again, but I would never know his fate – and I would still be prisoner to my uncle's whims.

I must have dozed. A sound woke me, a small noise like a satin ribbon sliding through a woman's hands. I sat up. The sky outside the window was pitch black. The oil in the lamp sputtered, throwing shadows across the walls. Although our apartment was one of the lucky few to have electricity, Olga preferred the peasant romance of an old-fashioned lantern, insisting that the *Ilych* lamps, naked electrical bulbs designed to hang from the ceiling, could never set the right scene for her tales.

Mamochka? Are you there? I let my mind become quiet, imagining I was standing beside a curtain in the stalls, like the one always reserved for Olga and me at the Bolshoi ballet. I imagined my mother on the other side, her shadow falling across the heavy crimson drapes, her hand just out of reach. I waited, holding my breath. I had a feeling that if she did not speak now, she never would again. I hesitated, wanting to be angry with her, but also afraid that if I banished her, she would not return. *Mamochka, I forgive you.*

Nothing.

I sighed. A vast emptiness yawned inside me. This was the truth, then. I was now all alone.

And then very faintly, I heard her. *I am here.* I sat up, my skin tingling. Her voice was soft. I strained to listen. *The tin!*

I jumped up and knelt beside my bed, drawing in a sharp

breath as my knees banged on the floor. Thrusting my hand beneath the frame, I felt around until I found what I was after; a loose board, its edges worn smooth. I wedged my thumb beneath its lip, levering until I felt the board give way and I could thrust my hand inside. My fingers met the rough surface of the metal. I pulled. It slid out into the pool of light thrown by the lamp: a biscuit tin, speckled with age.

As I flipped open the lid, dust flew into the air. It singed my throat, but I didn't care. I waved it aside, impatient for it to clear, my mind focused only on the objects nestled inside.

When the air settled, I could see them clearly. An old lace shawl wrapped around a tattered book. A photograph, its edges curled with age.

They were the only items of my mother's I owned. I had salvaged them as servants moved back and forth the week after her death, carrying her belongings out of the room. My uncle had ordered everything to be removed. Her beautiful *takhta*: the vanity table with its gilt-edged mirror. Her fur coats, her silver-backed brushes, the nylon fibres still woven about with long strands of her white-gold hair. Everything was piled up in a lorry downstairs, ready to be taken away. Watching between the banisters of the staircase, I had known that if I did not hurry, there would soon be nothing left. Waiting until the men were distracted by the bulk of an ornately carved armoire, I darted in, my heart beating like a thief's, grabbing blindly at whatever came to hand. The result lay before me now; perhaps not what I would have chosen had I been given time to think. But the combination seemed a message in itself, or perhaps it was that I had never looked at them in quite the same way, thinking of them only as touchstones to a past I could not reclaim. At first, I had hidden them in my cupboard, bringing them out each week to pore over, trying to glean every last memory, imagining my mother's hands placed over my own. But with Uncle's surveillance everywhere, I grew fearful they would be discovered. When I had stumbled on Stepanov, one of my uncle's bodyguards, reading my diary after school, I knew I needed a better place to store them.

The book was a small volume of Estonian poetry and folklore, some of it handwritten. Flicking back the cover, I read the inscription recorded inside. The ink had faded from black to brown but some of the words were still visible. They were written in Estonian, the strange symbols such a contrast to the Cyrillic we used.

For dear little Ana,
A gift for you from your fatherland to remind you
always. Until we meet again.
P.S. Do not drop your stitches!

The signature had faded. I ran my finger over the page, wondering for the hundredth time who the mysterious writer had been. Who had given this book to my Mamochka? I had never thought to ask until it was too late and she was gone. Skimming through the book of poems now was like meeting a long-lost friend. I understood most of the Estonian words from the lessons my mother had given me in secret as we sat in her boudoir each morning while Olga stood guard outside. As she read from the book's pages, Mama's beautiful language had flowed around me like dust motes in the air, the words settling on my skin. After each session, Mama had sworn me to secrecy. She'd told me that the poets featured in the book were all dead now, but they had been the forebears of Estonian culture, inspiring their countrymen to rise up against their oppressors, back then the Baltic Germans and the Russian Tsar, and to demand their independence. No wonder Uncle had not liked to be reminded of my mother's culture. It was too close for comfort, too great a reminder of the power of ordinary people to do extraordinary things.

The photograph showed my mother as a girl of seven or eight, clothed in a white summer dress, standing outside a large building – a town hall with fluted columns and dormer windows. The sun beamed down on her shining hair and the oversized bow tied on one side of her head. I remembered my mother telling me it had been taken in Haapsalu, on the coast of Estonia. The Town Hall was where my grandfather worked, along with his brother, my great-uncle, who had a large estate that included a farm, a sauna and a little lake where my family would go in summer to picnic beside the shore. It was there, in Haapsalu, that my mother had been taught to knit by the local women. Her lessons were interrupted when my grandfather had a falling out with my great-uncle and moved the whole family away to Moscow when my mother was fifteen. My mother told me that her aunt and uncle later lost the farm and moved away without letting anyone know their destination. One of her greatest regrets, she often said, was never going back to search for them or to speak again to the women who had shown her how to bind off a single strand of yarn to make the lace edges sewn onto the centre of the shawl I now held in my lap.

Draping it across my hand, I marvelled again at the shawl's tiny stitches. The pattern was a mystery. It ran in a series of repeated images down the middle, finishing in small bobbles knitted to the corners. Although it was soft, its weight was comforting. I remembered the way my mother had thrown it into the air as I sat in her room, allowing the folds of it to settle upon my shoulders like snowflakes.

What would she say now, my Mamochka, if she could witness me trapped here in this place at the mercy of my uncle? Would she advise me to stay put, as meek as a mouse, or to find shelter elsewhere until he came to his senses and forgave me my indiscretions? What if my Olga was arrested next on some made up charge? I could not bear to imagine her locked away. The guilt would be too much. Where could we go, though? Any place we tried to run in Moscow would not be far enough, even if I did have friends who would be brave enough to defy my uncle and take pity on me. His guards would find us and I would be dragged back to face a greater punishment than the one I had endured yesterday.

As I ran the shawl through my hands, an image appeared suddenly before me. A pine forest. A farmhouse. A sauna nestled deep in the woods. Waves lapping at a shoreline.

A seed of an idea began to unfurl. What if I went to Papa? What if I begged him to shelter me?

Putting the shawl back in the tin, I rummaged in my drawer, moving aside my stockings to take out the book Joachim had lent me; a worn copy of *Crime and Punishment*. Inside were roubles he had asked me to put away for safekeeping. The apartment he lived in was shared with six others, and it was not safe to leave personal belongings about. Although I was allowed a monthly stipend from my uncle, it was carefully meted out, each account recorded in a ledger. Another form of control.

I hurried to Olga's room and knocked on her door. 'Olga?' She appeared in the doorway, her silvery hair loosened for sleep. I saw her flinch and remembered how my face must look, the imprint of Uncle's hand on my cheek darkening.

I shoved the roubles into her hand, and she looked down at them in surprise.

'I want you to go to the train station first thing tomorrow,' I whispered. 'And buy us two tickets.'

Her mouth fell open. 'Where are we going?'

'To Papa,' I said. 'In Estonia.'

'Estonia?' She looked horrified, as if it were the other side of the world. Casting a look up the empty hallway, she dragged me into her room. The lamp beside her own bed was lit. A book lay open on the bedspread. 'But your uncle, Lida!' she hissed. 'He won't allow it.'

'I will write to him,' I said. 'I promise. Once we're away. Papa, too. We must write to him before we go, to let him know we are coming, but we mustn't give him a chance to say no. We must send word and then leave straightaway.'

Olga was shaking her head. She pushed the roubles towards me. 'I cannot.' She lifted her chin. Her eyes flashed. 'I will not let you do this, Lydochka. It is madness.'

'Is it madness for me to want to see my own father? Is it madness to want to see with my own eyes the place my mother was born? I have questions only Papa can answer.'

Olga's lips pursed. I knew what she was thinking but I fancied I could also see a glimmer of sympathy in her eyes, a tiny scrap of doubt. It would be easy to give up meekly and return to my bed. But I could not stay here any longer. I would not die alone, like a flower pressed behind a glass.

I forced myself to speak coldly. 'If you won't help me, I will have to go alone.'

Olga's shoulders stiffened, but then her eyes filled with tears. 'If I promise to help you, you must follow my instructions, Lida. No lying. You do exactly as I say. Agreed?' She held out her hand. I pressed the money into it. Leaning forward, she hugged me, taking care not to press her face against my bruised cheek.

When Olga left the next morning, I flew around the apartment, packing the things I thought we would need. Into my suitcase went Mamochka's shawl, her photograph and book. Enough clothes to last me a week. I dragged out an old school book, tearing a page loose and scribbling my note to Papa on its lined surface. When I was done, I folded it and placed it in an envelope, ready to be sent. I spied the copy of Joachim's book still on my bed and put it in, too. *Crime and Punishment*; a reminder of what he had sacrificed. A reminder of my uncle's cruelty, his despotism. Soon I would be free of him.

A day later, we crossed the border from Russia into Estonia. I felt the air change.

It was subtle. It began with a tingling in my feet; a feeling of spreading warmth that twisted around my ankles and climbed steadily up my body until I felt my heart begin to thaw. The fear of being pursued and the heavy guilt of leaving Joachim behind were beginning to fade, at least for now.

We had slipped into Serafimovicha Ulitsa just before dawn, hurrying through the empty lobby of the building complex during the handover between the night and day security officers, when both men were distracted. Moving through the back streets of Moscow, we had caught an early trolley car to Kazanksy Station and waited in the shadows until it was time for our train to depart. Although Olga grumbled about being tired and the weight of her suitcase, she had done as I asked, organising our passage and sending the letter.

As the train thundered along, I rubbed my hands together and wriggled my toes, pressing them against the inside of my sandals. I was glad of them now; I could not imagine travelling in heels, even if they were fashionable. Through the window, I could see a pine forest, the trees spreading their arms wide as if to touch each other and the snaking form of the train as it rounded a bend, leaving the border checkpoint behind, a grey plume of steam ribboning up from the funnel into the sky.

Impulsively, I jumped up and lifted the sash.

Smoke and coal dust filled the compartment, speckling the air with tiny black dots. I gagged, pressing the back of my hand to my mouth. Pine trees scraped past, scattering fir needles onto the compartment floor. The fresh scent of them rose up, zesty and intoxicating. It was the scent of my freedom.

'*Bozhe moi!* My God!' With a hand tented across her face to shield her eyes, Olga shoved me aside and slammed the sash shut. She turned, her face red, her expression aghast. 'What were you thinking?'

I straightened up, willing my chest to stop hitching as the air cleared, one hand still pressed to my mouth. 'It was . . . hot.'

In her haste, Olga had knocked my suitcase to the ground, spilling Joachim's book along with my mother's shawl. Olga saw it and her eyes narrowed. Bending down, she plucked at a corner of the lace. Her mouth fell open.

'This was your mother's,' she said. 'How on earth did you find it?'

'I – I stole it from her bedroom. The day her things were taken away.'

Olga peered closely at it. 'Extraordinary! I thought it was lost!'

I moistened my lips. 'I wanted to tell you, but I couldn't. I didn't want you to get into trouble.'

Olga was rubbing the lace between her fingers. 'She loved this shawl. You know, she made it herself. A woman taught her.'

'She told me.'

'I envied such talent. Me, I will never be one to sit around and knit. Eating, perhaps, I can do. Cooking a little. Stories, certainly. But knitting? I have not the patience. Here,' she held it out, strung between her hands. 'You should wear it.'

Her fingers brushed my neck as she wound the lace around my throat. Now that the air had cleared, I caught the scent of dust in the shawl, like the lingering whiff from old books or parchment and the faint sweet scent of biscuits from the tin. Reaching up, I adjusted it, so that the fringes hung down my back in a triangle, the way my mother had shown me when I was a child.

When I stepped back, one hand against the wall to steady myself as the train swayed, it was to find Olga's eyes glistening with tears.

'Your eyes are so much like hers,' she said. Then seeming to remember herself, she rubbed her nose with the heel of her hand and turned to her own large suitcase. 'Well. If we are confessing to things we were not supposed to keep . . .' She rummaged through the contents, emerging a moment later with a huge bearskin coat bundled in her arms. 'Here,' she said. 'I saved it for you!' It gleamed in the swaying sunlight from the window, the edges of it trailing on the ground. I recognised it at once, and my stomach lurched. It had never occurred to me that Olga would keep something so awful. Now I understood why she had grumbled about dragging her bulging suitcase with her.

'Olga, please . . . no.' I bent to pick up Joachim's book. Its cover was wrinkled, the pages dog-eared. Joachim's fingers had folded them. I imagined him lying on his bed, the book propped up in his hands, surrounded by the sounds of the other tenants in his block laughing and arguing. What would he be hearing now? The screech of train wheels? The voices of men and women sobbing for the lives they had left behind? With trembling hands, I placed the book carefully back in the bottom of my case. I would have to trust that wherever he was, Joachim would want me to seek safety. He would not want his sacrifice to be in vain.

'You must wear it.' Olga's face startled me as she appeared around the side of the coat. 'You promised you would listen. Do you think I want your father to know how I have neglected my duties?'

I threw her her an exasperated look.

'It's spring! It's warm.'

'The air is changeable.' Olga glared at me. 'Your mother might send a demon to punish me. She will know I have failed to take care of you. How I have undone the promise I made to her the day you were born and I held you in my arms for the first time. Your mother was weak from childbirth. She bled so much she thought she might not survive. Of course, she did, but she made me promise then that I would care for you if she was gone.' Olga stared solemnly off into the middle distance. '*Olga Andreyevna Konstantinova*, she said, *do you promise to protect my child, Lydia Volkova; to stay with her, no matter where she might be sent; to do everything in your power to keep her safe from illness and violence, from the vile intentions of men who would corrupt her with evil words and deeds?*'

Her voice had grown louder with every word. Now it boomed around the small compartment, audible over the clatter of train wheels. She lifted her hand, fist curled, a fiery glint in her eyes. For a woman of sixty-five and of diminutive height, she was an impressive figure.

Bundling up the coat, she sank onto the seat. 'I suppose I should not complain. I've been lucky. You have grown into a beautiful woman. Your mother would be proud. The end is the crown to any work.' Pressing her lips together, she leant her head back and closed her eyes.

My heart gave a sharp, guilty twist.

I had promised her I would listen.

I took the coat from her hands. The fur strands clung to my skin as I lifted the coat and shrugged it on. The heavy folds swallowed up the silky fabric of the pleated black skirt I had pulled on this morning and the cream-coloured blouse with pearl buttons and scalloped collar. It fell in swathes to puddle around my feet. Slipping one arm into a sleeve, I felt the weight of it against my shoulder. The satin lining slithered against the bare skin at my wrist.

Thoughts buzzed like flies in my head, looping around and around in disconnected circles. I remembered the warm afternoon at the dacha in Zubalovo when my uncle, smiling triumphantly, had emerged from an afternoon's hunting with my father, dragging the body of the brown bear he had shot, vowing to have it made into a coat for my mother. I remembered seeing my mother wear the coat for the first time, her frown as she examined her reflection in the long mirror that hung over the *takhta* in her room.

Had she felt it too, the suffocating weight of the coat, the claustrophobic crush of the fur that seemed to constrict movement, squeezing tighter with every breath?

Sweat beaded my forehead. I reached up to brush it away.

Outside in the train corridor, the conductor called out, informing passengers that the next stop would be made within the hour to allow passengers to disembark, and that a short time after that, we would arrive at our destination in Tartu.

'Not far to go now.' Olga creaked an eyelid open. 'Ah. I see you've come to your senses.' A satisfied smile played over her lips. 'You see? It *is* cool. Best to be prepared for the change in climate. Estonia.' She gave a small shudder. 'Why your uncle sent your father here is anyone's guess. So far from Moscow. So very far from home. Still, your mother always spoke of it with such fondness.'

I resumed my seat beside her, tucking the coat around me so the ends didn't drag, as meek as the child she insisted I still was. The spiky ends of the fur pricked against my neck. I could not help but imagine it a collar, growing tighter the further away from Uncle we drew.

Peacock Tails

Kati

'Stand up, damned of the Earth
Stand up, prisoners of starvation
Reason thunders in its volcano
This is the eruption of the end!'

I SMILED AS I CROSSED THE COURTYARD TO AUNT JUUDIT'S apartment block. It was not yet ten in the morning, but her gramophone was working overtime, cranking out '*L'Internationale*', the loud orchestral tune that had been chosen by Lenin, before his death, to celebrate the grandeur and might of the Communist party. The origin of the song itself was French but the Russians had adopted it as their anthem. They had even expanded it from four stanzas to six, the better to capture its spirit of revolution. Stalin, Lenin's successor, was said to love it so much that it was often referred to as 'Stalin's Song'.

Aunt Juudit appeared in the doorway of the apartment block holding a broom. Her hair had faded from the bright red I remembered from childhood – the same shade as the crimson geraniums spilling from the wooden planter boxes beside the door – to the dull silver of old coins. As I approached she continued to sing, oblivious to everything, swinging the broom and swaying her body in time with the music. She had a beautiful voice; a powerful alto-contralto, cultivated through many years of training at the Conservatory in Tallinn.

If she had continued, she might have gone on to be one of the greatest opera singers Estonia had ever known. But an unfortunate bout of bronchial illness had befallen her in her twenties, robbing her of breath. Her lungs had never been the same. She had come here to Tartu to live on the farm with my parents and Grandmother, before she met and married my uncle, a professor at the university. Although she had done her best to be content with a quiet life, it was not possible for her to give up singing altogether; music beat in her heart and pulsed in her veins. When our old choir mistress died, it was Aunt Juudit who took over, marching in with her record player in its box beneath her arm to teach us songs. Every fifth year she travelled back to Tallinn to sing with her old choir friends at *laulupidu*, the song festival, and when I was eight she had taken me with her. We had reached the stadium to find a brass band in full swing, the trumpeters blasting notes while the trombone players sent out rippling *glissandos* of sound. I heard hymns from Viljandi, fishing songs from island settlements like Saaremaa. My favourite was *regilaul*, runo song, which was poetry with a little melody mixed in. Like the sagas of Iceland, it told the stories of everyday people, but our runo was mostly sung by women, so the stories were flavoured with the preoccupations of women's lives: births and deaths, betrayals. Hardships and heartbreak. All the things that had not changed in more than two thousand years since the first runo was sung.

Although there was a chance the song festival would go

ahead in three years' time, it would be the Russians who organised it. There would be no runo. *L'Internationale* was the Soviet-approved anthem now. Although I found its melody stirring, the meaning behind its popularity left a sour taste on my tongue. Its showy brass and bluster could never match the quiet power of '*My Fatherland, My Happiness and Joy*', the song Estonians had chosen as their anthem, as a reminder of their independence and their faith, a song nobody dared to sing now in the face of arrest and execution or deportation. With a pang, I remembered what Papa had told me the day Oskar's mother was murdered; all it took was one tune sung in front of the wrong people for the Russians to act. We were a tiny minority living on a knife's edge.

Catching sight of me, my Aunt Juudit glanced up. A smile illuminated her features. A lace shawl was knotted around her neck, decorated with her signature pattern of peacock tails. She drew me to her side, and we sang the last line of the anthem together, Aunt Juudit's soft, papery cheek pressed against my own.

> *This is the final struggle!*
> *Let us group together and tomorrow*
> *The Internationale*
> *Will be the human race.*

The trumpets gave one final triumphant blast and faded away.

Above us, a window banged open. A man's face appeared, grizzled features twisted into a scowl. He rubbed at his eyes with a scarred knuckle, cursing at us in heavily accented Russian.

Aunt Juudit radiated a smile. 'Ah! Good morning, Mr

Vachenko! Would you care to join us? It's never too early for a bit of patriotism, is it?'

The old man's eyes narrowed, but he clamped his lips shut. The glass rattled as he slammed the window closed.

Aunt Juudit turned to me, one eyebrow raised. 'What do you think, Kati? Another round?'

I shook my head, trying not to smile.

Since her dismissal as choir mistress last year when the Soviets arrived, Aunt Juudit's small rebellion was to play '*L'Internationale*' as loudly as possible each morning.

'Let them dare to complain,' I'd heard her say. 'Let them be dragged off for treason. It won't be me!'

So far nobody *had* dared to complain; not the new Russian residents in the units above, nor any of the remaining Estonians in the surrounding buildings in this small corner of Tartu.

Aunt Juudit lifted her shoulders and sighed in mock disappointment. 'Ah well. Another time, perhaps.' She cupped my cheek. 'It's good to see you, Kati. I was starting to worry.'

'I'm sorry I'm late,' I said. 'I couldn't catch a lift this morning. It seems all the lorries were headed in the other direction.'

Waving off my apology, my aunt picked up the broom and shuffled backwards to prop open the door. 'Never mind. Come in, come in. The others are waiting.' As I began to move past her she reached out to squeeze my arm and lowered her voice. 'Kati, Viktoria has finished the pasque-flower shawl at last. Make a fuss, won't you? You know how fragile she is. I think, between you and me, that she's finally starting to improve.'

A fresh chord of guilt plucked at my heart. How could I tell them about the wool?

I scurried past before Aunt Juudit had a chance to say more.

The apartment was not a large one; there was no grand entrance. The door opened straight into the cosy parlour. Although from the outside the apartment seemed quiet and unassuming, inside it was a hive of activity on a morning like this, the last meeting of knitting circle before the market next week. Women were crammed into every available space. Some, like my cousin Etti, were squashed into armchairs near the window, their knitting in their laps, their tongues already busy imparting the latest news. Others, like the sisters Miri and Helve, were busy on the balcony outside. Their laughter drifted in through the open door. They were stretching a shawl across a birch wood frame. They looked up, their cheeks pink, holding the frame between them. The shawl's lace edges were hooked across the bordered nails like a net designed to catch leaping circus performers. A bucket sat at their feet, filled with warm soapy water. Each shawl we made had to be hand washed gently in rainwater collected in buckets and heated to eliminate any impurities. Once blocked and dried, the yarn would relax into its final shape and any loose stitches were woven back in.

'Hi! Kati!' Their voices rang out warmly in greeting.

I raised my hand.

Other women murmured greetings at me before turning back to their neighbours to resume their conversations. Today was not just a day of tying up loose ends. It was also a chance to talk and catch up on the latest news. Since the arrival of the Soviets, our local newspaper *Postimees* had been full of stories unrelated to the annexation. It was clear that the journalists were being held to ransom; they could not print the truth, so the only way to glean any real knowledge was to listen to local gossip.

Snatches of it trickled through the room.

'Did you hear about Helju Jänes from Pärnu county? Her husband was arrested last month.'

'Those poor children!'

'She took her last roubles to the *upravlenie* administration office to ask them for help. She was hoping they would exchange them for food.'

'And what did they do?'

'Well, they turned up in the middle of the night and turned her house upside down, didn't they, searching for more! Of course, they found nothing. Then they took her away, too.'

An indrawn gasp. 'Where did they take her?'

'Nobody knows. The children will have to work on the *kolkhoz* farm now. No more school for them.'

There was a pause as this depressing news sank in before the gossip resumed.

'In Ülejõe, the Police Captain let some Russian prisoners out of jail,' said Tuuli. 'Gave them a pardon. They told my cousin the men had been "wrongfully imprisoned" by the old Estonian government. Now my cousin is afraid to walk down the street without her husband. When she complained, the militia laughed at her and told her she had better exercise harder in case she had to run and escape. Animals. I told her she must write to me weekly and let me know she is safe. I can't bear to think of her and those children in their flat all vulnerable and alone the nights Karlos is away.'

More outraged muttering. I saw Etti lean forward in her

chair and pat Tuuli on the arm in sympathy. Tuuli gave my cousin a sad smile but then lifted her shoulder as if to say, 'What can be done?'

The answer, of course, was 'nothing'.

It was not safe to speak the truth in the street. We each of us knew that what was said in the knitting circle must remain there, but we had also an unspoken contract that we would not keep secrets unless they were not ours to tell. It made the import of what I had come to say feel even heavier. How could I tell these women, who had so much invested in the knitting of shawls, that there was no longer an opportunity to knit, to tell stories and share the collective burden of our pain?

I could feel Etti's eyes on me. My poor cousin knew the pain of overwhelming grief and the need to share it in some safe place. Eight months had passed since her husband's death, but her face had not lost its gaunt, haunted expression. Sadness had suppressed her appetite, so she was even thinner than the rest of us, her arms thin ropes, devoid of muscle. I turned quickly away, busying myself with my own shawl, unlooping it from around my neck and hanging it on the old timber hallstand next to the door. I recognised a scrap of my grandmother's knitting still hanging there; the final sampler she had ever made, a wolf's paw print pattern identical to the one woven into my own lace. It always gave me a little jolt of sadness to see it, to remember her in this very room, her slippers whispering as she moved among the women, the rise and fall of her voice as she made suggestions of improvement or pointed out necessary corrections that would save the knitter the agony of having to unpick rows of yarn down the track. Although the other samplers she had made were carefully preserved, my grandmother had told us she wanted this one to remain visible in Aunt Juudit's apartment, to be always in view to remind us that she was still around, still part of the group even if only in spirit.

'There you are, Katarina Rebane.' The most senior woman in our group, Helle, had set aside her knitting and shuffled forward, her elderly face creased into a smile. Helle was so old she resembled a little bird who had long ago lost all its feathers. Her scalp was visible through the fine wisps of her hair. A faded grey housecoat swam on her small frame. Each time I saw her, she seemed to have shrunk a little more. I held her hands while she pecked at my cheek. Her kiss was as light as the brush of a sparrow's wings, but when I drew back I saw that her eyes were sparkling knowingly and when I squeezed her fingers gently she gripped me with such surprising strength I had to laugh.

'*Tere hommikust,*' she whispered in Estonian. *Good morning.* She was always formal despite having known me since I was just a scrap of a child playing about my grandmother's ankles while snippets of gossip eddied overhead, punctuated by the rhythm of clicking needles. Helle and my grandmother had been close friends, united by their love of knitting and by their dreams that one day their handknitted Estonian shawls would be sold in department stores all over the world. It was not such a foolish dream; when the Crown Prince of Sweden visited Estonia in 1932, my grandmother and Helle had travelled to Haapsalu to present him with a shawl made in his honour. Its pinecone pattern, *kroonprints* as it came to be known, had been adapted from a well-known one found on an antique mitten on the island of Muhu. There had also, at one time, been interest from an American investor who had fallen in love with the Haapsalu shawls and planned to entice a group of master knitters to return with him to his department store in New York. Imagine, my grandmother had said with wonder in her voice, every American girl wearing an Estonian lace shawl! The outbreak of war in Europe had put an end to these plans. It was probably for the best; the trip to Haapsalu had taken Helle weeks to recover from. The journey to America, if she had tried to undertake it, might have finished her off altogether.

'*Väga hästi*,' I whispered in return. *Very well*. Then in Russian: 'How did you go this month?'

Helle lifted her chin proudly. 'Ten shawls.'

Some of the women around us looked up from their knitting, muttering in surprise. One woman, Leili Poska, made a disbelieving sound in her throat and set down the practice sampler in her lap. 'Ten? I don't believe it.'

'It's true. I would have made more, if I'd been allotted more yarn.' Helle stooped to lift the lidded basket at her feet onto the empty chair behind. Pulling back the lid, she lifted out a shawl. The other women crowded around as Helle shook out the lace. Gathered eagerly together, they looked like hungry birds cooing over a crumb, eyes shining brightly in pale faces above the grey threadbare dresses they had cinched around their waists. Each woman wore her own lacy shawl, which at least made the clothes seem less tattered than they ought. Material had been increasingly hard to find the past few years; first the war between Germany and Britain had proved restrictive, then there was the lack of clothing available in the Soviet stores. Those who were skilled at sewing, not just knitting, were able to refashion their dresses and skirts but there was a longing among us, especially the young ones, for something new, a nostalgia for the warm memories of St John's Eve when our mothers would gift us with new clothes to celebrate midsummer. At least we could still have a new shawl even if we had to wear our old rags. It was a tiny comfort.

'It's a twig pattern, as Kati suggested,' Helle said, tracing a bony finger along the pattern that zigzagged up the centre of the shawl. 'I added some *nupps* for extra weight. See?'

She tossed the shawl's frilly edge so the *nupps* were visible. Murmurs of envy rose up around us.

'They are all of the same high quality,' Helle said. She pulled the other shawls out and laid them on the chair. 'Kati, you will check them.'

I hesitated. It was not necessary. Helle was a master knitter and her work was always polished. But it was my job to ensure that each shawl we sold was of an acceptable quality; that there were no loose ends or untidy seams. No reason for a buyer to bring it back or raise a complaint.

My grandmother had told me once that there must always be a leader, someone to take charge. *Sometimes it's a burden, sometimes a gift. Never take the responsibility for granted.*

I gave the shawls a cursory glance, testing their weight and splaying them across my hand before folding them up again.

'They are fine,' I said. 'More than fine. They are perfect.'

Helle shrugged her shoulders, as if she had expected nothing less, but a smile teased the corners of her mouth. Master lacework like this was the culmination of years of practice and dedication to the craft. There were not many other areas in which women could boast of such superiority in our world. 'My grandson helped me wash and block them yesterday,' she said. 'He was not pleased when I reminded him of the knitting

I made him do when he came to stay with me each winter as a boy. He told me I should keep my information to myself, if I did not want to find someone else to do my laundry work.'

Laughter erupted from the women nearby. Helle's smile widened. Boys were taught to knit, too, from a young age although they usually gave it up when they were old enough to help with the heavier chores. During the long winters, when snow and darkness made it impossible to go outside, whole families would sometimes work together, carding sheep's wool between paddles to rid it of burrs and then refining it on the spinning wheel, making sure the baskets were always full of yarn.

Helle began to place her folded shawls back in the basket.

'Wait a moment,' Leili said. She turned to me, unsmiling. 'You haven't tested them properly. With the ring.'

Helle's lips compressed and she turned around, scowling. 'What are you talking about?'

'The wedding ring,' Leili repeated, drawing out each word slowly as if Helle were hard of hearing. 'The test.'

The women around us muttered. I saw the flash of teeth as they grinned, excited by the prospect of a little conflict. There had always been competition between Leili and Helle. Rumour said it went back to the time when they were girls and Helle's future husband, then a youth, had swum naked with Leili in Lake Peipus.

'Kati isn't married.' Helle cast Leili a look sour enough to wither grapes. 'So, she doesn't have a ring. Besides, she has already given her approval.'

'Here.' My cousin Etti came to stand beside me. Reaching into the pocket of her skirt, she drew out her wedding band and pressed it into my hand.

I tried to hand it back. 'This is unnecessary.'

Some of the women's eager faces fell.

'No, Kati,' Helle insisted. 'If Leili thinks we should do the test, then we must. I've nothing to fear.'

She handed me the top.m.ost shawl on the pile. The women in the knitting circle leant forward eagerly to watch as I held Etti's ring between my fingers and poked the end of Helle's shawl through. As I pulled the remainder of the lace through, I heard my grandmother's voice. *Each shawl must be fine enough to be drawn through a wedding ring. Just as smoke from a chimney is a sure sign that a woman is knitting inside, so is the ring test a way for us to know a shawl's quality.*

When the shawl pulled clear through, some of the younger women clapped. The mood in the room lifted. Laughter and conversation began to flow as they flocked back to their seats, the older ones relating stories of the other times they had seen the trick performed.

'There, you see?' Helle's eyes were bright. She turned her back pointedly on Leili, who unfolded her arms and hobbled back to her chair. Helle handed me the basket and I took it to the bureau that held the completed shawls awaiting market day.

One or two other women brought forward their shawls for my inspection and then added them to the growing pile in the bureau. Aunt Juudit emerged with a tray from the kitchenette, where she had been heating up water brewed with nettles and strips of birch. Some of the young women wrinkled up their noses at the broth, but others, Helle and Leili included, took up their chipped mugs and muttered a small blessing, grateful for the warm drink that they swore eased their knotted joints and aching bones.

Aunt Juudit restarted the gramophone and led the younger women in another rousing rendition of *L'Internationale* while behind her back, my cousin Etti paused in her knitting to throw me an exasperated look.

With the women occupied, I found a moment to pull out my own yarn and knitting needles. *This shawl will be my last*, I thought, and the knowledge was bittersweet. What pattern would I make? I sat in quiet reflection a moment before taking up the needles for the *veniv kootud serv*: stretchy knitted cast-on. I would make a wolf's paw shawl. It seemed fitting that my grandmother's pattern would be the last I made before I was forced to stop. The pleasant rhythm of the knitting soon took over. I felt my body slowly relax, the tension leaving my arms and legs.

'Kati!' I turned to find Viktoria standing beside me. A wisp of a girl with bad skin and teeth, she smiled at me from beneath a curtain of hair that fell in mousy ringlets down to her waist.

I stood, giving her my brightest smile. 'How are you, Vikki?'

'Good.' Viktoria was twisting a shawl in her hands. 'Look, I finished the pasque-flower! It was hard; you were right, about needing to keep just the right amount of tension in the yarn. I had to unpick a few rows, but it's finished now.'

As I took it from her the lace was warm from her hands. I unfolded it carefully, noting the delicate openwork leaves with twisted stems, the double strand of yarn Vikki had used to strengthen the finer parts. I could feel her watching me anxiously. The bottom edges had been worked carefully so that they draped and did not curl. It was the sort of shawl my grandmother would have praised; although it was not embellished with *nupps*, the foundations of the shawl were secure, the stitches evenly spaced.

'Viktoria,' I said, my heart lifting with pride. 'This is beautiful work!' I turned the shawl in my hands, marvelling at how far Viktoria had come since she first joined our knitting circle last year. If anyone had told me then that it was she who had crafted this fine shawl, I would have shaken my head in disbelief. Viktoria had been living upstairs with her father until the night of the Soviets' arrival. He had been beaten to death after rushing out to protest as the Russian military moved through the streets, rounding up members of political parties and local policemen who would not comply. It was said that half a million troops moved across the Baltics during the first days of the Soviet occupation, their number far outweighing the armies of Estonia, Lithuania and Latvia. Only some people had dared to resist and those who chose to fight, like the Estonian Independent Signal Battalion in Tallinn, soon found themselves surrounded, forced to negotiate and surrender before they too were killed.

A week after the annexation, the same day the Nazis occupied France, Aunt Juudit had found Viktoria wandering dazed in the courtyard outside the apartment block, her hands raw and bleeding. Through her tears, she'd explained how she had gone to search for her father and found a group of soldiers kicking his lifeless body. When she cried out, they chased her. She'd taken refuge in the cellar of a shop which had been looted and set on fire, too scared to return home, too afraid to go back and find her father's body to arrange a burial. When she at last found her way back to the apartment block, Aunt Juudit had organised for her to stay with Helle in the apartment down the hall, and encouraged her to join us, in the hope that the knitting would keep her mind away from the horrors she had witnessed. Even so it had taken at least two months before Viktoria's hands were steady enough to hold the needles properly and another three months of practising by copying my grandmother's lace samplers before she was ready to knit her first shawl.

The Viktoria standing before me was different to the one I remembered from her first knitting circle, that shy ghost of a girl who refused to speak, and winced when I first handed her the needles. This Viktoria stood more confidently, her shoulders pushed back. Her hair shone like copper and even her skin was less red than usual, which probably had something to do with the bars of pine tar soap Helle cooked up in her apartment kitchenette.

'Do you think it's good enough to sell at market next week?' Viktoria said.

'Of course it is.' I began to fold the shawl up, pressing the corners together. 'It is more than good enough.'

Viktoria shuffled from one foot to the other. 'Aren't you going to test it? With the ring?'

I paused, the shawl pinned between my fingers. Viktoria tried to smile but her eyes were troubled. 'That's just a trick,' I told her, trying to soothe. 'It's an old saying. It means nothing these days.'

'No.' She curled her hands into balls. Her mouth was determined. 'I want it to be tested like the others. I need to know if it's good enough. Truly good enough.'

I was about to argue but something held me back. Perhaps it was the memory her words sparked in me. I had said almost the same thing to my grandmother when I was eight, when I had finished my first *rätik* shawl. I brought out Etti's ring again. It glinted in my palm. As I pulled the shawl through, I heard Viktoria draw in a breath.

The shawl slipped through the golden band like a cascade of foamy water.

Viktoria sighed.

'You see?' Refolding it quickly, I strode to the bureau and placed it with the others. 'You have nothing to worry about. You've made amazing progress, Vikki.'

She beamed at me, bouncing on the soles of her feet. 'Perhaps I could try the peacock tails next. Or even the Muhu pine. And one day, I would like to try my hand at the wolf's paw. That is, when you think I am ready, of course.'

Laughing, I shook my head. 'Why not? You can do anything. It's just time and practice now, a matter of patience. Why don't you start with the peacock sampler? When you've mastered it I will help you cast on and you'll be on your own after that.'

'Patience. Yes.' With a last grin and a wave, Viktoria disappeared back to her chair.

'She is like a different girl,' Etti said, coming to stand by my shoulder.

'I was only thinking that,' I said. 'The knitting has changed her. This is yours.' I offered her the wedding ring. Etti took it but did not put it on. 'My fingers are too swollen. Like the rest of me,' she said, glancing down at her body. I had to admit that it did not seem possible that Etti could grow any larger. Her round belly was pulled taut against the white linen of her blouse. She pressed one hand against it as I watched, and then froze as if waiting for a response. A moment passed and her face relaxed. She patted the lump, a furtive smile transforming her face from its usual strained lines into one of pure happiness.

'Is it painful?' I said, not wanting to offend but unable to stem my curiosity. My cousin and I had not been close as children, although we had played together whenever our families met. A few years older than me, Etti had struggled with various childhood illnesses – fevers, colds, wheezing in the lungs – that had kept her from school most days and prevented us from developing the kind of warmth I had seen in other extended families. Then when she was eighteen, she had married a Jewish friend of my uncle's and gone to live with him in Pärnu. Although he was Jewish, David did not observe religious practice, choosing to stay home with his young wife instead of attending synagogue and to work in the fabric shop he had set up in Pärnu's busy market district. In turn, Etti was happy to support him, helping choose the stock and run up samples of dresses and skirts. It was a good match, it seemed. When the Soviets arrived, they had taken David away to work in the mines at Kiviõli along with ten other men from the Pärnu Jewish community, leaving the women to fend for themselves. A heartbroken Etti had returned home to Aunt Juudit's only to receive a letter a month later informing her that David had been crushed in a mine accident along with his crew. For weeks, Etti had been inconsolable. She had rallied, spurred on by the discovery that she was carrying his child, but the sadness had never truly left her.

'It's strange,' she said now, measuring each word slowly. 'It's not what you imagine. Sometimes it's like I have a fish inside me, at other times I can feel hands and feet, it's more like one of the tadpoles Jakob used to tease us with when we were children.'

I rolled my eyes. 'He was a terror.'

Etti grinned. 'The worst.'

'Not much has changed. Does he come here much? He hasn't been home for months. Mama is ready to come and drag him back if he doesn't visit soon.'

Etti rubbed her belly with the flat of her hand. 'I've not seen him for weeks,' she admitted. 'He used to come here almost every night just to feed himself – I think the food at the dorms is not to his liking – but he stopped.'

My thoughts shifted uneasily. Why had my brother turned his back on us? My thoughts, my worries for my brother, led me in a twisting path back to my purpose. I needed to tell the women the truth: that I had not come merely to coordinate the shawls for market day.

I cleared my throat, hoping they would all look up, at the same time dreading the horrified gasps that would accompany my news.

Before I could speak, Aunt Juudit clapped her hands.

'Let's have some more music, ladies,' she said. 'No, not more *"L'Internationale"*. Something better.'

'I thought there was nothing better than *"L'Internationale"*, Mama!' Etti called.

Aunt Juudit pretended to look shocked at both her daughter and at the tittering laughter. Her fingers danced across the records in their folders, flicking them back until she found what she was searching for. She slipped the disk from its sleeve and placed it on the turntable, carefully manoeuvring the needle. The speaker crackled. Then a burst of music erupted into the room.

'That's better!' she said. 'Much less Russian, don't you

agree, Kati? In fact, the opposite!'

My stomach swooped. It was a snippet of 'The Ride' from the opera *The Valkyrie*, by Wagner.

I nodded, trying to keep the smile on my face although it felt stiff and frozen now. Oskar's words echoed in my mind. *The pact will not hold.*

'Kati, are you quite well?' Aunt Juudit crossed the room and laid a hand on my arm.

I swallowed, my chest tight. 'I just need some air.'

Aunt Juudit nodded. 'Come out to the balcony.'

I followed her and Etti out through the timber doors, the triumphant strains of Wagner's opera following on my heels. The balcony was a narrow space, no more than ten paces wide, but Aunt Juudit had managed to fit two timber chairs and a large tub of bright red geraniums onto it, along with the frames on which Miri and Helve's shawls were drying. Beyond the balcony, I saw the grand pillared buildings of the university glowing white in the sun. Far up the hill, I knew, were the red-brick ruins of the Dorpat Cathedral.

A light, warm breeze caressed my face, carrying with it the porous scent of the geraniums. It was peaceful here. If I tried, I could almost forget the importance of what Oskar had said. If I let the breeze tickle my closed eyes, I could almost pretend that it was simply another warm spring in Tartu without the ever-present shadow of the Russians watching over our shoulders, always waiting for their chance to capture the last fragments of freedom we held in our hands.

'Kati? You looked so pale in there.' Aunt Juudit's face was lined with concern. 'Tell us what's troubling you. We're your family. We can help.'

I bit back a sob. I could tell my aunt and my cousin about the Germans, but they would want to know how I came by the information. By talking about our meeting with Oskar, I would be drawing them into danger. Anyone found to be sympathetic to the Forest Brothers and their cause would be arrested or shot. There was only one piece of information that was safe to impart.

'It's the shawls. Papa says we have no more wool. The knitting circle will have to be disbanded. At least until we can find another source. Or until the Soviets leave.' I allowed myself a bitter laugh. The idea was so ludicrous. The only way they would give up the Baltics was through war. A war that, it now seemed, was imminent.

Etti worried at the fringe of her shawl.

Aunt Juudit was silent. Then she nodded slowly. 'Is that the only thing that's troubling you?' She fumbled with the shawl around her neck, her thin fingers unknotting the lace. A sea of peacock tails danced as she waved it at me. 'Tell me, Kati, what do you see?'

I frowned. 'Peacock tails?'

Aunt Juudit laughed. 'No, Kati. You're being too obvious.' She draped the shawl across her arm. 'Look. Do you remember when your grandmother showed me how to knit peacocks? Do you remember what my stitching was like, before she helped me?'

'You picked it up so quickly.' I shrugged. 'I can hardly remember what you were like before.'

'Can't you?' Aunt Juudit flung the shawl around her neck, knotting it nimbly at her throat again. 'Let me remind you: I was dreadful! Etti remembers. Don't you, dear one?'

Etti nodded.

Aunt Juudit pursed her lips. Bending down, she grasped my hands firmly in her own. 'Now listen to me. Selling these shawls was never about money. Yes, the money helps. But we will all share what we have. We will survive. We've survived so far, haven't we? So. What this is really about is you.' She paused. 'You've helped us. Since your grandmother's death, you've kept this group together. Even after last year, even after everything that happened with the Russians. Helle, Viktoria, even Etti here. We have all kept going because you are there to give advice when needed, you are there to show us how and why we knit even when our spirit fails us. Do you understand?'

Her eyes bore into mine until I nodded. It was the reason my grandmother had left me in charge. She would be proud of what we had achieved.

'Good,' Aunt Juudit said. 'Then let's have no more talk about disbanding the knitting circle. It isn't necessary. I'll speak to your father myself. He can't object if we aren't making any sales. What will we do if we have no more yarn? We will unpick all our old shawls and start again. We will teach ourselves to be better. Then, by the time we have found more wool, we will be masters like your grandmother. Like you.'

I blinked hard to force back my tears.

'Good.' Aunt Juudit released my hand, satisfied. 'Now if I can only convince Etti not to call my grandchild Hezekiah or Mikaela, I will consider my duty done.'

Etti's mouth tightened. 'It's my decision, Mama. I think David would have wanted the child to have a Hebrew name.'

'I understand,' Aunt Juudit said, her features softening. 'But perhaps a mixture of both first and middle names?

There are so many fine Estonian names. Your grandfather for instance: Endel. Or Erich, like your uncle. Or Evi or Leelo, if it's a girl.'

Etti touched her belly lightly. 'Well, I will give it some thought. What do you think, Kati?'

I opened my mouth to reply but before I could, Etti moved suddenly. 'Oh!' she exclaimed, bending double to clutch her belly, her mouth stretched in a wide grimace. I watched her face convulse with pain. After what seemed like a lifetime, the pain receded. Her features unknotted and she sagged. 'I'm sorry. It happens more frequently these days.' She placed her hands on either side of her belly. 'You haven't felt her kick yet, have you, Kati?'

I shook my head. I allowed my cousin to place my hand on her belly. For a second, there was nothing, but then I felt something press against my palm, something solid and forceful that said, *Don't ignore me. I am here*. Etti laughed at my sharp intake of breath.

'She's relying on you to teach her,' she told me as the kick came again, knocking against my hand. 'By the time she is our age, she will be the best lace weaver in Tartu.'

'Perhaps she will be a fighter,' I suggested, 'with a kick like that.' It was only afterwards, as Aunt Juudit linked arms with Etti and they moved towards the balcony doors, that my own words sent a chill along my spine. The burden of secret knowledge weighed heavily on my heart. What kind of world would Etti's child enter? What would happen to us if Oskar's prophecy of war came true?

Ring Pattern

Lydia

'*FREEDOM!*'

At first, I thought I'd imagined it; the catchcry of my own heart, the result of exhaustion, of too many hours spent travelling and too much introspection. But it was real, as was the sudden burst of gunfire, deafeningly loud – *rat-a-tat* like the first moment a wireless radio is flicked on and static floods the airwaves.

Through the window, smoke drifted across the platform. Figures moved like shadows behind a glass lamp. Every few seconds, the smoke would clear to show the timber posts scaffolding the station platform's roof, or a person running past.

'Lida? What is happening?' Olga's voice was hoarse with fear.

'I don't know.'

Our train had paused at the small station platform in Tiksoja to drop off passengers before the final leg to Tartu. The whistle had just blown before the rattle of gunfire sent everyone into panic.

I pressed my face against the glass. A cloud of smoke was dispersed by a puff of breeze, revealing the body of a Soviet train guard lying motionless, face down on the platform, a pool of dark blood puddled around him. I drew back sharply, my stomach churning.

'What is it?' Olga cried.

I shook my head, unable to answer. I had never seen a dead body like this before. Mama's corpse in the funeral house had looked almost real, her features smoothed by the embalmer's hands. There'd been no trace of blood, no real evidence her spirit had fled except the lack of movement and the coldness of her skin. This was altogether different. There was a rawness to what I'd witnessed, a sharp edge to the vision like a blade touching skin. I fought the urge to look again, horrified but compelled.

The gunfire resumed. People screamed. Boots thundered in the hallway, and Olga and I clung to each other as the door to our compartment was flung open.

A man in an unfamiliar brown uniform stood before us, hefting a rifle in his arms. 'Out, out!' he yelled. 'Leave everything behind.'

I threw off the heavy fur coat and we obeyed, filing into the narrow corridor with the other passengers. Most of them were sobbing. One woman tripped and fell. Nobody moved to help her. Instead, people stepped over her outstretched limbs, ignoring her pleas for help. Once outside, we heard more voices shouting. The rattle of gunfire was louder, relentless. The stink of it lodged inside my nose. Passengers flung themselves to the ground, and Olga and I did the same.

Small pebbles dug into my cheek. Raising my head slightly, I swivelled my head in time to see boots clomp past.

'Olga!'

'I am here.' Fingers clutched my wrist, digging in. I felt

a hand snake around my waist, Olga's leg pressed against my own.

As suddenly as it had begun, the gunfire ceased. Dust floated down amid the sounds of muffled whimpers.

'Is it over?' I whispered.

Olga's arm tightened around my waist. 'Be quiet.'

More boots filled my vision, moving past us. I dared to raise my head a fraction, and saw that the boots belonged to a group of men, all dressed in the same brown uniform as the man who had boarded the train. *Bandits*. They were running in and out of the train, emerging with their arms full of suitcases and carpet bags. Some were openly rummaging through the luggage, discarding anything not of value. Most had rifles slung over their shoulders. A few stood guard, guns ready, their gaze sweeping the station, watching for any sign of resistance or retaliation, but nobody moved. Nobody resisted. The bodies of the Soviet guards who had been riding the train with us were strewn about the platform.

My heart jumped into my mouth at the sound of something heavy being dragged along the ground. I half-turned and saw a bandit wrestling with a trunk, a monstrously large thing papered over with official-looking stamps and crests. He managed to heave it off the train and onto the platform, where he kicked it and it toppled over onto its side, spilling its contents into the dust. Frilled petticoats and ladies' under-garments disgorged in a tangled heap.

The man bent over them, rummaging like a pig seeking truffles, shoving the petticoats aside until finally he straightened, his prize – a jewellery box – clutched in one hand. Something inside it dazzled as he flicked the lid open.

'Stop!'

A woman nearby had half-risen to her knees. Her face was smeared with dirt, but I recognised her from the station platform in Leningrad. Olga and I had watched the train guard shouting orders to the porter as her trunks were loaded in, while she preened nearby beneath the attention of a handsome man in uniform; a diplomat or a high-ranking officer, most likely. A man of enough importance to secure her a compartment alone in the first-class carriage. Olga had pursed her lips as the train began to hiss steam and the man and young woman enacted a tearful farewell, complete with kisses loud enough to make me turn away.

Now the woman was trembling, one hand clutched at her lace collar.

'Please,' she called, voice husky with tears. 'My fiancé gave me that ring. It belonged to his mother from Kiev. You can – you can take the rest. All the roubles, but . . . please. Let me keep the ring.'

'Fool,' I heard Olga mutter.

The thief paused, one hand still tucked inside his pocket. He had a young face beneath his dirty blond hair that hung down in ragged strips, as if he'd hacked it off with a blunt blade.

'Jaak?'

Footsteps crunched beside us on the gravel.

'*Jah*, Kalev.'

I raised my eyes to see another man stride into view. The two men spoke rapidly in Estonian, and the shift of language jolted me. It had been so long since my mother taught me, but many of the words jumped out. *Ring*.

Russians. Roubles. Their words in my head were like the currents of a river that flowed together then broke apart.

I studied them. This man – Kalev – carried himself differently to the other boys, although he could only be slightly older. Twenty-two at most. While his companions were hunched, as if they thought to make themselves invisible, Kalev held himself erect like a statue carved from rock. His blond hair was close-cropped. He gestured with his fingers as he talked. The confident flick of his hand conveyed the weight of his authority. *A leader*, I thought, my mind accustomed to placing power where it naturally belonged.

As if he had heard me speak, he turned his head suddenly and looked directly at me, eyes narrowed. I dropped my gaze to the dirt beneath my face, heart bumping painfully against my ribs. I waited for fingers to grip my collar, to be dragged to my feet and searched for valuables.

'*Tanan*, Jaak.' *Thank you*. Footsteps, coming closer. I squeezed my eyes shut.

The footsteps went past. I dared to raise my head.

Kalev was standing beside the Russian woman Jaak had been speaking to. She flinched as he knelt down, and whimpered softly as his rifle slid forward on his arm. He lifted his shoulder, nudging it back.

'This is your ring?' he said, in accented Russian.

The young woman nodded.

'Take it.' He held it out. The diamond twinkled between his fingers. When she didn't move, he reached down and grasped her hand, forcing her stiff fingers open so he could slip the ring into her palm. The woman's mouth fell open as she stared up at him, her face tear-streaked.

'We might be thieves but we aren't animals. Perhaps you will remember that the next time your countrymen shoot at us in the forest.'

He straightened, adjusting his brown suit.

'Kalev!' Shouts echoed at the other end of the platform. The young man tensed instantly, dropping into a crouch. The ground began to vibrate, and gunfire crackled in the distance amid more yelling from the lookouts as they called the men back. 'Jaak! Walter!'

Their boots kicked up dust around us, sending pebbles flying into the air. My eyes stung. Through the dust haze, I saw them run towards the edge of the forest and disappear. Moments later, Russian army soldiers flooded the platform.

More dust. More chaos. More voices shouting, this time in Russian.

I covered my head with my hands to block out the noise.

'Lida.' Olga was shaking me. 'It's over.'

Pushing myself upright, I stared into Olga's face. Dust had wormed its way into the creases, giving her the appearance of an old marionette doll carved from wood. White hair billowed around her shoulders, freed from the many combs she usually employed to keep it in place. I reached out to squeeze her hand. Around us, the passengers were in various stages of relief and anger. Many of the women were crying. Russian soldiers moved among them, asking questions and taking notes. One man was shouting at the train conductor, telling him he should have attacked the thieves and defended us all. The train conductor was ashen, oblivious to the irate passenger as he stared off into the forest, as if he expected the thieves to run back out.

Suddenly, he pitched forward and vomited all over the ground.

I turned away, my own stomach cramping in sympathy.

'Ladies,' said a voice near my elbow. I whipped around.

'Apologies.' The man held up his hands. 'I didn't mean to startle you.' He was dressed in a grey uniform, a medal bar dangling over his breast pocket. The chevron insignia and the red stars on his collar distinguished him from the other officers moving about. There was a coldness in the line of his features, the way his deep-set brown eyes turned down at the corners. I had seen eyes like that before in the faces of my uncle's colleagues. They were the eyes of someone who is used to having their orders obeyed.

'You are a lieutenant,' I said, unable to suppress my knowledge. It was one of the only things that had interested me at my uncle's State dinners: picking out the colonels and officers, the police captains and sergeants based on their uniforms. A small game to hold back the flood of boredom that always accompanied such events.

'Very good.' He straightened his shoulders. Even at full height, he was shorter than me. I found myself bending slightly at the knees so I would not be looking down at him, and being thankful for the flat sandals strapped to my feet. 'Lieutenant Dimitri Lubov,' he said. He had a broad nose with large nostrils; what Olga called a 'Lenin' nose. His chin wobbled as he smiled. 'Tartu division.'

'What took you so long to get here?' Olga rasped.

'There are no soldiers stationed here in Tiksoja. Although that may change now.' The smile left his features, replaced by a hard expression of distaste.

'Who were they?' I glanced back at the forest. The fir trees swayed slightly, their branches creaking in the sudden breeze. Soldiers with rifles were stationed at the tree line.

'Thieves. Bandits.' Lieutenant Lubov sniffed. The wind riffled his black hair. He jammed it down flat with his palm before raking it back into place with long fingers. 'Resistors and saboteurs. They call themselves Forest Brothers. Usually hole up together like foxes in some stinking bunker. Rest assured, the Soviet army will find them.'

'I've never heard of such a thing,' Olga said. 'I thought the Baltics surrendered peaceably.'

'There was no surrender,' Lieutenant Lubov said sharply. 'None was needed. The Baltics have always belonged to Russia. She has just welcomed them back to the fold.'.

'Of course.' Olga dropped her eyes to study her dusty shoes.

Lieutenant Lubov took out a notebook. 'I will need your names,' he said. 'And a record of everything you saw. Anything you can remember, any details, will help us identify the thieves if they should be so stupid as to show their faces.'

Our names. I wondered if I should lie, but what would be the point? 'I am Lydia Volkova,' I said. 'And this is my companion, Olga Adreevna.'

At my words, Lieutenant Lubov looked up from the notebook, large nostrils flaring like an animal that has caught the scent of prey.

'You are the Partorg's daughter?'

'I am.'

Lieutenant Lubov's eyebrows lifted. 'How strange. He did not mention you were coming.'

'We only sent word yesterday,' I said. I felt slightly affronted. What business was it of his what arrangements we had made? Perhaps he was my father's confidante. I wondered if they were close, aware of the disadvantage of being so distant from Papa all these years. At least in Moscow, I knew most of the players. Who preferred flattery to direct questions.

I waited for him to say more, but he merely stared at me intently until I grew uncomfortable.

'What happens now?' I said eventually. I shielded my eyes against the sunlight that gleamed on the green paintwork of the train. Sweat was forming on my back, making me glad I had thrown off the bearskin coat before we left the train. Perhaps one of the thieves had snatched it up.

My voice seemed to snap him back. He flipped the notebook closed and pocketed it, his gaze sliding away to the soldiers at the edge of the forest. 'There will be a short delay while the train is set right,' he said. 'And then the driver assures us that the service will continue to Tartu. You should reach there by the afternoon.' He pressed his lips together. 'Once they reach their dens they become difficult to track. But I hope I will see you in Tartu. Excuse me.'

'Wait, Lieutenant.'

He turned back, frowning. Ignoring Olga's warning squeeze, I pressed forward, close enough to catch the sharp whiff of cologne and cigarettes, mixed with the faint, fading scent of gunpowder.

'What will they do with them if they are caught? The thieves.' I was thinking of Kalev and Jaak, imagining them back at their camp or wherever they lived, dividing up the spoils, which would be slightly less after the clemency they showed the young woman.

Lieutenant Lubov's eyes were hard pebbles. 'They will be shot. On sight.'

I swallowed hard. 'No trial?'

Lieutenant Lubov leant close. I felt the hairs rise on my neck as his breath tickled my skin.

'We don't give trials to animals.'

Squaring his shoulders, he strode away.

It was past noon when the train finally pulled into Tartu, belching to a stop beside a dusty platform and a peeling timber building that had seen better days.

Footsteps pounded the corridor outside as passengers disembarked, greeting the people waiting for them on the platform and disappearing into the thick coils of steam. I understood their haste, their desire to be away as quickly as possible and to leave the ugly incident of this morning behind. I, too, was eager to forget the cold reality of my first robbery.

Olga was dozing, her mouth half-open. I shook her awake, trying to summon up the energy to gather our things.

We had been lucky. The bandits had found little of value among our belongings, and though we returned to find them scattered about, it had not taken long to repack them. Others – those travelling with jewellery or items easily sold on the black market – were not so fortunate.

We stumbled out onto the platform, as dusty as two cats fresh from an alley scrap. Beside me, Olga clutched her case. She had regained some of her spirit.

'I hope your papa has been given decent lodgings,' she said. 'A man of his stature. I am dreaming of a Tsar bath like the one Catherine the Great presented to Potemkin.' She half-closed her eyes as if she could see it shimmering in the shabby waiting room nearby; a great granite tub carved from a red monolith. A bath fit for a lover and his Queen.

Despite my exhaustion, I laughed. 'I doubt Papa has been given such grand utilities, Olga.'

Olga sighed. A breeze raced up the platform. The passengers had largely dispersed, and the few train staff hurried back and forth across the platform, eager to be on their way again. Olga and I stood alone.

I searched for any sign of Papa's retinue. A car, a guard waiting.

'You did send the letter, Olga?' I said. My stomach was beginning to twist itself into knots.

'Of course!' My companion sniffed. 'What do you take me for?'

'Stay here,' I said, not wishing to worry her.

As the train released a blast of steam, I made my way to the ticket office. Through the glass, I spied an empty chair. I banged on the glass and called through the window.

Nobody came.

I rapped again.

Nothing.

Panic beat in my chest. With no car to collect us and no way of knowing the location of Papa's office, we were stranded. Could we walk there or must we drive? Were there trams, or was this city too small for such modern conveniences?

I looked around in despair, taking note of a small square of car park behind the peeling ticket office, weeds poking up between the gravel.

'There's no more services today. They've all been cancelled,' said a voice from behind me. I spun around.

Tall. I had to squint up to see his face. Big hands poking out beneath the sleeves of a shabby jacket a few sizes too small; threads hanging down against pale skin flecked with freckles.

I took an involuntary step backwards.

'Do you work here?'

His voice trailed off and he spread his palms helplessly. I studied him as if he were a strange specimen I had never seen before. I felt a tingling in my hands; the first stirrings that my mother was near.

Important, she was saying. *This one is important.*

I chewed at my lip, allowing my gaze to run across his thin shoulders and down to the ends of his freckled fingers. He did not look important, but I could not force my eyes away. With a jolt I realised I was staring. I felt my face turn hot as a brick left in the hearth.

But the man did not seem offended. 'Yes,' he said. 'I'm Estonian. Among other things. Jakob Rebane.'

He held out his hand. I took it quickly, and then let it drop.

'Lydia Volkova.'

'Volkova?' He frowned. 'Like the Chief of Security.'

'Yes. He's my father. You know him, then.' I felt relieved. If this man knew where my father worked, he could surely direct us there.

'Know him?' Jakob blinked rapidly. 'He's the Partorg,' he said in a low voice. 'Everybody knows him. He has offices on Vaksali Street but I believe he's most often found at the Grey House. Põder Street.'

I waited for him to speak again, to tell me about my father's achievements, or his rapport with the local populace. To tell me about the great things Estonia was now achieving beneath Soviet rule. The things I had read about.

Instead, an awkward silence opened up between us.

His eyes raked over me, coolly assessing. The train huffed and puffed on the track nearby, hissing steam. I felt exposed. I wrapped my arms around my body, wishing suddenly for the bear coat, with its imposing pelt of shining chestnut fur. But the coat was now buried at the bottom of Olga's case. 'I need to find a car,' I said at last. 'Well, I need a driver too. My companion and I are here from Moscow to visit my father. But there seems to be some mix-up. Perhaps it was the incident this morning at Tiksoja that caused the delay.'

He tilted his head. 'I heard about Tiksoja. There are crazy rumours flying around everywhere; the station master said it was resistance fighters. Forest Brothers from Tartu. Did they do that to your face?' He sounded shocked.

I lifted my fingers to my cheek, frowning. I had forgotten about it.

'No,' I said. 'No, they didn't hurt me. That was . . . someone else.'

'Oh.' He seemed relieved. He unfolded his arms. 'I see. I can give you a lift.'

'You have a car?' I could not help but look down at his shabby pants, which were faded to a dull grey.

Jakob shrugged. 'It's not fancy. But yes. I run people back and forth sometimes, diplomats, visitors . . . I even offer a guide service for an extra fee. Assuming, of course, you are interested in a small place like Tartu. Many people pay me extra just to stop talking.'

'Well . . .' I stared at him, chewing my lip, my mind searching and discarding an ever dwindling array of possibilities. Suddenly, something warm pressed itself against my side.

'Lydochka?' Olga lifted her chin to scrutinise the man. 'You've found our driver?'

'Someone to take us, yes,' I said, coming quickly to a decision, wrapping an arm about her as the train wheels began to grind, pulling the train out of the station. It was my fault Olga was here. I could not ask her to walk. I held the man's gaze. 'We would very much appreciate a ride. Thank you.'

Jakob's face relaxed. 'Excellent. It would be a pleasure to escort you.'

I caught the quick flash of his smile before he turned his head, steering us towards an old vehicle with scratched panelling and windows darkened so that the interior was strangely obscured.

'It's not the finest vehicle around,' Jakob was muttering, opening the passenger door. 'But it will get you to your father's office. Here.' He extended his hand for my case. Nestling it below the front passenger seat, he helped me in, shielding my head with his hand to avoid bumping it on a flap of fabric that had come loose from the car's roof.

Muttering an apology, he tacked the roof back up, pressing it into place with his thumb. He ran around to open the back door for Olga. 'Are you comfortable?'

He seemed so anxious to please, I did not have the heart to complain about the cramped space or the faintly sour whiff of body odour lingering in the fabric seats. 'I am. Thank you.'

Grinning, he slammed the door closed. I heard the boot open behind me and the sound of Olga's heavy case being pushed inside, then Jakob climbed in and started the vehicle. The engine coughed and sputtered, an alarming sound. Olga cleared her throat pointedly and I read what was in her mind: this was not how she had imagined arriving at my father's office. But it was too late to change my mind now. I fumbled in my skirt for the remaining roubles. Jakob pocketed them and then he was turning the wheel, the car circling the small car park to join the traffic on the road outside.

Tartu was a city of cobblestones and high whitewashed walls. Hidden gardens flashed past, screened by iron gates. The streets were not as crowded with people as those in Moscow. I saw mostly soldiers, their grey uniforms and gleaming guns. On a street corner, I spied a group of women in faded coats huddled together, white scarves knotted around their heads. I swivelled in my seat to catch a better look, but the car moved off and they were gone, just a blur of white lace and drab clothes in the distance.

Jakob kept up a steady stream of chatter, only pausing every now and then to ask a question about Moscow. What did people think of the war? How did Muscovites view the annexation of the Baltics? Did my father talk much about what was happening? He kept his gaze fixed on the windscreen as I tried to answer. I was sure he was only asking to be polite, and when I told him I had not spoken to my father in some time, he did not reply.

At an intersection he pointed past a building to a set of ruins high on a hill. The broken brick battlements stuck up from the ground like sharp teeth. 'Dorpat Cathedral,' he said. 'Built in the . . .' He screwed up his face. 'Twelfth century? No, that can't be right. Anyway, it was captured by Prince Dimitri of Pereslavl. He was the son of Alexander Nevsky.' He spun the wheel, rounding a corner so the cathedral vanished from view. 'Fourteenth,' he said suddenly. 'Fourteenth century. I was wrong.'

'I thought you said you were a tour guide,' I said.

He grinned apologetically. 'I never said I was a good one. My sister Kati is the historian and folklore expert in the family. She knits, too.' His eyes swivelled to the lace shawl around my throat. 'Shawls like that.'

'Oh.' I looked down in surprise and touched the shawl's hem. I'd forgotten I was wearing it. It weighed almost nothing. 'Do you think she could identify the pattern? My mother knitted it when she was a girl.'

Jakob snorted. 'There's nothing my sister doesn't know about knitted shawls. Nothing.' He took his eyes off the road to peer at the lace, and suddenly I was conscious of his gaze on my throat. Olga coughed again and Jakob looked away quickly, then turned the car into a wide avenue where tall government-looking buildings stood shoulder to shoulder. 'Almost there.'

A moment later, we pulled up in front of a tall grey office building with arched dormer windows hedged on either side by similar-looking buildings. A Soviet flag hung on a long pole over the doorway. Jakob jumped out to open the doors for us.

I looked up at the building where my father worked. It was only now, facing the grey building that seemed to stare back at me, the windows striped with bars and the huge doors looming imposingly, that I realised how cold I was, despite the warmth of the shawl at my neck. I wanted to banish my fears but they continued to crowd about me.

'Will you be staying long?' Jakob was standing at arm's length, holding out my case. His fingers brushed against mine as I took it. They were warm. I fought an unnatural desire to climb back into his shabby car and stay there. But Olga was at my back, and Jakob was watching me.

'I don't know.' What would Papa say when he saw me? Would he be pleased or worried? Unconsciously I reached a hand up and bunched the lace at my throat.

Jakob nodded. 'Well, I wish you luck.'

He turned back to his car. I heard the engine cough twice before it finally turned over. Then the car was gone, sliding around a corner and lost to view. I realised with a shiver that without its presence, the street was silent. No pedestrians. No trilling birds.

The silence was absolute.

Kringle Pattern

Kati

'I SUPPOSE I SHOULD BE GETTING HOME.' STRETCHING MY arms above my head, I tried to stir the life back into my limbs. The lace I'd been unpicking slipped sideways across my lap. I hooked it with one finger just in time, before it could slither in a soft silvery pile to the floor.

'And I should be getting ready for work.' Etti put her own knitting on the faded armrest and began to struggle out of her chair. 'Since Tiina Tamm disappeared last month, I've been taking on her housekeeping shifts as well as my own.'

I paused, suddenly curious. 'Does the Partorg ever talk to you?'

Etti gave me a strained smile. 'He's never there. I haven't seen him since the agency first sent me. It's just Tiina and me.' Her eyes clouded over. 'Or it was. Now she's gone.'

Gathering her things, Etti hurried out, leaving an uncomfortable silence in her wake.

Perhaps the other women were also thinking of Tiina. I saw some of them cast a glance at the place she used to occupy near the long window casement when she joined us at the knitting group. Her husband had circulated pamphlets on behalf of the Forest Brothers, calling for action and the need to support the old Estonian home guard army, what was left of it. Tiina had begged him not to be so foolish, to keep his mouth closed. But he hadn't listened. Maybe he had hoped Tiina's position as housekeeper of the Partorg's apartment meant that they would be spared. He had soon discovered his mistake.

Calling out my own goodbyes, I hurried to the door of the apartment, my mind already racing ahead to the sheep, which would need to be let out when I reached home. I twisted the handle and crashed straight into something hard outside in the hallway. Too shocked to cry out, I could only mutely register the brown curls and the checked jacket, the long thin fingers clasped like a manacle around my wrists.

'Jakob!'

Before I could say more, my brother leant around me, closing the door firmly behind my back so we were alone in the corridor. In vain, I struggled to free my hands but Jakob's grip was as tight as I remembered it.

'Thank God it's you,' he said, brushing back his hair with one hand. 'I thought I would have to wait hours. I had to hide in the shadows when Etti came out. I'm probably covered in cobwebs.'

'Why?' I demanded. 'What are you up to?'

My brother put his finger to his lips, a frown deepening the groove between his brows. 'Hush! I don't want the whole knitting circle after me. I don't need their questions.' He began to lead me down the steps, taking them two at a time, our footsteps clattering in the stairwell.

'Not so fast!' I wrenched my hand away.

When we reached the bottom I turned him back to face me. 'Well?' I hissed, rubbing my wrist. 'What's the big secret?'

There were circles beneath Jakob's eyes, I realised. He

had jammed his hands into his pockets. His jaw moved back and forth as if he were chewing invisible gum, a habit I knew from childhood. It was the same gesture he made whenever he was debating the best course of action, usually the kind that involved the fastest way to absolve himself of chores so he could join his friends fishing at the riverside.

'Have you eaten?' he said suddenly.

The question startled me. 'Not since last year.'

Jakob grinned, but the smile was wonky. It made the hairs prickle on my arms.

'Funny.'

I let out a breath. 'No. You think I have roubles to waste on food?' I couldn't resist the chance to highlight the advantages he had been given. 'You think our parents give me an allowance the way they do you?'

Jakob stared at me for a fraction of a second. And then he turned. 'Come on.'

The door groaned loudly as he pushed against it.

Outside the wind had come up, whipping through the branches of the linden trees lining the courtyard and stirring up dust, making golden motes dance in the cold sunlight. The shadows were lengthening.

'I have to get home, Jakob.' My shoes slipped on the cobblestones as I hurried to keep up with his long strides. 'I shouldn't even be here.'

'We aren't going far.' He threw a glance back at me over his shoulder. 'Did you catch a ride in?'

'Yes.'

'I'll drive you home.'

I looked up in surprise. 'You bought a car?'

'No.' His gaze shifted. 'It's on loan from a friend.'

'Which friend?' I demanded.

'It doesn't matter. Are you coming?'

I sensed his growing irritation but it only made me want to stand my ground. 'Besides, shouldn't you be in class?'

Jakob came to an abrupt halt and swung around. 'Stop asking so many questions. Just trust me. Can you do that?'

I raised my chin, but the seriousness in Jakob's eyes made the retort die before it reached my lips. We crossed the courtyard in silence, heading back towards the towering university buildings and then down a street that ran beside the marketplace.

Jakob stopped outside the big glass window of a café, one I had passed before but never entered. A striped awning extended over the entrance, the colours bright strips of green and grey. The name 'Werner's' was written in curly script across the tinted window. I frowned. Back before the start of the occupation, it had been bursting with students; now the only ones who could afford such luxuries as coffee and beer were the Soviets who had been assigned good jobs at the university or the men who were lucky enough to work for the Partorg or the NKVD.

I raised my eyebrows. 'A café, Jakob? Really?'

Jakob didn't reply but grasped the door handle. The scent of tobacco unfurled from the open doorway, along with the faint hum of voices and – overpowering, intoxicating – the rich mahogany scent of coffee. Real coffee, not bitter ground-up hazelnuts.

'Hurry up. You're letting the draft in.'

Still frowning at him, I stepped inside.

It was dark inside. An old man with whiskers sat snoring in an armchair, while at a long counter that ran the length of the room four Russian men in business suits nursed steaming cups of coffee. Their voices carried on the swirl of their tobacco smoke. They turned to us as the door slammed shut, cigarettes still dangling from their lips, and I felt my cheeks colour. But we were of little interest – just another shabby-looking pair of students – and they soon turned away.

'Stay here.'

I watched Jakob weave between the tables, his knees brushing against the backs of chairs. I realised with a pang that he was thin, too. His trousers and jacket did not cling as they had when Mama presented them proudly on his last day at the farmhouse. They hung loosely, the jacket too short in the arms. When we were children I had teased him about his height, calling him stork-legs, asking him if the air in the clouds above was warm or cool. I had missed him since he stopped visiting. The months at home had been lonely. He began to talk with the man behind the counter, gesticulating with his hands.

I pushed away the small guilty niggle that whispered I should be heading back to the farm, and sank down into a chair near the window. I should not be here with Jakob, indulging my senses in the long-forgotten aroma of coffee. The noise of footsteps outside made me glance up sharply. But it was only a group of soldiers marching past, filling the street with the sound of their boots.

'Surprise!'

I stared in disbelief down at the plate Jakob had set in front of me.

'A kringle?' Glistening and caramelised, the pastry was

heaped on a small white china dish, a powdery pelt of sugar coating its gentle curves. I looked up to find Jakob grinning.

'I told you this was a special place. Remember how you used to ask for a kringle every birthday instead of a cake? You even created that special stitch with Grandmother, "kringle stitch", and you knitted Papa a scarf full of little pastries. You told him the kringle stitch was magic; it would protect him from sickness and bolting horses, and highwaymen who intended to rob him. What a funny child you were.'

'I remember,' I said. My eyes were drawn back to the plate. I could not recall the last time I had seen a kringle, let alone had one placed in front of me. The ingredients alone must have cost more than six months of Jakob's yearly allowance. It took all my strength not to reach out and press my thumb against the sugar-flecked china. Jakob's eyes were still eagerly on me, his expression as bright and boyish as a child watching presents being opened on Christmas Day.

'Well?' he prompted. 'Aren't you going to eat it?'

My mouth was watering, and with an effort that surprised me I pushed the plate away with one knuckle and then sat on my hands, crushing my fingers to stop them betraying me and creeping out to snatch up the whole pastry and cramming it in my mouth.

'Jakob, what is this about? Where did you get the money to buy such a thing?'

Jakob's smile froze. 'What are you talking about?'

I was about to reply when a waiter appeared carrying a tray laden with cups of steaming coffee. He was a young man with a thin moustache. His hands trembled slightly as he set them down, the teacups rattling. My brother thanked

144

him and a secret look passed between them.

'*Danke*,' my brother whispered, so softly I almost did not hear him. The waiter's lips tightened in a small smile before he withdrew and moved away. I watched him return to the counter, my curiosity kindled. The café was called Werner's; a German name. I wondered if the waiter was one of the few Baltic Germans who had stayed behind when the war between Germany and Europe began. Hitler had called them home after the signing of the pact with Stalin, keen to unite all the German-speaking people together. Those who had remained behind in the Baltics risked the same fate as the rest of us who were minorities. There was no protection from the Russians and their campaign to convert everything and everyone to their side.

I turned to ask Jakob to confirm my suspicions about the waiter but he was staring out the window, blowing on his coffee, one of his long legs folded over his knee, maddeningly calm.

He glanced over at me and smiled. 'Aren't you going to try your coffee?'

The coffee sat between us, dark as treacle. There was no milk. Scented steam rose up from the surface, a bittersweet aroma mingled with memories of better days before the invasion, when such things were readily available. The idea that Jakob might have been here in Tartu enjoying himself while we suffered at home festered inside me. How could I indulge myself knowing Mama and Papa would not eat today until they finished delivering apples to the factory depot and made their way home?

My voice shook. 'Is this where you've been wasting

Papa's money, treating yourself while we've been slaving away to keep you in your studies?'

Jakob's nostrils flared. He spread his hands out on the table, his nails digging into the timber. 'I haven't touched Papa's money. Not for months. I'm surprised at you, Kati. This is how you thank me for taking you out?' He shook his head, disbelief etched in every feature. 'Maybe you like eating broth every night. You've grown accustomed to it, so you think everyone else should be starving too.'

His words hit me like a slap. I saw the pain register in his eyes, a mirror image of my own misery. He snatched up my hand even as I swivelled my legs sideways, ready to take flight and leave it all behind; my brother, the Russian businessmen, the thick tantalising scent of coffee.

'Kati, wait. I'm sorry.' Jakob's voice trembled. 'Did you hear me? I said I'm sorry. That was uncalled for. I—' He crushed my hand between his own. 'I apologise. A thousand times. Just listen to what I have to say. Please. Just stay a little longer. I have to talk to you. It's important.' He sighed, then continued. 'Perhaps I shouldn't have brought you here. I just thought you deserved something nice. A treat, before . . . I know you think I don't understand, that I can't possibly guess how hurt you were when they chose to send me to university, but I do know. I know and I'm sorry.'

My brother's eyes were warm. I heard the sincerity in his voice. He had never apologised for what happened two years ago, when my parents had drawn us into the kitchen one cold December day to inform us that Jakob would be moving to the university in Tartu to study teaching; he had just scraped by with enough marks to get in.

'It's not my choice!' Jakob had raged later when my parents were out of earshot. 'You think I want to spend my life teaching kids how to tie their laces? I want to travel and meet new people.' I had watched numbly as he scattered the embers of the fire with the poker, churning them so the sparks flew up the chimney, swirling like angry fireflies. Was it fair that Jakob was the one charged with passing on our history and our special tales? Jakob, who mixed up all his dates. Jakob, who was more content when he was chatting with strangers than up to his elbows in books.

Now my brother bowed his head. When we were children, we had sometimes played that Jakob was my student and I his teacher. When he struggled with a piece of homework, such as an essay on the liberation of the serfs during the Estonian Enlightenment, I was the one who helped him, guiding him gently towards the answers while letting him feel he was in charge.

'What I said to you before is true,' he said. 'The money isn't from Papa. It's from . . . another source. That's what I need to talk to you about. I need your help, Kati. Please. Stay.'

Sighing, I sank back into my chair. 'Tell me everything, then,' I said, reaching for the kringle. I bit into the pastry, and sugar exploded between my lips in a delicate puff and then melted on my tongue. I must have made a small noise of pleasure because Jakob laughed. It had been so long since I'd tasted anything so good. In a few moments, the pastry was gone and only small flecks of sugar remained. I dabbed at them with my finger, the sticky paste of the ground walnuts clogging my throat.

My brother took a deep breath. 'I've been suspended.'

'Suspended,' I repeated.

Jakob nodded. He crossed his arms. There was a note of defiance in his voice. 'I'm not ashamed of that part.'

I rubbed my forehead, trying to process the words. A lump of pastry was lodged in my throat and I sipped at the coffee Jakob had bought me. The brew was as smooth as silk, but it didn't bring the kind of comfort I remembered. 'And they suspended you for what?'

'Unsavoury connections. It could be worse,' he said, seeing my shocked expression. 'They only *suspected* my involvement. If they knew for sure, I wouldn't be sitting here with you. I'd be in a cell at Tartu Prison.'

'Oh, Jakob.' I pushed the plate away, feeling sick. 'What exactly have you done?'

Jakob glanced around as a roar went up from the businessmen. I suspected they had moved from coffee onto the bottles of liquor lining the walls behind the counter.

My brother wet his lips. 'I joined a group,' he said, sitting up a little straighter. 'Of resistance fighters.'

'Forest Brothers.' The words were bitter on my tongue.

Jakob nodded. 'They sent a recruiter around to the dorms a few months ago. Kati, it was Oskar. You remember what they said about him, what they accused him of?'

He paused, waiting for me to answer, his expression revealing only mild wonder. He'd been away at school when the bodies of Oskar's mother and sister were found. He and Oskar had never been very close, but even Jakob had agreed in private that it was impossible for Oskar to have killed them. We had discussed it only once, in the safety of the barn.

'I do.' I ran my thumb along the edge of the table, avoiding his eyes.

Jakob nodded. 'It was all a sham, as we suspected.' He lowered his voice. 'Oskar told me. The Russians killed them. And Oskar ran. He's been working with others all this time, building a resistance group. I've been helping them; Torvid, too. Selling things for them on the black market, amassing arms. They gave me a car – I use it to run them back and forth between towns when it's not safe for them to walk or catch lifts with strangers. Sometimes I take diplomats or officials to their offices, pretending I'm a guide. Anything I overhear, any scrap of information from outside, I feed it back to Oskar.'

'Jakob!' I lifted my hands to my mouth. 'Spying?'

'Don't say it like that.' Jakob's eyes grew stony. 'It's not just me. There are other students, too. We pulled down all the Soviet flags in the university square one night and replaced them with Estonian ones.' He smirked. 'That was my idea. We made the flags ourselves, by dying some old scarves and sewing them together. You should have seen the Partorg's face! He was visiting the university the next day with some important diplomats from Moscow . . .' Jakob's voice trailed off as he caught sight of my expression. 'You don't have to look so disappointed. I don't regret joining.' He set his jaw stubbornly. 'If anything, I think they are our only option. We can't go on for much longer, licking the Russians' boot heels, subjugating ourselves to the whims of Stalin and the Partorg. I just need you to help me convince Papa to join, too.' He raised his chin. 'You see, I don't plan on going back to university. Torvid will; he's gone home to his parents in Tallinn to lie low and then he'll come back next term when the storm is over. But not me. I'm going to join my friends in the forest. Live there, sleep there. I'm going to do everything I can to help win this war with the Partisans that the Soviets have started. What good will a degree in teaching do me when all the jobs go to Russians anyway? How will staying at university help our country? Kati, Papa has always listened to you; you have a way of softening him. So, that's it. That's my plan. We will return to the farmhouse together and I'll collect my things. This time next week I'll be a real resistance fighter.'

He sat back, waiting for me to speak.

A real resistance fighter. My brother's words chilled my skin. 'Have you . . . Have you seen Oskar lately?'

Jakob narrowed his eyes, but he was still smiling. 'Not for a few weeks. He can be . . . mysterious. General Pilk of the Estonian Home Guard – he is the man in charge of this area – he says Oskar is one of their best fighters, but he takes off sometimes and it's hard to know where he goes. He is in charge of his own unit. They always come back with all sorts of things to sell and weapons and useful information, so he's always forgiven. Why?' Suspicion sharpened his words. 'You haven't seen him, have you?'

I nodded. It seemed that no matter what I did, I could not escape the association with these renegades. First Oskar, now Jakob. There was the scrape of sugar as Jakob stirred his own coffee, the chime of a spoon rebounding against the china.

'He came to the farmhouse last night.'

Jakob paused, the spoon stilled in his hand. 'Why would he do that?'

I shrugged miserably. 'To do the same thing as you, I

suppose. To convince Papa to join this crazy movement that seems to have turned all your heads.'

'That bastard!' he said. His hand was shaking. The spoon rattled against the saucer as he set it down. 'He never said he was going to . . . He had no right.' His face suddenly crumpled, like a child's. He raised one trembling hand and cupped his forehead. 'Oh God. He's ruined everything. What did Papa say?'

'He told him to go away.' The words brought a fresh wash of guilt. 'He swore if he ever saw him again, or any of his brethren, he would notify the Partorg and have them all arrested for treason!'

Jakob was shaking his head. His coffee lay abandoned. 'This is terrible. Kati, do you think he realises what he's done?'

'Why didn't you tell him to wait until you had spoken to Papa?'

Jakob gave a mirthless laugh. His face had gone very pale; freckles stood out against the pallor. 'Oskar does what he wants. Didn't I already say that?'

'He must have had his reasons for coming to Papa early,' I ventured.

Jakob's head snapped up. 'Oh, so now you're defending him?'

His tone made me prickle. 'I never said I was defending him! But he mentioned something about . . .' I lowered my voice. 'Germans. And parachuters. That they needed somewhere safe to land.'

My mind was suddenly filled with a vision of our moonlit fields. I heard the hum of planes, the whoosh of parachutes filling with air and saw our farmhouse as if I were circling it from high above, smoke curling up from the chimney, the bright lamplight from the windows like shining beacons against the oily blackness of the night.

A chair scraped against the floor. Jakob was rummaging in his pockets. He threw a bunch of roubles down onto the table. His mouth was a thin, taut line. 'Come on. We're going home.'

I jumped to my feet. 'Now?'

Jakob said nothing but began to push towards the exit. I hurried to keep up with him, bumping my hip against a sharp table edge and almost sending a chair crashing. The look Jakob threw me was not of reproach but one of surprising softness. When I reached him, he linked his arm through mine and pushed open the door with one hand. He waited until we were out in the street until he spoke, and then his voice was low, soft in my ear. 'Have courage,' he whispered.

He squeezed my arm, but it did nothing to repel the feeling of dread in my stomach.

Wallpaper Pattern

Lydia

'THERE YOU ARE.'

In the stark reception room at Papa's offices, Lieutenant Lubov stood smiling behind a polished walnut desk. His uniform was clean again after this morning's incident in Tiksoja, the grey suit pressed. His dark hair had been oiled into place. He was a model of Soviet perfection; the kind of man the girls at Model School No. 25 would have given anything to meet. But something about him unsettled me. Perhaps he reminded me too much of my uncle: outward friendliness concealing a moody interior. And why was he here? I frowned.

Struggling with her case behind me, Olga let out a cry of surprise. 'Lieutenant!'

He rounded the desk and plucked the case out of her hand, lifting it easily onto a chair nearby.

'We did not expect to see you,' I said. 'What happened to the bandits? Did you catch them?'

'No.' For a moment, his visage slipped. I caught a flash of irritation in his eyes before he concealed it. 'They escaped. There did not seem any point lingering.' He held out his hand for my case. I pulled it closer. Lieutenant Lubov let his hand fall, his smile still fixed in place. 'I thought I would come and file my report here in person, though.'

'You must have rushed through your paperwork.'

Lieutenant Lubov shrugged. 'Paperwork is never-ending in my job. I owe you an apology.'

I raised my eyebrows. 'Oh?'

'Yes. I should have offered you both a lift from Tiksoja. I should not have let you endure the rest of the train ride unescorted. Two ladies, far from home, one of them the Partorg's daughter.'

I studied him. 'We managed, Olga, didn't we? A man at the station was kind enough to give us a lift. An Estonian,' I added. I noticed a muscle flicker in Lieutenant Lubov's cheek.

'Ah.' His smile had faded a little. 'A small warning: you should be careful who you accept lifts from. Those bandits you met earlier? They have friends and families who help them in Tartu and the villages roundabouts. Sometimes they even dress as women to conceal their identities. They have their own network of spies. Do you by chance recall this individual's name?' He took out his notebook. 'I can run a check. He may already be on a list of people with unsavoury connections.'

I opened my mouth to tell him but paused, remembering Joachim. My heart squeezed tightly as Jakob's questions floated back to me. They had been quietly probing but nothing like an interrogation. I shook my head. 'I'm sorry. He didn't tell me his name.'

Lieutenant Lubov stared at me a second longer and then seemed to let the thought drop. He pocketed the notebook. 'No matter. Let me show you upstairs to your father's office, then. I'm sure he will be delighted to see you.'

His words sent a chill across my skin. I hoped he was right, but the lack of reception at the train station made me wonder if Olga's letter had reached him yet. My letters had always gone through my maid, who I presumed sent them on to the correct bureau for processing. Had I misjudged the time it would take for my letter to arrive? What if Papa was taken off guard? Then I gathered my courage. This man was my father. *Your loving Papochka*. He would not have written that if he did not miss me. *I think of you often*. Those were not the words of a man who had forgotten his only child. They were perhaps the words of a man who had to comply with directives, a man who must put his position before his family. But they were not a rejection. I had to believe Papa would protect me. I tried hard to suppress the churning nerves in my stomach.

Everything would be all right. I was here. Mama had called me.

I was hardly aware of the steps Lieutenant Lubov led us up to a thick oak door. A brass plaque announcing my father's name sat at my eyeline.

Lieutenant Lubov knocked smartly and waited for a response.

'Come in!' a voice called. It was a stern voice. Imperious. A voice used to being obeyed. I waited for a feeling of recognition, a connection to the voice's owner. But I felt nothing.

Lieutenant Lubov opened the door. The room was a haze of warm colours; green leather chairs, a timber desk. Hundreds of books lined up in neat rows in glass-fronted timber cabinets. A man sat behind the desk. When he looked up, his spectacles flashed, little silver half-moons reflecting the light from the window.

'Yes?'

I hesitated. I wanted to step forward but my feet would not obey.

I looked around to Olga. She was smiling.

'Yes?' the man said again. 'What is it, Lieutenant?'

Lieutenant Lubov cleared his throat. 'Excuse me for interrupting, Captain. But your daughter is here.'

The man behind the desk blinked. He laid down the pen in his hand, placing it carefully in the centre of the documents stacked before him and then he stood up, scraping his chair back. 'My daughter?'

Footsteps. He was coming towards us. The brass buttons shone on his uniform. His beard was speckled with white hairs. Up close, I realised he was old; much older than I had imagined. I could not place him with the image I remembered of Mamochka. The young woman she had been, full of spirit. I forced my legs to move, so we came face to face in front of the bookshelf. He peered at me over the top of his glasses. A long nose. A heavy brow that jutted out over his eyes, forming a cliff to which his grey eyebrows clung. I tried to remember the picture I had drawn of him, the one still hanging on my wall in the House on the Embankment. But the picture would not reconcile with this stranger. It was a child's fond remembrance, each pencil stroke a wish of longing. It was not reality.

I found my voice. 'Papochka?'

I was eight years old again. The meeting hall of the Octoberists' group had high ceilings. It smelt of pine sap and varnish. The timber had been recently cut, built specifically for our private group, and the scent of the forest lingered in the wood. My papa's face was shadowed, but I knew he was smiling. Papa was proud of me. He had taken time away from his important work to come to my ceremony. His fingers brushed against my shirt as he pinned the badge on my scarf. *Always ready!*

'It's me, Papa,' I said now. I tried to smile. 'It's Lydia.'

He said nothing, just continued to stare at me.

'Captain?' Lieutenant Lubov looked from me to my father. 'Are you quite all right?'

My papa ran his tongue between his lips. 'Leave us,' he said sharply. His gaze darted to Olga. 'Take the woman with you.'

I heard Olga begin to speak before Lieutenant Lubov hurried her out, pulling the door closed firmly behind him.

I waited for Papa to reach for me, to embrace me. But he simply stood, staring, his arms hanging limp by his sides.

'What are you doing here?' he said at last. His face was twisted up, as though he had drunk week-old tea and the shrivelled skin was clinging to the roof of his mouth.

'Olga sent a letter,' I said. I could hear the quiver in my voice. 'Letting you know we were coming.'

'I did not receive it,' he said. He sounded incredulous. 'The communications lines have been busy. Your uncle knew?'

I hesitated. But this was not the moment for secrets. This was the time for revelation, for all things to be made clear. 'No,' I said, sounding bolder than I felt. 'I planned to let him know once we arrived. It did not seem necessary to tell him. After all, I am grown up, aren't I?'

He didn't answer.

'You aren't pleased to see me,' I said. The words were painful but I said them anyway. Adults did not shrink from telling the truth. They swallowed their bitterness and their disappointment. That was what Mama had done; but in her

157

case, it had been a draught, medicine crushed into liquid form, pounded down until the flakes were small enough to dissolve on her tongue. I was not Mama, though. I was myself and I wanted to live. 'I'm sorry,' I said. 'We should have waited. But we're here now.'

He drew in a deep breath. 'There's been a mistake.'

I tried to answer, but my tongue felt too big for my mouth. Suddenly, understanding made the words come. 'I know about Mama,' I said. 'I know how she died. It wasn't your fault.'

He made a strange sound. 'It's not that.' He lifted his chin. 'You will have to go back.'

At first I thought I had misheard him. It was a simple mix-up. My uncle would be upset, but my father could talk him around, surely. My absence was nothing that could not be fixed by a telephone call and then we would perhaps take our dinner together at Papa's residence, Olga fussing about, overseeing each course as Papa and I shared a look of secret exasperation. And then he would excuse himself, dabbing his lips with his napkin and take himself off to his study to finish some work while I slipped into my new bedroom and stared at the lights twinkling over Tartu, a place so foreign and yet, with Mama's heritage and her stories and the language she had so carefully taught me, so strangely and achingly familiar.

'You poor child,' he said. 'You have no idea who you are. Do you?'

And then the meaning of what he had said hit me.

I took a step backwards.

My father opened his mouth as if he had more to say, more commands to impart. But then he sighed, and the telephone wire twisted around his arm as he picked up the mouthpiece. A moment passed. 'Comrade Stalin?'

I heard the muffled reply. His eyes darted towards mine.

'Comrade Stalin . . . your daughter is here. Lydochka. She's safe.' A pause. 'She brought the woman with her. No, I don't know how they slipped away.' His tone sharpened. 'Isn't that the role of her bodyguard, to know where she is at all times?' He bent to listen to the response, wincing. 'I'm sorry, Comrade. Of course. I apologise. Yes . . . I suppose. That seems best. I'll tell her. Don't worry.' He turned slowly in a half-circle to pin me with his gaze. 'I'll tell her,' he said again, his voice softer now. Complacent. 'I understand.'

The telephone clicked as he replaced it on the cradle. Then he came slowly back to the middle of the room and took me by the shoulders. I wanted to turn my head, to shake off everything I had heard. The meaning of his words could not reach me if I let them sit on my skin, like oil on feathers. *Your daughter. Lydochka.* If I could simply ignore them . . .

'Lydia.' I had never before realised that Papa's eyes were green. They were as green as the rippling grasses in the fields outside Uncle's dacha in Zubolovo. They were different to mine. They were not the shifting hues of the sea, changeable, moody, at once peacock blue then grey and stormy.

'How?' I said. 'My mother . . . she would never . . .'

His mouth puckered. 'Your mother had no choice in the matter.' His words made me stagger, but his strong hands held me upright. 'What your father wants, he takes. And I think perhaps at the start, she cared for him . . .'

My legs were weightless as he guided me towards a chair, the timber seat sliding beneath me. Bright light filtered in from the window beside me, melting the room's sharp edges. The man I had believed my father, who had given me his name – Captain Volkov – was talking, pacing back and forth as if conducting a meeting. I tried to concentrate on his words but they slipped from me.

'. . . already pregnant at sixteen when I married her,' I heard him say. 'When she died, I was sent away and told never to contact you again.'

Had I known? I cast my mind back, a wash of memories flooding in while I snatched at them. My mind snagged on an image of myself as a child being jostled on my uncle's knee at the house in Zubolovo while my mother lay with a book propped on her knees, watching on from a shaded place beneath the canopy of a linden tree. Uncle's hand was warm on my back, holding me steady, keeping me from falling. Ripe peaches lay half-eaten at our feet. In the hazy afternoon sunlight, the lake glimmered like blue silk. Uncle patted my hair and then said something – I couldn't decipher it but I knew it was about me, something favourable, a compliment ground out around the cigar clutched between his teeth. My mother laughed. She pushed herself up; her book thudded to the ground. Her shadow fell over me; her fingernails brushed against my skin as she stroked my hair away from my face.

'Yes.' Her voice was uncharacteristically proud; all hint of vulnerability gone. She paused midstroke, her fingers digging into my scalp. 'Yes,' she continued, straightening her spine so that we were both, Uncle and me, cast in her shade. 'Yes, Josef. You are right. It is just like yours. It is exactly the same.'

The memory receded, pulled away as if the tide had dragged it out. In its place, I saw my mother the week before her death, darkness encircling her eyes. She was not sleeping well, I heard

Olga say to Zoya. She woke each night, disturbed by terrors nobody could explain. I had hidden myself behind the curtain as I listened to their whispered discussion, knowing I should reveal myself but unwilling to admit I was eavesdropping. I heard Olga say that Mama was homesick; she wanted to go home and take me with her. She had begged and begged but *he* would not allow it. Later that day, Mama had taken me out into Red Square to watch the autumn leaves flutter down from the bare boughs like birds coming home to roost. She had squeezed my hand and told me I should always keep what was in my heart a secret. It was the only place that was safe.

At the time, I had thought the 'he' to whom she referred was my father, and I thought it odd. Papochka was not a cruel man. If my mother had begged him, surely he would acquiesce to her request. But now an idea grew clearer in my mind. I recalled the times, more recently, when Olga would pass on gossip about girls of my age who had had affairs with married officers and diplomats and found themselves pregnant. If they were lucky, they became mistresses, their children taken care of; if they were unfortunate, nothing was ever heard of them again.

What if mother had been one of these women? What if it was not Captain Volkov she had been referring to – what if it was someone else, someone whose control extended to everything: family, friends, colleagues, former lovers, the State?

'You wrote to me,' I said suddenly, remembering with a jolt the letters I had hidden between the pages of my schoolbooks. My hands were shaking. I fisted them together.

'I felt sorry for you.' Captain Volkov paused in his pacing. 'Abandoned at eleven by your mother and a man who would never claim you as his own? Who would not.

I see now that it was a mistake. My mistake. I regret it bitterly. I encouraged you. I should have . . . left you alone. I only did more damage. It was not my intention. Your mother would be angry, if she knew.'

I did not want to hear any more. I put my hands to my ears, and the room spun and spun, a kaleidoscope of shapes and colours, jagged sunshine and fragments of shade. I heard my own voice speaking, although I was so detached now it was like hearing a stranger. 'Why did she kill herself?'

He shrugged sadly. 'Shame. Grief. Loneliness. Perhaps she thought he would give you to me, once she was gone. She was wrong. Instead, he has claimed you . . . unofficially.' His words bit painfully into my skin. 'She escaped him, you see. In a manner of speaking. But you . . .' He shook his head. 'You're always there to remind him of what he lost.'

'Why did you agree to marry her?' I asked.

'That was not my decision to make.' The sudden coldness in his voice made the hairs bristle on my arms. 'I was following orders. Your father already has a family, if you recall. It was a practical arrangement; I was promoted to Security Chief, your mother was allowed to stay with you and enjoy a life of comfort. I would visit every few months and play my part. Nobody was the wiser, except that nursemaid she hired to baby you.'

Nursemaid. I stared at him, disbelieving. Olga knew? She had *known*?

'I gave you my name and a happier childhood than you would have known. It should have been enough. I never imagined you would seek me out.' He frowned suddenly. 'I did like your mother. She was a beautiful woman. Estonian, as I think you know. Your father met her at a Party meeting before your grandparents died. But he was already married by then with children of his own. A public scandal would have exposed him to ridicule.' He pursed his lips and then turned away and bent down to pick up some fallen pieces of parchment, slipping them back into the file on the desk. He tidied them with his long fingers, squaring them until they were perfectly aligned.

I sat watching him, helpless, alone. 'What will happen to me?'

'You will stay at my townhouse until arrangements can be made to send you back,' he said. 'You have come at quite an inconvenient time. Russia is on the brink of war with the Germans. Olga will have to stay with you. Your father wants you to write him a letter. An apology. Perhaps you can do that while you're waiting. I will ensure it is posted.' He had picked up the telephone again. 'I will organise a car to take you to my lodgings,' he said. He was calm, businesslike. There was nothing of the man I remembered. Nothing of the man in the letters, the man who had written *Your loving Papochka.*

'Did my mother love him?' I asked.

He paused, the receiver halfway to his mouth. 'Of course she did,' he said, a flicker of warning crossing his features. 'Who doesn't? He is always right. I would advise you to consider wording your apology carefully. Your future may depend on it.'

I dragged in a shaky breath. Everything I had thought about myself was a lie. The man I had believed in and trusted to protect me was merely a false front, an invention of my own imagining, helped along with a little bit of misplaced information from Olga. Her round face sprang into my mind. She had lied to me.

163

But why? I knew she loved me. She had loved Mamochka, too. It could not all have been pretence. The demands she had made of the staff in the House on the Embankment to ensure we were given enough food and that our rooms were always spotless. The lengths she had gone to to hide my mother's secrets, standing guard at the door while Mama taught me her language and shared her stories of Estonia. The many times I had left her half-dozing on the lounge in our living room, determined to make sure Mamochka arrived home safely from her parties, no matter how late the hour. She had loved Mama and when Mama abandoned her, she had kept her greatest secret safe.

Me.

In spite of everything, Olga was the only person who looked out for me. If she had lied, there must be a reason. I would have to trust her. I had no one else left.

I heard him speak abruptly into the receiver, the short, sharp sounds of an order. Then he moved around the desk, his footsteps creaking on the floorboards. When he reached for my arm, I yanked it from his grasp. Captain Volkov said nothing, merely ushered me to the door.

'Go downstairs, now,' he commanded. 'The car will be waiting. Tomorrow you'll go back to Moscow and be your father's daughter.'

Without another word, he pushed me out onto the landing and slammed the door closed.

In the hallway, I stood staring at the walnut panelling with the sign attached that bore half my name. Volkov. Lydia Volkova. That name was a lie.

I reached out and touched the brass. It was warm. My

fingers left a smudge over the letters that I did not bother to wipe clean. A gust of air blew along the corridor, carrying a whiff of tobacco smoke from the rooms either side of Captain Volkov's office. I could hear typewriters whirring, men's low voices. A row of windows ran alongside the corridor, overlooking the courtyard behind the office block. I walked over and stared down between the bars that cast bands across the carpet runner. The courtyard was fenced, crowned with coils of wire. So different from the street façade, with its bland windows and columns, its arched door.

What other secrets was this building hiding?

From somewhere to my left, a scream pierced the air, shocking me out of my thoughts. It came again, louder but less shrill now. It was primal, a sound of unearthly pain. I ran back towards the stairwell Lieutenant Lubov had led me up earlier, my feet thudding on the concrete.

The screaming ceased. Just like that, it was gone. But the sound of it continued to echo, trapped in my head. Blindly, my feet found the bottom of the stairwell and I stumbled out into the reception hall.

'There you are, Lida!'

Olga hurried towards me, a worried look on her face. I hesitated, resisting the urge to shout at her, to demand to know why she had lied to me all my life. But the shock was too much. I fell into her arms.

'There now.' Olga's arms were around me. 'There, Lydochka. What's wrong?'

I shook my head. I wanted to sob and bury my head against her shoulder. To confess everything my 'father' had told me. But I could only hug her as tightly as possible. 'Did you hear it?' I said, instead. 'Somebody was screaming.'

The reception hall seemed cold after the warm brightness of the corridor upstairs. I shivered in my thin blouse. There was a police officer standing guard near the front doors and Lieutenant Lubov lounged against the wall beside him, engaged in conversation. It was as if they hadn't heard the screams at all.

With her arm still about me, Olga shuffled towards them. 'Lieutenant!'

He turned towards her, his grin fading.

'Yes, comrade?'

'Lydia tells me she heard screaming.'

The Lieutenant glanced at his companion and then back at Olga. 'Nothing for you to worry about. There are holding cells upstairs. Sometimes informants are taken there.'

'To be tortured?' My voice choked. I had heard of such places, of course, but the sound of that gutteral screaming sent a tremor of horror up my spine. Was that how Joachim had sounded as they questioned him? Had he screamed and begged for mercy? Or had he agreed to whatever false crime they had accused him of, haunted by the cries of those in the holding cells around him? The thought made me want to retch. I couldn't tolerate standing in a place where such horrific events were even now occurring. The very air seemed tainted and sour with fear. I placed my hand flat on my stomach, pressing hard.

'An unfortunate part of the judicial process, I'm afraid.' Lieutenant Lubov strode across to our waiting luggage and handed me my suitcase. 'Some people won't give up their information easily.'

'But who are they?' I asked through dry lips. I knew. Deep down, I knew.

Lieutenant Lubov shrugged. 'What does it matter? Some are farmers, intent on withholding their land, unwilling to allow the state to collectivise. Others help bandits like the ones you saw this morning, giving them shelter or food.' At my sickened expression, Lieutenant Lubov raised his eyebrows. 'They are always offered a choice. Most of them are happy to comply. Sometimes they need a little encouragement, though, to be convinced.' He nodded at me. 'I have arranged a car to take you both to Captain Volkov's townhouse. It is waiting out the front.'

'Oh.' Olga's creased face drooped a little. 'I had hoped to speak with your papa, Lida. It's been so long since I saw him. He is well, I hope?'

I bit my lip, feeling the sweat gather beneath my arms, unable to meet her gaze.

'He is well,' I mumbled. 'He wants us to return to Moscow, though.'

'So soon?' Olga said. She fussed with her hands. 'But why? We've only just arrived.'

Her confusion was painful to see. I needed to tell her I knew the truth but I could not do it with Lieutenant Lubov hanging about. I would have to wait until we reached the townhouse, where we could speak in private.

She watched me, waiting for my reply. I tried to answer her but the words stuck in my throat, tiny crumbs of truth I could not swallow.

Lieutenant Lubov moved quickly between us. 'Captain Volkov is well but, sadly, very busy. Your arrival has coincided with a very delicate operation and although he probably wishes he could be a better host, I imagine he will not be able to give you the full force of his attention until

167

it's concluded. I'm sure he will send for you then.'

Olga pursed her lips in disappointment but she could not argue. 'That's kind,' she said. 'It's been many years since we spoke, the Partorg and I. Too long.' Pacified, she allowed Lieutenant Lubov to usher us into the street.

Outside, a cool breeze danced with the Soviet flags attached to poles on the façade above us. A car waited beside the kerb, black and glossy, its engine purring. Olga began to berate the driver for not helping with her suitcase. Pink-cheeked, the young man hurried out to assist her.

Lieutenant Lubov moved to the other side of the car to swing the door open for me. 'That's twice today I've rescued you, Lydia Volkova. Once at Tiksoja and just now, with your friend.' His gaze lingered on my face as I eased myself into the car's interior, breathing in the scent of carbolic soap mingled with the sharp fumes of alcohol. A familiar smell, the same as all the cars in Stalin's fleet. A reminder that everything, even the truth, could be scrubbed clean.

I rolled the window down as far as it would go so that air rushed into the car.

Lieutenant Lubov lingered near the door. I wanted him to go, but like a wraith he continued to hover. I turned my head away, hoping he would leave. Instead, he stood beside the window, his shadow falling across my face.

'Your father seemed surprised to see you,' he said.

I looked down at my skirt. It was stained with dust. 'I fear the note we sent did not reach him. There was a misunderstanding.'

'Ah.' He shifted slightly.

I shielded my hand against my face to block out the

sunshine slanting in the window. 'Is there something you wanted, Lieutenant?'

He muttered beneath his breath and then leant in suddenly, so close I could smell the cloying pine scent of his aftershave. 'You should be careful not to go out tonight. Don't try to leave the complex.'

A gust of wind blew up the street and the flags snapped in their holders. Golden sickle. Glittering star. Moscow's symbols of triumph.

I thought of Stalin, my father Stalin, waiting for me to return. My cheek tingled, as if anticipating the strike of his hand. I had questions – so many questions – I wanted to ask him about my mother. But I knew he would not answer them. He was a monster. He had sent Joachim into exile. He had authorised the torture and execution of so many people, including members of his own family, while surrounding himself with men like Captain Volkov; people who were too afraid for their own lives to tell him no. Had my mother been afraid? Was that why she'd killed herself? Had she suspected he would one day turn on her; that her only way of protecting me would be to leave me with Olga?

A dull ache throbbed in my head. If my 'father' was truly mad, what hope did I have of surviving?

'Comrade Volkova? Did you hear me?' Lieutenant Lubov tapped the edge of the window.

'Why shouldn't we leave the complex?' I said. I could not go back, but I would not be given a choice. I would be dragged back. I was not a person. I had no more freedom than the prisoners in the holding cells.

'The operation I was telling you about . . . it is due to begin tonight. So, there may be a little disruption.'

'What kind of operation?'

A muscle flickered in his cheek. 'A standard one. Relocation of undesirables. Weeding out those who would help the Partisans – like the bandits you saw earlier today. Their families assist them. Their neighbours hide them and then tell bald-faced lies in the interrogation room. Not everyone complies easily, as you just heard. I would hate for you to be hurt or caught up in any resistance. I'll be overseeing things at the train station. I won't have time to check on you.'

Something snapped inside me. 'I don't need looking after!' I said. 'No matter what everyone may think. I appreciate your concern, Lieutenant. But I'm more than capable of taking care of myself. And I have Olga.'

'Ah yes.' His lips twitched. 'The nursemaid.' Straightening up, he glanced up at the high façade of the Grey House as if he could hear the Partorg calling him like a master summoning his dog, his voice an invisible beacon that only Lieutenant Lubov could discern. 'I meant no offence. Simply thought you should know.'

Before I could say more, he walked away, his shoes clipping the cobblestones.

Pearl Pattern

Kati

JAKOB AND I DROVE HOME TO THE FARM IN SILENCE. WHEN we reached the house, Jakob switched off the engine and sat staring through the windscreen. I watched his expression darken as his gaze swept across the mouldy thatch on the roof and down to the house's windows. A few months ago, a huge thunderstorm had swept over us, throwing hailstones like cannons and pouring rain down between the thatch to stain the floors. The largest hailstones had cracked the glass in some of the windows, leaving holes the size of my fist and a cobweb of fractured lines that radiated out towards the timber frames. Shawls had been stuffed into the holes – not delicate lace ones, but my mother's thick old woollen ones with the frayed ends. Jakob's gaze burnt. He turned to me, his eyes narrowed in accusation.

'Why didn't you tell me?'

'What good would it have done?'

Jakob shook his head, then climbed out of the car, slamming the door behind him and stalking into the house. I let myself out and went to the barn to release the sheep. As I heaved the barn doors apart, I tried not to see the broken windows, or the rust that peppered the iron door handles and left smears of blood-red speckles against my palms. It had been my father's plan to renovate the farmhouse; he had been saving for years, storing all of his kroons in the Estonian National Bank, waiting until the time was right, until the farm could spare him. But when Papa had gone to line up outside the bank one day in March, he'd been informed that all our savings were now worthless. Kopeks had replaced cents, roubles instead of kroons. Estonian tender was now worth less than a withered apple skin.

I could hear my brother banging around in the rooms upstairs and wondered if perhaps I should go in and speak to him. But my parents would be home soon. He could say what he had to say to them without me. I was not his keeper. He was old enough to join the resistance group. Old enough to make his own choices.

I led the sheep outside into the paddock, watching their flickering tails. They were restless after so many hours cooped up inside. Grass stalks snapped beneath my boots as I drove them out to the very last paddock, the one furthest from the house. Let Jakob be the one to greet my parents when they returned from another degrading trip to the factories to give away our apples for the good of the state, I thought, switching the grass savagely with my birch stick. Let him be the one to tell Papa about his subversive activities. I could not shake the feeling of helplessness. We were at the centre of a storm; no matter which way the currents pulled, we were destined to follow. The peace I had experienced briefly at Aunt Juudit's this morning was gone, the threads of it scattered like a shawl unravelling in the wind.

I saw Jakob emerge from the house and begin dragging things out of the barn, cleaning them with a rag and sudsy water. The timber crates made from sanded birch logs which we used for storing apples, to prevent them being jostled. The old milk canisters we filled with water and dragged inside when the frosts arrived so we had a source of water always and could avoid the shocking sting of the cold pump on our hands. When he lugged the old dogsled through the barn doors, I almost called out. It was still sturdy, despite many years of use, with enough room for two people to sit side by side with room for the crates behind. We had used it until last year to transport goods to our neighbours when the snow fell thickly. Rasmus Poska from town always hired his dogs out to us. But the Russians had seized them two months ago and slaughtered them for barking through the night. There would be no dogsledding this year.

Jakob slapped the rag against the side of the sled and scrubbed vigorously. Guilty, I thought. He feels guilty that he's left all the farmwork to us, that he's been at university all this time. I did not feel smug for being the one who had stayed while Jakob went ahead. When he glanced up at me, I turned away, unable to bring myself to tell him his efforts were wasted.

My anxiety about Mama and Papa increased as the day began to fade. I'd driven the sheep as close to the road as I dared, watching for a glimpse of Papa's white lorry. The field here was mostly brown, full of stones and tangled bushes. The clover was so shrivelled that the animals did not nibble at the ground but huddled together in a knot, bleating with displeasure each time a truck roared past.

I stopped before my brother, squeezing my hands together. It was useless to pretend any longer. 'Where are they?'

'Perhaps they stopped in at Tartu.'

'Why would they do that?'

'I don't know.'

I tried to still my racing heart as I handed my brother the

birch switch. 'Help me bring in the sheep. I'll need to see to supper. If they aren't home by then, we'll drive back to Aunt Juudit's and look for them.'

My brother frowned but took the birch switch and followed me, poking at the sheep, who tossed their heads and glared at him. When I commanded them, though, they began to move as a unit, their feet stirring up the mud, straining their necks as they shoved and jostled their way towards the farmhouse and the safety of their pens.

We had just reached the last field when I heard it – the distinctive splutter of the lorry's engine.

I whirled around.

There it was, jerking across the ground, the tyres churning.

Sheep bleated around me, clamouring for protection. I broke through the circle of their warm fleecy bodies and ran towards the fence. I was up and down the other side before my father had even brought the lorry to a stop, careless of the way my muddy skirt slapped against my shins.

'Mama!' I ran straight to the passenger side and reached up to wrench open the door. My mother was hidden in the shadows of the lorry's cabin, but I saw her hand, tanned and speckled from the work she now did in the orchards with Papa. Leaning in, I clutched it with my own. Mama's skin was cold. I rubbed her fingers, trying to warm them, but she did not move or react. She was still as stone.

My father appeared behind me, his face stricken.

'What's wrong with her?' I stared at her still form leaning back against the fabric seat of the cab. Her eyes were closed.

'She's fine.' My father pushed me aside and braced

himself against the open cab door. 'Marta.' He leant in and gently shook her. 'Marta. We're home.'

My mother did not open her eyes, but jerked her head away from Papa.

I heard Jakob's feet squelching in the mud. 'Kati, what's the matter?'

'Mama's ill.'

'She's not ill. She's in shock.' My father lowered himself from the lorry. His face was shiny with sweat.

'Jakob?' I heard my mother call, her voice faint.

'He is here,' my father shouted. Gasping, he reached forward and grabbed my brother by the shoulders, pulling him hard against his chest. 'Thank God.'

Jakob looked over Papa's shoulder at me, his eyes wide. 'What's going on?'

My father pulled back, wiping his eyes with the back of his hand. 'They've commandeered the lorry. The Partorg's men were waiting for us in Kobratu. I'm supposed to report tonight in an hour's time at the Town Hall to hand it over. Juhan Vunder refused to give them his vehicle. They shot him and arrested his son and took it anyway.'

'But why?' Jakob said, his face shocked. 'Why do they need the lorries?'

My father's hands shook. He ran them through his hair. 'Elvi Tamm said he saw railroad cars lined up at the station. Dozens of them.' *Railroad cars.* The memory of the first deportations rose up around me like hissing steam. *They take the educated ones first*, that old woman had said. The government officials, the teachers. I looked at my brother, his face ghostly pale, and realised my father was staring at him.

Perhaps he was thinking of the old woman's words, too.

'They expect us to help them.' Papa drew in a deep, shuddering breath. 'But we're not going to. We are going to run. The way we should have done last year. I was wrong. We're not going to stay and be part of this crime.'

'We should fight,' Jakob said. He curled his fists by his sides. 'We're not alone in this. We should stay and show them we are not afraid.'

From inside the lorry, I heard my mother moan softly.

Papa ran a hand across his shiny forehead. 'Jakob.' His voice shook. 'You aren't thinking clearly. I'm the head of this house. Stop talking nonsense. I will decide when we fight and when we go.'

Jakob's jaw tensed. 'It isn't nonsense.' He turned. 'Tell him, Kati! You agree with me, don't you? We can't leave! We must just hold out until help arrives. We are part of this family, too, Papa.'

'Kati?' Papa swivelled to face me. 'What do you have to say?'

I looked between my father and my brother. I was torn. How could I leave Oskar without telling him goodbye? I could imagine his pain when he found our house empty, all of us gone. His heart would break, as my heart was breaking. I'd slept last night with Oskar's gloves beneath my pillow and woken with them clutched in my hands, the soft wool wet with tears. What if Oskar knew I had gone without resisting? Yet how could I stay when Papa, my strong Papa who had weathered so much, was staring at me with wild, shining eyes as if he might suddenly cry? How could I cause him more worry and heartache by asking him to allow us to stay behind?

176

Another second passed before Papa shook his head. 'You see?' he said to Jakob, as if my silence was confirmation.

'I have weapons,' Jakob said, stubbornly. 'A pistol. A knife. You have a shotgun. I know you do, I know where you hide it—'

Papa looked shocked. Then his face lengthened. 'A pistol, Jakob? A shotgun? These are your weapons? Against their rifles? No. Enough.' He held up his hand as Jakob started to answer. 'You're upsetting your sister. Your mother.' He called up to Mama. 'Marta, hurry!' Swinging himself up, he helped her to climb down from the cabin.

Mama's colour was better, but her legs still shook as we ran towards the house and began to gather our things. The farmhouse was dark and quiet. The only sounds were our feet scuffing the floor, and the bang of cupboard doors.

'We will drive north,' Papa said. Objects rattled in his knapsack as he swung it up onto his back. 'I know a man in Tallinn with a boat. We will have to cross the Gulf and hope we can find a safe way into Finland. And from there – who knows?'

I looked down at my own knapsack, hoping I had brought the right things for a journey to an unknown destination.

'You are a good man, Erich. We trust you to guide us.' Mama tapped my shoulder and passed me the last of our dry food, clothes and candles. My fingers fumbled with the strings on the bag. The room was dark with shadows. There was no time to light the lamps.

'Here.' Mama reached across and deftly knotted the bag closed. For a moment, her fingers stayed on mine. I could smell the familiar scent of home on them; the earth on her hands, the pine tar soap on her skin. The bittersweet tang of apples.

'We don't have to go.' Jakob's voice floated out of the darkness. 'We could stay.' I could just make out his shadowy form. He stepped forward, drawing in a long, slow breath. 'Papa, please. Listen. I came home to convince you to join the others in the forest. We could fight. We should fight.' My brother's face was shadowed but his eyes burnt with purpose. He raised his chin. 'We don't have to run like cowards.'

'And what,' my father said softly, 'do you think will happen to Kati and your mother? Do you think they will fight with us to dispatch the Partorg's men and the hundreds of Soviet soldiers they've been sending into the forest this year?'

'Hundreds?' Jakob's face was pale. His mouth faltered. 'I thought . . . perhaps a few dozen. Oskar said—'

My father moved suddenly. I flinched, thinking he might strike my brother. Instead, he embraced him. Jakob stiffened, but after a moment he wound his arms tightly around Papa as if he were a child again.

'I am not a fighter, Jakob,' my father said, his voice slightly muffled by Jakob's hair. 'I'm a farmer. I could not hold a gun to a man's head or shoot him in the back. I'm sorry.'

They stayed for a moment locked in the embrace. Finally, my father straightened up and shouldered his pack. The darkness blurred his edges. It was as if he were already disappearing, our presence swallowed by the night. 'If there was another choice, I would take it. But there isn't. This time it's our turn to run.'

'Did you pack them?'

In the cab of the lorry, my mother clutched my arm. She seemed to have revived a little but her hands were still cold.

Outside, I could hear my father and Jakob in the yard, ushering the sheep out into the field. Although we could not take them with us, Papa could not bring himself to keep them penned indoors.

'Yes. I brought them.' From my pocket I drew my grandmother's pearl earrings, passed down to her from my great-grandmama. They glimmered in the starlight, as perfect as two teardrops made of ice.

'No. Not those,' Mama hissed. 'The samplers!'

I gaped at her. My mother made a clucking noise. 'Your grandmother never cared for those earrings. It was the lace samplers she always fretted over. Did you bring them?'

I was too surprised to speak. I had emptied the lace fragments into my sewing bag along with Oskar's gloves and left the beautiful oak storage box on the dresser in my room. The box was too heavy to carry, too bulky to fit in my knapsack. 'Yes,' I said finally. 'I have them.'

My mother cleared her throat. 'Good girl.' She paused, worrying at her shawl with her fingers. 'I know she asked you to take over the knitting group. And to look after her lace. I–I was never trusted with those things. I was not a good knitter. My stitches were clumsy. I was impatient. But I want your grandmother's spirit to rest easy, knowing they are safe.'

She turned her face to the window so I could not see her expression, but her words circled around in my mind. I saw her suddenly the way she must have been as a child, sitting by my grandmother's knee, growing more and more frustrated as the lace in her hands refused to flourish. My grandmother's sharp voice commanding her to re-pick the rows she had muddled. My grandmother had always said that anyone could learn to knit, but we both knew this wasn't really true. A real knitter

179

had an eye for patterns, and hands that remembered. A way of looking further ahead than just the stitch or row of the moment. My mother had neither of those things. I could imagine her throwing down her work in a temper and never taking it up again, rejecting my grandmother's traditions. How my grandmother would have been hurt, and how that pain might have hardened into distrust. When I was born, my grandmother must have seen it as a chance to try again. She had been more careful with me, perhaps, more patient. And to her delight, I had been the one with the eye, and my hands itched if I went too long without knitting. I could see now how Mama's disappointment might have simmered into resentment. My grandmother and I had been close in a way she could not understand. Our knitting had bound us, as had my grandmother's stories and the history she had brought to life through the hours we spent together. Those lace shawls and those tales had formed a bond between us that Mama could never break.

I looked at my mother anew, wishing I could apologise for the times Grandmother and I had laughed at her, or teased her about her crooked stitches, but I couldn't make my mouth form the words I needed to speak.

Too late. Footsteps stirred the pebbles outside. Jakob pulled open the door and climbed up next to me and Papa clambered in on the other side. Squashed between my mother and Jakob, I found it hard to breathe. The air was close, tinged with sour sweat.

With a sharp pang, I thought of Oskar again. I would have to trust that he knew I'd not wanted to go; that we'd had no choice but to run.

Outside, the darkness had spread, eating up the fields.

Cars and trucks were visible up on the road, their lights flickering. How many were carrying people back to their homes, where they would eat their meagre dinners and fall into bed, exhausted, unsuspecting of the fate that awaited them in a few hours' time? The fatal knock, the indignity of being given only minutes to gather their things and pushed outside in their nightclothes. If only we could warn them . . . But as the lorry's engine rumbled and I listened to the strained breathing of my family, Papa's grunt as he shifted the gears and propelled the lorry away from the house, I pushed away the guilt that weighed on me. It was just as Papa said. It was our turn to run. We would escape. That was what mattered.

My father cursed.

Two sets of headlights had broken away from the road. They bounced across the ground as the vehicle drew closer, winding around the path that led through our fields. It was not a car, I realised, but an army truck. I felt my father tense beside me. His elbow dug into my ribs as he spun the wheel and sent the lorry bouncing onto the side of the road. The brakes squealed.

'Out!' He leant past me and threw open the door. 'Get to the forest now. Run!'

My legs were frozen.

The oncoming lights were dazzling. Tyres scraped on gravel as the truck closed the distance between us.

'Erich?' Mama's voice quivered.

Papa grunted. 'I'll join you afterwards. Jakob!' he barked.

Jakob shook himself then grasped my arm, forcing feeling back into my limbs. My feet thumped onto the earth. With Mama between us, we tore towards the forest. Mama stumbled; Jakob grabbed her coat and dragged her to her feet. He helped her when we reached the first fence, holding the wire apart so she could scramble through. Mud sucked at our shoes and caught at the edge of my skirt. Mama's breathing was loud in my ears, sobs escaping her lips.

Behind us, doors slammed. I heard men's voices, speaking guttural Russian. They grew fainter as we moved towards the edge of the forest, still ahead of us. The darkness there was thick, impenetrable.

We reached the last field, where the apple trees were spaced in rows, and flung ourselves against their sheltering trunks, Mama behind one, Jakob and I behind another.

When I peered around the tree I saw Papa on his knees between three men. They were shouting at him, their words echoing across the fields. *Liar! Traitor!*

One of the men reached into his pocket and produced a pistol. Almost casually, he aimed it and fired.

Papa crumpled. From the tree on my right, my mother's scream rose up, shattering the night air. Blood seemed to flood every chamber of my heart at once. I thought my chest might burst. I heard a voice cry out. It was my voice.

'Papa!'

I started to move. If I could reach him, I could help. I could save him.

Jakob's hands gripped my shoulders tightly. I tried to fight him off. It was useless. I heard him whisper, but his words could not penetrate the thick fog of shock in my mind. What was he saying?

No.

I stopped struggling.

For a moment, everything was still. Then Mama was gone. She was running, slipping and sliding between the fence wires, heedless of the mud and the waiting men.

I felt Jakob tense behind me, ready to race after her. My own legs were burning, aching to run. But neither of us moved. Jakob's grip relaxed slightly. His arm slipped to my middle, his hand searching in the dark until it found mine.

Helplessly, we watched Mama fall to her knees. She was sobbing, cradling my father's head.

One of the soldiers shouted at her to get up, but my mother didn't seem to hear him. He shouted again and then, as if losing patience, he raised the gun again and fired. Mama slumped forward.

I screamed, unable to contain the sound that burst from my mouth.

The men turned, and with them a torch beam bounced across the ground, illuminating the grass, the mud, the fences we had scrambled through.

Jakob and I turned as one and tore our way across the last field. The torch beam zigzagged across our path. Men yelled behind us. A shot exploded into a nearby tree. I heard Jakob grunt, saw him stumble and then right himself.

Together, we staggered to the edge of the field and through the last fence.

Footsteps squelched through the mud behind us.

I looked back. Figures were running through the field, closing in.

Jakob seized my hand and dragged me into the trees. In seconds, the light from the torch had vanished. The darkness of the forest had swallowed us whole.

Cornflower Stitch

Lydia

'OLGA.'

My nursemaid paused and looked back at me from the little path leading to the Partorg's townhouse. The late afternoon sun threaded her white hair with silver. Tired rings circled her eyes but she seemed happy enough, pleased to have reached our destination at last. The Partorg's residence stood behind her, a charming two-storey building with whitewashed walls rising above a sea of foaming flowerbeds.

She gripped her suitcase between her hands. I heard the car drive off. The residential street beyond the iron gates was quiet, almost deserted. People hurried past without glancing up, their heads bowed.

'Olga.'

'What is it Lydochka?'

When she smiled, Olga's teeth were revealed, the yellow stains on them clear as tidemarks drawn in the sand. The stains were relics of the years after the revolution, when she had struggled to find food and her body had suffered from malnourishment and lack of vitamins. She had told me those stories of horror, woven among her fairy tales. Stories of a city that had been starving. A country in the grip of famine. Children screaming on the streets, bellies bloated from hunger. No wonder Olga now ate everything set before her. She knew what true hunger was.

I almost changed my mind, then. She was everything to me and I to her. She had known so much pain in her lifetime; the death of her husband and my mother. Famine and disease. The purges of the last ten years, when many of our neighbours had been, wrongfully or otherwise, arrested or killed. How could I force her to acknowledge the truth, to relive the past when she already had suffered so much?

'I need to speak to you.' I watched her smile slip. 'I think it's best we talk now, before we go inside.'

'Is it about your Papochka?' she said. 'Why is he sending us home so soon? I had hoped to stay a little longer, not only to speak with him but also to honour your mother's memory by seeing a little of the country she loved. I remember the stories she told me about—'

'It's about my father, yes,' I interrupted. 'My – my real father.'

Olga's eyes widened in surprise. We stood looking at each other. Bees hummed in the rose bushes nearby, lifting off the fragrant blooms as they felt the vibration of my footsteps beside them. Their scent was warm, enveloping. It was so pleasant to stand in the afternoon sun. I wished I could go on standing there, that I was indeed coming to live in my new home. Instead it would be another holding pen until I was sent back. I wished I could unlearn the things I had discovered; about my past, about Olga. About my parentage. *Lydia Stalina.*

I said the name out loud, heard Olga's breath draw in sharply.

That was who I really was. The daughter of a murderer and a tyrant.

I watched Olga's face slowly deflating. She dropped her suitcase to the ground and lifted her hands to cover her mouth. She began to cry. Tears splashed over her hands and dropped off her chin. My arms tingled with the need to comfort her, to hold her as she had held me all those times in my childhood. But I let her cry. I was callous and cruel. I was my father's daughter, even if nobody else knew the secret but two men who had made a business transaction and an old woman protecting the secrets of her dead friend.

'Who told you?' she said at last, brushing away her tears with the heels of her palms.

'Captain Volkov did.' I could feel the sun beating upon my back through my shirt. 'He had to. Stalin has ordered us back.'

'I hoped he would leave us alone.' She drew up her trembling chin. 'I hoped he would let you go. That he'd be glad to be rid of the . . . responsibility. I should have known he would not give you up easily. He controlled your mother, too. Everything she wore and read, the people she saw. His spies were everywhere. And Captain Volkov, as you saw, has a will which is as weak as a kitten. He had no power to say no. The only place we were safe was in her boudoir. Just the three of us. When you were practising your Estonian and your mother could speak freely about her past. Her family. But your father found a way to ruin that too, in the end. That was why she killed herself. She couldn't stand it any longer, the threats and his endless taunts. The shame.'

She began to cry again. Emotion overwhelmed me.

I reached for her hand. It was slippery from her tears. I covered it with my own.

'I know why you lied,' I said softly.

Olga sniffed hard. She looked away. 'I did it only to protect you. I could not bear to see you disgraced, shut out.'

'I know.' I squeezed her fingers. She looked up at me, eyes slanted against the sunshine.

'I'm thankful you kept her shawl,' she said. 'She would have wanted you to have it. I would have saved it, if I had the chance.'

'There was a little book of poems, too.' I lifted my case. 'I kept them. And a photograph.'

Olga's mouth worked. 'I'm so glad. I was too upset. I could not rouse myself. By the time I got to her rooms, there was nothing to be had except a few of her coats and a letter written in Estonian. I kept the letter to give to you but I could not read it, then I lost it . . . everything else she owned was taken off and burnt. Stalin did not even give her things away. He had them all thrown on a fire. Your mother's treasures. Her beautiful clothes. Her books.'

'At least you can remember her.' My heart felt heavy. 'I sometimes worry I'm starting to forget.'

Olga lifted her head. 'I will never forget her. Never. She saved me. I only hope you can forgive me, in time.'

'Will you tell me about her?' I said. 'How could she bring herself to be with him?'

Olga sucked air in through her nose. 'Yes, Lida. Yes. I will tell you everything. Nobody else knows the truth. Your Mama trusted only me. But first, let us eat and rest. I feel so hungry I could eat all these flowers.' She waved her hand at the nodding roses and row of cornflowers and sprays of white blossoms lining the path.

Questions burnt inside me. I was on the verge of begging Olga not to wait, demanding that she tell me everything. But she was tired and old. There would be time enough for us to talk of Mama later. I let Olga walk ahead and ring the bell beside the door. Through the large front window, I glimpsed glossy timber furniture and damask curtains pulled back. More colourful flowerbeds were banked up against the panes. It was a beautiful place, with the sky beginning to move towards dusk and the fragrance rising up from the blooms. I almost wished I could stay there on the warm flagstones, surrounded by bright cornflowers, steeped in memories of walking through the Apothecary Gardens with Mamochka and Olga outside the Kremlin.

I could recall as if it were only this morning the way Mama had held my hand, her bracelets jingling, our shoes making small puffs in the dust as we wandered along the avenue of linden trees towards the greenhouse. Olga had been idling behind, content to watch us walk ahead.

'Lydochka!' Mama's hand had slipped away. I watched her shift her pale braid back over one shoulder as she crouched beside the path. 'See here,' she had said, pointing between the trucks to a patch of blue flowers shooting up amid the grass. Their vivid blue stood out against the green, the colour shifting like a kingfisher's wings. 'Estonia is full of cornflowers,' she said, smiling so that her cheeks dimpled. 'I asked the gardener to plant these here to remind me of home. You know the story of the cornflower?' Reaching out, she had plucked a spiky blue blossom from its stem and tucked it behind my ear, weaving the soft coils of my hair deftly into a braid like her own. 'When Queen Louise of Prussia was fleeing Napoleon's forces, she hid her children in a field of cornflowers. She kept them quiet by weaving wreaths for them. Can you imagine the fear in her heart, the terror, knowing that at any moment they might be caught and dragged back?'

I had shaken my head then. Now I could imagine how that might feel, being taken against your will, forced to live an existence subservient to a man's will.

At least Olga would be beside me.

The door of the townhouse opened to reveal a young woman in a black housecoat. A white lace shawl was settled across her shoulders. The sight of it jolted me – it was just like the one I wore. Mamochka's shawl.

'You're the captain's girl,' she said, glancing at me quickly and then looking shyly away. 'I'm the housekeeper. Your father sent word to expect you.' She drew back the door and stood aside, her back pressed against the wall. Although her face was thin and pinched, she could hardly be older than me. The shapeless housecoat ballooned around her but even its formless shape could not disguise the round swell of her belly.

As if she had noticed my gaze, her hand drifted towards her stomach and she rested her palm on the protrusion; an unmistakable gesture of protection.

I felt a sudden affinity towards her. How desperately must she need to work, to be so close to her time and yet be here.

'Lydia Volkova,' I said. 'And this is Olga Andreyevna.'

She shot us a quick, frightened glance, her hand still cupping her belly. 'I know. I'm Etti,' she added, clasping my outstretched hand. Her fingers were callused, ridged by small bumps that had obviously burst and healed. She withdrew her hand quickly.

'You look too young to be a housekeeper,' I said.

The girl gave an embarrassed shrug. Leaning over, she took the suitcase from Olga's hand. 'I was just a maid until last month. There was another woman here, Tiina Tamm. But she's gone now, so it's left to me.' She began to lug Olga's suitcase up the hallway towards the stairs. 'Thankfully the Partorg doesn't use this residence often. It is used more for guests or special visitors. The bedrooms are upstairs. I have made the beds up for you already and drawn a bath. I imagine you must be exhausted after your travels.'

'That's kind of you, but unnecessary.' I drew in a breath, thinking of the letter I must write to Stalin; to my real father. What would I say to him? What could I say? I would have to be contrite, apologetic, when all I wanted to do was ask him how he had let me believe for so many years that I was the daughter of another man. I wondered if he would accept me, now that I knew the truth. Or would he shun me, as Olga suggested, refusing to admit it? It seemed more likely I would become another of the Kremlin's dark secrets, like the men and women who had been wrongfully accused.

I imagined the letter I would write.

Dear Stalin.

Dear liar.

You do not deserve an apology. I have learnt the truth. I know you were the reason Mama killed herself. I know about the trials and executions carried out in your name. I know what happened to Joachim and why you had him arrested, your efforts to control everything. You are the worst kind of man. I'm ashamed I spent so many hours trying to please you, worrying that you would be angry with me for disturbing you, thinking that I was dear to you when in fact, it was the opposite. If you cared about me at all, if you felt bad about your role in Mama's death, you would have accepted my happiness. You would have set me free. Instead, you have made me hate you. I will never be your daughter, not in name and not in my soul. Those things belong to me now. They are mine alone.

Of course, I couldn't write that.

To do so would be suicide. I would have to be meek and simpering and subservient. I could never reveal my parentage. It would be dangerous. I remembered how Stalin had paraded his legitimate children before world leaders like Winston Churchill, pretending that he was a true family man.

I knew the truth now, but my tongue was sealed.

It would be better to get the distasteful ordeal over with as soon as possible.

When we reached the stairs, I watched Etti struggle for a

moment, trying to manoeuvre the suitcase onto the lowest step. Unable to still myself, I moved forward to help. Mama had always instilled in me a respect for servants. *Treat them as if they were your family*, she had once said, and although I imagined she had been referring more to Olga, who was indeed like a mother, the words had stayed with me. Besides, was it not the principal teaching of communism, for everyone to be equal?

'Here. You can't lift that,' I said. 'Not in your condition. Please, don't protest.'

She fell silent. Her fingers brushed mine as she released the suitcase into my free hand.

'Up here?'

Etti nodded. Ignoring the resistant ache in my muscles, I heaved Olga's suitcase and my own up to the next floor. A moment later, I heard Olga mount the stairs behind me, grudgingly praising all the lovely things in the rooms downstairs.

At the top of the landing, Etti paused to lean against the timber wainscot that ran along the wall and catch her breath. Her skin was mottled pink.

Olga peered at her down the bridge of her nose.

'You are close to your time,' she observed, reaching out without permission to run her hand over Etti's belly, splaying out her fingers. I thought Etti might protest but the Estonian woman said nothing.

'It is a girl,' Olga declared, tossing back her head. 'I am certain. You see? The stomach is round and soft like a big ball of dough ready for kneading. If it was a boy, it would be a different shape, more narrow.'

'A baguette?' I suggested.

'Perhaps.'

Etti blinked in astonishment at the informality of our conversation and then she smiled hesitantly.

'Superstitions,' she said. 'It seems they are everywhere. Let me show you to your rooms.'

The second-floor landing led into a corridor and a number of bedrooms. Two of the doors were open, revealing double beds covered by knitted bedspreads. A narrow bathroom, cleverly concealed to look more like a linen closet, was sandwiched between them. The scent of rose soap floated towards me on a cloud of steam. I was all too aware of my own odour and suddenly I could think of nothing I wanted more than to submerge myself beneath the surface of the water.

The letter to Stalin could wait.

'I've changed my mind,' I said, setting Olga's suitcase in the doorway of the first bedroom. 'I will bathe. Thank you, Etti. It was very kind of you. I don't know how many days I will be here.' I bit down on my disappointment. I couldn't tell her I would be staying only one night; she would want to know why. 'But I'm glad my father appointed you the housekeeper until Tiina's return.'

Etti's expression was sombre. 'I'm not sure that she will return, to be truthful.'

'Oh.' Grasping her meaning, I fidgeted with the hem of my blouse. An awkwardness stretched between us. Had Tiina been yet another victim of my father's tactics?

Etti filled it at last. 'In any case,' she said, 'you can ask me for anything you need. I will go now and prepare your supper.'

'I will help you,' Olga said. Etti raised her eyebrows and looked from Olga to me, her curiosity clear.

'My husband was a chef,' Olga offered. 'He worked in a grand hotel. Sometimes he would sneak me in and I would help him prepare the food before a particularly important guest arrived. This was years ago, of course, long before I came to look after Lydia, at her mother's request.'

'A grand hotel?' Etti pursed her lips. 'Then I'm sorry, you will find our meals and our ingredients meagre by comparison.'

Olga shrugged. 'I have not cooked in a good while. And besides, that does not matter,' she said. 'My husband used to say it is not the ingredients that are important, but how we use them. Kneading dough, slicing vegetables, making bread dumplings for the soup. These are all the things he taught me.'

'I would be glad of your help,' Etti said. 'But it would be unconventional for a guest to cook for herself.'

'Nonsense,' Olga said. 'I miss cooking. Zoya did not like me to interfere with her methods. She was always offended if I tried to help.' She began to roll up her sleeves. 'Let me make myself decent first with some water on my hands. My dear friend Ana, Lydochka's mother, often spoke of the delicacies of the Estonian palate. She knew how much I appreciate food.'

Etti still seemed uncertain. 'Well, if you insist.' She began to move away but turned back as she reached the stairs. 'You are not what I expected,' she said, her brow furrowed. 'Either of you.'

* * *

The unmistakable scent of frying fish engulfed me as I stepped out of the tiny bathroom. Saliva flooded my mouth. What had I last eaten? Breakfast on the train: a pot of coffee and lumpy biscuits studded with raisins. It seemed a lifetime ago.

Running my fingers through the waves of my damp hair, I hurried to the bedroom. Olga had laid out fresh clothes for me. As I buttoned on my skirt and blouse I spied a figurine of a provincial milkmaid on a nearby shelf. A mantle clock ticked the seconds quietly away, behind a glass dome surrounded by spinning golden baubles. Beautiful objects. Someone with taste had selected them. Curious, I pulled open the wardrobe door. It was filled with women's clothing, dresses and gloves. Hats and shoes. I realised that they must have belonged to the person who had lived here before. They must have left in a hurry. Perhaps the captain did not realise their things were still here, cluttering the wardrobe. I let the door fall closed.

When I turned to leave, I saw my mother's shawl folded on an old rocking chair near the window. As I drew it towards me, something caught beneath it fluttered to the carpet. It was an envelope which had once been cream. Now it was yellowed at the corners, mottled with age. I wondered who had left it there. Perhaps the person who had owned this room before had forgotten it, in their hurry to leave? I turned it over. My breath caught suddenly.

It was addressed to my mother.

The handwriting was faded, drawn across the paper in long elegant loops. Olga must have left it for me. I stood frozen with the letter pinched between my fingers. Although

I wanted to rip it open, some part of me was hesitant. I could not suppress the fear that some further stain upon my mother's character would reveal itself. How many more secrets had she kept?

My stomach gurgled with hunger. I slipped the envelope into my skirt, resolved to read it once I had eaten and bolstered my courage for what lay in its folds.

The working kitchen was situated at the back of the townhouse. Copper pans hung from hooks on the ceiling. Late afternoon sunlight flooded the room. In here, the smell of fish was both rich and delicate, perfumed with spices.

Etti and Olga stood side by side in front of the stove with their backs to the door. They were peeling potatoes and chatting as I entered, tossing the skins into a bucket. I heard Olga say her husband's name.

'. . . candelabras everywhere,' she continued. 'And a great circular pool with lights and fat carp swimming around.'

Etti drew in her breath. A slippery spiral of potato peeling flew from her hand to the floor. 'I cannot even imagine.'

'Yes. And sometimes Ivan would come out and catch a fish for a special guest. And sometimes a guest would join the fishes for a swim if he'd consumed too much vodka. And Ivan would be sent in to fetch him out, all dripping.'

Etti burst out laughing. Olga laughed too.

Steam swirled from a pot and Olga bent over to stir it with a spoon.

Etti paused in her peeling, her finger on the blade.

'I remember when David was alive he would often rise early to make *challah*. He would sprinkle it with spices and brush it with egg yolk. The smell of it baking would warm the house. I think he enjoyed baking.'

Olga tapped the spoon on the edge of the pot to loosen the sauce. 'David? He was your husband?'

Etti nodded. Her lips were pursed. 'He was a good man. He would have been a good father. Now it's just the two of us.' She looked down at her stomach.

Olga tutted. 'I'm sorry,' she said.

Etti shrugged but I could see she was trying not to cry. Her distress made me think of Joachim. How could I ever forgive myself for not fighting harder for his release?

I remembered Mama telling me once that Estonian women were proud. They did not like to cry in front of others.

I stepped forward. Olga turned, smiling.

'Lida. You look much happier.' Her voice grew softer. 'Did you find the letter I left for you? Your mother's?'

I nodded. My throat ached as if a fever burnt inside. I could not bring myself to tell her I had not had the courage to read it. She seemed so pleased.

'I found it when I was unpacking my things,' she said. 'It was in the pocket of the fur coat all this time! Who could tell?' She shook her head in wonderment and glanced at the bubbling pot. 'I think we are nearly done here. Just the potatoes to go.'

'I can tell.' I sniffed again at the rich aroma. Fat sizzled and popped in the pan. 'It smells heavenly.'

'Our friend here was showing me the way to make *mulgipuder*,' Olga said, lifting the spoon in the pot near her elbow to reveal a dripping lump of barley groats. 'I remember your Mamochka saying it was her favourite.'

Drying her eyes on her sleeve, Etti picked up the chopping board and slid the potatoes into the boiling water. 'And your companion certainly picked up some tips from her time at the Metropol. I would never have thought to use dried parsley to bring out the flavour of salted fish.'

She shot Olga a grateful smile, the fading light glinting on her bronze hair. 'I appreciate the help. Tiina was a better cook than I am. I suppose I've been spoilt; my mother was always good with the stove. But I find it difficult. Trying to coordinate everything to come out at once. If you'll both be seated, I'll serve you shortly in the dining room.'

'Please don't fuss on our account,' I said, wishing my blunt words were prettier, more convincing. 'I'm sure Olga and I would be happy to eat here.' I glanced around at the plain timber table and the scarred chairs I'd spied shoved into a shadowy corner. 'There's no need for such formality.'

Etti's forehead crinkled. 'Are you sure?'

I thought of the dinnertime rigmarole we endured back home; the silver knives and forks, the various courses each set out on their own dishes. Somebody had to clean it all up when we were done. Back home, there was an army of invisible service personnel who saw to it. Here, there was only Etti, belly straining against the folds of her housecoat.

'Quite sure,' Olga said, as if she had read my mind.

Etti pursed her lips but the wrinkle between her eyebrows disappeared as if an invisible iron had smoothed it out. 'If you insist. It's for both of you to say.'

Turning away, she grasped the handle of the frypan and slid the fish out onto two plates, then poured the bubbling sauce from the pan across a ladleful of the *mulgipuder*. Catching up the plates, she waddled over to the table and set them down, returning a moment later with knives and forks clutched in her fist.

I hadn't realised just how hungry I was until the food was before me. My hands shook as I separated the fish as cleanly as I could from the bone and shovelled a forkful of the flesh into my mouth. Etti watched me, stroking her distended belly absently with one hand.

'You must be hungrier than you thought,' she said, but a teasing smile lit up her eyes.

Olga ate more gracefully, picking at her food with care, her fingers moving elegantly around the plate as if they were dancing.

After watching us another moment, Etti hauled herself to her feet and began to wash the pans, first filling the sink, then sliding the cooking utensils in one by one so they didn't splash. She started to hum as she worked, scrubbing energetically at the pan that had contained the fish, picking at the black bits with her nail until they lifted away. Suddenly she recoiled. The pan sploshed into the sink. Etti spread both her hands on the cabinet bench for support. A waiting plate rolled off the edge of the bench, teetered and then arched over, splintering upon the floor.

Olga and I sprang to our feet.

'Etti?' I said.

She gave no sign she'd heard me, but moaned softly. Her knuckles were white, her body tensed like a cat's, the muscles of her back straining against the fabric of her dress.

After a long moment, she relaxed and drew in a breath.

Her shoulders slumped. 'I'm sorry.' Pulling out a crumpled handkerchief, she dabbed at her face.

'You should be resting,' I said.

She shook her head but her skin was white.

Olga took Etti gently by the arm and I took the other, and together we guided her to a chair. She grunted as we eased her into it. 'Where is the broom?' Olga said.

'In that cupboard.' Beads of sweat rimmed Etti's hairline. I heard the door of the cupboard open and Olga rummaging inside. The shards of porcelain chimed as she swept them together.

'Does that happen often?' Although nobody close to me had ever had a baby, I could recall Mama talking to Olga about women in their social circle who had recently given birth. It had fascinated me at the time: the blood, the ritual, the prayers for mother and child; always whispered, since religion was frowned upon by the Communist state. Now that I was older, though, I also understood how dangerous a time it might be. How a woman could lose her mind with worry or allow fear to paralyse her body at the critical moment.

Etti's colour was beginning to return. She dropped her eyes, embarrassed now. 'More often this past week.'

'It's your body preparing for the rigours of childbirth,' Olga said, tipping the contents of the broken plate into the bin. 'I remember Lida's mother describing it to me as if it were yesterday.'

Etti grimaced. 'I can only hope it will be over quickly. If this is the warm-up, I imagine the real thing will be quite something.'

Olga nodded. 'You will need every bit of strength,' she warned, the dustpan still clutched in her hand. 'I remember Ana saying it was like a gigantic mountain she had to climb and each step felt as if she was not moving forward. It seemed she would never reach the other side. Then all of a sudden, at twilight, just when she said she could no longer go on, Lida was born. Sometimes you can't see your progress until you look back.'

'Did you never have children?' Etti said.

'No.' Olga's eyes shifted to me. 'It was not my fate. But I have my Lida. She is my daughter now.' Replacing the dustpan and broom in the cupboard, she fetched a dishcloth and ran it beneath the tap, then wrung it out and handed it to Etti, who wiped it across her face.

'I will take my bath now,' Olga said. 'And leave you two to talk. I imagine Lida will have questions to ask you, Etti. Ana was Estonian, you know.'

Etti cocked her head. 'Really?'

'Yes. You should ask her about the lace, Lida,' Olga prompted. 'She might be able to tell you about the pattern.' We watched her disappear out into the hallway. A moment later the floorboards overhead creaked.

When I looked back at Etti, it was to find her studying the lace shawl around my throat.

'Did your mother knit this?' she said.

'Yes,' I said.

'It's lovely.' Etti's fingers wound through the lace. 'It's an unusual pattern, but not altogether uncommon. Different to mine.' She touched her own shawl. 'As you see, mine is a lilac leaf pattern. It's a very old pattern. Estonia is full of lilac bushes and we use the wood to make knitting needles. Who taught your mama? Where did she learn?'

'Somebody showed her how. A woman – a friend – from Haapsalu. Mother lived there for a short time with family.'

Etti's face brightened. 'Haapsalu? You know Haapsalu?'

'Only the little my mother told me about it.'

'Perhaps your mother's family are still there,' Etti suggested.

I shook my head. 'I don't think so. I don't know anyone here; I haven't met any other Estonians anyway. Except for you and a young man called Jakob Rebane.'

Etti froze, her hand still wrapped around the lace. 'Jakob? You know my cousin?'

I stared at her. I felt my mother's shadow pass behind me. 'I wouldn't say I know him, exactly,' I said, my mind wondering at this unexpected connection. 'I met him today, very briefly. He gave us a lift from the station when we were stranded.'

Etti sighed. 'That sounds like our Jakob. He can never resist a pretty face. Oh—' She frowned suddenly. 'I didn't mean that to sound as if he's impulsive, or that he has a lot of girlfriends. He doesn't – I would know; Tartu is not such a big place.' After studying the shawl a moment longer, she let the lace fall. 'Are you a knitter yourself?'

I shook my head. 'No. But I would love to learn. Mama taught me to speak Estonian. I think she always hoped we would come back together.'

Etti's gaze was thoughtful. 'That is impressive. It's a difficult language. One of the hardest to master. You should learn to knit, if you can. It will give you something to do here in the evenings. A few years ago, everybody knitted or carded the wool. In the winter, there's little else to do. Now everybody is busy working, scraping to get by. Even children are expected to work in the mines or pull turnips at the *kolkhoz* – the collective farms, you know. People don't have time for knitting. And there's a shortage of wool to contend with, too, which is a shame. But there are more important things than knitting to think about. Who even knows if I'll have a job to come back to once this little one is born?' Her expression clouded. 'While they're replacing Tiina they may replace me as well. There's plenty of others who'd love to have a job like this; one that doesn't carry the risk of the mines or breaking your back in a soggy field. All we can do is make the best of our time, I suppose.'

'But doesn't it bother you?' The question burst out before I could hold it back.

'Does what bother me?'

I thought of all the things I had learnt about the Estonians today; the desperation of those men to do what they did at the train station this morning, the anxiety Etti must feel at the uncertainty of a future dependent on the Partorg's favour.

'It's not your fault,' I said, eventually. 'And yet you are punished. You and your family, your fellow Estonians. How do you stand it? Don't you want to – to fight back?'

Etti's gaze flicked towards the kitchen doorway, but it was empty.

'No,' she said, loud enough to make it obvious she was speaking not just for my benefit. 'I do not want to fight back.' She lowered her voice. 'But since you are interested in our shawls, let me explain it this way.' She unknotted the shawl around her shoulders and held it up. 'I think of life here as being like this shawl, Lydia. A triangle. Before, it was us on top. We were the tip of the triangle. Now . . .' She flipped the shawl upside down and draped it across my lap. 'We are on the bottom. But one day, perhaps we will be on top again. For now, we must make do.'

I bit my lip and looked down at the shawl Etti had spread across my skirt. The pattern was different to my mother's; it was a series of small triangles, with lace bobbles attached at each of the points.

Etti pushed back her chair. 'Don't trouble yourself, worrying about us,' she said, quietly this time so that even if Olga did happen to be treading down the stairs, she would not be able to discern the words. 'If you'd like me to, I can take your shawl with me to knitting circle the next time I go. My cousin Kati would be excited to see how far this shawl has travelled. She's about your age. It's so rare for any young people to be interested in these things now. Especially half-Russians.'

She smiled to let me know this was not an insult. Removing her hand, she bent and gathered up the shawl, draping it around her shoulders. 'Well, I should start for home. Mama will be finished her shift soon and if I'm not there, she will worry. It's her—'

The sound of sudden, wild screaming filled the air. Etti and I exchanged frightened looks.

'Stay here.' The bobbles on her shawl bounced as she crossed into the next room. I heard her inhale sharply, and I jumped up. Through the window, I could see purple dusk sifting down over the trees. Sounds filtered in: birds lifting from the trees, boots running on the pavement outside.

'What's happening?'

As if in answer, a man began to shout in Russian, his voice filling the street outside. 'Get your hands off me!'

There was the sound of scuffling and then a grunt of pain.

Etti and I hurried to the window, where we saw a man behind the long iron bars of the fence. His arms were being held by a soldier in uniform. Beside him, a woman stood silently, hugging a small child to her chest.

Blood seeped from a wound on the man's forehead, snaking down his face and into his eyes. A pair of cracked glasses were perched on his nose. He struggled against the iron grip of the soldier.

'Let me go!' Ripping one arm free, he staggered forward until his face was pressed against the fence.

'Partorg Volkov! I know you are in there!' The man's voice was so loud it was as if he had stepped into the room with us.

Etti took an involuntary step backwards. I could not move. I was frozen in place, transfixed by the desperation in the man's voice.

'Captain Volkov! Please! They are dragging us out of our homes. My wife, my son; you have to help! I said *let go*,' he snarled at the guard, shaking his arm in a useless effort. The woman behind him had begun to sob. 'I used to work for you!' The man was struggling now, his face straining against the bars. 'I drove your car last year, you remember? Captain Volkov! Captain Volkov!'

His cries were cut short as the guard brought the butt of his pistol down on the man's skull. Blood spurted from his head and he sagged, a lifeless ragdoll. If not for the guard clutching his arm, he would have tumbled to the pavement in a heap.

The soldier turned to the man's wife, still struggling to quieten her son. 'Shut that child up!'

The woman whimpered, hugging the shrieking boy so hard I thought he might suffocate. The guard began to drag the man towards a police wagon that waited on the other side of the street. The woman followed, holding her child. The guard thrust the man's body into the wagon and pushed the woman and the boy in, too. The doors of the wagon banged shut and a moment later, the car was gone.

A figure dashed past the gate, no more than a grey blur, head bowed.

'What was that?' Olga appeared on the stairs, knotting a bathrobe around her waist. Her white hair was still damp, hanging loosely around her face. 'I heard shouting.'

Neither Etti or I answered straightaway. Eventually Etti spoke. 'I've seen this before, when the Soviets arrived last year.' She hugged herself and drew in a ragged breath. 'It's a deportation. It's begun.'

She sat down suddenly.

Lieutenant Lubov's voice echoed in my head. *Relocation of undesirables.*

In the silence, I heard the distant rumble of approaching trucks.

Twig Pattern

Kati

PINE NEEDLES STUNG MY FACE. JAKOB'S BREATH WAS HOT and loud in my ears.

We kept running until we reached the river, where the water rushed over the stones in a great roaring gasp. Moonlight glimmered on the trees, gilding them a soft silver and poking through the bristled firs to pattern the ground. Jakob's head was bowed, his hands resting on his knees as he fought for breath.

Despite the heat pounding in my head and soaking my body, I felt cold. My legs seemed to be frozen, now that we had come to a stop, my feet rooted to the earth.

Mama. Papa.

'We need to find Oskar,' Jakob said.

The whip crack of gunshots. The stench of cordite. Mama's body crumpling to the ground.

'Kati.' Jakob shook my arm.

I shrank away. 'We have to go back!'

Jakob's grip tightened, his fingers digging into my skin. 'No, Kati.'

I tried to make out his features. 'She might be dying,' I said. 'She needs help.'

Jakob cursed. For a moment, I felt his whole body tense and then he softened, his shoulders slumping. 'Kati, they're gone. Do you hear me?' His voice cracked. 'Both of them. They're gone.'

His arms snaked around me. His cheek pressed against my neck. I saw the moon, a glimmering pearl in the watery sky, and scattered stars like tiny fish, silver and gold.

Everything looked the same as it had always been. How could it be possible that my parents were gone?

'We need to find Oskar and tell him,' Jakob said. 'There might be a way to save others. And we can't wander around all night in the forest, alone.'

Why not, I wanted to ask. I felt strangely detached. An image came to me of my wolf, Elina, padding softly through the undergrowth. My wolf, with her moon eyes and soft, grey pelt.

She was always alone.

I will send you a sign. You will know it's me. I will wear the pelt of a wolf, my grandmother had told me.

Was she watching us now? Had she heard the gunshots and seen us running for our lives? Had her presence last night not been a coincidence, but a warning?

'There's a bunker.' Jakob drew back but did not let go of me. 'It's not far from here. Downriver. I've left messages there before in an old tin. That's where we'll go. Oskar will be there. Can you walk?'

I heard his words, but they came from far away. I looked slowly towards him and realised he was waiting for an answer. I made my lips move. 'Yes.'

'Good.'

Drawing in a deep breath, he let go of me and moved away, weaving through the trees on the shoreline. His boots crunched on the leafy undergrowth.

As I followed him my thoughts continued to spin, drifting like the seeds of a dandelion blown helter skelter by the wind. All the plans my parents had made for the farm, for Jakob, for me – in the end, everything had been for nothing. Papa's assistance to the Partorg and the new Soviet state had been worthless. It had cost him his life and Mama's.

I heard Jakob call my name, softly, in the dark.

I swallowed. I needed to bury this pain. I could grieve for my parents later. But a slow burning anger was moving up my legs as I followed my brother's steps. I saw the Partorg's face the first time he had visited our farmhouse. I had listened from my bedroom as he spoke to Papa, assuring him that there would be enough food for us to last the year, that what we were doing would help everyone.

He had lied. He had fed us the illusion of freedom, all the while knowing we were animals trapped in a cage.

I knew in my heart that if I saw the Partorg again, I would not hesitate to plunge a knife into his heart or send a bullet into his soft flesh. I already hated him for the rumours they had spread about Oskar being a murderer. My hands trembled, imagining the suffering they would cause him. I stilled them by gripping the straps of my knapsack until the canvas bit into my palms.

I flung my thoughts out into the universe. I would not be afraid of fighting, like Papa. I would hold tightly to the possibility of revenge. If Papa and Mama could not come back, perhaps this was the thing that would keep me alive.

* * *

We followed the river for some time, until Jakob stopped abruptly near a clearing of tall birches just visible.

'It was here.'

His feet stirred up the dirt as he walked the perimeter of the line of trees. He peered into the darkness. It was pitch black. Impenetrable.

A breeze rustled through the trees. 'Perhaps you're wrong. It's dark.'

'No.' He straightened up. 'It was here. I know it was.' He sent his foot into the leaves.

I took a step away, straining to see, and suddenly the point of something sharp pressed against the base of my spine.

A woman's voice hissed in my ear. 'Don't move.'

'Jakob!' I called, and my brother whipped around. A torch glared in my brother's face. He raised his hand to shield his eyes from the dazzling light.

'Please,' I started to say, but the tip of the knife digging through my clothes silenced the rest of my words.

'Hilja?' Jakob dropped his hand and leant forward, squinting. 'Hilja, is that you? It's me. Jakob Rebane.'

The knife quivered.

Jakob held up his hands. He hesitated then took a step towards us. 'Do you remember me? From the meeting in Torvid's dorm? I remember you. You helped us get the dye for the flags. Right?'

The woman behind me sniffed, but I felt the knife withdraw a little until only the faintest edge of it was touching my jumper. 'So. I remember you. Jakob Rebane. What are you doing out here? You're lucky I didn't slice you open.'

The knife pulled away. My whole body was tingling.

Jakob grimaced. 'We need to speak to Oskar.'

'What do you want with Oskar? Nobody gave you a message to pass on, did they? I would have known about it.' Her voice was accusing. 'And who is this? You know what Oskar said, about bringing outsiders in. They have to be checked. Approved.'

The torch beam tracked over me. I could not see my interrogator, only her dark outline against the trees.

'I know.' Jakob shifted. 'But there was no time. This is my sister. Kati. It's important we find Oskar. We have some information he needs to hear.'

'Information.' The torch beam wavered. 'It's urgent?'

'Yes. Why else would we be out here, in the dark?'

'Maybe you've got nowhere else to go,' she said. With a click the torch beam disappeared. 'Fine. I'll take you. He's at the bunker. There are . . . others there, too. You will see.'

Her words made me shift uncomfortably. What if she led us into a trap? I remembered Papa speaking about the NKVD agents who paid informants to catch out resistance sympathisers. But then, Hilja would not have been so reluctant to help us if her intention was to trap us.

Understanding swept through me. 'Germans,' I said.

Hilja clucked her tongue. 'Hush.'

I pressed my lips together.

The sound of rushing water faded a little, muffled by the trees as Hilja led us through the clearing.

'Over here.' She was bending in the dirt some feet away. The torch flicked on, making a puddle of light at my feet. Hilja pulled back a screen of shrubs that had been cleverly

211

drawn down to conceal the bunker's entrance.

Beneath the foliage, the entrance was a dark open maw, as narrow and damp smelling as the doorway of a crypt.

'Don't worry.' I heard the smile in her voice. 'It's bigger inside than it looks.'

'I'll go first.'

I watched as Jakob scrambled inside, hunching over to fit his body into the space, moving forward on his knees.

'Now you.' Hilja jerked her head at the dark hole. 'Quickly; it doesn't do to hang around, waiting for patrols to find you.'

I nodded, trying to accept her reassurance, although every fibre of my body screamed at me to back away. What if there was no air in there? What if the supporting beams collapsed, crushing us into the earth below?

From somewhere behind me, blackbirds began to caw, beating their wings. An odd sound at night.

Hilja raised her head, like an animal sniffing the air.

'Inside now,' she barked. It was not an invitation but a command.

My knees scraped against the dirt floor. It was pitch black in the tunnel, but there was light ahead, a small golden circle. It was this light I focused on as I inched myself forward, trying to ignore the walls that seemed to press around me, squeezing what little breath was left from my lungs.

The tunnel widened suddenly into a room lined with timber bunks. A dirty oil lamp cast an amber glow over everything. Pushing myself up, I looked behind me to see Hilja emerging from the tunnel, the lamplight catching the glint of her dark eyes and the bare skin of her forearms collared by the rolled-up cuffs of her shirt. A grey handkerchief was knotted over her hair. She brushed the dust off her trousers then straightened up and pointed, unsmiling.

'Oskar is in there.'

At the end of the room was another entrance, a door made of rough-hewn timber, hanging slightly ajar. It led into another space, a room no larger than our threshing room but containing at least fifteen men bent over a table made from crates pushed together to form a flat surface. A radio sat in the middle, a lump of black with wires poking out. Maps overlapped each other, their edges pinned down by rocks.

They all turned as we entered, the conversation dying. The light from the oil lamp transformed their faces into planes of yellow and grey. Most of them were young, hardly older than us. They wore uniforms like Oskar's, made from mushroom-brown wool. Two were clad in grey and stood slightly apart. Small swastika emblems were emblazoned on their armbands. *Nazis*. My heart tapped out a staccato rhythm. I tried not to stare at them, but their presence unnerved me. These were not the Baltic Germans we had grown up hearing about, but foreigners from another land.

I tried to remember what my grandmother had told me about the Germans who had lived next door to her when she was growing up, in the little timber house in Haapsalu. She had told us they were Christians who prayed at the tiny Lutheran Church and chose to eat the crops grown in their own yard rather than slaughtering animals. Was it possible we would have no choice but to side with the Germans again now? The thought made me uneasy. What would life be like under the Germans? What conditions would they set down in exchange for helping us? Our old president Konstantin Päts had banned the National Socialist Magazine and forced the elected member of the Baltic German Party to resign after he made unsettling comments about Jews. But that had been before the Russians arrived. When they had, President Päts was placed under house arrest and eventually deported. There was nobody to protect the rights of the Jewish people now.

I had a terrible sense of foreboding and felt Jakob shift uncomfortably beside me. Perhaps he, too, understood the danger of this association. When I glanced at Hilja, I realised she had moved back, out of the lamplight, leaving us to speak for ourselves.

Somebody broke away from the group and came forward. A rush of relief made my legs tremble.

'Kati?' Oskar's pale eyes widened. 'What are you doing here? And Jakob.' He turned to my brother. His eyes travelled down Jakob's rumpled clothes and came up to rest on Jakob's face. 'You better explain.'

Jakob and I glanced at each other.

'Is it your father?' Oskar's voice had hardened. 'Did he send you out here to spy on us for him?'

'He's dead.' The words turned to dust on my tongue. 'He was killed tonight by the Partorg's men. Mama too.'

Oskar's mouth dropped open.

'We've come to ask you for protection.' Jakob's eyes roved over the knot of men watching us. 'And to warn you about an operation that is happening right now, as we stand here.'

Oskar moved so quickly I barely registered that he had grasped Jakob's arm. 'What kind of operation?'

'A mass deportation.' I cleared my throat. 'That's what Papa told us.'

Oskar's eyes flashed. 'How many?'

'We're not sure.' Jakob prised Oskar's fingers off his arm. 'Perhaps thousands. Papa said he heard about railroad cars lined up at Tartu station.'

'He was supposed to help them but he couldn't.' A lump burnt in my throat. 'He tried to run but they caught us in the yard. They shot him. And then they shot Mama.' I stared hard at the ground, my vision swimming with unshed tears.

Silence filled the room.

Then everybody began to talk at once. German. Estonian. A little Russian thrown in.

A cacophony of voices clamouring to be heard.

Oskar moved towards me. Beneath the hubbub of noise, I heard the pain in his voice. 'Kati, I'm so sorry.'

I squeezed my hands tightly. 'You didn't kill them. You tried to warn us.'

He grasped my shoulder. 'It doesn't mean I don't care. Your mother was dear to me. As for your father—'

He closed his mouth suddenly, as if afraid to say more. I could feel the pressure of his fingers squeezing in sympathy. I sniffed back my sobs. I wanted to hold him, but I was afraid that if I did, the last barrier of my composure would collapse. Mama and Papa's faces rose up in my mind. Speaking about their deaths had made the pain of their loss seem suddenly raw and real. Oskar's hand slid up to cup the back of my head. His eyes were wide, dark with grief, a reflection of my pain. He began to speak again, but the voices around us lifted and he released his hold on me, as if remembering where he was, his purpose.

I heard Jakob saying, '. . . but we must do something!'

'We'll speak later, Kati,' Oskar said softly, touching my arm. 'This is not the place. Not the time. You understand?'

I nodded. I could feel Hilja watching us. When I turned to look at her, she glanced quickly away.

'Quiet!' Oskar banged his fist on the makeshift table. The Forest Brothers partisans fell silent, though the Germans continued to speak in low voices to each other. Oskar ran a hand across his cropped hair. He moistened his lips with his tongue. His broad shoulders lifted and fell. 'We need to find out if the information about the deportations is accurate.'

Jakob took an angry step forward. 'I just told you—'

'I know, Jakob.' Oskar frowned. 'But they might have fed your father a lie. Perhaps they suspected he would run, or that he wasn't loyal and they wanted to prove it.' Jakob opened his mouth but stayed silent. 'I'm not saying he was wrong. Only misinformed.' Oskar jerked his head. 'This is Officer Weber and Officer Geyer from the SS Cavalry Brigade. They were brought in across the border a few weeks ago. Gentlemen, this is Jakob Rebane and his sister, Katarina.' His eyes lingered on me before darting away. 'Kati has not yet taken the oath but I think we can trust that they are telling the truth. As they see it.'

The older German tugged at his collar. 'It sounds as if the Russians are mobilising.'

'If it's true, they will take aim at the farmers. The people we rely on to help us,' Oskar said. 'They will deport anyone who is sympathetic to our cause. Soviet patrols will begin combing the forest before morning. Those who run will be shot.' He glanced at me. 'Like Kati's father. This is how it goes.'

'What would you advise?' Weber mopped at his forehead with a handkerchief. 'We don't want to die like trapped rabbits down here.'

'So, tell them.' Oskar placed his hands on his hips. He nodded at the transistor radio on the table. 'Tell your colleagues at the border.'

The Germans exchanged looks.

'There will never be a time like this again.' The lamplight glowed on Oskar's face. The soft expression he had worn earlier when he'd spoken about my parents was gone, replaced by a hard look of determination. I had seen him like this before, during our school days when some of the boys had waited behind the trees to pelt him with acorns as we walked home, calling out insults about his mother's poverty, asking if he even remembered his papa. Oskar had ignored them all, keeping his eyes fixed on the road ahead.

'One day,' he had told me between gritted teeth, 'when I'm a carpenter, they will be begging me to build their houses and fill them with fine furniture and I will refuse.'

The boys' taunting laughter had followed us, but Oskar would not look back. He'd taken my gloved hand, wrapping it in the crook of his arm to keep me warm. But the fierce intensity in his face had made me shiver. How much of that boy was left in him now? Perhaps more than I had guessed.

Perhaps that fierceness had kept him alive this past year.

'Right now, the Russians will be distracted,' he said. 'Every Russian guard and soldier will be involved in some way. Once the dust settles, there'll be nobody left to fight here when Hitler finally makes his move. We know these forests. So do the other partisan groups. We know there are people ready to fight in Latvia and Lithuania, too. Do you want your men stumbling around, circling each other, uncertain of which direction to shoot in?'

I saw the Germans weighing up his words. The younger man threw a long, agonised look at the radio. 'But if we are wrong . . .'

'If we are wrong, I will take full responsibility.' Oskar turned away, moving towards the back of the room where long wooden crates rested against the packed-earth wall. 'If we are wrong, I will personally hand myself over to the *Sturmbannführer* for whatever punishment he decides I deserve.'

The other partisans groaned. 'No, Oskar,' said one. Oskar silenced him with a glance, then turned back to the crates. He lifted the lid of one with his foot. It creaked open to reveal gleaming rifles. The partisans glanced at each other, their young faces brightening at the prospect of a fight.

'So, we stay here and make contact while you enjoy your hunt.' The German officer sounded resigned.

Oskar lifted a rifle from the crate. Weighing it in his hands, he ran his thumb gently over its ridged curves. My breath shortened. The sight of him holding the gun made the blood pound in my head. 'We cannot hope to get to town to warn others,' he said. 'Besides, the Russians are paranoid and would kill everyone – the trains would be chock full of bodies, not people.' My stomach tightened as I thought of Etti, Aunt Juudit. The others from our knitting circle. Oskar and Jakob, lying dead in the forest.

Oskar hefted the gun onto his shoulder. 'But we can give them a chance if they make it this far. We will fan out towards the edge of the forest.'

'We have to find our cousin, Etti,' Jakob said. 'She's expecting a child. And her mother is an older woman. She'll find it hard to run.'

Oskar shook his head. 'If they make it to the forest, we'll help them. But they are two among many hundreds, Jakob. I'm sorry.'

Although his words were aimed at my brother, Oskar looked at me. His eyes were full of sympathy but the words were an ice shard through my heart.

He turned towards the young men who were already lining up and began to hand out the rifles. 'Jaak. Joosep.'

One by one, the boys took the weapons and began to rummage in another crate for ammunition. The Germans were already turning the dials on the radio, chattering in German, and I caught only snatches of what they said; my German was limited to the little we had been taught at school. All I could think about was the sound of Mama's body hitting the earth. I could not bear the thought of Aunt Juudit or Etti, or my unborn cousin, suffering the same fate.

'Jakob.' Oskar held out the rifle. A hesitant look passed over Jakob's face and he glanced at me, his shoulders hunching guiltily. But a moment later he was reaching out a hand to grip the metal tightly.

Oskar nodded. 'We were right to trust you,' he said. The ghost of a smile flitted over his features.

I wanted to cry out and rip the weapon from Jakob's hands. What if he was killed? Then I would truly be alone.

He ducked his head as he joined the others filing out into the other room, avoiding my narrow gaze.

'I will look after him.' Oskar's shoulder brushed against mine. I could not bring myself to look at him, so I focused on the collar of his jacket. It was flecked with mud that had dried and formed a speckled crust over the fabric. 'I will keep him at the back, close by me. I swear to you. Kati. Look at me.'

I raised my chin, summoning every scrap of fear and anger so I would not be tempted to cry.

Oskar's mouth twitched. 'I promise.' He raised his hand and tucked a strand of hair off my face with his thumb. I could smell the rifle on his fingertips, an oily bitter scent.

'Just see that you do,' I said. 'Please.'

Oskar nodded. 'I don't want you here,' he said, straightening. His tone was authoritative; the voice he had used before with the partisan boys under his command. 'It's too dangerous. There are no exits, if you're caught. You're to go with Hilja. There's a safety point not far away. That's where people will flee to, when they get wind of what the Russians are doing. Once there's enough of you, Hilja will take you all into the deep woods to the camp. It's where we try to keep the young and the elderly. Those who aren't fit enough to fight. It's safer; fewer patrols there. And there are guards and places to escape to, if you're found. We'll join you there when we can.'

'Where is the safe point?'

Oskar hesitated. 'My old farmhouse.'

I felt myself sway, as if the ground were buckling beneath me. Oskar's hand shot out and caught me. His fingers locked around my wrist, and he stroked his thumb across my racing pulse.

'I can't go back there.' I heard the lowing of cows. Smelt the thick rivers of sticky caramel. Saw the blood staining the floorboards. 'Too many ghosts,' I whispered.

'Nonsense.' Oskar smiled sadly. 'My mother and Aime are long gone. They won't come back, not in any form. And I'm not intent on becoming a ghost myself.'

'You promise?'

Oskar glanced around swiftly. The room was empty. We were alone.

Shouldering the rifle, he stepped towards me, slid his arms around my waist and kissed me swiftly, his lips gently touching mine before he pulled away.

'I promise,' he said. 'No secrets. You see? I do remember. You will listen to Hilja, won't you?'

My heart thudded in my chest. *I want so badly for you to stay here*, I thought. But I could hear the Germans murmuring and feet shuffling as the men waited outside for Oskar to lead them. I made myself nod stiffly.

Moments later, I heard Oskar's voice in the corridor outside.

My throat ached, raw with pain, everything I had not said trapped inside.

Ladybird Pattern

Lydia

'I NEED TO GET HOME.'

Etti's voice was soft, *home* drawn out on a breath so quiet it was almost a whisper. If we had not been huddled together with Olga behind the window of the Partorg's apartment, watching the shadowy forms of deportees being marched past the fence, I might not have realised she had spoken at all.

The sound of shuffling feet and voices shouting orders in Russian had lessened now, changing from a steady flow of noise to a faint hum, like the static on a wireless. None of us had spoken as the horror played out in the street. Men and women. Children and elderly people, carrying walking sticks and shuffling with difficulty down the steps to where the cars were waiting. The soldiers spared no one but herded them all into waiting wagons, destined for the train station. We heard them shouting in Russian as they evicted people from their homes.

'No razors! No weapons of any kind! One suitcase only! *Davai*: hurry! The train is leaving! *Davai!*'

I bit my lip hard, recalling it all.

My fathers had caused this. Both of them; the real and the imposter.

'You're safer here.' But even as I said the words, I heard

the lie in them. Who was I to comfort Etti?

'Mama will need me. What if her friends have been taken?' Etti's face, when she turned towards me, was haggard, her eyes circled by shadows. As I watched, she flinched and closed them, pressing down on her belly as if it pained her.

'I think you should stay,' I repeated. 'Olga, don't you agree?'

My companion looked small and shrunken in her worn dressing gown. 'I think so, yes. I remember what it was like, in the Revolution. The streets were full of gunfire.' She cinched her dressing gown tighter around her waist. 'Whatever is happening out there, at least if you stay here, there is less danger of being shot.'

Etti tilted up her chin. 'You don't know my mother. She will panic, grow angry. She might say something ridiculous, trying to defend the others. No.' She shook her head. 'I have to go to her. I've no choice.'

I began to protest but she raised a hand and then hurried to the kitchen, emerging a moment later with her basket. With one hand, she pulled the edge of her shawl up so that it half-hid her face.

'Lock the door once I am gone, and stay inside,' she said. 'No matter what you hear.'

She threw a fearful glance towards the window. Outside, the wind had begun to blow. Shadowy figures drifted past the gate, blurred shapes moving against the purple twilight. I could feel her terror as if it were my own, a place just beyond the threshold of the doorway.

The despair in her face made me think of Joachim. It

seemed like so long ago now. Could it only have been days? I knew I would never forget his bloodless lips, the words he had mouthed at me. And the way people had turned away until the car moved off with him inside. All those faces averted, as if he had already ceased to exist.

And I had turned away, too. Would I ever forgive myself for letting him go?

'Wait!'

Etti jumped, her hand already on the door frame.

'I'm coming with you.'

'Lida! You can't.' Olga tugged at my arm. 'What would your mother say? She would want you to stay safe!'

'I don't care.' Olga gasped. I softened my voice. 'I'm sorry, Olga.' I pressed my hands together to stop them shaking, filled with the memory of Joachim's desperate face. 'I have to do this. I'll be back as quickly as possible. I'll just see Etti home. I promise.' I tried to dig up a smile for her but it wouldn't come.

Olga stared at me, seemingly robbed of breath. Then she moved quicker than I thought possible, clomping up the stairs without a backward glance. Etti and I exchanged looks.

Moments later, Olga appeared wrapped in the enormous chestnut bear fur, her tiny frame making the coat seem even larger as it trailed on the floor after her. There was a determined look in her eyes. Kissing Olga's cheek, I turned back to Etti, still waiting at the door for us to escort her into the night.

I am doing this for you, Joachim, I thought, gritting my teeth, before we stepped outside into the dusk.

Moth Stitch

Kati

Hilja did not utter a word until we reached the clearing and Oskar's farmhouse. She moved silently, slipping through the trees like a spirit. I followed as best I could, tripping sometimes, trying to imagine we were simply two friends walking together, to push down the fear of being discovered by Soviet patrols. Finally, she stopped at the edge of the trees and straightened up, her hands on her hips, eyes roving across the glade as she searched for signs of life.

The house was a shadow against the dark trees. Hilja clicked on her torch, its beam disturbing a fox. I caught a glimpse of its bushy tail and red fur against the foliage before it streaked away. She directed the light towards the house, running it across the porch, making silver moons in the windows, past the empty rocking chair where Oskar's mother used to sit peeling plums for her pickle jars. Everything was still.

As we waited until Hilja was satisfied enough to switch off the torch, a smell drifted towards us on the wind, filling my nostrils with the ripe scent of rotten fruit laid over an undercurrent of sour decay.

I lifted my hand to cover my nose, but the stench lingered in the back of my throat as if I'd swallowed it. I gagged, trying to suppress my heaving stomach.

Hilja grunted and flicked off the torch. The light died – and the day of the murders came back to me in vivid colour. *Imbi. Aime.*

In the sudden darkness, I had a terrifying delusion that their bodies had never left. Perhaps they were still trapped in there, waiting for me to find them again, their poor corpses buzzing with bloated flies.

'Hilja . . . what is that smell?'

Hilja sniffed and began to move again, sticking to the darkest shadows, edging closer to the farmhouse.

'Dead animal,' she said shortly. 'We leave them around the house to deter patrols from getting too near.'

'It doesn't deter refugees from seeking help?'

Hilja didn't bother to reply. The long grass shivered as she picked her way through it, heading towards the back of the house, passing the half-filled woodpile still stacked against one wall. After gulping in a breath, I moved after her, trying not to be sick, moving as quietly as possible. Despite my best efforts, a family of rats began to squeak noisily as my boots stirred up the pebbles near the woodpile. Hilja flung me a look over her shoulder, but the shadows of the eaves above us hid her face. I could only sense her disapproval, reaching out to me, curling around my legs like tendrils of smoke.

The back door opened silently when she pushed it, revealing the dark interior of Oskar's cottage. After a moment's pause, Hilja reached out and pulled me inside after her, closing the door behind us, sealing us in.

The blackness inside was all-encompassing. The scent of decaying flesh was less strong with the door closed, but my stomach still gurgled.

'You'll get used to the smell.'

Hilja struck a match. From its light, I could see that the windows had been blacked out. The kitchen was as I remembered it, but cobwebs were stranded on the shelves. Sadness pricked at my heart. Imbi Mägi would be so ashamed for people to see her cottage this way, undusted and in such a state. Although it was a small place, she had made it a home for Oskar and Aime. Oskar's father had made the furniture himself before the illness claimed him. The curtains I had helped Imbi to sew now lay abandoned on the floor, the lace edges yellowed. The benches she had been so proud of were speckled with rodent droppings and dust.

Hilja set the match to a small stub of candle, then sat down heavily, crossing her legs and leaning her back against the wall. Her face was creased with frown lines. She was older than I had thought, nearing forty I guessed.

I hovered near the door, unsure whether to stand or sit. I was afraid to look around the cottage. I could feel the presence of Imbi and Aime close by, as if they were ingrained in the walls, the floor. Beneath the smell of rot and decay, I fancied I could still detect the sweet burnt sugar caramelising in a pan.

'You might as well sit down and rest,' Hilja said, closing her eyes. 'It's going to be a long night.'

The ground was spongy beneath my feet, the floor sticking to my shoes. Water must have worked its way in and swollen the boards. *I should have come back*, I thought. I should have come back after Imbi and Aime's bodies were taken away but I had been too afraid. The house had stayed empty. Even the Russian settlers did not want it. It was haunted, they

227

said, and nobody had disagreed. I remembered the NKVD agent's face as he explained how Oskar must have murdered them and taken off. His skin had not even flushed. He had not stammered. Every word had been delivered perfectly smoothly, every lie told with not a trace of guilt or shame. I'd found myself wondering if he was the one who had shot them, or if he had merely been covering for his colleagues. I was thankful for Papa's hand on my arm. If they had seen my rage and my hatred, they would have killed me, too.

I found a spot on the wall opposite Hilja that felt dry and settled myself, pulling my knapsack into my lap.

The house creaked and groaned around us. Mice moved in the walls, rustling against the sawdust and timber.

'How do you know him?'

Hilja's voice startled me.

'Oskar.' She opened her eyes, pinning me against the wall with her gaze.

'We're old friends.'

'Lovers, you mean. I saw you together.'

I felt myself prickling. 'That's not your business.'

Hilja lifted a shoulder. 'Maybe not. But Oskar doesn't need distractions right now.'

Her words sent a trickle of unease down my spine. 'I'm sure Oskar can decide what he needs for himself.'

Hilja pushed herself further up the wall, arching her back. 'He's important. Perhaps you didn't realise. He has a special role to play in the Forest Brothers. Without him, the Germans wouldn't take us seriously. He's brought everyone together. When I first met him, he was scared. A boy. Then he killed his first Soviet soldier in a raid on a collective farm up near

Rapla. This soldier had been raping workers on the farm, taking whatever, whoever he wanted.' Her eyes flashed. 'You should have seen Oskar. He was terrifying. Crept up on him when he was eating supper and shot him point blank. Blood and brains all over the walls, along with the mashed potatoes.'

She paused and her dark eyes bore into mine, unblinking. I glanced away, trying to banish the sudden image of Oskar holding a pistol, blood spattered over his face and hands. Those same hands which had stroked my cheek and held me close not an hour ago. Those same hands I had dreamt about holding this last year. They were the hands of a killer now. How could Oskar not be changed by what he had done? What he had been forced to do?

The room seemed colder, sour damp rising through the floorboards. I caught the quick flash of triumph in Hilja's fleeting smile. 'They tell stories about him,' she said. 'The others. Sometimes they call him Kalev.'

I shivered, remembering the stories my grandmother had told me about Kalevipoeg, the guardian of the underworld. In Estonian mythology, he was a great fighter, renowned for his resourceful use of weapons to defeat his enemies. In the most ancient versions he was a giant, a titan with the ability to slay men and beasts. With a sharp jolt, I remembered, too, how he had met his fate: bleeding to death at the hilt of his own sword after giving the wrong directives to his followers. Even demigods could make mistakes.

Hilja's face sobered. 'So you see, he is needed to keep everything turning. Oskar's mind needs to be sharp. I simply think it would be unwise for you to expect—'

I cut across her, my temper flaring. 'I expect nothing.'

The light from the candle shuddered. A puddle of wax was already slipping down the side of it, bleeding onto the floor.

I took a deep breath. 'We are friends, Hilja. That's all. I told you. Nothing more. There was never any time . . . and . . .' I shook my head, unable to find the words. A moth sailed suddenly past my face. Its wings whirred in my ears. I watched it soar on a current of air towards the flame of the candle, attracted to the glow. 'When we knew each other before, things were different. We were different. Children, I suppose. The past year has changed everyone. It would be foolish to pretend that things could go back to the way they were. It would be like asking the moon to shine during the day. Impossible.'

Impossible.

As the words left my mouth, I felt the weight of them crush me like a giant fist laid on my heart. This was the new truth, I realised, a reality I had not wanted to imagine, preferring to think that Oskar would want me in the way that I had once wanted him. When I had entertained ideas back then of marriage, perhaps even of children, my parents had always been in the background, able to offer guidance, to counsel us when challenges arose or when we quarrelled, as we inevitably would. Every couple did. My parents' presence was something I had taken for granted, just as I assumed Oskar's mother would always be around, ready to sweeten our lives with her concoctions and ease any misunderstandings with her belly laugh. I had imagined my mother, her back bent from years of apple picking, sitting in the orchard with her grandchildren, showing them how to count out the pips.

Now all that was gone. Oskar and I were alone in our

pain. More than alone. We were facing a future fraught with uncertainty. Love had no place in such a world.

It was only by being apart that we could hope to survive.

The moth was still dancing, but slower now, as if the light had drained it of energy. It circled in slow, lazy loops around the slippery wax.

When I looked up, Hilja was watching me, her chin thrust forward. Something about my face must have satisfied her, because she relaxed back against the wall again, bending her knees and drawing her legs up to her chest. Her trousers rode up, revealing the space between her shins and her boots. The skin there was puckered with dozens of round scars.

'Cigarette burns,' she said, following my gaze. 'They're all over my body.'

She smiled, showing crooked teeth. 'And the others wonder why I don't smoke.' She held out the back of her hands for me to see. They too were covered in shiny brown spots, crowded together over the surface of her skin like the mottled pattern on a leopard's fur.

Although I wanted to turn away, I forced myself to look at them; to acknowledge her suffering.

'I felt nothing after a while.' Hilja folded her scarred hands over her knees. 'Nothing. They kept burning me. They wanted to know where the others were hiding. But I stopped screaming. That's when they brought Luksa's body in. I didn't realise they had caught him already. His body was ruined. Torn apart by bullets. Decomposing. They told me . . . to make love to it.'

Another woman's voice might have broken. Hilja's did not change.

She picked at a scab on her hand, peeling away the crust and flicking it into the darkness beyond the candlelight.

'Sometimes it's better.' She looked at me evenly and it was only now, with the light shining directly on her, that I realised the creases in her face were not age lines but small scars, made lightly with an instrument like a scalpel. A sharp blade that would leave only the barest marks. The hand that had made them had been tender, like a lover's caress, but every stroke had ensured that she would appear wizened forever, her youth nothing but a distant memory. 'It's better not to love at all. You don't know the things you will do. The things they can make you do.' She touched her face gently, running her fingers over the creases. Then she sniffed and leant forward, batting the moth from the candle with the back of her hand. It whirled away, confused, into the dark. 'When the others arrive,' she said, 'if they make it this far, that is, you will need to think of nothing but running. The camp is a little way from here; we'll need to move as quickly as we're able. Patrols may come. They know we will try to get as many people into the deeper woods as possible. You must prepare yourself.'

'What if there are children? Old people, like Oskar said.'

Hilja blinked. 'Help them. Of course.'

'But if they can't run . . .'

'Do what you can.'

'What if they fall or get left behind?'

Hilja gave the slightest shake of her head. 'Just keep moving. Not everyone makes it, Kati.' For the first time I saw an expression of pity in her eyes. It made her ravaged face seem young again. 'Not everyone survives.'

Birch Pattern

Lydia

'YOU WILL BE TRANSPORTED TO TARTU STATION. FROM there, you will begin your journey to your new home. You have been granted an allowance of one suitcase each. Anyone who resists will be arrested.'

The soldier's voice boomed in the street. Despite the cacophony of noise, his words were clear, ringing out over the heads of the people being steered into police wagons and shoved into the back of trucks. Timber crates lay heaped and broken on the footpath, cleared out so the trucks could accommodate as many bodies as possible. All the soldiers had lists. As each person came forward, they were to give their name to be checked off and then bundled into the wagon where their families were already waiting.

Ahead of me, I saw Etti freeze, her shoulders lifting as if someone had shone a spotlight on her face. But the soldier closest to her had already turned away, distracted by a question from his colleague. We hurried past him, Olga holding fast to my arm as if I might be swept away on the river of people being ferried towards the police wagons. In turn, I reached out to hold onto Etti, anxious not to lose her in the crowd. My fingers knotted in the weave of her shawl; we moved slowly until the deportees peeled away and it was just the three of us, making our way towards a courtyard surrounded by apartment blocks.

When we reached the courtyard, Etti groaned, coming suddenly to a halt, both hands pressed flat against her belly. My grip on the shawl slackened.

'What's the matter?' Olga said. Her face glittered in the light from the streetlamp. She lifted an arm, swiping at her face with her sleeve.

Etti was bent double, her breathing ragged. I wound my arm around her shoulders. 'Etti, do you need to rest?'

She shook her head. Her mouth was pinched, her face screwed up in pain. She let out a long exhalation of breath. 'There's no time. It's just ahead.' She jerked her head towards a doorway harboured on either side by boxed geraniums. The noise of the streets – the clop of horse hooves, the grind of wheels – seemed muffled here. Nobody wailed with fear or shouted instructions. The sounds were muted, as if the blank walls and darkened windows of the townhouses clustered around the courtyard had absorbed them. Or as if there were nobody left inside.

Olga's face appeared beside me, knotted with worry. 'Perhaps you could wait here,' she said to Etti. 'Lydia and I can go.'

'No.' Shaking her head, Etti tried to push herself to her feet. Swaying, she let out a sharp gasp.

'Lida, you take that side,' Olga said, slipping shoulder beneath Etti's arm. 'Come now. Quickly!' I obeyed, helping to heave Etti to her feet. Together, we half dragged her across the courtyard, her breath coming in short gasps. When we reached the doorway, she seemed to rally, shaking us off to stagger inside unassisted.

Although the stairwell inside was dim, lit only by a single bulb, I could smell the dust that clogged the carpet, the tobacco that had soaked into the wallpaper from years of tenancy. Together we struggled up the stairs, Etti stopping every few steps to lean against the wall, panting.

At last, we reached the landing. 'In here.' Etti reached past me, gripping the handle of a door painted a faded blue. I heard her gasp. Bracing myself, I followed her inside.

The apartment was full of women. At least, that was how it seemed. Their pale faces stood out in the glow of an oil lamp on a sideboard. Their shadows stretched behind them, making dark impressions against the wallpaper. They huddled in the centre of the room as if knitted together by an invisible thread. The puddle of light thrown out by the lamp created a wide circle around them. At the edges were shards of gleaming china, pieces of glittering crystal that lay in a heap like jagged jigsaw bits.

As we entered, the women let out a sigh and broke apart.

'Dearest!' An old babushka wobbled forward, hands clasped together as if in prayer. She was as thin as a bird, her stockingless legs poking out beneath a grey housecoat belted around with an old piece of flowered fabric. Her faded slippers crunched on the glass fragments and she halted, looking down as if afraid to go any further.

Etti moved towards her, catching up the old lady's frail hands. 'Helle! What happened?'

The old woman's face crumpled. She began to cry noisily. The other women shrank together, murmuring uneasily like nervous hens in winter when the foxes circle round.

They all wore plain dresses and white shawls around their shoulders. The ripe scent of sweat and onions rolled over me, mingled with the fumes from the oil lamp sitting on the floor at their feet.

'It was the Russians.' Helle dabbed at her eyes with the edge of her shawl. Her eyes lingered on Olga and me curiously before shifting back to Etti. 'They came into the building and took away the Saar family. All of them! We heard them being ordered to dress and march downstairs. Those poor children.' Her voice cracked. She pressed the back of her hand in front of her mouth.

'They said Papa Saar was carrying out subversive activities,' one of the younger women volunteered. She pushed back a loose brown ringlet that had fallen across her eyes. 'You know he was assigned to work in the bread shop last year. They said he was favouring the Estonians, giving them the better bread while the Soviets were given bread made with sawdust and old papers.'

'That's ridiculous.' Etti's face flushed. 'How can that be possible?'

The young woman lifted a shoulder helplessly. 'Etti, your mother argued with them!'

'She was a force to be reckoned with.' Helle lifted her chin. Only the slight tremble of her mouth betrayed her. 'She said the same thing you did. That they were obviously mistaken. But oh, Etti . . . they took her.' Fresh tears leaked from her eyes. 'I'm so sorry. Your mother tried to fight them off. That only made it worse. They didn't even give her time to pack a case or take her coat. Animals.' A flash of anger suffused Helle's tiny pointed face. 'Then they came

236

back in here and took everything of value they could find and smashed the rest. We gathered here to wait for you.'

'Where did they take her?' Etti's face had blanched.

'Same place as all the others.' Helle shook her head. 'The train station.'

Etti gasped and swayed, holding onto her belly as if it were a lifeline.

'Perhaps they will hold everyone there until morning,' I said, thinking quickly. 'There are so many. It's surely too hard to organise so many people onto trains in the middle of the night.'

The women turned to me. I felt their interest sweep over me like a searchlight in the dark. I could almost hear them thinking, who are these Russian women?

Helle moved towards Etti as if to protect her from us. Her voice was wary. 'Etti?'

The Estonian woman drew in a long, ragged breath and waved a hand. 'They are friends, Helle. Trying to help. Lydia and Olga. You can trust them.'

Helle's shoulders relaxed. 'If you are sure, dearest.'

'I am.'

A train whistle shrieked suddenly, shrill and insistent, the sound cutting through the night. All the women turned towards the window. The lamplight picked out the sharpness of their cheekbones.

'Too late.' Etti's voice was dull and mechanical. She sank slowly to the floor and remained squatting there, hugging herself. 'She's gone.'

'She's not gone yet,' I said, but Etti did not seem to hear me. Her head was bowed, her shoulders slumped in defeat.

My mind was racing, searching for possibilities. Etti's mother was not imprisoned yet. She might not even be on the train. If we could find someone to speak to, a guard . . . Lieutenant Lubov's face leapt into my mind.

Kneeling beside Etti, I brushed the sparkling shards of a crystal vase to one side so that only the glittering dust remained. 'I know someone, Etti. Someone who could help us.'

Etti raised her eyes to mine. Deep pain was etched there, but the shock of it all was keeping despair at bay.

I squeezed her shoulder.

'You'll have to come with me to the train station. But if this – person – is there . . . if he is where I think he will be, there's a chance we could save her. Our only chance.'

'We will all go.'

I looked up to find the little old woman, Helle, shuffling forward, adjusting the shawl on her shoulders, pulling it up so that it shrouded her hair. The other women did the same. They looked like brides going to church to meet their husbands. Helle shrugged at my raised eyebrows.

'If there is a chance we can save Juudit, we must go. We will all stay together, in the shadows, and look after Etti. Juudit will be easy to spot.' Helle sighed. 'She'll be the one shouting, if I'm not mistaken.'

'Are you sure you would not rather stay here?' Olga said.

Helle's small mouth thinned to a determined line. 'Impossible. Juudit Koppel is one of us. And the train station is not far.'

The train whistle shrieked again.

My skin tingled and sweat prickled at the back of my legs. How could I lead these women out into the chaos of the night? What had I ever done that was brave, that had prepared me in any way to march off and demand that a woman I did not even know be spared when so many others were resigned to their fate? They were all watching me, even Olga, her face a wrinkled map.

The answer came unbidden in my mother's tongue. *You can do anything.*

The lace shawl around my throat was a warm caress. I touched it with my fingers, the tiny holes, the bobbles. My mother's hands had made it and she had loved it. Like the lace shawl, I was her legacy.

'My mother made this shawl,' I said softly. 'She was Estonian. From Haapsalu.' I heard the women's intake of breath. 'She would not want me to stand by and do nothing. Perhaps we will be safe together. But Etti should stay.'

I knew she would protest. 'My mother is strong headed,' she said. 'You may need me to reason with her.' I threw an exasperated look at Olga but she shook her head, so I reached down and offered Etti my arm. A small grunt escaped her lips as she stood up but her face was set in determination.

'Mama needs us,' she said. 'Let us go and find her and bring her home.'

'Have you seen my husband, Meelis?'

The woman grabbed at me. Her fingernails scratched at my arms. 'He is a tall man with blond hair and a birthmark here.' She lightly traced the skin beneath her right eye with a shaking hand. The glare of the floodlights the Russians had set up around the small, overcrowded station gleamed on her face and on the fox-fur sable arranged fashionably about her neck. 'He's a policeman. They came for him a half-hour ago.' She turned her head to look out at the long line of railway cars that ran the length of the station platform, coupled together like the ones that took oxen from their homes to the slaughterhouse factories. The doors of the railway cars were open, and the ones at the front of the line were already half-full. Rows of waiting people stood before them while uniformed guards consulted their lists.

I shook my head. 'I'm sorry,' I said. 'We have only just arrived.'

The woman released me. 'Please,' she said. 'He doesn't belong here. Do you think they might have taken him elsewhere?'

Before I could reply, a dozen more police wagons pulled up nearby. The woman staggered towards them, craning her neck, searching for her husband among the deportees spilling from the doors.

'This is madness.' Olga's mouth was pursed. 'Madness,' she said again, her gaze sweeping the thousands of people waiting to be herded into cattle cars. More trains waited in the sidings, half-hidden in the shadows. The noise was terrible; worried mutterings, the howls of children who could not be pacified, the rough scrape of shoes on gravel as the deportees shuffled forward to be assigned a train carriage. Then there were the noisy sobs of those who had come to bid goodbye to their families; some men, but mostly women in shawls, mothers and grandmothers who had not yet been ordered to leave but risked the displeasure of the Soviet authorities by following to say farewell. Olga hugged the bear coat closer around her even though the breeze that blew along the platform was warm and the press of bodies around us made sweat gather on my lip. 'How do you hope to find one woman, amid all this?'

'We'll find her,' I vowed, although my heart was already sinking. Etti's arm was tucked into my own. It felt limp, as if the bones in it had been removed. When I dared to glance at her, her mouth was turned down. She shook her head, her eyes filling with tears.

Olga was right. Finding one woman amid this chaos would be impossible.

Unless.

I scanned the crowd again, trying to separate the grey-uniformed men from the sea of deportees. When I spotted him, he turned his head, as if even from such a distance he could smell my fear. I fought the urge to fling myself behind Etti, behind Olga, and disappear into the crowd. But our gazes connected. I saw his eyes widen and then narrow. As much as I wanted to, I did not look away. I let the harsh light from the flood lamps illuminate my features. I even moved apart from the others, letting go of Etti's arm, finding a little space of my own so that the cluster of women would not shield me. The breeze lifted my hair off my neck, teasing the tendrils that had worked free of their pins.

I saw him pause. He said something to the officer beside him, shoved the clipboard at his colleague and began to wade through the crowd towards us. There was a curious, hungry expression on his face, the same one he had worn earlier. Only now, amid this weeping, shifting mass of human misery, it seemed even more out of place. He brushed past an elderly couple, careless of the way the woman stumbled over her suitcase and had to clutch at her husband for support.

Could he hear my heart thudding against my ribs as I waited for him to reach me?

'Lydia Volkova. You don't take advice easily.' His face shone in the floodlights. 'Aren't you afraid to be here? Someone might mistake you for a resistance sympathiser.'

I tried to speak, but my throat was painfully dry. 'I need your help,' I said.

'My help? The Partorg's daughter wants my help?' He drew back, placing a hand on his chest, but the look of wolfish shrewdness didn't leave his face. 'I'm surprised! You seem more than capable of doing things for yourself. I know your father is a clever man, but I'd not expected his daughter to be so independent. And here I thought you would be tucked safely away. No need for you to witness all this.'

He waved his hand, as if his fellow officers were dividing up livestock instead of people. People jostled around us. I saw men being shoved towards the waiting carriage at the end of the train, while women were pushed together, many of them holding children tightly to save them from being crushed. I caught the flash of a man's clear spectacles, the bright green of a headscarf, the bright burgundy of a child's woollen jacket as people drew together and broke apart.

A woman appeared next to me suddenly, as if she'd caught sight of Lieutenant Lubov's uniform and had been working her way towards him. She wore a frightened expression and carried a screaming toddler on her hip. The toddler's face was brick red and blotchy, his nose leaking greenish mucus.

'Please help me!' she said, her voice hoarse, desperate. 'My child is sick! He has the measles. My husband is a doctor.' She nodded towards the end of the platform where men were being loaded into a carriage. 'Please let us stay together!'

Lieutenant Lubov grimaced as the child shrieked. The woman tried to quieten him, but he only screamed louder. 'There!' the woman cried, her face lighting up with hope. 'There is Andrus!' I looked to where the woman was pointing. Far down the end of the train, a man was struggling against the surge of the crowd. He had a brown doctor's bag in his hands. As we watched, he raised it above the crowd and tried to push towards us. A guard blocked his path.

Lieutenant Lubov shook his head. 'Impossible,' he said. 'Men and children separate.'

The woman's face crinkled in confusion. 'But my child—' She cast a look at the wailing toddler, heaved him higher up her hip. 'I cannot look after him myself. He needs medicine!'

A man's voice shouted. 'Kaarin!'

The woman's husband was holding out the bag, dangling it over the shoulder of the guard blocking his path. The guard pushed him with the butt of his rifle. The man stumbled back. The bag flew from his hands to land in the dirt at the soldier's feet.

'Please!' the woman cried. 'Please let me see him for just a moment!'

She reached out and grabbed at Lieutenant Lubov's arm, almost dropping the toddler, who slid down her waist and wailed louder. Lieutenant Lubov's face darkened. Wrenching his arm free, he shook his head in disgust and pushed the woman away. He seized my hand and began to drag me away from the heaving, jostling crowd towards the edge of the station where the bright haze from the floodlights was blocked by the corner of the waiting room. I caught a glimpse of the woman's desperate face before it was swallowed up by the rest of the flock.

A curdling horror bubbled inside me. The air was charged. It would take only a moment's panic for a stampede to occur. Forced together in these circumstances, these people were more like animals than humans. They had not been given a choice to be otherwise. This was how Stalin saw the world, I realised. And by closing my eyes, by ignoring what was right before me, I was complicit, too. Was this what Joachim had seen, experienced: this wave of terror and desperation? What cruel indignities had he been forced to participate in on his journey north?

I tried to slow my breath and my pounding pulse. 'There is a woman,' I said. 'A friend. I need to know where she is. If – if she has already gone. Or if she might be in one of the carriages here. Her name is Juudit Koppel. She was wrongfully arrested earlier this evening.'

I tried to ignore the way Lieutenant Lubov's eyebrows formed an unbroken line over his eyes. 'Do you think you can find out?' I said, my voice rising. 'Can you help me?'

He continued to stare.

'Please,' I added, reminded of the woman with the shrieking child.

He took his time answering, straightening out the sleeve of his uniform, which was, I noticed with a sharp stab of horror, speckled with dark brown stains. Finally, he looked up. 'I'd like to help you. Really, I would. But I'm very busy, Lida. May I call you Lida?'

His words took me off guard. I nodded, unnerved. 'Yes. Fine.'

He flashed me a small smile. 'Lida, then. Your father gave explicit instructions that the operation is to be completed by daybreak, if possible. How will it look if I'm searching for one woman among so many others? What will your father think of me?' He swung his head around to gaze at the mass of people. 'So, if I help you, Lida, what can you do for me? What do you have to offer?'

I dreaded the softness of his voice and worse, the slow tick of his smile. It froze my thoughts and dried up all the words on my tongue. I tried to speak but even my stammering came out as nothing but a hoarse squeak. Narrowing his gaze, he leant forward until our bodies were almost touching, his head tilted to one side as if he were concentrating hard on listening to me above the clamour of noise on the station. After a long moment, he shrugged and straightened up.

'Then you must excuse me. There are still a lot of people to process.' He breathed in through his nose. 'I really can't stand around any longer. Goodnight, Lida.'

He pivoted on his heel.

'Wait!' My fingers scrabbled for his jacket, slipping off the smooth material. 'I have something. Some information. You may find it . . . useful. I'm not sure.' I shook my head, my thoughts whirling. 'It's all I can think of.'

'Information.' He crossed his arms. 'What kind of information?' Behind him, in the distance, I saw Olga looking around for me, craning her head over the crowd in search of my face. I shrank back into the shadows of the ticket booth.

'It's about the Partorg.'

His face stilled. 'I am listening.'

'I'm not his daughter,' I said, garbling my words in the effort to get them out.

Lubov's lip curled. 'So, you're a bastard,' he shrugged. 'What does that matter? Why should I care which man is your father?'

I closed my eyes against the crudeness of his words. 'Not just any man.'

'Then who?'

I watched his face change as I told him, the interplay of shadow and light transforming his features like clouds scudding before the sun. He startled me by seising my shoulders suddenly, thrusting his face into mine. He began to march me away from the platform.

Panic rushed through my body. 'Where are we going?'

He shot me a quick, hard glance. 'Back to the Grey House. I'm taking you back to your father. Your real father. You're too valuable to be out here. Clearly.' He shook me. 'Now that we're friends, I think we need to stick close together, don't you? I'm sure the Partorg will be pleased to have you safe and sound.'

I stared at him, and hatred surged through me. I knew in that moment that I was Stalin's daughter. I was everything I hated about him: his unpredictable temper, his ability to obfuscate the truth until he believed his own lies.

I closed my eyes as the whistle screeched again. Steam hissed from the wheels. I had imagined I would feel unburdened, now that my secret was shared. Instead, when I saw the thirsty way Lubov was looking at me, I felt heavier.

'Wait.' With an effort, I threw him off. My arm ached where he'd gripped it. 'The woman,' I said, swallowing hard. 'Juudit Koppel. You said you'd find her. You promised. If you don't help me, I will never help you. I will fight you all the way back.'

Lieutenant Lubov shot me a long, hard look and then suddenly, he let me go. I watched him hurry away towards the train, pushing aside those unlucky enough not to see him coming. I watched his dark hair bobbing through the crowd and let out a breath.

My feet dragged as I made my way back to where Olga and Etti were waiting with Etti's mother's friends. The small group of women exclaimed when they saw me. Olga hurried over and hugged me, her eyes moist.

'I thought you had been taken!'

I wanted to kiss her cheek, but there was no time. The train gave a blast, making the people on the platform push back, knocking over those behind them.

I searched desperately for Lieutenant Lubov's face. Suddenly, it blazed out at me. He was standing halfway down the platform. When he saw me notice him, he lifted his arm slightly. He pushed someone in front of him; I caught the blur of her grey dress, silver hair falling around her shoulders as she tented her eyes from the glare of the floodlight.

Hope lifted my heart. 'She's there!'

'Where?' Etti was at my side instantly. I began to push my way forward, bumping into knees and legs, keeping Lieutenant Lubov's face in constant view as I dragged Etti along behind me.

Panting, we reached the carriage.

They fell into each other's arms, Etti's sobs mingling with her mother's soothing cries. Her knotted hands stroked Etti's hair, coming to rest on the white triangle of shawl that hung down her back.

'You see? I keep my promises.' Lieutenant Lubov's voice rang close in my ear. I looked up to find him staring down at me. He smiled, showing sharp teeth. 'You'll learn to trust me. Now it's time for you to keep yours. Time to go back.'

I could not answer him. I could only stare down at the hand he had placed on my arm.

The crowd moved suddenly between us, filling the spaces we had made with bodies as the soldiers at the back began to urge them forward. I heard Lieutenant Lubov curse. Somebody's elbow pressed into my back. The sharp edges of a suitcase jabbed the back of my legs, almost sending me crashing to my knees.

A guard shouted and grabbed a young boy by the collar, thrusting him up into the carriage nearest us. It was so full of people crushed together that he teetered on the edge; the guard jumped up and tried to slam the sliding door shut.

The boy cried out as the guard shoved him backwards.

'Leave him alone!' Juudit had flung herself forward and grabbed the guard's trousers.

Etti gasped. 'Mama! Hush!' She tried to shield Juudit's body, but the older woman continued to tug at the guard's leg. His feet slipped. He lunged out as he fell, his hand grasping a metal bar on the side of the train and holding on while Juudit continued to berate him, her voice shrill.

Gunshots cracked.

People screamed. The crowd swelled, broke apart, surged back together. Somebody shoved me against Etti and I staggered, catching her around the waist. We crashed to the ground. Stamping feet kicked up dust around us. Above me, a sea of faces blended in and out of view. Under a rain of blows, I dragged myself to my feet, pulling Etti up beside me. Soldiers ran back and forth, their rifles raised. Bullets struck the air around us.

We cowered. People fell to the ground, shielding their heads.

Somebody seized my other hand and began to drag me through the surging crowd of panicked deportees. I caught a glimpse of Olga's frightened face, before she turned back and continued to pull me towards the back of the station. Desperately, I clutched Etti's slippery hand with my fingers, hoping she would follow. A man stumbled into me, loosening my grip. Suddenly, my hands were empty.

'Olga!'

She turned, smoke billowing around her head from the discharged guns.

I looked back to see Etti kneeling in the dust. People wove around her. Guards were still shouting.

I began to fight my way back to her, before I realised why she'd stopped.

Etti was hunched over her mother, her shoulders shaking. A river of blood soaked the dust and stones around Juudit's body. Bullet holes riddled her chest. Even before I reached her, Etti had torn off her shawl and was trying to plug up the holes. I placed my hands on the shawl as I fell to my knees beside her. Blood bubbled up through the lace. When I pulled my hands away, the shawl came with them, sticking to my fingers. Juudit's face was grey and still, her white lips parted. The cold glow of the floodlights was reflected in her wide, unblinking eyes.

Somebody tripped over her leg, sprawling in the dust beside us. Someone else's shoe caught on Juudit's hand as they jostled against the panicked crowd. There was the crunch of bone.

Etti began to scream.

I grabbed her wrist, and this time I did not let go, but used my own body as a weapon, driving myself against the crush of people, focusing on nothing else but reaching the edge of the station. I collided with something hard, sending pain bursting through my shoulder, but I pressed on. In the distance, I saw a group huddled beside the ticket booth. If we could only reach them . . .

Etti's arm sagged in mine. I yanked it, hard.

Finally, we reached the edge of the crowd. Soldiers paced up and down, brandishing their guns, shoving people into the railway cars without consulting the lists in their hands. There was an urgency to their movements now. Some of them looked frightened, alarmed by the gunfire and the

250

crush of the crowd. One soldier I passed could not have been older than fifteen. An old lady in a headscarf tried to speak to him as he herded her towards a carriage. I saw him glance away, pretending not to hear, his mouth trembling. Perhaps he was thinking of his own babushka. He had no choice but to obey orders. I waited until the guard closest to us turned his head, then I pulled Etti behind me, ducking as low to the ground as possible, praying that she and Olga would do the same.

The women cried out as we reached them, huddling around Etti.

'We thought you were gone!' Helle sobbed. 'The soldiers told us if we went to find you we'd be taken, too. Oh, Etti! Where is Juudit?'

Etti did not answer. Helle turned to me, seeking answers, eyes wide.

'She's dead,' I said.

There was a moment of silence before Helle released a sharp cry of unbridled grief.

I wiped my hand across my sweltering forehead, daring to glance back. The train was already full; they were taking no chances now, but shoving everyone into the carriages, packing them in without regard for lists or names. Poor Juudit's body was there somewhere, crushed beneath the crowd.

I turned to ask Olga whether she was hurt, but the space beside me was empty.

A terrible panic rose through me. 'Where is Olga?'

Etti stared at me. Her mouth was slack, her eyes dull.

I shook her, ignoring the gasps of Helle and the other

women. 'Where is she?' I could hear the panic deepening my voice.

Desperately, I scanned the seething mass of people crowding the station. Where was she? Doors slammed. The guards had filled their quota.

'Olga?' My voice cracked. I could not hope to be heard over the crowd.

As a guard approached the last van, I spotted her. The fur coat glistening. Her creased face, so familiar, like the lines of my own palm. I tried to call again, but the words were strangled in my throat.

I imagined she saw me. That one arm lifted. That her lips moved. A prayer, a proverb.

Then the guard slammed the door closed, and a moment later, the train moved off, snaking into the dark.

Somebody grasped me. Words swirled and swooped, and I tried to catch them, to comprehend what was being said.

'We are sending you to a safe place.' Helle. No, Etti. The girl with the ringlets. Their voices, faces, mingled together, a blur of colour, a cloud of sound. A man's face loomed in the darkness. A stranger. 'This man has a truck that will take you to the edge of the forest. Go with him.'

A hand gripped mine, the palm sticky. I held on. I let myself be anchored, although I wanted nothing more than to drift away.

Snowdrift Pattern

Kati

'TELL ME THE STORY OF THE WOODCUTTER.'

Oskar's elbow touched mine. Meadow grass prickled my neck. Clouds unspooled above us, fringed by the overhanging canopy of spruce trees. The leaves were just beginning their transformation from bright green to the russet red of autumn. The faint scent of woodsmoke drifted across the fields to where we lay, our schoolbooks abandoned beside a small timber acorn Oskar had whittled from a lump of oak. A cow huffed nearby, releasing a scent of sweet hay.

'I thought you didn't like my fairy tales.' I propped myself up on one elbow.

'I was lying.' Oskar's blue eyes flicked from the sky to me. His hair was long and in need of cutting, bleached by the sun from its usual gold to the colour of pale straw. His lips twitched. 'I like them. I only lied about it for Jakob's benefit. I don't need any more trouble from the other boys.' Without looking down, he located a strawberry with his fingers from the pile we had gathered and brought it to his mouth. I watched him bite into it. A trickle of juice dribbled down his chin.

'Are you certain?' I said, folding my arms and attempting to sound stern. 'I wouldn't want to waste my breath.'

Oskar grinned. Strawberry seeds glinted in his teeth. 'I promise.'

'Well then.' I settled back, still watching him, and pinched a blade of grass between my fingers. 'There was a woodcutter who went into the forest. He went to cut down a birch but in a human voice it shouted, "Do not kill me! I am young! I have many children!" So he took pity on it. He chose an oak tree instead. But the oak tree called out, "Do not kill me! I'm not fully grown! If you kill me now, no oaks will ever grow here again!" Next he tried an ash tree. "No, no!" cried the tree. "I was married but yesterday! What will become of my bride?" It's no use, thought the woodcutter. I can't do it. My heart is not made of stone. But what shall I do? If I don't cut down trees, I shall starve. Just then a little forest spirit appeared and, in reward for saving the trees, gave the man a golden staff not several inches long and no thicker than a knitting needle. The staff had magic powers – it could summon food and beat his enemies and make barns spring up from nothing. And so the woodcutter never wanted for anything ever again.' I scrunched the grass blade up in my hand.

'And he lived happily until the end of his days,' Oskar said softly.

'So he did.' I tossed the grass away and watched a flock of spotted skylarks swoop over the trees. From the distant farmhouse came the sound of someone calling.

'Your mother wants you,' I said.

Oskar's smile faded. 'Probably needs me to cut more firewood and bring the cows in.' He sat up, shaking his hair out of his eyes. 'It's not her fault.'

I picked up our schoolbooks and climbed to my feet. When I

looked back, I was surprised to find that Oskar had not moved.

'I wish I had a golden staff,' he muttered. He reached out and plucked the whittled acorn from the grass. Rolling it in his palm, he said, 'I would use its magic to summon up a feast every night. And to give Aime a new dress each month. And to buy new tools so I could make furniture to sell and mend the holes in our roof. I'd use the money to buy you the finest gold necklace and you'd be happy.'

He sounded so low it made my heart ache. Kneeling down, I placed my hand on his shoulder. 'I don't need a gold necklace.' I plucked the acorn from his hand. The timber was warm, the top ridged and the bottom smooth. 'I'm happy here now, with you. I'd rather have this acorn than a gold necklace. Where would I wear it? And the trees might object to your felling them just to buy me things. They might cry out in protest. Listen.' I inclined my head. 'I think I can hear them now saying "Please Oskar, have mercy! Think of our poor wives!"'

Oskar wrinkled his nose but his lips were pinched together, as if he were trying not to laugh. I stood and held out my hand to help him up. Our palms met.

An owl screeched loudly. *An owl?* Owls did not fly in the day.

My eyes snapped open. Everything rushed back with horrible clarity. Mama and Papa were gone. The Russians had shot them. Grief flooded my body like bitter poison. My chest ached with loss as I replayed their final moments, watching them die over and over again. Not only were they gone, but Jakob and Oskar were gone too. And I was in the farmhouse with Hilja.

My neck was stiff on one side. The candle near my feet

guttered. Beyond its puddle of light, I could see Hilja's outline. She shifted, drawing up her legs and then stretching them out.

'You were dreaming,' she said. 'I could tell.'

She hadn't slept, then. I tried to brush off the vague discomfort I felt as I imagined her watching me while I dozed. 'What time is it? How long did I sleep?'

Hilja leant forward and rolled her shoulders, then slumped back against the wall. 'Not long. It's still night. There are many hours—' She sat up suddenly, her face alert. 'Did you hear that?'

My pulse quickened. Yes, I had heard it – the swishing of branches being pushed aside. Feet vibrating the ground. Loud whispers and panting gasps, like the collective breath of a hundred different voices erupting all at once.

Hilja sprang up, and I scrambled to my feet. She turned as someone tapped on the door, the edge of her boot catching the candle. For a second the flame danced, a quivering orb of crimson and orange.

Then the door fell open, snuffing out the light.

The sudden darkness breathed in ragged gasps. It shifted and cursed and cried. It was muffled sobbing, the squeak of shoes, a child's questions cut short by a stifled hand. The acrid stench of body odour and dirt in a confined space.

Hilja's torch flickered on. Its beam crossed the floor and swung in a wide arc across the refugees who had flung themselves into the farmhouse and now stood pressed shoulder-to-shoulder in the room. Old lined faces, young tired ones. A woman with a toddler slung across her chest, its face buried against her shoulder. They all turned away from the light as it roved across them, as if seeking the protection of the darkness.

Something touched my leg, and I started. All my nerve endings sang with tension.

A man stepped forward, shielding his eyes. 'Hilja?'

Hilja froze the beam on him. 'Yes, Jaak.'

He lowered his hand as Hilja swung the beam away.

'How many?' Hilja said.

'Around twenty. We picked them up near the station.'

Hilja muttered something under her breath. The torch beam wavered. 'Any injuries?'

Somebody whimpered softly.

'None that I could see.' Jaak shuffled his feet. He seemed nervous. Before the beam had left him in shadow, I'd caught the sheen of his ragged hair and, more worryingly, a long scarlet stain near his jacket collar. But Jaak did not seem injured. Was the blood Oskar's? Was it Jakob's? I imagined their bodies laid out like Imbi and Aime's; Jakob's back hunched, the too-small jacket stretched across his frozen shoulders. Oskar with his arms flung out, eyes clouded with death. I thought of asking Jaak for news, but he was already backing away, as if he did not want to linger. 'You'll be leaving soon?'

'Now.'

'Good.' Jaak glanced behind him again. 'Be careful.' He gave her a curt nod. The wind blew through the open door as he slipped away.

Hilja trained the torchlight on her own face.

'I'm Hilja,' she said, speaking in Estonian. 'I will take you to the camp. You need to keep up. Anyone who doesn't will be left behind.' The newcomers muttered quietly as Hilja reached into her knapsack and passed a slim water bottle to the nearest person, an old man with unkempt

257

white hair. 'We will stop once for water. Once for food.'

'We have nothing,' one of the women said, her voice quivering. 'There was no time to gather anything.'

'I have dried cakes you can share,' Hilja replied. 'They're not appetising but they'll have to do until we reach camp.' She paused. 'You must know that there can be no going back once we reach the camp. Your lives, as you knew them, are over. Until Estonia is returned to us, you will be outlaws. Shot on sight by the Soviets. If you betray us, we will kill you. There is no middle ground. You are Forest Brothers now, or Sisters. Eventually, when things settle, you will take an oath. You may be given new names, if it is considered too dangerous for you to be known by your old one. Is everybody of the same understanding?'

The group was silent.

'Good.' Hilja handed me the torch, tracking its beam onto the floor. 'Kati, can you organise them? Single file. Women with children at the front, elderly in the middle. Men at the back. I need to check outside. I will wait in the trees across the glade; when I give you the signal, we will move out.'

Obediently, I moved among the group, examining them to determine which place they should occupy. The task was a welcome distraction from the images of Jakob and Oskar's corpses which replayed themselves in my mind. When the weak torch beam hit the last two figures – two women, holding hands – I gasped and dropped the torch. It rolled away, sending fractured light spinning in all directions.

'Etti?' I leapt forward, clasping my cousin to my chest. Her rounded belly nudged my hip. 'What happened to you?'

Etti did not respond, and immediately I felt the beginnings of dread creep through me. I said her name again, shaking her gently, but she turned her head away.

'She's in shock,' said a voice from the darkness. 'We all are. Please. *Aita meid*. Help us.' I scrambled to retrieve the torch. Its light spilt over the features of a young woman. Her hair was the shade of stewed berries, a deep auburn, almost black.

'Who are you?' I frowned at her, trying to place her face. Etti did not have friends I didn't know. Our world was small; and yet this woman, this girl, was clasping my cousin's hand as if they were sisters who would not be wrenched apart.

She sighed. 'It doesn't matter.'

'It matters to me.' I stepped closer to her. 'You are Russian, I can tell by your accent. How do we know they haven't sent you in here to gain our trust? How do we know you won't go running to the nearest outpost as soon as we stop?' Fear made me bold. I snatched at her arm, forcing her to turn towards me so I could push the light into her face. 'Who are you?' I repeated, louder this time, forgetting the others lined up outside, waiting for Hilja's signal to move into the trees.

The girl dropped Etti's hand, and lifted her tired, defeated eyes to mine. 'I'm Lydia Volkova.'

I realised with a start that her orange skirt was stained with blood. And then her words registered in my brain. 'Like the Partorg?'

She nodded, her shoulders slumping. 'He's . . . my father.'

Cold spread through my body and I turned away, unable to look at this woman. 'I must tell Hilja. She'll know what to do with you.'

I took a few steps towards the open door where the others were huddled.

'Kati, Mama is gone.' Etti's voice was soft. It was the voice of a lost child, of someone who has become untethered from the world. In the torch's fragile light, she shook like a leaf bent by the wind. Her eyes stared at the ground, seeing nothing. 'They shot her. She's dead.' Lydia and I moved towards her at the same time. Our hands met around Etti's shoulders and I pulled away, feeling as if her skin had burnt me.

'Lydia must come.' Sobs now racked Etti's body. 'You must bring her, Kati. She's not one of them. She's like us. I won't leave her behind.'

'The signal,' somebody hissed through the open door. 'Hurry!'

'We have to go,' I said. I began to shuffle Etti towards the door. I shot a dark look at the figure of the girl who had stayed behind, her shadow already blending into the darkness. 'Etti, you're delirious. The grief – I know, it is—'

'No.' Etti dug her shoes into the sticky floorboards. 'I won't leave her, Kati. She tried to help Mama. And her mother was Estonian. She is a friend.'

I sighed. No matter how I tried to force Etti forward, the bulk of her would not shift. 'Etti, please.'

'What is going on?' Hilja's razor-sharp voice hissed in the doorway. 'I gave you the signal, Kati! What are you doing? This is not a game!'

Sweat was forming all over my body. 'I found my cousin. She's in shock.'

'Good for you.' Hilja grabbed Etti's arm roughly. 'Get her out, then. Get her moving. We don't have time for this.'

She marched Etti towards the door. The moonlight rimmed Etti's face as Hilja shoved her outside. My cousin gave me one last, despairing, pleading glance.

I took a step forward and then another, the torch beam shimmering ahead.

The darkness gathered in the room behind me, a thick wall, silent save for a small noise, coming in mechanical intervals. The short, sharp intake of breath; a deep expulsion of panic from the lungs.

I swallowed, trying to calm myself and make a decision. I looked back at the darkness that held the Partorg's daughter. Hilja would kill her. I could leave her here; she would find her way to somewhere, eventually. This safe point would no longer be safe, but at least my conscience would be assuaged.

Beyond the open door, the trees shifted and swayed. I heard the low hum of voices.

My cousin's face swam before my eyes; her eyes hollow, leaden. Aunt Juudit was dead. My parents, too. Oskar's family. The women from the knitting circle would be gone too. Even if they had survived the purge, we would probably never see them again. To try would be to put their lives in danger. Jakob was somewhere in the woods, perhaps wounded or dying. Etti was the only one I could protect; and in her grief she had attached herself to someone who could turn on us at any moment. What had she said? *Like us.* The girl was like us.

Another thought rose up. Something my mind had missed in the shock of seeing Etti again and the overwhelming anger the Partorg's daughter had stirred in me.

A lace shawl. The torch beam had picked it out, wound around the girl's shoulders. And she'd spoken Estonian, although the words were strangely curt, heavily accented.

I turned back, swinging the light across the floor. She was standing against the wall, her hands grasped beneath her chin. Her blue eyes stared straight ahead and although she could not possibly see me, standing behind the glare of the torch, I had the strangest feeling of connection.

It was as if I were seeing my wolf, made human. Alone, hunted. Something in me recognised that ache, the hunger that would never cease. She shrank back. A corner of her shawl slipped, and she tugged it up over her shoulder. The white lace enswathed the cream blouse she was wearing. The torch beam trembled as I moved towards her until we were inches apart. She smelt of faded perfume.

It couldn't be, and yet it was.

Lightning pattern, long rows of it. And at the very bottom a wolf's paw, half-hidden in the lace like a footprint buried in the snow.

'Where did you get that shawl?' I demanded.

The woman flinched as I reached out and fingered the lace. I rubbed my thumb over the wolf's paw and felt a surge of response, a current travelling through a wire. Up close I could see the stitches were not my grandmother's; they were not fine enough. But the wolf's paw . . . It could not be a coincidence.

'It was my mother's.' Up close, I could see dust smeared on the woman's face. A branch had torn the skin of her cheek. '*Ta oli eestlane*. She was Estonian, as Etti said.' She lifted her hand and wiped it across her forehead. 'Leave me here,' she said. 'Go. I would not blame you.'

An owl screeched again outside. A warning? I licked my lip, tasting salt.

I should leave her. Why risk taking someone who would be searched for, hunted? I had no doubt the Partorg would come looking. I let the lace shawl fall from my fingers and the woman shrank back, nodding, as if she'd already decided her fate for me.

I began to turn away.

My grandmother's voice came back to me, loud and clear as if she was standing behind me, hidden in the shadows. *Why do we make shawls? Not only for ourselves but to send our Estonian traditions out into the world.*

Here was a shawl which had come back.

Before I could change my mind, before I could quieten the voice of warning screaming in my head, I seized her shoulder and dragged her outside with me, into the night.

'Over there.'

Hilja's voice rasped. I rubbed at my bleary eyes, trying hard to focus where she was pointing. The others shuffled around me. I gazed down at the twisted nest of fallen birch logs. The grey light of dawn turned their trunks the colour of faded bruises.

'Climb up.' Hilja grunted as she hoisted herself onto the nearest trunk, then straightened. She held her arms out for balance. 'Walk to the end. Then make sure you jump across to the other side. We can't leave track marks for the Soviets to find.' She jerked her head at the copse of trees ahead. 'Camp is there, beyond those spruces.'

A buzz of excitement thickened the air.

'Etti, we are close.' I turned to look at her. 'We are here.' My cousin's face did not change. She still wore the same weary expression. Dark shadows were gathered beneath her eyes. Her dress was stained with mud. Spider webs clung to her hair. When I brushed them off, she closed her eyes and drew a long breath in through her nose. I kissed her cheek. It was cold. The faint scent of vomit lingered on her breath.

For hours, we had stumbled along, slapping at bugs, fighting the branches that scratched at our faces. We hadn't spoken, too busy concentrating on following the flash of Hilja's torch.

Only once had we heard a volley of shots break the silence. Hilja had pulled us into the undergrowth, where we had lain for what seemed like hours on our stomachs, unable to move as the insects crawled across our skin, waiting for Hilja to tell us it was safe to keep moving.

Etti had been the last to emerge. She had shaken off my grasp on her shoulder, wanting to stay curled beneath the bracken and the coiled fronds.

'I can't move,' she said, her voice edged with panic. Her arms were wrapped about her waist. 'Something is squeezing me! It won't let go!' Her breathing came in short gasps. I watched helplessly as she shuddered, arching her back against my hand, her sobbing muffled by leaves.

'Please try, Etti.' I could feel sweat soaking into my hand. I looked in desperation at the line of refugees moving away from us, through the trees. What if we were left behind?

'You must get up!' I said. 'Come, I'll help you!'

Etti twisted and writhed. When I put my hand under her arm, she ripped it fiercely away. I was on the verge of calling out for Hilja when Lydia appeared, her white shawl gleaming in the darkness.

'Etti is ill!' I said, although the words seemed so insufficient. 'I can't get her to move . . .'

'Let me see.' Moving the ferns apart, the Partorg's

daughter knelt beside Etti's prostrate form. I heard them whispering and moments later, Lydia stood up and helped my trembling cousin to her feet.

'It's gone, now,' Etti said. She sounded weary and exhausted. 'The feeling.'

'You are sure?' Our breath mingled in the darkness.

'Yes.' She took a wobbly step forward, clutching Lydia's arm. 'Come on, Lida.'

The line of refugees was already disappearing through the trees. Hilja's torch beam bounced off the trunks of white aspens. We hurried to join them. When we stopped for food, Etti took one bite of her cake before thrusting it at me and stumbling away to be sick. She returned, wiping her mouth with her hand, her legs trembling and shaking like a child who is learning how to skate on ice for the first time. Hilja had not noticed, too busy handing out the cakes. Sometimes we had lagged behind, waiting for Etti's pain to pass before we moved again. The long night stretched out taut as a length of yarn, broken only by moments of panic where I prayed we would not be left and times when I almost wished we would, so that Etti could rest.

At long last, the sky had begun to lighten, the birds warbling their dawn songs. It was both a relief and a source of sorrow. So many would not wake this morning. So many were gone.

I pushed down my grief. People began to help each other climb up onto the fallen trees as Hilja had instructed, edging their way towards the spruce trees. Some people crawled on hands and knees, afraid of slipping.

Levering myself up on my belly, I managed to stand,

only wobbling a little before I gained my balance. 'Etti.' I reached down a hand.

She glanced away. 'Where is Lydia?' she said.

'Here.'

The Partorg's daughter melted out of the line of people waiting behind me, as pale as a spirit, her hair like a streak of dark blood spilling onto her shoulders. Hiking her skirt over her knees, she crawled up beside me. Etti stretched out her hand, and Lydia grasped it. Together, they struggled onto the log.

A pang of jealousy stabbed at my side.

Turning away from them, I shuffled forward. A breeze danced through the trees, shaking the leaves, stirring up the scent of warm pine and balsam. The day would be warm and cloudless, as beautiful as any ordinary day. But everything had changed.

I leapt lightly across the gap as Hilja showed us, my boots slapping the shelf of rock, and squeezed myself between the spruces. I heard Lydia and Etti behind me; Etti's grunt as her feet hit the rock. I wanted to turn and ask her if she needed help, but I feared she would shun me.

I entered the camp alone, and as I stepped into the clearing, my heart sank.

Sometimes when Jakob and I were children, we had camped in the forest near our farmhouse. A tent, a bed roll. A fishing line. We had not needed much to keep ourselves happy. It was the very act of being in nature that delighted us; the warmth of the sun filtering through the leaves, the sandy riverbed where silver fish darted or came to nibble at our bait. The thick perfume of musk flowers and the tang of mushrooms hiding beneath tree roots. We had found an old sauna and placed hot rocks inside and stripped naked, daring each other to see who could stay in the searing heat the longest, emerging at last to feel the night air tighten against our skin. We had declared ourselves wild spirits, refusing to return home when Mama hollered across the fields, demanding we fulfil our chores. It had never occurred to me that the appeal of it all was the possibility we could return home whenever we liked.

Now, that illusion was gone.

The Forest Brothers' camp was a dreary place. Dozens of lean-tos dotted the landscape, roughly constructed from bark and timber logs and lashed together with coils of wire. A blackened fire pit lay half-submerged in front of them, wind skimming the ashes. People moved around, speaking softly, their gait stiff and wooden. Those not in uniform wore grey, shapeless outfits, faded and scrubbed from many washes in a tub of black, scummy water. Their limbs were thin, faces gaunt. A child emerged suddenly from one of the makeshift shacks. Her hair was a tangled bird's nest, eyes bright with the kind of fever that comes from having too little to eat. When she saw us, a group of newcomers, she did not move but stared with her lips pressed thinly together.

I read her mind as keenly as if I had stared into her head. *More people. Less food.*

I glanced away from her challenging gaze, searching for Hilja. I saw her talking to two resistance fighters, rifles slung across their backs. She caught my eye and although she did not break off her conversation, she inclined her head ever so slightly.

Suddenly, she broke away from her companions and strode towards me.

'You'll want to know about your brother.'

My stomach lurched. 'Yes.'

'The shots we heard last night.' She lifted her chin. 'They were partisans. Two Soviet groups were killed in the forest. Your brother is safe. He did well, it seems.'

I let out a breath, my thoughts immediately turning to Oskar.

'He's on his way, with Oskar and the others,' Hilja continued. 'They should be here before—' She broke off as a commotion behind us interrupted her thoughts. I followed her gaze.

Etti was squatting in the dirt, with Lydia beside her. Her face was white, covered in a sheen of sweat. As I watched, she gave a long groan. Her hand tightened around Lydia's arm, the knuckles whiter than her face. Dirt clouded up around me as I ran to her.

'What's wrong with her?'

Lydia looked up at me. 'It's her time, I think. She told me. She's certain.'

Etti gave another groan, loud enough that the other deportees stopped and began to whisper.

'She can't.' I looked around. The trees seemed to be gathering, crowding around us. 'She can't have her baby here.'

For the first time, the stench of the latrine hit me full in the face. It was the rank stink of rotten meat in summer, mixed with the dead scent of river water dried to muck in the sun. My mind was a sudden frenzy of churning thoughts. I had seen many sheep born, had even once watched Papa pull a lamb from its mother's body. I remembered his arm reaching deep inside the ewe, the tautening of his shoulder muscles as he twisted the lamb this way and that, carefully guiding it through the birth canal before at last it spilt out, slippery with fluid, the birthing sac a shrivelled skein around its throat.

I swallowed. This was not like those times. A baby was not a sheep.

Hilja was frowning at us. I ran back to her.

'My cousin's baby,' I said. 'It's coming. Are there any doctors here?'

Hilja shook her head. 'Not that I know of. But there are plenty of women. There's bound to be someone who can help you.' She called out to a group of women watching us. 'Johanna!' An older woman with eyes like chips of ice and knotted hands came forward. A lace stole was netted around her shoulders; not a shawl, but a narrow scarf. A pattern of snowdrops swirled across the fabric.

Hilja jerked her head. 'This is Katarina. She thinks her cousin is in labour. Johanna has a daughter here, Liisa, and three grandchildren she delivered herself,' she told me. 'She was a midwife in her village outside Kulli before the Russians killed her son.'

'I'm sorry for your loss,' I said, worried that my words would sound callous. 'But my cousin is having a baby. It's her first time. She's frightened. And I don't know anyone here except the other woman we came with.'

Johanna pushed back her sleeves and turned back to the other women. 'Liisa. We are needed.'

Her daughter Liisa was a fair-skinned girl with a sleeping toddler draped over her shoulder. She handed the child to another woman and came towards us. Her eyes were small like Johanna's, her nose a slim stroke beneath fine pale hair; the soft Danish features of the people from northern Estonia who had mixed less with the Russians and so retained their pale fairness. I led them both to where Etti was crouched in the dirt, Lydia still holding her hand. With surprising flexibility, Johanna knelt beside her, her hands moving across my cousin's stomach, prodding gently. Etti let out a sob, which became a long cry. It sent the birds in a nearby bush flapping into the air. Johanna waited until Etti's pain had passed then, with a swift look around, lifted the rim of Etti's dress and peeked beneath. When she let it fall, she was frowning. 'This girl has been in labour for some time. Did you never notice?'

'She didn't say anything,' I said, guilt suddenly weighing on me. 'I didn't know.' Etti had been running all night, pausing when the pain became too much. And I had yelled at her to hurry, pushing her along. I had not seen what was happening, too terrified of being caught and captured to notice the early signs of her labour. And Lydia had said nothing.

I glared across at the Russian woman. Johanna's eyes followed my gaze.

'And you?' she said to Lydia, raising her eyebrows. 'Did you not notice?'

Lydia shrank a little, bunching up her shoulders. 'She asked me not to say anything. Made me promise.' Her Russian accent was even more pronounced since we were surrounded by women speaking only Estonian. I saw Johanna and Liisa exchange a look of surprise. 'She didn't want to worry you,' Lydia said, directing her words to me. I saw a flash of something in her eyes; defiance? Or guilt?

I continued to glare at her. If Etti had only told me. Why had she not confided in me? Surely she knew I would want to help her. But in the same instance, I knew that I would have kept pushing her, too afraid of Hilja leaving us behind if we lagged. I would not have changed a thing.

Johanna held Etti's other hand as she whimpered. 'Liisa, find them a lean-to. Some blankets. Clean water. And fetch me a knife.'

'Lydia can help you,' I said, my voice prickly.

'No.' Etti's voice was taut with pain. She gripped Lydia's hand. 'I want both of you to stay.'

'Hurry,' Johanna warned, as Etti began to whimper again, squeezing Lydia's hand until the Russian woman's lip curled in pain. 'It will not be long now.'

'It's all right, Etti,' I said, trying to soothe her, but I had to force myself to ball up my fist in the pocket of my skirt to resist slapping the Partorg's daughter across the face.

Stork's Foot Pattern

Lydia

'HOW IS SHE?'

From the doorway of the lean-to Kati's shadow loomed over me. Her voice was brittle, shards of ice. I could see her hands were tightly clenched. She was angry. One word to Hilja and I would be dead.

I brushed Etti's hair back from her face, hoping that the small gesture would serve as a reminder that Etti needed both of us. Heat flared in Etti's cheeks as if a fever had her in its grip. She was panting, her gaze unfocused. 'The same,' I said.

Etti had stopped speaking some time ago. Now she only growled or grunted, guttural animal sounds of pain interspersed with laboured breathing.

'That is normal,' Johanna had said. The Estonian woman was sitting at the edge of the cassock, every now and then laying her palm across Etti's belly, murmuring reassurances. I wasn't sure if Etti even knew she was there; she had retreated into a place we could not follow. The minutes dripped past in agonising slowness. I could not help thinking of my mother. Had she suffered giving birth to me? Olga had told me she laboured for hours and had bled badly afterwards. Had it been like this, each contraction hemmed in by these waves of calm where Mamochka drifted in a trance, unaware of her surroundings? I saw Olga's hands where Johanna's lay on Etti's stomach and imagined my old nursemaid kneeling beside my mother. I wished she was here now. Olga would know what to say and what to do. Grief squeezed my heart like a fist. Where was my Olga? Where had the train taken her with its cargo of screaming, crying children and their exhausted mothers?

Of all my losses, I knew Olga's would cut the most deeply. Olga had been the last link to Mamochka. Now I was alone, surrounded by strangers. The only one who'd shown me kindness was Etti and she was floating in her own mind, distracted by the brutal pain of childbirth. I'd seen the other women's faces when I opened my mouth to speak my badly phrased Estonian; the curiosity written on their features. Would Kati tell them who I was? She'd thrown me such a look of hatred earlier, I could not now be sure.

I risked a glance at her, wondering if she was here to denounce me. But she was still standing in the doorway, her hand squeezing the wet cloth Johanna had sent her to fetch while it dripped a puddle onto the dirt.

Etti's breathing changed, and once again her body shook. I felt my bones grind together as she squeezed my hand. A scream wrenched itself from her throat. Kati's eyes widened. 'Don't be alarmed,' Johanna said, rubbing Etti's back. 'Wait for the pain to pass.' When it did, Etti eased back, her eyes open but sightless.

'You seem so confident,' Kati said, shifting her legs beside the old woman so that they were tucked up beside her. Her pale hair was pulled into a thick braid like a sheaf of wheat that hung down her back. It was the sort of style I had worn when I was younger and I had attended the Young Pioneers, the kind of style the girls at Model School No. 25 would have teased each other for wearing. But it suited her, softening the sharp yellow-green of her eyes. A few knotted strands of pale hair had escaped the weave. She tucked them in away with impatient fingers. 'I always imagined Aunt Juudit would be here, doing this, helping to bring Etti's baby into the world. Now I find it is me who must help her. And strangers. And a Russian girl.' She lifted her chin, levelling her gaze at me. 'She trusts you.'

'I don't know why,' I said. 'I don't deserve any of her pity. Or yours.'

'She said that you helped her save Aunt Juudit.' Kati spread one of the blankets out on her lap, picking stray hairs from it.

'I tried.' I lifted a shoulder. 'I failed.'

'It's not what your father would have wanted you to do.'

'Sometimes we have to do what is right,' I said. 'Sometimes it's more important to do right, than to be right.'

Kati said nothing.

Etti's breathing shifted, changed. She began to low like an animal, the sound digging under my skin and entering my bones.

'The pain is coming now,' I said, partly to her, partly to myself. I could feel it cresting within her, like a wave carrying a tiny shell on its lip. I was hardly aware of how I knew, but I was somehow certain that the crescendo of agony ripping her apart must soon reach its peak.

Kati watched us, her eyes wide.

Etti's scream filled the hut. It seemed such a long time before she released my hand. When she did, we were both gasping.

Johanna moved herself, lifting up onto her haunches. 'You must unplait her hair,' she said to Kati, who merely stared at her. 'It will ease the birth pains,' Johanna continued, rubbing her hands with a cloth Liisa had given her. 'We should really be in a sauna.'

'I will do it.' Letting go of Etti's hand, I carefully unknotted the strands of her hair, allowing them to fall across my lap. I used my fingers to unfasten the tangles, stroking with smooth movements before remembering with a wrench of my heart that this was the way Olga had always soothed me. The enormity of her sacrifice was like a sudden blow. My fingers seized, tangled in the copper strands.

Holding Etti's skirt over her knees, Johanna spread a blanket across her own lap. 'You will need to push soon,' she told Etti. 'There will be great pain, but listen to your body – it will guide you.'

Etti tossed her head, her hair spilling over my knees. 'I can't. Kati!' Her voice cut the air, as thin as a razor. Kati shifted instantly to her side. She clasped her cousin's hand, wincing at the intensity of Etti's grip.

'I'm here, dearest.'

Etti screamed again and then sank back onto the pallet, her breaths filling the air. 'You promised to sing for me,' she said at last, her voice a croak.

'I did?' Kati's hand fluttered to her throat.

'Yes. You said, if Mama forgot the words, you would do it. Remember?' Between the cries, Etti's voice was dry from the effort of voicing her pain. Another scream tore itself from her lips, whirling around the makeshift room, howling like the wind caged in a glass lantern.

Kati cleared her throat. She opened her mouth, but nothing came out but a squeak, a tiny sound that fizzled then died like an ember winking out.

In the sudden silence, Etti began to cry. 'I want to die,' she sobbed. 'Please. I can't endure this.' Her body bucked, driven by invisible forces. I looked desperately at Kati but she was frozen, helpless to do anything but watch. Rolling onto her knees, Etti clawed at the ground beyond the pallet, her fingers raking the earth.

I could not bear to see her suffering, this girl I had met just a day ago, this girl who had no husband, no parents. Something kindled in my throat. It started with a word; I strung it together to make more. Soon it was a sentence, a song I didn't even know I could remember. I heard it in my mother's voice, and it was as if she were moving through me, her spirit pouring out in a gush of song. Or as if we were singing an old lullaby together in Estonian, walking through the avenue of linden trees towards the greenhouse outside the Kremlin's walls.

> *Slumber gently my birdie*
> *I am watching over you*
> *I will not leave your bedside*
> *Now, go off to sleep*
> *In the morning, the wing of an angel*
> *Will wipe sleep from your brow.*

I paused to wait until Etti's next screams had subsided and she lay back, sobbing.

Sleep gently my birdie
You are without worries
Your eyes are still innocent
The world is still undiscovered
In the morning, the wing of an angel
Will wipe sleep from your brow.

It was a song Mamochka had sung to me, taught to her by her aunt.

My voice lifted and died until I could not go on. The pain of memory was too raw. I imagined my birth, my mother's voice hoarse with labour. I imagined her holding me, a shiny newborn child in her arms. She had not cared that my father did not want me. Everything that I was, it was due to her and to Olga. I wanted to thank her, for the things she had given me, and to thank Olga for being my mother when I had nobody left to care for me. But it was not possible. They were both so far now from where I was. I could only hope that what Mama saw in me and what Olga remembered did not disappoint them and that perhaps, wherever they were, they could hear my singing and it might soothe them.

Kati's face was streaked with tears. She opened her mouth to speak but Etti's cries blotted out everything. This time all the screams rolled together until they transformed into one long sound, stretched taut. I heard Kati cry out hoarsely, as if she was the one who was ripped apart. She stifled her cry quickly with her fist. Sunshine flickered in through gaps in the lean-to's walls, striking Etti's squirming body with tiny fragments of rainbow light.

'Push, now,' Johanna called, over the endless roar.

A gush of blood and fluid soaked the blanket on Johanna's knees. 'Push,' she commanded. Etti's legs were shaking so hard the pallet began to rip beneath the pressure, the loose stitches coming apart so the pine needles stuffed inside spilt out onto the ground. Adrenalin surged through my body. I gripped the skirt of my dress, twisting it in my fingers. Etti's cries were so piercing, I feared she was dying. I called on Olga and my mother, praying for them to help her and heard, very faintly, my mother's voice.

She was singing.

Moments passed as, inch by slow inch, Etti's baby emerged until at last it slid out into Johanna's waiting hands. Deftly, Johanna cut the cord with Hilja's knife, then bundled the infant into the blanket, wiping the baby's eyes and face with the corners of a rag. Johanna's face was calm, but her shoulders had lost their stiff look. I guessed she had been worried, but had not wanted to alarm us. My own body felt weak and insubstantial. I knew I had witnessed what so many other women had seen before me and yet the experience was unique. Sacred. Etti's baby would never be born again. This was her moment of triumph; hers and Etti's. Even Johanna, who must have seen many births as a midwife, was smiling now and her eyes were warm with excitement.

'She is a beauty,' she said admiringly, touching the baby's cheek with her thumb. 'A girl. Is there a name?'

'Leelo,' Etti said in a weary voice. 'It's what my mother would have wanted.' I saw Kati clasp Etti's hands, their fingers meshing.

'Leelo.' Johanna hefted the baby, testing her weight. 'Means *song*. A fine name.'

As if she agreed, Leelo began to grizzle, making soft yelping noises. 'Here,' Johanna said, holding out the bundle for Etti to take. Etti tried to reach up her arms but they flopped beside her. She shook her head. 'Kati, you hold her. I'm too tired.'

Kati glanced at me, as if seeking reassurance. I shrugged slightly. I knew as much as her about what happened after babies were born. Etti had sunk back against the bed, her eyes closed.

'She will need milk,' Johanna advised. 'Best put her to the breast now.'

Kati hesitated, then carefully laid the child upon Etti's chest, unbuttoning her blouse with one hand. 'Etti,' she said. 'You must feed her.'

'But I'm so tired.' Etti shook her head. 'I can't.'

'Like this.' Johanna lifted the baby easily from Kati's arms, positioning her so that her tiny mouth could close over Etti's nipple. Etti sighed but did not open her eyes. The baby's hair was the colour of wet sand, streaked through with blood. When she had suckled for a while, she pulled away. Kati lifted her off Etti's chest, holding her carefully. Still Etti said nothing.

'Let her rest,' Kati said quietly as she lifted the baby in her arms. Together, we peeked at her face. She was tiny but perfectly formed. While Johanna delivered the afterbirth and then bundled it away, Liisa handed Kati a damp cloth. Together, we wiped the remaining crusts of blood and mucus from the baby's face.

'She is an angel,' Kati said, kissing the baby's soft cheek. 'A miracle.' I heard the wonder in her voice and felt it shift beneath my own skin. Yes, it was a miracle to be born after a night of such heartache. *How could anyone want to hurt her?* I thought, touching her tiny ear with my thumb. How could anyone who had witnessed the act we had just seen be so twisted by fate that they could think of harming something so pure? And Johanna, Liisa, Kati . . . all those women who had helped bring her into the world. What had they done to deserve deportation? To have their lives cut short or be banished to a far-flung place as Joachim had been, as Olga had been? My father had caused this misery; my real father.

I had a vision of him shouting down the telephone wire at Captain Volkov. What would he do when he realised I was missing? Would Captain Volkov send Lieutenant Lubov after me? Lubov would tell them I had been at the station. Perhaps he'd even seen me with Helle and the others. If he sent his soldiers and agents after me, they would eventually track me here. I knew suddenly that I could not stay any longer, surrounded by the thick stench of blood, haunted by the terrible truths that had blinded me until now. Stumbling past Kati, I staggered out of the hut towards a knot of people sitting side-by-side near the remains of the fire, catching the last of its warmth. They looked at me curiously. I edged past them towards a small copse of trees near a bucket of water on a tree stump, their muttering following in my wake.

I leant against the scratchy bark of a tree trunk and closed my eyes.

I would have to leave. I would have to go on alone, with only my memories for company. I'd not even been able to return to the townhouse to retrieve Mama's volume of poems or her photograph. Joachim's book. All the mementos of my past were gone. Everything except the shawl and –

My hand flew to fumble in the pocket of my dress. *The letter.*

I pulled it out, fingers trembling. The envelope crackled in my hands.

I stared down at the unfamiliar handwriting. My mother's

name was printed first, followed by our address at the House on the Embankment. Flipping the envelope over, I withdrew the contents; a crinkled piece of writing paper, tissue thin.

I unfolded it carefully, aware of how my heartbeat had slowed, how the sounds of the camp seemed to have faded.

The words were all in Estonian, black symbols like scattered twigs. One of the hardest languages to learn, Etti had remarked. But I could read every word. It was as if my mother had prepared me for this moment.

My dearest Ana,

How good of you to write and tell me of the safe delivery of your little girl. Lydia. A beautiful name. And Volkova! The wolf. I know she will be a strong girl. I am so pleased to hear you are both fine. How does she look? Is she dark or fair? Does she have your eyes? I'm sorry. Too many questions. You must forgive me. I do feel I know you, after so long. Does she sleep? Is she a good child? Enjoy this special time. In a year's time, you will not know her. I can tell you this because I already see my own granddaughter changing. When she was born, she slept much. Now she is always watching, always reaching, wanting to touch and experience the world for herself. She loves best to watch me knit; she thinks the needles are playthings. One day she will hold them herself. I look forward to that day. I look forward to teaching her to make shawls, as I taught you. I suppose you don't knit now. You must be too busy. But I hope that when you wear the shawl I helped you make you recall our time together with fondness. I too miss those days. I miss Haapsalu, its little winding streets and the promenade and the bandstand where the musicians played. You were a good pupil. You had the eye for patterns. Such a shame we did not get to spend more time together. I encourage you to write again, when you feel stronger. And remember you are always welcome to stay with us if you visit Tartu. I hope our paths will one day cross again.

Yours in good faith,

Elina

The letter ended with an address in Tartu I did not recognise. But at least the missive revealed the link between my mother and Elina, the mysterious woman who had taught her to knit and gifted her the little book of poetry.

I stared at the letter a moment longer. It was strange to read about myself, even stranger to imagine Mamochka sitting at her writing desk, penning the story of my birth to this woman, her friend. How tragic that Mama had never seen her again. I could almost feel the burden of her sadness as she waited and waited for a reply, then the hope when the letter arrived.

I tucked the letter back into my pocket and touched the shawl at my throat.

It was time for me to go.

Every minute I stayed, I was risking the women's lives, exposing them to danger. Had Etti been through so much only for me to jeopardise Leelo's survival with my presence? Had I learnt nothing from what happened to Joachim?

'Lydia?'

I froze.

'Lydia, from the train station?'

I squeezed my eyes closed, then opened them.

Jakob Rebare stood before me. I recognised his face at once, the soft curls of his hair. Only, this time he did not look like a dishevelled student on his way to class. His features were sharper, his look wary. In his hands, he carried a gun. Blood flecked his jumper. It coated his hands and made tide marks up his wrists.

'It is you. Isn't it?'

We stood very still, facing each other. 'Yes,' I said, at last. 'It's me.'

I thought perhaps he might raise the gun. Would that be so bad? I felt the bite of the bullet nicking my skin, the sting as it buried into my flesh. My heart beat slower, anticipating the flow of blood from the wound.

'Hilja said there was a Russian here.' He blinked. 'I didn't expect it to be you. My sister Kati told everyone you were one of Etti's friends who's been living in Leningrad. Why would she do that?'

'Kati is your sister?' I shook my head in wonder. *Is this a sign, Mamochka*? My mother had told me Jakob was important. Did she want me to stay?

'You will have to ask her.' I nodded over his shoulder at the hut, relief and excitement mingling. 'She's in there. With Etti. And your new baby cousin. For want of a better term.'

Jakob's eyes widened. 'Etti's baby . . .'

'Has been born.' I wiped a tired hand across my eyes. 'Yes. And she is beautiful. Like her mother.'

He shook his head in wonder.

'I am going to clean up,' I told him, aware of the blood

soaking my clothes. 'I have not told anyone else of my connection to Captain Volkov. You can shoot me. Or report me. The choice is yours.'

I turned towards the water tub.

When I looked back, he was staring after me. But he neither raised his gun, nor called for Hilja.

The water in the tub was brown. A thin layer of grey scum floated on the surface. I hesitated a moment, before plunging my hands in. This was life now, as Hilja had said last night in the cottage. There would be no warm scented baths in porcelain tubs. There would be no soft mattresses and no dresses with collars of Ukrainian lace. I let the water soak over my arms, lathering with the tiny scrap of grey soap beside the tub. Something crawled across my neck. I reached up and felt behind my ear. My skin tickled. I pinched my fingers together and drew out a tiny brown spider which had been hiding beneath the dark-red mass of my hair. Its legs were drawn up over its body, its many eyes blinking. I flicked it away, horror tugging at my stomach. My scalp prickled. I could feel more of them shifting there; my fingers had disturbed them. They'd probably leapt on me as I stood beneath the trees. Before I thought better of it, I plunged my head into the cold water, relishing the rush of the liquid across my tingling scalp, trying to obliterate the insects along with the guilt in my heart.

Refugees continued to flood into the camp as the day went by. We watched them stumble between the rocks, many of them bleeding. Most of them were women wearing shocked looks on their faces and dragging exhausted-looking children behind them or carrying babies wrapped in blankets, towels or tablecloths. Anything they had been able to find at the last minute before they fled. The few men who did come were elderly folk assisted by their daughters or wives. Some of them brought suitcases, others knapsacks. Some brought nothing at all, just their aching bodies and their tears, their stories of watching their husbands and sons loaded into police wagons before they ran into the forest, not knowing what awaited them but unable to turn back for fear they would be dragged off and shot or thrown onto the trains headed east. One adolescent girl told us about seeing the train pass through town and about the notes which had littered the sleepers in its wake; balled up bits of paper containing scrawled letters to loved ones who had not been able to say goodbye. The young girl had collected as many as she could with her mother and brought them to the camp in her knapsack, hoping she could reunite them with their intended recipients, assuming some of them had made it to the camp where we were staying. Although the women all gathered around her, each one of us taking a letter to decipher, it seemed like a hopeless task. Thousands of Estonians were being deported all over the country. Not just in Tartu, but in Tallinn, Estonia's capital city, and other places I had never heard of. Reuniting their letters with those left behind seemed too great a challenge when survival was at stake.

'Here.' I handed the scrap of paper back to Kati. I felt sick to my stomach. 'It's for a woman called Arina.'

Kati took the letter in her hand. Her eyes skimmed the page. She bit her lip as if she might cry, before placing it in the growing pile of papers on the floor of the lean-to.

It was from a woman called Noora whose children had been staying at her sister's farm when she and her husband were arrested. The letter was addressed to her sister.

We are in a train, the woman wrote, *which sat at the station for four hours before it finally left. It is hot and airless. There's no food and no water. Babies cry because their mothers' breasts are empty. We do not know where we are headed. Please keep my children safe for me. Kiss them each night. Tell them I will never forget them.*

There was nobody called Arina in the camp that we knew. The letter would go back into Riina's knapsack. Perhaps one day it would reach Arina, or perhaps it would not. Her children might never know what happened to her, whether she was killed or deported. They might wonder each night where she was, how she was suffering, their thoughts circling as they imagined the worst.

'I heard they are deporting people from Lithuania and Latvia, too.'

I turned to find Jakob standing in the doorway. His presence made the blood rush up into my cheeks. In the hours after his return, I had found myself so on edge I could not eat or rest as I waited for him to turn me in. I'd sat stiffly beside the dead embers of the fire, waiting for my damp hair to dry, anticipating the shout and then the scuffle of feet outside the lean-to. But so far nothing had occurred. Now it was almost evening, the blue sky shot through with pink, the moon a slim white fingernail glowing brighter as each minute passed.

I reached for another letter, trying to make myself invisible but I felt Jakob's attention shift to me.

'Five thousand at least from Riga,' he said. 'Perhaps more.'

'Oh, no.' Kati sighed. She sniffed, rubbing at the tip of

her nose with her thumb. 'So many gone.'

I stayed silent.

On the mattress behind us, Etti's baby made a small noise. We all glanced over. Leelo was tucked into Etti's arm, swaddled in a blanket. She was beginning to stir, nudging the blanket with her tiny limbs. She looked so small and alive, her skin so pink, it was hard to believe that only yesterday she had been waiting to be born. Etti's eyelids fluttered open as Leelo's movements grew more restless. I watched Etti's eyes dart round, resting on each of our faces, before she looked down at the child cradled in her arms.

Kati reached out her hand and patted Etti's leg gently. 'Etti? Leelo needs feeding.'

'Yes.' Etti nodded slowly, but she was still staring at Leelo as if she was a rare animal who had come close. Etti's blonde hair was matted, and hung limp over her shoulders. She pulled herself up higher on the bed, rubbing at her tired eyes with her free hand.

'Yes. Feeding.' Holding the baby in one arm, she began to unbutton her blouse. Her fingers fumbled clumsily at the buttons. Leelo began to slip awkwardly off the cot. I reached out automatically and scooped her up. She weighed no more than the expensive porcelain dolls I had played with as a child. Her blue eyes latched onto me and she blinked slowly, like a person waking from a pleasant dream. I heard Jakob cough behind me and Kati's brief intake of breath.

Too late, I realised my mistake. Fear engulfed me. I pressed the baby quickly into Kati's arms, muttering apologies. I could not look up to meet Jakob's eyes but I saw him turn swiftly and march away, leaving an awkward silence behind him broken only by the sounds of Leelo's hungry yelps.

'It's all right,' Kati said to the grizzling Leelo. 'Shhh. It's all right, now.' She glanced at me warily and I sensed the fragile trust between us unravelling. Had Jakob gone to tell the others? She looked away as Etti held out her arms for the child and brought her to her chest.

I stood up and walked outside. If I was going to be executed, I did not want Etti or Leelo to witness it. I would go as far away from them as possible. Etti had seen enough violence and I did not want Leelo's first experiences of the world to be of bloodshed.

Darkness was closing in outside. Some of the women had rebuilt the fire in the centre of the camp, lighting bits of kindling and throwing them in until a blaze crackled. It was summer and warm but people gathered around it anyway, leaning against each other, their hands fanned against the flames as if they were trying to burn away the bad memories. Liisa handed out small mugs of water and ladles of vinegary broth that people slurped before passing on to their neighbours. Some people were crying while others held each other, talking softly or humming. I caught snatches of their songs, the words both familiar and strange. I had never imagined to hear my mother's language spoken again.

Nobody spoke to me, but nobody came to kill me either. I tried to see Jakob, to make him from the few men moving about but he remained invisible. I huddled as close to the fire as I dared, letting the heat lick up my arms and fill my belly with warmth. I felt utterly alone, apart from the group despite the fact that I understood what they were saying. One man began to mutter curses at the Russians, heaping bad omens upon them. Other voices called out in agreement.

One woman spat in the dirt and vowed to kill as many

Russians as possible if she was captured, even if it meant dying herself. In a tearful voice she recounted how her husband had been reported by a neighbour because he refused to hand over their last cow, which they kept for milk and cheese. The woman's husband had been arrested and the cow butchered into parts and carted off.

Her voice shook as she clenched and unclenched her hands, trembling with unspent rage. 'His life was worth less than a stupid cow! The first Russian I see will be slaughtered. I do not need a weapon. I will use my hands, so help me!'

I winced as if her words were rocks against my skin and shifted away until I could not hear. I could not blame her. Until four days ago, I had not known any better. I'd supposed that the people reported had done something wrong; their arrest was proof enough. And if they were innocent, they would be pardoned. I knew the truth now. My own Russianness felt like a mark upon my skin. I shuffled closer to the fire, wondering what it would take, how many years of regret and guilt, to wash away the stain.

'Careful. Too close and you'll catch alight.' I turned to find Kati's brother standing over me. My pulse sped up. I unknotted my hands from around my knees, ready to shield my face and waited for him to point his gun. Instead he fell to his knees beside me and slung his rifle onto the pine needles criss-crossing the ground.

I watched him, muscles tensed. But he did not seem aggressive. Cautiously, I lowered my hands and hugged my knees again.

'You didn't tell me your mother was Estonian.' Jakob splayed his fingers before the fire. They were clean now, the blood washed away. 'I thought you were pure Russian through and through.'

'It makes little difference. It doesn't change what I am. Who my father is.' I hunched away from him, holding my hand out, the heat licking my skin. A small ember drifted from the fire and stuck to my palm. I cried out and snatched my hand away, curling it in my lap.

'Let me see.' Jakob held out his hand. Reluctantly, I allowed him to uncurl my fingers. It throbbed and stung where the ember had touched it. A tiny spot of red burnt in the centre like a jewel.

'I wasn't judging you. Does it hurt?'

'No, it doesn't,' I said, trying to pull my hand away. Looking back at the people on the other side of the fire, I lowered my voice. 'You might not judge me, but they will. I don't belong here.'

Jakob smiled. It was a sad smile, laced with sympathy. 'Your mother was Estonian. You didn't kill anyone. And you tried to save Juudit. I would say you belong well enough.'

I shook my head. 'You don't understand.'

Jakob lifted his eyes. 'Try me.'

I opened my mouth but nothing came. Jakob waited, his hand curled around mine, a patient expression on his face. How could I tell him who I really was? I was a secret wrapped in a secret. I did not deserve to be spared.

'You—' I began, then stopped again. 'Everything is clear for you. Russians are bad. Estonians are good.' I bit my lip. 'Things for me are complicated.'

'But you must know that you have chosen. Even if you didn't intend to.' He looked around. 'You've chosen us. It doesn't matter know who you are. You can't go back. We'll keep you safe.'

I wanted to argue with him – nobody could keep me safe from Stalin if he wanted me back – but I could also see the sense in his words. Even if I was caught, I could not return to the world I had grown up in. Joachim's ghost would haunt my memories. And Olga, my Olga, was gone. I allowed my arm to relax a little and felt the slightest bit of pressure of his fingers as he squeezed them and looked back at my hand, as if he was studying it. His breath caressed my palm.

A long moment passed.

'What are you doing?' I said, growing uncomfortable and trying without success to pull my hand away.

Jakob smiled again. 'My grandmother would tell fortunes on New Year's Eve. Don't you want to know what yours says?' Reaching into his pocket, he drew out a handkerchief, which he swiftly knotted over the wound.

'Are you saying that Estonians are as superstitious as Russians?'

'So it would seem.' He released my hand. 'My grandmother called it "luck pouring". We'd use an old bucket and a molten tin. Papa would throw a ladleful of the melted tin into cold water and grandmother would read the shape.'

I leant my head on my knee and watched the flames dance. I was so tired, but so afraid that if I slept, my dreams would be full of blood and death and screams. 'What did she see for you?' I asked.

'Always the same thing,' Jakob said, staring at the fire. I waited. 'Well?' he said. 'Aren't you going to guess?'

I shook my head. 'I don't know. A gun?'

Jakob smiled. 'No. A stork.'

Goosebumps spread across my skin. 'A bird is a bad

omen in Russia,' I said. 'If it taps three times on your window, death is near.'

'A stork, though?' Jakob lifted a handful of dirt and scattered it towards the fire, sending little sparks dancing into the sky.

'I don't know about storks. I've never seen one.'

'Here they are symbols of hope and fertility. Children.' He raised his eyebrows. 'They are good parents, storks,' he continued. 'Both of them. They like to nest on power poles and in rooftops. The women in the knitting circle – my Aunt Juudit and Kati, Grandmother, the others – they had a lace pattern called Stork Stitch, like birds' feet. The Scandis even think there was a stork present at the crucifixion; that it called out as Christ was dying.' He cupped his hands around his mouth. '*Stryket! Stryket!* Have strength!'

Some of the Forest Brothers on the other side of the fire looked around, wondering at the sound.

'Hush!' I said, not wanting to draw attention, but Jakob just chuckled and they turned away.

'I hope to have children one day,' he said after another moment had passed.

I made a sound in my throat, incredulous. 'After everything you have seen, everything you have been through these past few days? How can you say that?'

Jakob shrugged. 'It changes nothing.'

'Are you crazy? It changes everything.' I thought of my mother, taking her own life as I slept in the room down the hall. I thought of her face in the glossy coffin, the terror of realising she was truly gone and would never return. The memory cut deep into my heart. 'It's a foolish statement. To

292

have children . . . and then abandon them to fate. It is . . .' I struggled to find the right words. 'It is reckless and selfish.'

Jakob did not seem troubled by my reaction. His face remained as calm as ever. 'I won't let what has happened alter those parts of my future, Lydia. You should not let it change yours.'

I shook my head at him.

'We have a saying. Perhaps your mother didn't teach it to you. *Igaüks on oma õnne sepp*, Lydia,' he said. 'Everyone is the smith of his – or her – own happiness.'

'Jakob.' He turned. A Forest Brother stood behind us, holding out a tin mug. His face was familiar; I realised with a jolt he was the bandit I had seen during the raid on the train station, the one they had called Kalev. I recalled how different he had seemed to his companions, the way they had looked to him for leadership. The confident way he had spoken and the compassion he had shown in returning the ring to the woman when he might easily have ignored her troubles. His eyes were cold. It was as if the heat from the fire could not reach them. He made a gesture with his hand, shaking the mug for Jakob to take. Jakob hesitated, then took it.

'Vodka. For courage,' the other man said roughly. 'Jaak retrieved it earlier from a fallen soldier.'

'*Aitäh*,' Jakob said. 'Thank you.' Kalev moved away to join his comrades. Jakob tilted the mug, looking into its depths, then raised it to his lips and swallowed. Wiping his mouth with his hand, he held it out to me. There was plenty left. The sharp scent made my stomach contract but I gulped it down anyway.

Heat spread through my body. I settled down onto the ground, not caring how it must look. Pine needles tickled my cheek. The stars spun above me, laced by dark leaves.

'Why do you need courage?' I asked. I held out the mug and Jakob reached for it. The tips of our fingers met.

'We are going out again tonight,' Jakob said, downing the last bit of the vodka. 'There are Russian patrols at the forest's edge. Oskar – that is, Kalev – wants to draw them away from the camps and meeting points. Distract them so the refugees can find their way to us.'

I swallowed, the sour taste of the vodka lingering in my throat. The flames of the bonfire merged and mingled, first arctic blue then red then bright orange like a Catherine wheel. Sleep blurred the edges of my vision.

'Aren't you afraid?' I mumbled.

'I'm more afraid of doing nothing. I don't think my parents should have died just so I could give up and surrender. I don't think Aunt Juudit would be proud of me if I just slunk away like a dog with its tail between its legs. And my grandmother; she would not want us to leave. This was her home. This was where she raised her children and knitted her shawls. These trees, this earth. These forests and lakes. Even if we cannot live in cities, we will live here. Where else would we go?'

I tried to mumble something else – good luck, perhaps – but I was already half-dreaming, my mind weaving images together. I saw a young woman in a lace shawl sitting beside the hearth, holding a nursing infant to her breast, comforting and rocking him before the fire while outside a great stork landed in the yard and shook off its feathers. They floated like snow onto the ground, leaving the stork's pink flesh exposed. The stork straightened up and he was a man, plucked clean, his face like Jakob's, shining with hope. Lifting the infant, the woman ran out to greet him. They kissed and then turned to walk inside, his hand cradled around the head of his infant son.

Something soft drifted over my shoulder. Feathers? Snow? But it was summer.

A blanket. I felt the rough edge of it brush my cheek. A voice whispered in my ear, a spell to banish nightmares.

I slept and my dreams were blank.

Ash Pattern

Kati

'GIVE ME LEELO, KATI.' JAKOB'S VOICE WAS IMPATIENT.

I stared down at the infant's tiny face. A whisper of golden hair clung to her scalp. Her eyes were closed. She grunted in her sleep, disturbed by some nameless dream. I stroked my thumb against her soft skin and she yawned, stirred, then settled back into my arms, a look of deep contentment spread across her face.

Only six days old and she was already disproving everything my mother had warned me about babies; that they screamed all day and all night, that you could not get anything done for watching them. Leelo was a perfect baby. She slept regularly, only waking to be fed and changed. She hardly ever grumbled, happy to be carried about in a sling made from a woollen blanket as we went about the camp doing what was required to keep everything running smoothly, her blue eyes fixed on the clouds that raced overhead. Even now, pressed against my chest while I sat with my brother and Lydia and Etti on a grassy tussock near the edge of camp, she was happy to doze, letting our conversation wash over her while she slept. A length of wire was strung between the trees on which clothes snapped in the breeze, the cotton shirts billowing like clouds.

'Kati?' My brother held out his hands. Just for a moment,

I hesitated, imagining they were stained with rust-coloured blood. But when I blinked, they were clean. His shirt cuffs poked out beneath the long sleeves of his fitted jacket. He looked smart in his brown uniform; a reward for the three Red Army soldiers he had killed in a raid at the edge of the forest the night after the purge. Two of the Forest Brothers accompanying Jakob had been shot that night, lured out by the soldiers who had wounded a farmer and left him crying out for help in his field. Jakob had been forced to listen to the farmer's terrified screaming while Oskar moved back into the forest to gather more men. Jakob's companions had raced out one after the other, trying to reach the man before the bullets of the Red Army soldiers found them. Neither of them had survived. At last, Oskar had come back and a bloody fight ensued, ending at last when the Forest Brothers were able to overpower the soldiers holed up in the farmhouse. The farmer had died of his wounds before they could save him. Back at camp the other Forest Brothers, Oskar included, had hailed Jakob as a hero. Only I knew what the transaction had cost him. Only I knew how the man's screams pierced his dreams, just as the faces of my parents haunted mine.

He jiggled his fingers impatiently. 'Come on. You've not let me hold her once. You've been keeping her all to yourself, just like you used to do when we'd bring kittens home or stray dogs. Do you remember?'

'She's not a stray dog.' I passed her gently to him, relinquishing my hold, already missing the caramel scent of her skin and the way her tiny fingers curled around mine. With a last look of longing, I took my seat on the timber crates we had set up at the edge of the camp, as far away from the latrine as possible. 'And you never looked after them,' I added, unable to stop myself. 'Once we got them home, you'd take off to go fishing and leave me to clean up all their mess. Stray puppies. Those girls you followed around, asking if you could walk them home. It was always the thrill of the chase for you.'

I saw Lydia glance up sharply from the wet blouse she was wringing. She was a different person to the one I had dragged here a week ago. Stress had sharpened her face, drawing out her cheekbones. Or perhaps it was grief. I had heard her mutter in her sleep, calling out for someone called Olga. Sometimes when I woke she was already outside, helping the other women prepare breakfast at the fire, her thick dark hair slick with water and tied with a piece of twine behind her back. So much of her was a mystery, but she seemed unwilling to talk to anyone about much except for Jakob. I'd seen them chatting together when he returned from patrol. He followed her about her chores, sitting behind her while she scraped the remnants of food from the pans into a bucket or scoured blood from the uniforms with a wooden brush.

I caught only fragments of what passed between them, busy as I was with Leelo and caring for Etti, making sure she had clean rags to staunch the blood that continued to flow in the days after the birth. Sometimes it was stories about Tartu or the games we played as children, sometimes Jakob told her jokes. I could not tell whether she encouraged him; she seemed always to wear a frown. But watching her now, I wondered how I had missed it; that bright kindling of yearning in her eyes. Jakob saw it, too.

'All lies,' he said quickly. Lydia's shoulders relaxed. She pegged the blouse out on the line. 'Kati loves to exaggerate.'

My brother held the sleeping Leelo close to his chest, nestling her into his arm. A smile flickered across his face. 'Etti.' He glanced over at where my cousin sat, staring up at the creaking branches of the spruce trees. 'Tell Kati she's a liar.'

Etti did not turn around.

Sunlight glinted on her blonde hair. The leaves on the branches sighed overhead.

Jakob glanced at me. I shrugged helplessly.

If Leelo had adjusted to the rigours of life quicker than other infants, Etti seemed to be struggling to find her way back. The loss of her mother had affected her deeply. Some nights she woke screaming, bathed in sweat, sobbing for Aunt Juudit. She would not be quietened until I stumbled from my pallet to sit beside her and comfort her with soothing platitudes. I could not tell her how hard I found it, to be woken suddenly from a deep sleep. It would not be fair to complain about the grief which shook my body each time I remembered how Mama and Papa had died. In dreams, I could pretend that my parents were still alive. Poor Etti could not even find comfort in her dreams.

Often, she would sit in the grass, staring at the entrance to the camp as if she expected Aunt Juudit to come waltzing in, singing 'L'Internationale' at the top of her voice. Leelo was the only thing that brought her joy, but sometimes she held the baby so tight I was afraid she would crush her, and Leelo seemed to prefer being carried to being held in one place, squeezed against her mother's chest.

I felt Jakob move restlessly beside me, Leelo in his arms. We both wanted to help Etti, but what could we do? She needed something else to keep her busy, to hold despair at bay. I wished we had a gramophone or a *kannal*, the six-stringed instrument which sounded a little like a lute. Surely there was somebody in the camp who could pluck a few strings. But nobody had thought to bring anything like that. We had fled with essentials; in my knapsack were saucepans, a ladle, a sharp knife. Oskar's gloves, which I now kept under my pillow. Nothing of comfort. Nothing that would say to Etti: *Life is worth living. There is still beauty in the world.*

My searching mind lit suddenly on the final addition to my knapsack: the samplers. Leaving Leelo with Jakob, I ran to the lean-to, where I unknotted my bag. I poked about inside until my fingers found the soft lace. I drew out the samplers and my grandmother's needles and the last ball of yarn I had snatched before we fled.

I hurried back to where Etti was sitting and laid the yarn in her lap. Etti looked down. I handed her the needles, and her fingers trembled. She held them awkwardly, one in each hand.

'Here.' Holding her fingers carefully, I made the slipknot with Etti's right hand and then brought her left up to meet it, the slender needle like an arrow. My grandfather had carved those needles for my grandmother from the boughs of a lilac bush. They were delicate but firm, pliable and stubborn; just like my grandmother. As I brought them together, I heard Etti sigh and felt her breath brush against my skin. 'That's it.'

As she began to knit, her fingers finding the rhythm, I dug through my grandmother's samplers until I found the one with the peacock tails. Placing it across Etti's knee, I stepped back, pleased to hear the steady sound of the needles working against each other like the ticking of a clock.

'I was hoping you would teach me.'

I turned to find Lydia beside me, her gaze fixed on the lace in Etti's lap. She was twisting her own shawl around her hands. I had noticed she never took it off, not even to wash it.

'I'd be glad to teach you,' I said. 'But alas, there's no yarn. Only this one ball.'

Lydia Volkova glanced down. Her fingers moved across the shawl, hesitating. Then she pulled it off her neck. 'Could you unravel this?'

I stared at her. 'You want to undo it?'

She lifted a shoulder. 'As long as you promise you'll teach me to knit it again the same way.' She held it out to me.

'It's fine work.' I took it, running my thumb over the lace *nupps*, unable to help the admiration that crept into my voice. 'This little pattern here, this paw print, is like my grandmother's. It was her signature. But others might have used the same motif, of course.'

Lydia watched me shake it out. 'It belonged to my mother. She made it herself.' She hesitated, as if deciding whether she should say more. 'A woman taught her to knit when she was a child; they wrote to each other for years. This shawl is the last of my mother's things . . . If I learn to knit it again, it will make me closer to her somehow.'

'I will unpick it tomorrow,' I said. 'Then I can show you how to start. You'll need to learn some basic stitches first though, before you can make a pattern as complicated as wolf's paw.' I folded the shawl carefully. 'It's my turn on food duty. When that is done, perhaps, I will have some free time this evening.'

Lydia lips curved. 'Thank you.'

301

I found myself smiling back at her. Etti's needles clicked beside us. Bees hummed through the flowers nearby, weaving on the air currents.

'Jakob.'

I looked up. Oskar was standing a few feet away from us. The sun shimmered around him. 'You're needed,' he said to my brother. 'We are moving out again.'

He stood very straight and stiff. His gaze swivelled towards me, lingering for a fraction of a second before darting back to Jakob.

I dropped my eyes, a feeling of hope expanding in my chest. Every day, I had expected Oskar to come to me, but there had simply not been time. Each of my days in the camp had been spent caring for others, especially Leelo and Etti, but also the refugees who arrived with bruises and bleeding shins where they had fallen as they stumbled through the forest escaping the Red Army battalions. I had seen Oskar briefly with the other men, but as they took turns to patrol, he was either preparing to leave the camp or settling down in the lean-to he shared with his fellow fighters. They slept all together like dogs in a pack, their guns resting against the wall, always alert even as they dreamt, always ready to spring up if danger was near. The few times we came face to face, we greeted each other and shared a smile but it was never possible to snatch more than a moment to talk. Hilja was always waiting for Oskar nearby with something that demanded his attention, or else it was Leelo who needed to be changed, her grizzling so loud in my ear I could not hear Oskar's words.

I kept telling myself there would eventually be a time for us to be alone, once the fighting between the Red Army and the resistance fighters died down. News had already filtered through about the number of deportees transported; at least ten thousand from Estonia, fifteen thousand from Latvia and sixteen thousand or more from Lithuania. The Red Army had been less active the past few days, since the trains filled with the exiled began to reach the prison camps. We had heard rumours that they might have caught wind of the German invasion. As each day drew to a close with no further contact from the Germans, though, I began to fear the rumours were incorrect. The German Army certainly had their hands full already fighting the British and their allies in the Middle East and unleashing the last of their air raids over London. I had not been able to get the image out of my mind of the night sky lit up by raining bombs. It seemed a dreadful omen of things to come, if the Russians did not give up Estonia easily. It felt as if our country was a child's boat caught in a riptide. Whichever way the currents turned, that was where we must go.

With so much uncertainty, there seemed little time for Oskar and I to share our private thoughts. I did not expect today to be any different.

As Jakob rose to his feet, I held out my arms to take Leelo back. To my surprise, Oskar stayed my hand and turned to Lydia. 'Lydia, can you take her? I want to speak with Kati alone.' Lydia's eyes widened at being addressed. I knew she was frightened of Oskar; she ducked her head each time she saw him coming or crossed to the other side of the camp if he entered. I saw her exchange a glance with Jakob, her eyes communicating a message I could not grasp. I watched as Jakob tipped Leelo's sleeping body towards her. Leelo's bottom lip pushed out, pouting in sleep, but she didn't wake when

Lydia's arms slid about her, one hand cupping her small rump. Relieved of the infant, my brother stroked Leelo's small snub of a nose with his thumb and then squeezed Lydia's arm before marching off towards the entrance of the camp where the men were gathering. For a moment, I marvelled at how easily my brother had taken to Leelo, how natural he had looked holding her. I had never thought that one day my brother might want children. I would have laughed a few years ago, if he had spoken the desire aloud. How could a boy look after a child when he could hardly care for himself? But I realised now that without my even noticing, my brother had grown up.

Lydia's gaze lingered on his back, and then, catching my eye, she turned away with Leelo to sit beside Etti on the grass. I drew in a breath, knowing Oskar was waiting.

When I turned to face him, he was smiling. It was so unexpected and pleasant I found myself grinning in return. Before I could speak, he took my hand and led me away from the clearing, threading through the trees near the back of the camp until we were surrounded by their tall trunks, masked a little from view.

Oskar kept my hand captured in his. 'Kati,' he said softly. 'You don't know how I've longed for this.' He raised my hand and turned it over to kiss my wrist. I swallowed, not daring to raise my eyes. Oskar's breath on my skin made me shiver.

'You've been occupied,' I said.

Oskar nodded. He released my wrist. 'Yes. I wanted to come earlier, but there was no time. It would not have been wise. But at last, today, there is cause for celebration.'

'Why?'

Oskar squared his shoulders, a hint of a smile flickering

on his lips. 'The Germans have marched on Russia. Moscow, Leningrad, Stalingrad. All of them will soon belong to the Wehrmacht. The Germans will be here in a day, if not hours. Stalin has already announced the war and the Russians are scrambling to defend their cities. They don't have the resources to defend the territories.'

I gasped. 'Then it is almost over. The Soviet occupation.'

'Yes,' he said. 'The Germans have promised Estonia her freedom. We must of course flush out the remnants of Russian battalions and any remaining Army corps. The Russians are leaving in droves, fleeing like rats from a sinking ship. Some of them are abandoning their posts and fleeing into the forest. We are going out to patrol today and kill as many of them as we can find. Clear the area of any stragglers. We have only to hold on for a little while longer. And then—' He squeezed my hands. 'Then we will finally be free.'

He watched me take in this news, his lips still curved in a smile.

I tried to process what he had said, but my emotions were muddled up. If the Germans and Russians were at war, many people would die. Many innocent people who had nothing to do with the power struggles of two huge nations. But the German invasion meant the end of the Russian brutality in the Baltics. There was hope we could return to our homes and rebuild our lives. Leelo could grow up without the shadow of violence blotting her future. I would not have to sit up late every night, worrying about Oskar and Jakob, imagining their deaths and replaying the horror of my parents' last moments.

I realised I was playing with the lace shawl around my neck, twisting it. Oskar took my hands in his own and drew me in, bringing me slowly closer until we were inches apart and I could trace the fine cupid's bow of his upper lip with my eyes. My breath caught as he leant forward and kissed me. As our lips moved, I could feel the earth spinning. Only Oskar's firm grip on my body kept me from falling.

An urgent longing fluttered in my belly. I made a soft sound, bringing my hands around to clasp his back and press our bodies together. Oskar jumped slightly in surprise. Then I felt his breath quicken. His arm tightened around my waist and his kisses grew deeper, more urgent.

Through the warm haze of pleasure, I observed that this was not like the few other times he had kissed me in the field behind the farmhouse. Back then, the merest brush of our lips had sustained us. Our kisses had been innocent, chaste. There had not been this charge, this invisible heat as our bodies strained together, desire kindling between us.

When at last we broke apart, Oskar groaned and kissed my forehead.

We were both breathing hard. 'You are killing me,' he said. I caught the flicker of his smile, but his words sent a chill over my skin. How could we forget ourselves so entirely when the world was now at war?

I pretended to smooth down my skirt, hoping for a moment to master myself. As I did so, I caught sight of the gun he always wore tucked into the belt at his waist. Although I tried not to stare at it, I could not help but think about the men he had used it on. It was a submachine gun, he had told me in one of our brief exchanges; a gleaming bringer of death given to him by one of the Germans. The others called it *ameeriklane*: the American.

I shivered, wishing he had left it behind at the lean-to but knowing it was a part of him. Even now, when we were safely sheltered in a bower of trees, *Amerikana* was with us, a reminder of the danger that was still present.

Hilja's warning rang out sharply in my head.

You don't know what you will do. What they will make you do.

I glanced over my shoulder, almost certain I would catch her standing there watching us. She followed Oskar everywhere like a faithful hound. But we were still alone, surrounded by the arms of the trees, the camp a grey blur behind the leaves. Insects whirred in the bushes nearby.

'Kati.' I turned back to Oskar. His cheeks were pink, his blue eyes very bright. 'You know what I will ask you.' He slid his arms around me again. His kisses fluttered against my neck, as soft as moth's wings. I wound my fingers through his hair. 'You must promise to marry me,' he said, his words flushing hot on my skin. 'No matter what happens.'

No matter what happens.

A spasm of pain pulsed through me. I drew back. It was agony, but I could not banish the memory that had reared up suddenly at his words. I saw again Hilja's face in the guttering light of the candle, her scarred skin. Her warning, branded in my mind.

With an effort, I stepped away from him. 'I can't promise that. Not now. When you return, we will speak of it.'

Oskar blinked. A look of confusion obscured his features. 'I don't understand. Is there someone else?'

'No. Of course not. I just feel that it's not safe,' I began, and then stopped. Oskar's shoulders had stiffened. I tried again. 'It's . . . It's dangerous. For both of us, but more so for you. A promise like that . . . it carries risk. There is no certainty that the Germans will succeed—'

Oskar made a small scoffing sound and opened his mouth to argue.

'Just listen.' I drew in a deep fortifying breath. 'Please. You can't afford to be distracted. You can't be thinking about marrying me while you are heading off into a fight. Can you really afford to put your life at risk? The lives of your friends?'

Oskar's mouth pinched. 'That's not your choice to make, Kati.' I could see he was clenching and unclenching his hands. 'You can't tell me who to love. Who not to love. If you don't love me back, then that's your decision. But do not try to tell me my own heart.'

'Oskar . . .' I shut my eyes. I willed myself to be strong, to foster arguments which could convince him that we should be patient, that we should wait. But I could not fight the powerful tide of his words. I felt tears gathering behind my eyelids.

Oskar clasped my hands. He turned them over and kissed them in turn, his lips softly caressing my palms.

'*You* have been my good-luck charm,' he said. His voice was rough, raw with emotion. 'It wasn't the gloves. It was the memory of you. Your stories and your history lessons. Your dreams and your knitting. It was knowing you were still there, safe in your parents' house while I was shivering in the forest, trying to forget what I saw the day my mother and Aime were killed. Trying to forget my own cowardice at failing to save them. It was knowing you were alive that kept me going. You think that I'll be daydreaming while I am dodging Russian bullets? No. I'll be thinking of us. Together.

Our future. If I could be sure . . .' his voice wavered. 'If you could promise me that you will be mine. That you will be waiting for me. Then I promise you that I will come back.'

I opened my eyes. The light was green and hazy, the air wood-scented and full of balsam. Oskar was waiting for my answer.

I made myself smile. It was not so hard, if I imagined the cottage Oskar had once promised he would build with the heart-shaped windows; if I thought back to those days which tasted of strawberries and smelt of sweet hay and sunshine. I pushed away the image of him lying broken in a field, screaming for me as the blood drained from his body from half a dozen bullet wounds. It was not I who had to face death. All I had to endure was the pain of loss if Oskar's promise could not be fulfilled. Surely, I could give him this, a vow which might sustain him through the next few days of horror and fear? My sacrifice was small. It was all I could offer, and I should offer it gladly, not think of myself when a greater threat loomed.

'All right,' I said. 'I promise. Yes.'

I heard him release a breath. 'All right.' In his relief, he kissed me clumsily, his mouth meeting the edge of my lips before he drew away and picked up his cap from where he had dropped it upon the pine needles. I tidied my hair with my fingers, ignoring a small voice which whispered that it was a bad omen for our last kiss to have been so weak. Oskar stood straighter with his cap on. It shadowed his eyes, but I could see he was smiling. *Good*. He reached out and brushed my cheek with his thumb. '*Hüvastijätt*, then, Kati.'

Farewell. The sound of his footsteps crunching away tore at the last of my resolve. Sinking to my knees, I allowed myself to cry. Finally. For my parents, for Aunt Juudit. For Etti and her husband and their child, born in the wilderness. For the fear I held in my heart for Oskar and my brother. For all the things I had lost and the things I still had left to lose.

When I finally stumbled back into the camp, it was to find Lydia's sour face waiting for me. She marched towards me, her hand shielding her eyes.

'Where have you been?' she said, her eyes flashing. 'You were such a long time. Etti was worried. I've left Leelo with her while I came to look for you.' It was more emotion than I had seen her display in the week we had known each other. I almost wanted to crow with triumph; at last, her exterior was cracking. But I was too drained to fight.

'The Germans are marching on Russia,' I said wearily.

Lydia stared. 'Truly?'

'Yes. The Russians are retreating, Oskar said. It's nearly over. The Germans have promised to return freedom to Estonia.'

'And you believe them?' Lydia said.

'Of course.' The cynical tone in her voice irritated me like nails scratching on glass. 'Why would they lie?'

Lydia folded her arms. 'They gave Stalin their word and look what happened.'

'Stalin is a monster,' I snapped. 'As is anyone associated with him. An alliance with the Germans guarantees us our independence. Can you really be so stupid? The Estonian home guard will be restored to full power. A new government will be formed.'

'And the atrocities the Germans have perpetrated in Poland? In France?' Lydia's face was flushed. 'What about their stance on Jews? What about Etti? And Leelo?'

My stomach lurched. Lydia's question was a valid one. 'They won't be harmed. David was Jewish but Etti never converted; Leelo is not considered Jewish. Besides, that won't happen here. Once order is restored, the Germans will leave. There's no reason to believe the Jews are in danger here. Estonia has always welcomed people of all faiths.'

Lydia continued to glare at me until at last I pushed past her, making for the wash stand where I could scrub my tear-streaked face. 'Oskar is going out now to patrol with the others. There are battalions everywhere. The Russian army is desperate.'

'Jakob, too?'

'Of course.'

Lydia's face knotted with worry. 'Then I must find him and say goodbye properly. In case something happens.'

'Why?' I stopped in front of her, blocking her path. Lydia froze. Confusion and panic fought for control over her features. 'First Etti, now Jakob,' I said.

She opened her mouth, but then closed it again.

'Don't you have your own family?' I said, clenching my fists so that I would not be tempted to shake her. 'Don't you have anyone you can go back to? You needn't be here. I don't know why you stayed. Your duty to Etti is over. Long past.'

I glared at her, my breathing ragged.

'Your friends are leaving,' I continued, relentless, hissing with rage. 'You should go with them. Consider your future. What will happen when the Germans get here? You think they will pardon you?' I lowered my voice so that the people around us could not hear. 'Do you think I have forgotten who you are? Who your father is?'

I saw Lydia's face crumple. I wanted to stop, but it was as if some demon possessed me. Black words and thoughts poured from my mouth, an unstoppable flood of pain.

'You may have fooled Etti and Jakob, but not me.' I folded my arms across my chest. 'I see you, Lydia Volkova. The wolf in sheep's clothing. That's what Volkov means, doesn't it? Wolf? Go back where you belong. Your place is not here.'

A buzzing filled my ears as I finally faltered, the words drying up on my tongue.

Somewhere in the distance, I heard the rattle of gunfire.

Lydia took a step back.

Somebody shouted, and we both turned to the sound. Some of the Forest Brothers had emerged from their lean-to, their boots slapping the ground, kicking up dust. They filed in one line towards the entrance to the camp, slipping between the narrow tree trunks. I saw Jakob among them, the familiar mop of hair sticking out beneath his cap. He caught my eye, raised his arm. Then he was gone, following the others out into the forest.

I watched Oskar emerge last; he raised his head, searching for my face. When he found it, he grinned and I saw his teeth flash white in the sun. I tried to paste on a warm smile in return but my lips felt stiff and frozen. Thankfully, Oskar had already turned away. He strode with purpose towards the entrance, *Amerikana* clutched beneath his arm. My heart gave a tug of longing. Then he vanished, too, and the only partisan left standing in the yard was Hilja, her face creased with scars.

I became aware of Hilja's eyes searing into me. Of course, she must have seen the change in Oskar. He was usually so serious and just now his face had glowed as if he had won the war single-handedly. My stomach turned uneasily.

Turning back to Lydia, I found she had gone. Run off, no doubt, to tell Etti how I had mistreated her. A small coil of guilt wormed its way around my insides. I could imagine my grandmother shaking her head at me, her face clouded with disapproval. But was I not allowed a moment, one opportunity to express everything that was in my heart; the disappointment, the grief, the jealousy? The fear I would have to live with until Oskar and Jakob returned?

Was I not allowed an outburst of my own?

I knew the answer, as surely as if my grandmother was standing before me, or as if she had sent her wolf to judge me in her place.

Moss Pattern

Lydia

I RAN. TEARS BUBBLED UP. I BRUSHED THEM AWAY WITH the heels of my hands.

Etti was not in the lean-to; she was standing with Johanna near the makeshift kitchen, giving Leelo a sponge bath from water heated over the fire's embers. I bit down on a desperate desire to join them.

Kati's words whirled round and round in my mind.

Go back and join them!

I couldn't stay.

Snatching up my mother's shawl, I bundled it together with the letter Olga had saved and an apple whose skin was already beginning to pucker. I slipped them both into a small bag Johanna had given me, sewn from the remnants of a torn skirt. On the threshold of the lean-to, I looked back at the tiny space which had been my home for the past week. The bedding was mussy from where Etti had been sitting earlier, feeding Leelo. A baby rattle lay on the floor, a small item one of Liisa's children had given us to keep Leelo amused.

On the pallet where Kati slept were her knitting needles. They were not the best ones; I had seen her show those to Etti. I remembered how she had held them between her fingers in the evenings when she knitted while the other women talked and sang songs and cleaned up the camp. These ones were short and made from apple wood.

Would she miss them?

I picked them up, expecting someone to lay a hand on my shoulder. Now I was a thief as well as a liar.

Pushing them into the bag, I ran outside. I kept to the edges of the camp, my head lowered until I reached the entrance. I saw Hilja some distance away, speaking to Kati. Kati's hair was braided in its usual plait, the sun catching its pale highlights. She was gesturing with her arms, her lithe expressive hands circling in the air. An unspeakable sadness washed over me. I would miss her, even though she hated me. Would miss her voice, softly singing to the baby in the warm darkness of the lean-to. The strength she gave so easily to the women who trudged into the camp, eyes wide with shock and to Etti, when she needed to rally to feed the hungry Leelo. It came to her unconsciously, the ability to issue directives and take charge. I would miss Etti and Jakob, too, Jakob perhaps most of all. He had gone now and I'd not even had a chance to say goodbye. He had not even looked around for me before he left. I'd become used to him hanging about as I washed up and helped Etti with Leelo in the afternoons. Somehow I had fooled myself that we were friends.

But Kati was right. I didn't belong.

I was better off on my own.

I pushed between the trees at the entrance of the camp. The forest danced around me, branches swaying while hidden birds sang. Where would I go? I turned one way and then another. I took a step towards the area where the trees were thinnest. My bag bumped against my leg, as if urging me on.

The grass was marshy. I felt my shoes sink slightly into the muck before I reached firmer ground. At least it was warm. It was summer. I would not need to find real shelter until the air grew cooler. I pushed on, walking until my breath was short. I came to a ring of rocks. The grass was dry.

I sat down, resting my back against a stone. The stone's warmth bled through the back of my dress. Moss grew beneath it, forming a soft mat. The lace collar of my blouse tickled my throat. It was the blouse I had been wearing when I arrived at the camp. The blouse Olga and I had collected from the dressmaker on Staropanskiy Parade. It seemed so long ago. Moscow was a half-forgotten dream. A memory flashed, like the click of a camera. Joachim in the cinema, his face silver from the light of the screen. His warm breath. His hands.

I opened my bag and drew out Mamochka's shawl. I spread it over my lap. My fingers found the edges and I began to unpick the lace. The yarn was thin as a cobweb. It came apart in my hands. I gathered the threads up and put them in the bag as I unravelled it and the longest length of yarn came loose. When enough of it was unpicked, I dug out the needles.

Kati had made it look easy. I'd watched her, trying to be invisible at the back of the group of women, trying my best to conceal my Russian accent although I knew they were curious. Make a loop stitch. Thread the yarn.

I tried it myself. The yarn slipped from the needle. It would not catch.

I tried again. When the yarn hooked, I almost cried out with triumph. But now what? I put the needles together, crossing them as I used to do with the shining cutlery we used in the apartment. No cutlery here. Fingers and mouths.

I had seen Kati earlier helping Etti, reminding her how to slide one stitch onto the other needle, while holding the yarn tight with her little finger to ensure the tension didn't slacken.

I slipped the stitch carefully onto the other needle. My heart filled with pride. I could do this myself. I could remake Mama's shawl. I did not need anyone to help me. If I could do this, I could survive alone. The next stitch slid perfectly onto the needle, a smooth little circle. I smiled. The leaves swayed overhead. Insects hummed in the bushes. I levered the needles together, keeping the yarn wrapped around my pinkie finger, making the small movement needed to create the next stitch. But the yarn soon slipped loose from my finger. I tried to catch it and as I did, the needles pulled too far apart. The stitches slipped off, returning to their original shape. The yarn grew flimsy. All my work was undone.

Frustration clawed at me. I gripped the needles until my fingers ached. My second and third attempts failed, although I got further. My fourth unspooled before I had even made the second stitch.

A sob was building in my chest. Afternoon shadows were slipping through the trees. Soon it would be night time. I wound the yarn around the needles, trying not to look at the damage I had made to my mother's shawl, unpicking the edge of it to try my hand. I shoved it with the needles back into the bag and sat back against the stone. The day's heat still lingered in it. After a little while, I dozed, dreaming of Mamochka with her hands full of wool, dreaming I was not utterly alone in the world.

Angel Pattern

Kati

I MOVED MECHANICALLY THROUGH MY TASKS THAT EVENING, throwing myself into the preparation of dinner for the civilians and Hilja, stirring together a batter of flour and chicken's eggs, spreading it over the griddle to make thin wheat cakes. With a little honey spread over them, they were palatable enough, but tonight of all nights I could not stomach them. After chewing the same piece for what seemed like forever, I managed to choke down a mouthful, then passed the remainder of my portion to little Hanna, a quiet five-year-old who often sat near me during meal times, her big eyes fixed on me.

Her eyes widened now as I forked the extra cake onto her plate. The look she gave me, joy mingled with adoration, chipped away a little of my guilt and gave me the strength to endure Hilja's resentful stares.

It returned though when I went to visit Etti after cleaning the plates, and found her dozing with Leelo beside her, tucked into a nest of pillows. Lydia was nowhere to be seen. The pallet she usually occupied was empty.

I remembered with a sudden pang that I had promised to show her how to knit once my cooking duties were completed.

The curtain of the hutch flapped in the breeze, ushering in the scent of fried wheat cakes. The sky was visible in the narrow gap between curtain and wall, the blue deepening to a cool purple hue. Stars were already flickering to life and birds cawed and wheeled towards their forest homes.

Uneasily, I lay down beside Etti, who whimpered softly in her sleep. I laid my hand on her chest and her brow cleared.

I will ask her, I thought drowsily, as my own breathing settled into a rhythm with Etti's, the warmth of the hut stealing over me. *I'll ask her when she returns. We can start with pasque-flower; Viktoria mastered that quickly.*

I touched Oskar's glove beneath my pillow made from pine-needles, aware of the comfort of the wool beneath my thumb. As my muscles relaxed I saw lace patterns drift before my eyes; peacock tails, lilies of the valley. A delicate wolf paw, repeated over and over, like a story retold a hundred times.

The sound of distant screams woke me.

Heart thumping, I sat up. My arm slipped off Etti's chest.

Gunfire rattled. Something boomed in the distance. The ground shook. The thin boards of the shelter creaked around us.

'Kati!' Etti's hand found mine in the dark.

Another boom. Light glowed orange beyond the curtain.

'Get Leelo.' Etti obeyed, scooping the infant up and thrusting a blanket hastily around her small body.

'Come on.' Seizing Etti's arm, I elbowed the curtain apart and dragged her roughly outside.

The night was on fire.

Trees burnt, their limbs dancing with ruby flames. Smoke billowed in the air and drifted across the ground in big coils, the stench scorching my nostrils and blocking my throat.

The screams started again, louder now, followed by a volley of piercing gunshots.

Through the coils of smoke, I saw Hilja running from shelter to shelter, yelling. People emerged, some in nightclothes. Many of them seemed bewildered, looking around as if they had woken up in some nightmare landscape.

Somebody stumbled past us, a dark shadow silhouetted against the burning glow.

Gunshots peppered the ground.

Etti cried out.

The figure pitched forward, face first into the earth, and did not move.

Holding Etti's hand tightly, I dragged her towards the back of the camp, past the grove where we had sat only hours before. I tried to see it clearly in my mind; to visualise the rocks that provided an exit to the camp. All we had to do was slip between them.

I imagined the feel of the rock sliding past my body, even as I heard voices shouting behind me, raised in terror. The rock formation loomed up ahead, between the thickly wooded trees. The trees here were not yet burning, but their leaves trembled, as if they feared the oncoming storm.

Suddenly a great whoosh of air reverberated behind us. I looked back to see that the shelters had caught. Some were already blazing, the thin frames as spindly as matchsticks. Figures ran past them, alight, their desperate cries for help making my stomach heave.

A spray of bullets cut across the clearing.

People fell, limbs flung wide. One small body was tossed upwards like a doll, imprisoned against the light. Then it thudded down, peppered by gunfire.

The trees that were alight creaked and groaned beneath the weight of their heavy boughs.

Leelo's wailing snapped me back.

I turned away from the chaos. My hands found the rock ledge. I pushed Etti through it, protecting Leelo's head with my hand before slipping through myself.

Beyond the camp, the air was clearer. We gulped it in, sinking to our knees.

An explosion shook the ground, and the roar reached us seconds later. Knocked flat, I tasted bitterness. Blood. I spat on the ground.

Leelo's squalling cries reached me and Etti's scream of terror. Coughing and gagging, I dragged myself to my knees, squinting against the darkness.

'Etti?' My cousin was curled in the leaf litter, holding Leelo to her chest. She was breathing, but in shallow gasps. I could see the whites of her eyes.

'I'm here,' she said.

'We need to move.' I touched her arm. 'Can you walk?'

Leelo shifted restlessly against Etti's chest, her bawling now one long series of hiccupping sobs. Etti looked down at her and then nodded. With my help, she struggled to her feet and we stumbled down a steep embankment until the stink of smoke lessened.

Propping Etti against the trunk of an oak tree, I sank down beside her, succumbing to the dank rich scent of earth and rotting foliage. I wrapped my arms around my cousin and her child. Etti's body was trembling. Drifts of smoke still wafted overhead. The sounds of screams and gunfire had ceased. The fire had burnt itself out, bloated on the trees and timber constructions in the camp.

Above us, the trees stretched upwards, fingers pointing accusations at the stars.

Leelo's crying lessened. Eventually, her breathing changed, and she slept.

I closed my eyes.

'Kati. Kati.'

Hands shook me. I tried to stir, but my limbs were too heavy. My head was full of smoke and singed flesh and the rattle of guns.

I inhaled the musky scent of fur, along with other night smells. Ash. Pine. Beneath my eyelids I saw glowing eyes. A flash of teeth.

'Kati, it will be all right.' Soft feet padded past.

Grandmother, wolf, a girl in a white lace shawl.

A fairy tale woven from the blackened threads of history.

Sunlight pierced my eyes. I jolted awake, and panic spread through me when I realised my arms were empty.

'Leelo!'

'She's here.'

Lydia held her out. I snatched her up, squeezing too hard, pressing her against my thudding heart. I nuzzled her neck, drawing a soft sound of complaint from her as relief rushed through me.

Lydia was sitting opposite me in the leaves, Etti's head was in her lap. Sunshine filtered down around them as Lydia stroked Etti's hair. My cousin's eyes were closed. Her chest rose and fell.

'She's sleeping,' Lydia said.

Birds trilled in the branches overhead.

Lydia raised her eyes to mine. Her dark hair was twisted into tangled ropes. Smoke streaked her face. Her skirt was torn, the lace collar of her blouse half-ripped away.

'Where did you go?' It was not what I had planned to ask. But it was all I could manage.

'Not far. I thought I should be alone. Perhaps I could live in the forest by myself for a while.' She shot me a sad smile. 'I was asleep when it started, out here under the stars.' She paused. 'It was a group of Russians. Soldiers, not agents. I think they stumbled on us by accident. They had rifles and petrol bombs.' Her voice shook. Tears sprang into her eyes. 'I heard them. I couldn't do . . . anything. I wanted to cry out, but I was frozen. All I could do was lie here like a coward. Some of them died in the big blast. I heard others running away, cursing.' She faltered, looking down suddenly at Etti, pressing her lips together.

'It's not your fault.' I drew in a shuddering breath. 'Have you been back?'

She shook her head. Her face tightened, a muscle flickering in her cheek. 'I . . . I don't think I can.'

Silence pressed around us. 'I'm sorry I shouted at you,' I said, at last.

Lydia lifted a shoulder, but the muscles in her face relaxed. 'You were right, to be protective. But I would never hurt your brother. You must believe me. I would not hurt any of you. My father,' her face darkened, 'he is a villain. But I am not like him. I am trying to make amends. That's why I try to help as much as possible. Why I tried to help with Etti and with Leelo.'

She fingered the tattered lace collar on her blouse. 'I have lost people too,' she said softly.

I did not ask her. I thought I already knew. The woman she called to in her sleep. Olga.

'I should go.' I slid Leelo off my shoulder. Her body was so small and warm. Lydia shifted Etti gently aside and held out her arms.

'You don't have to.' The freckles stood out on her pale skin like a smattering of stars. She reached out her hand, grasping mine.

I bit the inside of my mouth. How I longed to sink back down and drink in the sunshine, cuddling Leelo and pretending that we had slipped outside the camp for the morning. That everything would be the same when we returned, the chatter of the other exiles, the stench of the latrine. The occasional shout of laughter from one of the Forest Brothers as a joke was shared in Oskar's lean-to.

My thoughts lurched suddenly to Oskar. What if he'd come back to fight the Russians and protect us? He could be lying hurt and injured. The stench of the fire still lingered in the back of my throat. A rush of fear went through me. I did not want to go back. But I needed to see for myself.

I pulled away gently and started up the slope.

Sharp stones scratched at my feet as I edged through the rocks and into the camp.

The smell hit me first and a minute later, the sound.

Burnt meat. Buzzing flies.

Smoke rose from the blackened ground. A crater the size of a sheep's pen gouged the earth near the ruined wreck that had been our food tent. Oskar's lean-to was gone, the soil dark and moist as if newly turned.

Bodies lay scattered among the ruins. Some were unrecognisable, just blackened skeletons. Others bore the familiar marks of their former hosts. Hilja I knew from her brown uniform, with the sleeves rolled up. Her body lay near the churned pocket of earth. Half her face was gone, blown away by the grenade she must have detonated to kill the Russian attackers.

My stomach roiled and I lurched, stumbling away and nearly tripped over a small suitcase. Through the blur of my tears, I realised it was not a suitcase but the small body of Hanna, Johanna's granddaughter, her tiny childish limbs curled up in death.

I sank to my knees beside it, all semblance of hope lost, and began to sob.

There was nothing left but blackened soil and tarnished memories. Even with their last gasp, the Soviets had destroyed any possible shred of happiness, not content to allow us to live as exiles.

My fingers dug into the still-warm ground. I rubbed the ashes on the skin at my wrists and the back of my hands. *I will not forget you*, I promised them. Hilja. Hanna. Johanna. Liisa. All the people who had shown us kindness this past week and shared our meals and our stories. The women who did not have a voice, whose lives and heritage had been ripped away.

The black ashes coated the back of my hands, mottled grey and white. They looked like lace, the same fineness; like a pasque-flower weave, or a simple pattern of vine leaves.

I was still staring at them when I heard somebody call my name. Distantly, then growing closer.

I climbed unsteadily to my feet as Oskar appeared between the scarred skeletons of the trees. He ran towards me, his feet stirring up the ashes. When he reached me, he crushed me to his chest. Stubble pricked my forehead and his fingers stroked my hair as he said my name, over and over.

Eventually, he drew back. Grief lined his features. 'If we'd known . . .' He squeezed my hands, his face hardening. 'If we'd come back earlier.'

I shook my head, unable to speak.

'The Germans are here. They arrived this morning from Tallinn. They're executing any remaining Soviets. Anyone who has links to the Soviet regime.' My hand disappeared as he folded it within his own. 'You're safe,' he said. 'Safe, Kati.'

Safe. There was no meaning in that word. It was an empty promise. All we could hope for was to help each other to survive. Our new alliance with the Germans held no guarantee.

'Kati?' He frowned. 'Did you hear me?'

I wanted to shake my head at him. Instead, I opened my arms.

Spider Stitch

Kati
September 1941

THE SOUND OF JACKBOOTS RANG OUT ON THE cobblestones. Soldiers marched in uniform precision, their faces solemn, although some smiled fleetingly at the people lined up along the pavement. The people in the crowd shouted, smiling ecstatically, waving their hands and the Estonian flags they had fashioned themselves or brought out from boxes hidden in attics or basements. Women and children threw flowers; posies of cornflowers or 'bachelor's button', twists of green ivy woven around gleaming buttercups. A stream of cars clogged Tartu's main street, a shining procession of vehicles as black as hearses and moving just as slowly, navigating through the throngs of people, inching towards Tartu's Town Hall.

A warm breeze shook the boughs of the linden trees dotting the pavement and sent a shower of white blooms raining down on the heads of the crowds below. Some of the children tried to catch the whirling blossoms in their hands, voices shrill with delight. Watching them, I recalled my grandmother's stories about the sacred linden trees, her descriptions of the women who danced in the wild linden groves, praying for fertility and domestic peace.

The street was a picture of joy. A scene that should have

filled me with happiness, blotting out the horror of the past months and the oppression of the past years. The people of Tartu welcoming their saviours. Instead, a cold dread crept into my bones. Every time I saw a Nazi swastika flash past, I was reminded of the Soviet sickle and star. Every time I heard someone shout Hitler's name, I thought about Stalin; how people like my father had been forced to acquiesce to his demands, believing that we would be better off surrendering than fighting for our freedom. Where had it got us? What good had it done?

I turned away, reaching up to massage my temples, hoping that anyone watching would imagine I suffered from migraine. It was half-true. I could feel the pressure mounting already, building behind my eyes, a wall of solid buzzing pain like the swarm of bees before a honeypot.

'A good turnout.'

I glanced sideways. Lydia stood beside me, hands thrust into the pockets of her skirt; one of Etti's, the pattern of lilacs faded from once vivid purple to a dull grey. Although she had done her best to tie her hair with a black ribbon, bits of it had escaped, springing around her shoulders in twisted coils.

'People are glad to see the back of the Russians.' I kept my voice neutral, but all the same her face changed. Guilt suffused her features.

'I'm glad too,' she said, quietly, looking over to where Etti stood a short distance away with some of the other women from the knitting circle. Helle was rocking Leelo in her arms. The baby was asleep, exhausted by the day's excitement and the impact of a lingering cold she had battled all week. Now two months old, she had started to change, her lost newborn gaze replaced by one of keen interest in everything around her. Her blue eyes watched everything, following us as we prepared supper or knitted in the evenings as we dimmed the lamps.

All the women wore their shawls, either tied around their shoulders or over their hair. Helle and Leili's faces were solemn; I knew they were thinking of Aunt Juudit. Only Viktoria was smiling, one arm linked through my cousin's. Etti herself looked tired. Her hair was dull, her skin pale from so much time spent indoors. The nights of feeding wore her out, even with Lydia and myself helping, bringing the baby to her. Leelo's cot stayed in Lydia's room most nights, too, so that Etti could catch some sleep without waking every hour to check that Leelo was all right.

At least we had the ladies of the knitting circle to support us.

There had been tears and much embracing when we returned from the camp to Aunt Juudit's apartment. Helle especially had been glad to see us and and to learn that Etti had survived the dangers of childbirth. But only Helle and Leili had escaped deportation, taking refuge in Aunt Juudit's apartment, too afraid to risk even contacting their families. Very slowly, we had rebuilt our lives from what remained. The women of the knitting circle had slowly accepted Lydia as one of their own. They had given her a shawl to wear which had been knitted by Aunt Juudit. Peacock Tails. The circle met once a week now in Helle's apartment and Lydia was always invited to join us. There had not been much left to salvage from Aunt Juudit's after the Russians smashed everything. Only the larger furniture – beds and wardrobes – had been spared. I'd already begun to teach Lydia how to knit properly and I had mended her mother's shawl, piecing it back together with some spare yarn Helle had saved.

A roar of sound made me glance back at the procession. A group of brown-clad men approached, their rifles shining; the Estonian Home Guard. I spotted Jakob among them and lifted my hand. His brown eyes crinkled, but his gaze went past me. With a wrench, I knew I was not the one he sought. I stepped away, giving him an unobstructed view. I did not have to look to know that he was wearing the same smile he wore every time Lydia came near, or that she was returning it.

When I looked back, his curly head was bobbing away. Lydia pressed her hands together, staring after him. When she caught my eye a corner of her mouth lifted and colour rose to her cheeks. She turned to stare back at the apartment block that loomed across the courtyard behind us. The windows of Aunt Juudit's apartment were shuttered closed.

A frown wrinkled Lydia's forehead. 'It feels wrong to be out here. All this . . .' She gestured around. 'All this celebration. After everything that happened.'

'I know.'

The silence that stretched between us was filled with the happy chatter of voices, Estonian and German. But Lydia's eyes were troubled.

I hugged myself, realising with a jolt that my own fingers met almost around my middle. I could feel the spokes of my ribs beneath my hands. I tried to remember what I'd eaten last. Thin, watery grain. An overripe apple that turned to mush on my tongue. The departing Russians had taken with them whatever they could carry. What little remained had been seized by the Germans and, in fairness, by the

Estonian Home Guard and the Forest Brothers, who had needed energy to defeat the remnants of the Soviet Army. Any day, the Germans would depart, though. Then the fields would be returned to us, the *kolkhoz* collective farms broken up. This knowledge was bittersweet.

Our own farm was gone. It was now nothing more than a burnt-out husk, surrounded by blackened fields. My heart still ached as I recalled the way Jakob had staggered as we emerged from the forest the night after the Russians left. The way his mouth had worked as he struggled to keep control of his emotions. We had later learnt that Stalin had given instructions for everything of value to be torched. Nothing was to be left for the Germans – or for us. On the 9th of July, the retreating Russians had blown up the old stone bridge over the river Emajõgi. They had blown up St Mary's Church and the market where we'd once sold our shawls.

In a way, we were lucky. We had not been inside our farmhouse when the Russians destroyed it. In Kautla, a small township in Central Estonia, a battalion of retreating Russian soldiers had herded at least thirty people into their farmhouses and set them ablaze. The scene afterwards had been distressing to everyone, even the hardened members of the Erna reconnaissance group, a clutch of Finnish soldiers who had sworn to help liberate Estonia from the Soviets' grasp. It was the Erna group who had brought the news to Oskar after clashing with the Russian battalions. At night, when visions of flames distorted my sleep, I heard the cries of those men and women begging for their lives. My eyes stung with petrol fumes. My skin blistered, the flesh melting away until only charcoal bones remained. I often woke tangled in damp sheets, my throat choked with imaginary smoke.

Now, an arm draped around my shoulder. Jakob grinned down at me. He had removed his hat, and sweaty curls clung to his temples. His skin was tanned, warmed by the many hours he now spent outdoors training with the others. He looked exactly like the farm boys we had grown up with, arms corded with ropey muscle. Not the mild-mannered teacher my mother had yearned for him to be.

'Hello, sister,' he said, his brows knitted. 'Why so glum? Shouldn't you be with the adoring crowds, shouting my name?'

I shrugged his arm away. 'Shouldn't you be marching with the Home Guard instead of standing here, searching for compliments?'

He jammed his cap back on his head, the smile returning to his eyes. 'They told us to go when we reached the marketplace. We've been ordered to return home. Oskar's already gone. He's out at the farmhouse. He told me to tell you to meet him there.'

I swallowed. 'At the farmhouse? Why?'

Jakob shrugged. 'I don't know. He didn't say. You know how he is. The Boche have commandeered Werner's Café for the afternoon – you remember it, I took you there. I think they dread the competition we'll present. Can you tell me why anyone would prefer a hot-blooded German to a scruffy Estonian?'

He rubbed at the growth on his chin. It was thin and patchy, showing the bronze skin beneath.

When I didn't answer, my brother turned towards Lydia.

'What about you, Lida? You'd prefer a German, I suppose; someone who knows how to hold a gun properly and can grow a proper beard.'

Lydia had been staring at the pavement, tracing the toe of her shoe over a wedge of cobblestone split apart by thistles. 'I'm sick of guns,' she said, her words so quiet I almost didn't catch them.

The teasing look in Jakob's eyes faded. He took a step towards her then hesitated, his gaze darting quickly back to me and then to the women from the knitting circle who were all watching this exchange keenly. I wondered what he would do if we weren't there. Would he embrace her? Kiss her?

Lydia drew her shawl around her, turning her head away from us to face the crowd. The breeze teased her hair, sending tendrils of it spiralling over her face. She tugged them, winding them around her hands, tucking them into the back of her shawl to keep them from tangling. I saw Etti give Jakob a sharp look and raise her eyebrows, but my brother shrugged, uncertain of her message. Etti looked at me and rolled her eyes. Helle and Leili clucked at each other knowingly like hens.

Knots of people drifted past us, their faces wreathed in smiles. The unmistakable scent of smoked trout drifted through the air; somebody was cooking in one of the apartments nearby. The smell made my mouth water. Fishing had been illegal under the Soviet charter as all rivers were the property of the State and anything caught in them was to be shared equally among the masses. Some people had rebelled, sneaking into the woods to cast their lines in the crystal river waters. Perhaps the Germans looked more kindly on that behaviour. If our own crops were to be returned to us, it made sense the rivers would be, too.

'We should get back,' Lydia said, looking at Etti and the

sleeping infant Helle had returned to her mother's arms. 'Perhaps I can rest with Leelo for a while. My throat hurts. I'm worried I've caught her cold. Goodbye, Jakob.' She nodded at my brother.

Although it was only a glance, I read longing there and desire, a seed that would only need the slightest cultivation to burst into bloom. I felt a spurt of happiness for my brother which quickly mellowed. Lydia was not the kind of girl my parents would have wanted for him. They would have preferred a pure-blooded Estonian who did not mangle her words or burn the grain on the bottom of the pan when I left the kitchen. Lydia was an enigma. Perhaps that was why Jakob wanted her. Although we had spoken about her father the Partorg and some of her life in Moscow, I always felt she was holding back, unwilling to share all of her past. Etti still felt strongly about her. I often found them talking softly together as they watched Leelo stretching on the carpet and trying to kick her small legs. Despite her mystery, the three of us, Jakob, Etti and myself, had agreed to say nothing about her identity to anyone, not even to the knitting ladies. To expose her would be akin to murder. I could only hope that wherever my parents were now, they would want Jakob to be happy and would overlook any of Lydia's faults. I hoped they would give him their blessing.

'Why don't you go back to the apartment?' Etti said suddenly, breaking into my thoughts. 'Go back and rest. Kati and I have to visit with Helle for a while. She wants us to show her how to sew some *nupps* on her *kroonprints* stitch.'

Helle's face creased. 'What?'

'You remember, Helle.' Etti hitched Leelo up on her shoulder and patted her bottom. Her eyes glittered. 'The *kroonprintsi!*'

Helle lifted her chin. 'I know how to sew a *nupp*. Ouch!' She scowled, rubbing hard at the place on her elbow where Leili had pinched her, before understanding made her draw in a sharp breath. 'Oh yes. The *kroonprintsi*. Of course.'

Etti was shaking her head but she was smiling.

Lydia looked at Jakob and then at me, hesitating. I knew she was asking for my approval and although I felt an old flare of dislike, it was dimmed by the greater desire for Jakob's happiness.

'Go on.' I made an ushering gesture. 'You should. I've heard you at all hours of the night with Leelo, singing her songs and telling her stories. No wonder you're getting sick.'

Lydia's mouth curved. 'I suppose a rest might help. I muddle up the words if I'm too tired. Not that she knows.'

'I'll walk you back.' My brother stepped between us. He could not hide the eagerness in his voice, but I noticed his hands trembled a little. His nervousness made me want to laugh, a rare sensation now. It reminded me of the old days, how easy it had been to find pleasure in small things, before the shadow of the purge fell over everything. Things would be set right, I promised myself. When the Germans left and Estonia was restored. But there would always be a darkness, a shadow blurring the edges of the brightest moments. My parents and aunt were gone. Nothing would bring them back.

Jakob's boots clicked on the cobblestones. When he reached for Lydia's arm, she tensed. Then almost imperceptibly she moved towards him, leaning her body against his as they fell into step. The low hum of their voices was just audible beneath the burble of the dispersing crowd. The ease with which they came together made my chest tight.

I watched them, Lydia's narrow hips swaying as they reached the front doorstep of the apartment block. The corner of her shawl slipped off her shoulder, and Jakob's hand shot out and pulled it back up, smoothing it over the fabric of her blue blouse.

When I looked at my brother now, I no longer saw the tall, lanky student but the soldier, a man who had witnessed death first-hand. A man who carried that knowledge inside him. Instead of fearing it, though, he had embraced it like a gift, turning it outwards so everything he did was imbued with a gentle humour, a respect for the fragility of life. I watched him now hold open the door and stand back as Lydia slipped through. Then they were gone, disappeared inside the shadowy stairwell.

I realised I was smiling.

Etti's fingers prodded me. Her eyes were teasing. 'And you, Katarina? Where is your prince?'

I shrugged but my mind went instantly to the little string tied around the fourth finger of my left hand. Oskar had given it to me the day we exchanged our vows two weeks after the Russians surrendered.

I was Katarina Mägi now.

Although we had not had any money for rings, we had gone together to the marriage registry and records office the Germans had hastily arranged while they sorted out the papers which had been lost during the bombings as the Russians left. With Jakob and Etti as our witnesses, we had made our vows in a simple timber-panelled room and Oskar had tied the scrap of white yarn on my finger with quivering hands; a promise of the ring he would one day place there. Afterwards we had gone back to the apartment and toasted our future with vodka. Helle had invited our remaining neighbours to join us and they had all drunk too much. When they finally left us alone, we shrugged off our clothes in the dark and into bed, conscious of the paper-thin walls and Etti and Lydia sleeping in the next room. At last, we began to relax and for a few moments at least, I was able to forget all about our proximity to the others. But our pleasure was short-lived. First, the baby had begun to holler, then Oskar's Commanding Officer had sent an urgent message for him to return to the barracks. I'd been forced to hide my disappointment and assure him I understood his obligations, although I knew from the scowl on his face that the inconvenience had bothered him more than he could show. We were still at war and Oskar, as part of the Home Guard, was required to sleep at the barracks with his fellow soldiers. When we could, we snatched moments together in the apartment, always careful to keep our voices low so as not to disturb the others but there were days and nights where I wondered if I had dreamt our wedding up in my head and I longed for the day Oskar and I could finally be together and sleep under the same roof, not bound by the conditions of his leave.

'At the farmhouse,' I told my cousin. I felt a little frisson of anticipation shiver across my skin.

Etti was still looking at me. 'So? You should go there.'

I hesitated. The farmhouse still held terrible memories for me. But Oskar was waiting for me.

'You don't need me?' I said.

Etti heaved a long sigh that reminded me of Aunt

Juudit. 'Do you plan to make a professional career out of worrying once Estonia is restored, Katarina Mägi?' She pushed me with her free hand, using the other to hold the sleeping Leelo against her. 'Go!'

I made myself move, pushing people aside until I found a man with a lorry who was unloading his truck with crates that contained loaves of grey bread as hard as concrete. When I told him where I needed to go he motioned me up into the back of the vehicle. I squeezed myself between the rows of empty crates, the faint loamy scent of the bread drifting over me. The lorry started with a rumble. Seconds later, we were pulling out onto the road.

Oskar stood outside the farmhouse with one hand raised, his shirt a white smudge against the timber. The sound of hammering echoed across the clearing. As I reached the gate my foot snapped a twig in two. The sound reported like the whip-crack of gunfire.

Oskar spun around, his features tightening. Then his face broke into a smile. He dropped his arms to his sides and called out to me, the hammer still clutched in one hand.

'Mrs Mägi. You came.'

It was strange to hear him call me that. In my mind, Imbi had been Mrs Mägi until now.

I walked slowly across the clearing until I reached the garden and the little path that led up to the house. Most of the garden had been weeded, I realised, the soil turned. I made my way to where Oskar was standing at the top of the porch.

'I did.' I glanced up and my breath hitched in my chest. The house had been partially restored, the broken panes

338

replaced, new shutters folded over them. The broken front door had been removed and another of solid oak stood in its place, painted a bright cheery yellow like melted butter. The porch had been painted, too, and by the side of the door sat a new rocking chair. New thatch gleamed on the roof.

Oskar leapt down the steps and dropped the hammer in the grass. He took my hand. 'It's not finished,' he warned.

I stared in wonder. 'How did you manage this?'

I moved up the steps as if I was dreaming, running my hand along the wooden railing which stretched the length of the porch. The smell of paint and varnish filled the air.

'You like it, then.' Oskar's arm encircled my waist.

'Like it?' I could not stop smiling. 'It's wonderful!'

I tried to peer into the window which belonged to Oskar's bedroom but Oskar moved in front of it, blocking my path. 'Not yet.'

'There's more?' I pretended to peek around his shoulder, but he caught me and drew me to him and pressed his lips to my mouth. Desire leapt in my stomach. We stayed like that for a long moment, our lips joined, sunshine dancing on our skin.

When we broke apart, he looked so young, so much like the old Oskar it was almost impossible to believe how much had changed from that fifteen-year-old boy who had first kissed me in the field I could see beyond the porch railings.

'It's only the start,' he said. 'I intend to improve it further, in time, not just clean it. But I only have a few hours a week. And limited resources. What you see here is the result of what the Germans gave me in exchange for my services to the Home Guard. Whatever else I need I will have to trade or barter for. I want to fix up the garden, of course. I've cleared out most of the sodden boards inside. And the cobwebs are gone, you'll notice. No more spiders.'

And no more ghosts, I added to myself, unable to stop myself thinking of his mother, his sister and Hilja. And the others. All of them gone.

'I pity spiders.'

He raised his eyebrows.

'Everybody thinks so badly of them.' I leant against the porch, the timber pressing against my shirt to warm the skin on my back. 'But they're clever. They know how to play dead, how to wait and when to feed. And of course, they make lace. A sort of lace. They're weavers. And often overlooked. Do you remember the tale of the spider and the wind?'

Oskar raised an eyebrow. 'I must have forgotten it.' He kissed my hand. 'Will you tell it to me?'

'If you like.' As the scent of rampant weeds and wild juniper blew over us, I told him the story of the little spider who went to find the wind and was tricked by the fly.

'That's a sad story,' Oskar said, but he was still grinning.

'At least the spider always eats first,' I said. 'That is her consolation. And of course, she can make lace cobwebs. Like me.'

Oskar leant over and kissed my neck. 'Enough about spiders,' he said. His breath on my skin made me shiver. 'Come in, now. There's something I want you to see.'

We stepped inside.

I was aware of my body tensing. My eyes strayed to the corner where Imbi and Aime's bodies had lain. But the floor was clean and dry, the cobwebs gone as Oskar had promised. Was it possible that the ghosts of the past had finally found peace?

'Watch the boards.' Oskar's voice tickled my ear. 'I've removed the waterlogged ones, but I haven't replaced all of them yet.'

He guided me across the floor, nudging my leg with his knee if I came too close to a missing plank. Slowly, we made our way past the kitchen, heading towards the back of the house where the bedrooms lay. It was not so very different to skating, to moving as one across the ice while the wind blew cold enough to make our ears ache. In the old days, we had spent every winter sledding through the snow or spinning in circles across the glassy surface of the river beyond Oskar's farmhouse. Those memories glowed as brightly as baubles hanging on a Christmas tree. They were scented with cinnamon and spiced apple, laced with Aime's happy laughter and Imbi's scolding when we stayed out past dusk. One night we had witnessed an amazing spectacle as ribbons of light twisted across the sky – starry violet, glacial aquamarine, pink as brilliant as the rambling wild roses that burst into bloom in summer. My grandmother had once told me that the aurora lights were reflections of a celestial marriage feast taking place in the sky. The shimmering colours mirrored their glass sleighs and gilded plates and the coats of their giant stallions racing over the land. Unable to draw ourselves away, Oskar and I had clung together, our clouded breath mingling, children marvelling at a miracle that might never occur again in our lifetime.

We reached the door to the bedroom Oskar had once occupied. When he pushed it open, I expected the lingering smell of dust and rotten timber to envelop me. Instead, only the pungent scent of fir trees unfurled. I stepped inside, glancing up at the beams where bunches of pine needles had been tied. Their crisp menthol scent washed over everything, burning into my lungs, making my blood race and my heart pound. My feet creaked on the new floorboards below. I spun in a half-circle, taking in the other details of a room that had once been as familiar as my own. The bookshelf was still full of books, juniper branches twisted between them to ward off mice. A new timber bedstead had been pushed against the wall and a double mattress lain over it, covered in soft sheets and a knitted quilt.

'What do you think?' Oskar batted gently at a clump of pine needles, causing some of them to scatter. The sound was like falling rain. 'Do you remember when your papa would not let you camp in the forest with me, so I got Mama to help me hang fir branches from the roof so we could have our own forest for the day?'

A ghost smile teased his mouth. 'We were finding them for weeks; pine needles folded in my clothes, pressed between the pages of books. But the look on your face . . .' Bending, he grasped a pine needle between forefinger and thumb. The bruised scent of the fir made me want to cry. 'You were so happy. I think that was the day I decided I would marry you.' His smile became frozen for just a moment. 'How simple everything seems when we are children.'

Oskar closed his hand around the fir. He looked away from me towards the window where the sun was starting to shrink down behind the tallest trees. I sensed he was thinking of Imbi and Aime. He had stored up his grief after their death and there had never been a chance for him to release it. Like me, the memory of what had happened had become a poison running deep beneath his skin. Only by sharing the truth of what happened could he be free.

I moved towards him at last, fighting the desire to reach up and kiss him. Instead, I touched his shoulder gently.

'Oskar. Did you see them die?'

He stilled, one finger on the chest of drawers. I sensed him gathering the words, crushing them to his chest until the thorns pricked so hard he must release them or bleed.

Eventually he nodded. In a voice that shook, he described the way he had gone out early to collect blueberries for his mother. The terror when he returned in time to see the Russian agents enter the house. The screaming. The silence that followed. The guilt that had woken him each night as he lay shivering in the forest, imagining the ghosts of Imbi and Aime stood beside him, unable to rest due to the violent nature of their deaths. 'I've lived with it every day,' he said. 'Asking myself: what if I had come back earlier? What if I had taken my father's pistol from the box and killed those men when they appeared?'

He gripped his hands together tightly. I could see his knuckles straining through the skin. I laid my hands over his.

'You would be dead, Oskar,' I said softly. 'It's as simple as that.'

Oskar nodded. The bed groaned as he eased himself down on it, resting his elbows on his thighs. 'I'm sorry I never came to you,' he said, looking up at me. 'I couldn't stand for you to think I would do that. It ate at me like an illness and yet, I couldn't put you in that danger. I had to wait, and I knew that perhaps I would be waiting until

I was an old man. And now you're here. We are married. You know the truth about my mother and Aime. But I've changed. I've done things . . . I don't deserve . . .'

He broke off, lowering his chin, clasping his head in his hands.

Leaning down, I drew his face close and kissed him. His lips were soft. He tasted of rain and sodden berries. At first he resisted, but slowly, he began to respond.

I sank to my knees, and his arm slid around my middle to grip me tightly, as if I were the precious ballast on a ship that might suddenly disintegrate and leave him swirling in deep currents. When we broke apart, it was only to fill our lungs with air. Oskar's cheeks were flushed. I kissed his closed eyes, allowing my lips to linger before I moved my mouth to the soft curve where his jaw met his ear. Feather-light, I kissed the skin there, my body prickling as I heard him sigh. I drew back slightly and let my hands fan out across his back, delaying the moment of surrender.

Oskar's hands were warm around my waist as he drew me closer. In some distant part of my mind, I knew my knees were aching on the timber floor. I gasped as he moved my skirt aside and nudged my legs gently apart. He lifted me in one movement so that I was straddling him and his hands cupped my bottom, fingers splayed. As he pressed against me, heat shifted to my groin and a wave of longing crested through my body. Distantly, I was aware of my hand reaching down to unbutton his trousers. Perhaps it was Oskar's. I could no longer tell where I ended and he began. It was as if our pleasure had melted us together. When he paused to look at me, his hand resting between my bare legs, I could not tell if it was me who spoke, urging him on or if it was he who mouthed the words, seeking permission. I couldn't tell if it was really me who answered, in a voice so raw I imagined my skin peeling away, stripped to nothing by the fever pitch of our desire now allowed free rein.

I did not make a sound as he entered me, too lost in warm oblivion. There was nobody to stop us this time; no interruptions. Each moment was its own perfect prism, relief and solace combined. As our rhythm quickened, I felt my control slip. Tears stung my eyes. I gave in and heard myself cry out.

At last, when the tremors had subsided, we slipped apart. Our breathing slowed. Our hands were pressed together, our bodies cooling. I wriggled up to lay my head against his chest.

'Kati.' Oskar's breath stirred my hair. 'That was—'

He swallowed. Cleared his throat. I squeezed his fingers.

'I know,' I said. His lips brushed against my forehead. What could we say that we hadn't already told each other? I snuggled against him. I could easily have slept. My limbs felt heavy, my thoughts circling drowsily, reliving each moment of our love-making. But I forced myself up onto one elbow. The afternoon sun was beginning to cast long shadows against the wall.

'We should get back. Curfew starts soon,' I said.

Oskar grunted, one hand propped beneath his head, then he ran his thumb along my collarbone. I smiled as he shifted, moving down my body to draw lazy circles with his tongue over my breast. 'Just a few more minutes, then,' he said, his teeth grazing my skin. 'We've had such little time to practise being married.'

He resumed his licking and I lay back, drowning beneath the sweet sensations he conjured with his tongue. 'Just a few minutes more. Otherwise they'll look for you,' I said. 'You don't want to annoy the German officers. You know what they're like; such sticklers for rules.'

Oskar pulled away. I sighed. What I had said was true. The Germans did not forgive rule-breakers. When I opened my eyes, I realised Oskar was frowning.

'What is it?' I said.

'Kati, there is something I want you to promise me.'

'Anything.' I said. I could not stop a smile twitching the corners of my mouth. 'Is it something you want me to do for you? Because I—'

Oskar interrupted me. 'No. It's the barracks. I don't want you to go there. If you need me, just send word via telegram and I will meet you here. It's not safe. There are so many German soldiers in Tartu now. I can't stand the thought of anything happening to you. So, you will promise, yes?'

'Of course.'

He looked so worried that I reached down and grasped his fingers, bringing them slowly to my mouth to kiss the callused tips, the small whorls that creased his skin.

'I promise,' I said. Very gently, I drew his finger into my mouth. I half-expected him to laugh but instead, he groaned. A sense of power such as I had never known rippled through me, setting my limbs aflame.

'Kati.' He said my name with reverence.

A tiny network of scars shone in the hollow of his collarbone. I could not draw my eyes away from them; a tiny web that marked his skin. I would be the spider now. I would spin the lacy web that concealed us both and led him away from death and into the light.

Egg Stitch

Lydia

JOACHIM.

I heard his name in every step I took up the staircase to our apartment. Each excited thud of my heart felt like treachery. The squeak of my hand sliding up the peeling banister was the sound of Joachim's shoes slipping on the pavement as the agent dragged him into the Packard. *Help me.* I shook my head, trying to dislodge his voice, but I could still hear it, a wordless cry.

I had left him, abandoning him to death or deportation. It didn't matter much which one. I did not deserve the happiness I felt whenever Jakob was around. I certainly did not deserve the tingle of pleasure that ran up and down my spine as Jakob reached for my hand and led me out onto the landing. I fumbled in my pocket for the key and then took my time fitting it to the lock, twisting it this way and that, delaying the moment when I would have to choose whether to make the betrayal of my former lover complete.

'Here. Let me.' Jakob's fingers moved over mine. One twist. The door swung open.

Jakob extended his arm, waiting for me to enter.

'It's safe,' he said, when I didn't move. I almost smiled at his presumption. He thought I was uncomfortable when in truth, I had experienced so many firsts in this apartment in the past two months that it seemed to me almost as familiar as my childhood home. I'd grown used to the bare furnishings and the chipped mugs and the kettle which did not whistle when it reached the boil but shrieked loudly. I'd cooked my first broth here, with Kati's help, and sewn a button onto one of the blouses Etti had lent me. I'd started my own lace shawl, copying a pattern Kati had shown me in one of her samplers.

I knew all of the apartment's rooms; the sad one where Juudit had slept and which neither Kati nor Etti wanted, choosing instead to share a bed in Etti's bedroom while I took the small guest room. The tiny kitchenette with its peeling varnished cupboards and mismatched teacups. The courtyard with its view over Tartu and the geranium plants, the flowers now shrivelled and fading as autumn took hold.

The parlour was my favourite. When we'd returned after the Germans took over, it was to find that Helle and the others had swept up all the broken things and organised for the ripped armchairs to be thrown away. With so little furniture left, the room seemed a decent size and the big windows let in the warm sunshine, driving away the darkness of the deportations and the sad memories Juudit had left behind.

'So. We are alone,' Jakob said. He had taken off his cap and placed it with his gun on the hallstand. I was glad; I did not like the feel of his gun against my hip when we walked side by side through the marketplace, as evening fell or along the banks of the Emajõgi River.

My heart gave a sharp twist. 'Did you want to talk?' I said. 'Or I could make tea.' I tried to undo the shawl around my shoulders, ready to hang on the hallstand. A habit I'd picked up from the others. I could feel the lace tangling around my fingers. I tugged at it, not wanting to rip the stitches but unable to untie the knot I had fastened to stop it slipping and being crushed beneath the boot heels of the Germans as they marched up the street.

Jakob's hands appeared suddenly, snaking over my shoulders. He undid the knot with ease, and then slipped the shawl into my hands. I realised I was trembling. I glanced up at him, afraid he would laugh at me, but he had taken a respectful step away, his expression patient.

'Whatever you like,' he said. I caught the glimmer of amusement in his eyes. He was waiting for me to set the rhythm, as he always did. We had been talking for five months now. Talking and talking, endless stories. We would meet whenever he had leave, at the apartment or outside the barracks where the Home Guard were now stationed. As troops of German soldiers marched past and tanks rumbled over the cobblestones, we would talk about the events that had shaped our childhood, the places we dreamt one day of visiting. I retold Olga's stories and sang Mama's songs. As we became comfortable, I had found the courage to confide in him that Olga had been lost to me the night of the deportations. Jakob had promised to look for her name among the official documents left behind, but the outcome was not optimistic. There had been so many people deported that night it was impossible for all their names to be listed. Other lists had been destroyed in the bomb blasts that damaged the records office at the Town Hall.

The knowledge that I might have to live with the guilt of never knowing whether Olga survived was a crushing blow. Only Jakob's kindness and sympathy seemed to comfort me.

Sometimes we conversed in Estonian, and other times, out

of earshot, in Russian. My Estonian was improving. I could remember my mother telling me that Estonian was one of the most beautiful languages in the world. Each time Jakob and I met, it never seemed long enough. There was always more to say. It seemed as if my mouth could never catch up with my brain. As I walked back to the apartment, I would recall some little observation I thought would amuse that I had forgotten to tell him and as the week passed, I would hold it inside me like a small candle flame, determined not to forget. But when I saw him leaning against the stone wall of the barracks, a half-crunched apple in his hand, his lips shiny with juice, it was as if the words I had tried so hard to recall were no more than embers blowing away on the breeze.

And yet in all our conversations, two things had weighed upon my mind; the secret burden of my parentage and the truth about Joachim. A few times I had started to tell him about Stalin and then forced myself to stop, unsure if I could trust my own judgement. What if I was wrong? Jakob seemed caring. He seemed to want to know everything about me. But what kind of person could accept as his friend the daughter of one of the world's most dangerous men? In my worst moments, I imagined him running to tell the authorities. I imagined the looks of horror which would cross the women's faces as my secret was revealed. I feared Kati and Etti's rejection most keenly. Our connections were already so fragile, shaped by what we had witnessed the night of the deportations and then the decimation of the camp. We had built our own small world in the apartment with Leelo. Amidst the uncertainty of the changeover from Russian to German hands, we had grown close and created our own routines and habits to keep each other safe. I did not want to lose that now, when for the first time I had friends I could rely on and people who cared enough to involve me in their lives. I only wished Olga was with me, to share in my newfound freedom. I grieved her loss bitterly.

I stayed silent when Jakob talked with sadness of his parents, unable to share with him the immensely complex feelings my true parentage brought up. It was my secret, now that Olga was gone. I alone would be its keeper.

Jakob thought I was the Partorg's daughter and that was surely bad enough.

'Thank you.' I hung the shawl up now with the others. They looked like ribbons tied on the branches of a tree, the patterns all mingled. One day, I thought, I will know what each of those patterns is. One day I will get Kati to teach them all to me.

'You were quiet today.' Jakob perched on the edge of an armchair.

I moistened my lips. 'I'm always quiet.'

Jakob's eyebrows shot up. 'Really?' Slipping into the arm-chair, he leant back, his hands behind his head. 'This is the girl who swears to have seen every one of Greta Garbo's movies and can quote almost every line? The girl who can describe – in great detail, mind you – the exact formula for successful cutlery execution at a formal dinner party.'

I burst out laughing, despite myself. 'You don't understand,' I said, moving to stand at the window and let the sun warm my back through the glass. 'Today was . . .' *Disturbing? Troubling?* 'It was not a day for light-hearted chatter,' I said. I shot a look through the windows. Swastika flags hung from every corner of the street. German soldiers in their clean, pressed uniforms leant from the back of trucks, radiating smiles, happy to play the role of saviours.

When I looked back at Jakob, it was to find his face had changed. He ran a hand through his curls. 'I know,' he said, his voice low. 'I thought so, too. We must be careful. That is what Oskar says. We must wait and see.'

He was silent for a moment, looking down at his shoes before he raised his eyes to grin at me from beneath his curls. 'At the very least, we are together. I don't think we have ever been alone without the rumble of tanks around us or people rushing back and forth. Or Kati, fussing around with that awful kettle which sounds as if it's being murdered.'

'You don't want tea then?'

His eyebrows contracted before he realised I was joking. He laughed and shook his head. The armchair squeaked as he rose from it and came to stand in front of me. I felt my breath quicken, my pulse beating faster. *Do not think of Joachim. Squeak of shoes. Car door slamming.*

Jakob's warm brown eyes seemed to see right through me, right down to my soul. 'Lida,' he said and the breathless tone of his voice made my stomach flutter nervously. Very cautiously, as if he half-expected me to stop him, he leant forward and placed a hesitant kiss on my lips. I froze. When I didn't resist, Jakob kissed me again. Harder. Desire made my legs tremble. It surged through my body and I felt my heart soaring, like a bird freed from its cage.

And then suddenly, I was back in the cinema. I was tasting Joachim's cigarettes, the coffee he had drunk that morning. I was listening to him beg for his life as my real father's minders interrogated him and accused him of spying.

I was watching guards shove him into a dirty railroad car, hearing him call for his mother, his father. Begging them to save him. Begging me.

I pushed Jakob away, gasping hard.

'I'm sorry.' I put my face in my hands. My skin was cold. How could anyone want to kiss me? I was tainted.

Joachim's memory hovered just out of reach, still there like a shadow. If I could only purge it from my mind. I shook my head. 'It's not you.' To my horror, I realised I'd begun to cry. Tears leaked down my cheeks and dripped onto my blouse.

Jakob whipped out his handkerchief to blot them. 'I'm sorry,' I said again. I scrubbed at my nose, wishing I could ask Olga for the handkerchief she'd always carried. 'I've only had one boyfriend. And, you see, he was killed.'

Jakob's hand froze, his handkerchief halfway to my face. His face had paled. 'Killed?'

I nodded. 'I think so. If not, he was taken far away from his family and everything he knew. Nobody comes back from those places. He might as well be dead.'

Jakob's expression cleared. 'He was deported.'

'Yes. My father—' I paused. I could not tell him. He still thought of my father as the Partorg. 'My father had him sent away.'

'That's horrible.'

'Yes.' My sobs had lessened. 'Yes. It was horrible.'

'But not your fault.' Jakob dabbed his handkerchief against my skin, soaking up my tears. 'Not at all your fault. You mustn't blame yourself.'

I stared at him. 'But if he hadn't met with me, he might still be alive.'

'You've told me about your father,' Jakob said. 'Well, the little you know about him.' I felt a hot ember of guilt burn my throat. 'If I might suggest, your boyfriend knew the risks he was taking. He took them anyway.'

'But why would he?'

'Why?' Jakob looked at me as if I was mad. 'Because you are kind. And funny. And you almost always end up telling a rambling story about Olga or your mother. Because you know how to use fine cutlery and how to read poetry and about cinema and a hundred other completely useless bits of impractical knowledge.' I smiled. I did not believe everything he said, but the way he said it was almost convincing. Jakob pursed his lips as if he knew my thoughts. 'It's true.' Using his thumb, he raised my chin until our faces were level. 'I want you to promise you will let him go. Let go of that guilt. Your father was a horrible man. You are not your father, Lida. You will never be your father.'

I wanted to throw my arms around him and kiss him at the same time.

I did both. As our kisses deepened, I realised with a pang of longing that I had been blind to my own desires. Hadn't I wondered more times than I cared to admit what it would be like to trace my fingers along the ridge of his collarbone, or to tousle his curls or to run my hands across the flat of his back? Had I been so intent on sabotaging my own happiness that I had not seen what was in front of me? And Jakob, I knew now, felt the same. The last few times we met, he had seemed preoccupied, his hands always busy, fidgeting with his belt or hitching his gun up on his back or playing with the cuffs of his sleeve. I too busied my hands with other things; knitting needles. Baby bottles. Cooking implements. I had not realised that my hands would remain restless, empty until Jakob filled them and made the rest of the world disappear.

All my fears had been unfounded. Joachim was the past. Jakob was my future.

Now, at last, he stood before me and I was kissing him and for once, I didn't want to talk. I wanted instead to listen to the sound his breathing, to hear his heart quicken and the clamour of my own blood surge in my ears in response.

A rush of impulse flickered up my body. I moved away. The thin cotton of my blouse crinkled as I unfastened the buttons. The sun from the window warmed the bare skin of my back. Through the glass, I could still hear distantly the crowd of voices from the procession moving off.

My fingers were shaking as I fumbled with my waistband until the folds of my skirt fell in a soft puddle around my feet. Jakob was right. Joachim was gone and nothing I could do now could bring him back. I could not continue living as if I was already dead, as if my body was not able to experience desire and hope and love.

Jakob was watching me. When I'd begun to undress, he had looked wary. Now he was following my every move with his eyes. When I unclipped my stays, he made a sound in his throat and stepped towards me. His lips warmed my throat.

'You are sure?' he said against my skin. I could feel him trembling. It made me feel stronger, more confident, to know that he was as nervous as me.

'Yes,' I said, in Estonian, to please him. All my limbs were warm from the sun. I wound my arms around his neck and he kissed me swiftly and a little clumsily, his beard grazing my chin. My hands travelled beneath his shirt, exploring the hidden landscape of his body. His skin was covered in a fine soft down. It made me think of feathers and the dream I had experienced the night of Leelo's birth.

I thought of what Olga had said. *Love is complicated.* Perhaps it was.

'No bread today.'

Helga, the baker's wife, threw her hands down on the counter to emphasise her point. Clouds of white flour flew into the air. Through the hazy obscurity, her scowl was visible, her thick lips moulded into a stubborn pout as if someone had pinched them out of the doughy folds of her face. Flour dusted her cheeks and collarbone, speckling her apron like a drift of snow.

A hush fell over the group of women clustered beside me at the counter, conversation emptying until the only sound was the creak of the door between the back workroom and shopfront still swinging in Helga's wake.

In the queue beside me, Etti tapped her foot nervously against the tiled floor. I risked a swift glance at her. She was pale, her skin like chalk against the dull bronze of her hair. One of Juudit's old grey coats was buckled around her thin waist. I wondered with a sinking heart if I should have left her with Leelo at home. Kati and I usually collected our rations together, one of us heading to the bakery while the other queued up for the meat. Of all the days for Etti to come out.

I squeezed the ration tickets that Kati had given me tightly in my hand.

A sudden explosion in the street behind us made the people in the queue cry out and glance around in fear. Etti clutched my arm, her eyes wide. But it was only a truck backfiring. Some people smiled hesitantly, perhaps feeling foolish. Etti and I did not smile. We stayed pressed together. Etti's foot resumed its tapping and she cast me an uneasy sidelong glance.

I wondered if she was also thinking of the way the German presence seemed to have increased this past week. Their uniforms were everywhere. Trucks could be heard rumbling day and night along the streets, ferrying soldiers from the barracks to the Baltic borders where the fighting was worst. Tanks constantly rolled into Tartu, making the ground shudder. Posters had sprung up, too, seemingly overnight. They were different to the propaganda posters I had seen all over Moscow. Those posters with their bright, primary colours had seemed so innocent, with their fairy tale depiction of workers toiling in fields while farm overseers counted their profits with thick fingers.

The posters I had seen today plastered on the walls were openly hostile, dripping in vitriol. In small beady letters, they detailed an issue from the *Sicherheitspolizei* stating that Jews could not change their place of residence, or walk on the pavement or attend the theatre or school. All property owned by Jewish people was to be confiscated, and work to register any Jews remaining in Estonia would be carried out as soon as possible. Anybody who knew the addresses of Jewish people was encouraged to contact members of the *Selbstschutz*. Doctor Otto-Heinrich Drechsler, the High Commissioner of Ostland, had decreed that all Jewish residents must wear the yellow Star of David on the left side of their chest and back. Anyone of mixed race or who was suspected of having sexual relations with a Jewish person was considered 'mischling' and could be arrested for having Jewish sympathies.

Etti was safe for now, but things could change quickly.

Her husband had been Jewish by birth, but non-practising. She could not be arrested while the laws remained. I would also be at risk if the laws changed. If my mixed parentage was exposed, even the fact that my mother had been Estonian would not be enough to save me. I kept as low a profile as I could, never speaking more than was necessary to the baker's wife or the man who sold us our meat. I spoke only in Estonian or the German I had learnt at school.

There were other changes, also. Those people who had dared to hide their radios when the Soviet government outlawed them were encouraged to bring them out now, so that they could listen to Goebbels or Rosenberg, the Reich Minister for the Occupied Eastern Territories, outlining Germany's role in establishing a stable seat of government in the Baltics. Far from leaving, the Germans seemed bent on settling in and the longer they stayed, the greater the sense of dread which seemed to creep into everyday life.

The presence of their new propaganda was an unspoken weight. It stifled ordinary conversation and squeezed out any small pleasure that might be found in snatches of time spent bent over lacework. I wished I had Jakob to ask about it, but I had only seen him once over the past week and we'd been surrounded by others. I had suggested visiting the barracks, but Kati refused to go with me. I suspected that despite her calm, aloof manner, Kati was just as afraid as I was.

'Are you deaf?' Helga said. 'I just told you there is no bread. You might as well go home.' She raised her chin a little as if defying anyone to decry her claim. 'All of you!'

The crowd around us murmured. One of the other

women in the queue was brave enough to call out: 'There was bread yesterday, Helga!'

Helga's scowl deepened. She palmed back a wisp of hair with a dusty hand. 'I know. But that was yesterday. Today, there is none.' Her eyes roved over the crowd. Two small flames of colour danced in her pouchy cheeks. 'There are soldiers here who are defending your lands. They require food, sustenance. Their needs are greater. If you've any complaints, you may take it up with *Reichskommissar* Lohse. He's in charge now.'

The men and women muttered as empty baskets shifted from hand to hand. As if to torment us, a breath of yeasty air puffed out before the door to the workroom finally shuddered to a close.

Helga waved at us, making shooing gestures with her hands. 'Out! Out!'

People began to move, shuffling reluctantly towards the entrance of the shop.

'What are we supposed to feed our children?' a young woman asked, standing her ground against the shifting tide.

Helga squinted. 'That's not my problem. There are plenty of other foodstuffs to be had. Try the butcher; I saw a lorry pull up this morning with fresh slaughter from the factories.'

Grasping my basket, I guided Etti towards the front doors.

'I suppose we should be thankful Leelo has not started eating yet,' Etti said as we made our way towards the butcher's shop.

I flicked her a cautious smile, but she seemed unusually optimistic, swinging her basket so that it bumped against her knees as we passed a boarded-up pharmacy. An army truck rolled past, obscuring the window, flooding the road with petrol smoke.

Etti turned her head to look back. 'That was Mama's favourite shop,' she said, her eyes suddenly sombre. 'She always bought her soap there. Pine tar. It's good for the skin.'

She stopped so suddenly I almost crashed into her.

'What is it?' Starting to panic, I searched the road for danger. The truck had moved on, its wheels grinding on the cobblestones. It came to a stop outside an open wrought iron gate where a group of German soldiers were gathered around a dozen people. Most of them were men dressed in black suits but the few women who stood with them wore simple dresses of grey with black heels. Yellow stars like sunbursts stood out against their dark clothes. They clustered together, looking confused and wary. The tall façade of the synagogue loomed behind them, its arched windows reflecting the sky. Kati and I had passed it before, but I'd not taken much notice. We had similar synagogues in Moscow, although attending them was frowned upon as the populace was not encouraged to pursue any faith which could disrupt the teachings of communism. As we stood watching, the back doors of the truck swung open. The soldiers raised their weapons and began to drive the people towards the truck. Some of the men hesitated, while others began to do as they were bid.

One woman refused to go.

'Where are you taking us?' she demanded, thrusting her purse in front of her like a weapon. 'Who will tell our families?'

In answer, a ringing blow from a soldier's hand sent her sprawling. One of her shoes came loose and rolled away into the gutter. The soldier who had struck her dragged her roughly to her feet and thrust her into the truck where her companions waited. He did not bother to retrieve her shoe. We watched the truck lurch off, leaving four soldiers behind to stand outside the gates of the synagogue, preventing anyone from going in or out.

'Oh, Lida.' Etti drew closer to me, her hand seeking mine. Her bony hip dug into my side but I did not move away. Her trembling hand communicated everything we could not say in words.

Germany's intentions were now quite clear. It was not enough for the Jews to be marked as other, their movements restricted. They were being rounded up and taken to who knew where? Estonia was to be cleansed of Jews; *Judenfrei*. Next they would target the other 'undesirables'; those of mixed blood. The Roma people and the Russians and the Lithuanians who refused to be Germanised and had already organised a strong resistance movement to oppose the occupying force.

What did this mean for Etti and Leelo . . . and for me?

'What a time you've been.'

Kati's face in the crack between door and stairwell was pinched tight. 'I was beginning to think I would need to leave Leelo with Helle and come find you myself.'

Leelo cried out suddenly in the timber cradle beside the window, as if she had heard her name.

Kati crossed the room in a few steps, scooping her up and bouncing her in her hands, letting her small feet in their socks skim the floor. 'What took you so long?' Her voice carried a thin note of exasperation. She looked up and seemed to see our expressions for the first time.

I imagined how we must look; Etti with her eyes rubbed raw from crying. Me, with my lace shawl askew and my hair tangled by the wind. We had hurried home as quickly as we could, taking the shortest route possible, not daring to visit the butcher.

Kati's eyes widened. Laying Leelo gently down on her back in the cradle, she embraced her cousin. 'What on earth happened?'

I glanced at Etti. She was shaking her head, her lips clamped shut. She would not talk about it. Just as she had when Juudit died, she would internalise her fear and her suffering. I watched her scoop Leelo up from her cot and squeeze her tightly, closing her eyes as if she could keep the world at bay.

'Kati,' I said, trying to speak in a normal tone. 'Can you help me put these things away?' Kati's lips were white but she nodded.

The kitchen was a small square of space with barely enough elbow room for both of us. Cooking smells haunted the corners; fried fish, cinnamon apples, mutton stew. Their lingering odours were a kind of torment when all we had eaten for the past few weeks was hard loaves of bread or bone broth or watery grain flavoured with whatever dried spices remained in Aunt Juudit's pantry. I had barely placed the basket on the countertop when I felt Kati's fingers digging into my arm.

'Tell me,' she said, her expression grave.

I drew a deep breath. Like Etti, I found it difficult to put into words how terrifying the scene at the synagogue had been. Instead, I told Kati about the posters, the *Sicherheitspolisei* and their new laws about what Jews could and could not do.

Kati let go of me and clutched the bench top.

'What will we do?' I could hear the edge of hysteria in my voice. 'What if we're discovered?' I had heard rumours about what the Germans did to 'undesirables'. Whispers about internment camps like the gulags in Siberia, where food was scarce and the only clothing was whatever you arrived in. *I wish Jakob was here*, I thought. I wanted him to hold me.

'We will just stay inside,' Kati said after a long moment. 'We won't fetch our rations unless we need them. Surely we have enough now to last a week or so. Show me what you brought back.'

Before I could stop her, Kati reached out and snatched the handkerchief off the basket. She drew out the wedge of crusty hard-rimmed cheese at the bottom we'd picked up at the general store and then the wax paper containing the rattling beans.

'Cheese.' Confusion clouded her eyes. 'And . . .' She unknotted the twine. The shrivelled brown pellets slid from their sacking onto the bench. Kati ran a finger through them and they shifted, dividing into two small piles. It was barely enough to feed a fieldmouse.

She lifted her hand away suddenly, as if disturbing the beans might shrink them further and straightened, her mouth set.

'There was nothing else,' I said. 'There are food shortages.'

'What about bread?'

I shook my head. My limbs felt heavy. 'The Germans have taken everything. It's like a cloud of locusts passed over. That was all I could find.' I nodded at the cheese and the seeds. 'And we were lucky to get that. Others weren't so fortunate. I saw a woman weeping; someone had stolen the food right out of her hands and run off before she had a chance to cry out. And as for the butcher; well, we didn't go.'

Kati shook her head, her brow still creased. Anxiety and disapproval rolled off her in waves. My skin prickled with heat. I couldn't stand the thought that she might think I had deliberately avoided going to the butcher's without a reasonable cause.

'There is something else,' I said, mouth dry.

As I poured out everything we had seen at the synagogue, I watched the colour leach from Kati's cheeks. A look of pain crossed her face and she clutched her stomach with a knotted fist.

'That was the reason we didn't go to the butcher,' I finished. 'We thought it best to get home. Things are so uncertain right now; the Germans are still working out which Jews fled and who stayed behind. But they have started whatever they are planning and at some point, they will come to check on us. Oh, Kati . . . what will we do when that happens? What will happen?'

Kati said nothing. Muffled sounds echoed through the wall of the kitchen from the new residents next door. Somebody shouted in German, immediately followed by the sound of something heavy thudding to the floor – the dizzy clunk of a bottle spinning – and then the shouting resumed.

The sound seemed to stir Kati to life. Striding past me, she headed for the coat stand in the hallway, shrugged her worn brown coat off its hanger and thrust her arms into it. Pulling her lace shawl around her head, she grasped my coat and held it out to me, shaking it silently and warning me with her eyes not to disturb Etti and the sleeping Leelo.

She did not turn to me until we were both standing in the dim landing. Only the small sliver of light from the open door of our apartment showed the tired angles of her face.

Someone had stolen the corridor's light bulb weeks ago. Now we had to make our way up and down clutching the handrail and praying that no boards were loose.

'Where are we going?' I said. I wanted nothing more than to run back inside and slam the door closed on the world. I dreaded going back out into the street where the signs of German occupation were everywhere. *Jakob is out there,* a small voice reminded me.

Kati pulled the belt tighter around her coat. It was already a size too large, and her wrists were bone thin. Her face was gaunt and her once-glossy hair hung limp in its plait.

I shivered as the cold from the building seeped into my skin.

'We're going out to find help. I won't sit here waiting for them to come. That's what my father did; he waited too long. I'll ask Helle to come and help Etti with Leelo while we're gone.' I heard her footsteps scrape along the threadbare carpet runner, then the sound of her boots descending the stairs.

'What if Helle isn't home?' The handrail slid through my fingers.

Kati muttered something, but I couldn't quite catch it.

It might have been 'God help us' or something dramatic, like, 'We are damned'. I followed meekly after her and didn't ask her to repeat it.

In truth, I didn't want to know.

Teardrop Pattern

Kati

A MISTY RAIN BEGAN TO SIFT DOWN AS WE REACHED THE street of the barracks where Oskar and Jakob spent their time now. People hurried past, shielding their heads with their hands. I did not raise my hands but allowed the increasingly heavy drops to strike my head like bullets and soak into my hair, worm their way through the woven shawl. I shivered in grim penance. Why had we fooled ourselves into thinking the Germans would give Estonia back so easily? That they would not bring their hateful race laws into our country, along with their guns and their tanks and their promises to help rebuild our towns?

We wanted to believe the best.

I imagined the words being spoken in my father's tongue. The spicy fog of smoke from his pipe drifted across my vision. Hadn't he wanted to believe the Russians could do no worse the second time around? That we would be better off if we gave in, protected our own, helped them to achieve what they wanted while keeping our own heritage safe? But he'd been wrong. First the farms. Then the decree that only Russian should be spoken. Travel between towns and villages restricted. Soon, even something as innocent as a lace shawl was too dangerous. It would be the same now, I realised. The Nazification of Estonia had begun.

A cold finger of rain traced the vertebrae of my back.

I came to a stop beneath an awning outside an old pharmacy, Lydia pausing beside me. She ran a hand through her damp hair. Her teeth were chattering. We stared together at the barracks looming on the opposite side of the street, a drab grey building of sturdy bricks. A German soldier stood at attention before the doors, a rifle resting in his hands. Even from across the street, the swastika symbols blazoned on his uniform stood out. Squinting up through the haze, I tried to spy Oskar's face but the windows of the former gymnasium revealed nothing. Ghosts of school bells pealed out and the chatter of former pupils was almost audible beneath the patter of rain. Where were those children now?

The Germans had requisitioned the school along with a few other buildings for their soldiers. The education of children was second to winning the war against the Russians and their new Allies.

Thinking of Etti, I bit down on my fear and crossed the street, Lydia close on my heels.

'Good day.'

The German soldier blinked. He was a young man. Rain dripped off his peaked cap and spotted his collared shirt.

'I'm looking for a man,' I said, my voice rasping a little with nerves. 'He's a soldier,' I added, the colour rising in my cheeks. 'Oskar Mägi. One of the Estonian Home Guard.'

A frown twitched the corners of the man's lips, and I rushed on, gabbling my words a little. 'And my brother, Jakob Rebane. A fellow officer. Do you think you can help us?'

'Smile,' I heard Lydia mutter near my shoulder. I sweetened my expression, imagining I was just a woman visiting her beau, but the awkward moment stretched on.

The muscles around my lips began to ache.

After what seemed an age, the soldier lowered his rifle. 'Of course. Shall I fetch them for you?'

His eyes travelled over my body, lingering on my breasts and waist. I shrank instinctively inwards, my shoulders hunching. I felt Lydia shift. Her fingers prodded gently into my back. I straightened.

'Yes. It would be kind of you,' I said. 'We would be so grateful.'

The man barked a laugh. 'All right. Wait here.' He turned back to proffer a lopsided grin. 'Those Home Guard boys need to relax a little. Their gloomy faces are bringing us all down.'

A second later, the door banged closed. Lydia and I were alone again, shivering together to avoid the rain sluicing down from the eaves.

'Thank God.' Lydia shot me a dark look.

'What?'

'Are you really so guileless?' Shaking her head, she pressed the edge of her shawl to her damp hairline. When she pulled it away, raindrops clung to the cloth like glittering glass beads. 'I've heard it said the Germans consider Estonians the most Germanic of the Baltics. Your fair hair and your pale skin. Those kinds of things are pleasing to a group of people who want to stamp the "impurities" out of human existence.'

'We are not like them.' My eyes stung, as if hot ashes had suddenly blown in my direction.

'I didn't say you were,' Lydia huffed. 'But at least make use of what you have.' She glared up at the faceless windows. 'What do you think he meant? About the Home Guard?'

'I don't know.' I tried to remember what the guard had said.

That Oskar was gloomy? I was not surprised by this. Perhaps he was as disappointed with the Germans as we were. I had not seen him since the day of the procession days ago. The memory of the time we had spent in the farmhouse was enough to bring heat rushing into my cheeks; the scorch of his lips on my skin and the pressure of his hands locked around my waist ensuring my dreams were filled with pleasurable sensations.

A fountain of rain water suddenly erupted from the downpipe, coursing down onto the cobblestones. Lydia jumped back, cursing in Russian, almost knocking into me. She mumbled an apology.

'Katarina.' Straightening up, I found the object of my daydreams standing before me. He slipped out the half-open door. He was smiling but his eyes were cold. Taking my arm, his gaze scoured the rain-washed street. 'You didn't send a note.' His grip tightened.

'I know. I—'

'I told you not to come here.' His voice was low, each word punctuated by another squeeze.

'Yes, but . . .'

'Ah. You've found her.' The German soldier sauntered towards us, his features twisted with amusement. 'Good. You are a lucky man, Mägi.' Envy suffused his face.

'Yes.' Oskar grinned. 'Thank you, Koster. This is my wife. She's brought her friend to chaperone and make sure I am on my best behaviour.' He peered out at the rain sloshing down. 'Do you think . . . I realise it's unorthodox, but might I take the women inside, at least until the downpour ceases? We will stay in the reception room. Near the fire.'

The German soldier shrugged. 'I don't see why not.'

He gestured us inside.

As soon as the door slammed behind us, Oskar wheeled around, releasing my arm with such force I flinched. 'What are you doing here?' He ran his hand through his hair. His eyes were blazing. I was only vaguely aware of the bright fire flickering in the grate, the wood-panelled entrance hall that must once have been used for student roll call. School plaques adorned the walls. It was a much grander school than the one Oskar and Jakob and I had attended on Tartu's outskirts. Our schoolhouse had been a large timber structure, more like a barn, with a gabled roof and two fireplaces to warm the frigid air in winter so our stiff fingers could grasp the pencils. Lydia shuffled behind me, twisting her hands together. 'And you brought her, too?' Oskar threw up his hands. 'What were you thinking, Katarina?'

Anger bubbled up before I could smother it. 'I had no choice but to bring her! And why do you keep calling me that?' Tears pricked my eyes and I turned away, determined not to show him how he had wounded me.

Oskar sucked in a breath through his nose. 'I'm sorry.' He spoke softly. His tone was intimate. He touched my shoulder lightly. 'Kati. Turn around.'

Reluctantly, I did so but I kept my chin tilted up. Oskar's face was grave.

'I'm sorry,' he repeated. 'It was a shock to see you. After I specifically warned you not to come. I should not have argued. Forgive me.'

'Where is Jakob?' Lydia asked.

Oskar made a sound in his throat. 'He's upstairs.'

Something about the way he said it – and the fact that we hadn't seen another soldier in the barracks; it was eerily quiet

– made the hairs rise on my arms. 'What's wrong with him?'

Oskar tapped his fingers against his thigh, looking from Lydia back to me. Suddenly, he seemed to come to a decision. Wrapping my arm in his again, he marched me towards the staircase. 'Come. Both of you. You can ask him yourself.'

Lydia's footsteps clattered on the stairs behind us. A small wave of relief washed over me. *Jakob is alive.* But the relief vanished when Oskar opened the door to a narrow room, holding it back so that we could slip inside before shutting it firmly.

Jakob sat on a bed inside, nursing his head in his hands. Lydia gasped as he lifted his face. His skin was as grey as ash and lined with a thin film of sweat. A deep open gash the length of my palm ran from his cheekbone down to his chin. It looked red and angry, the edges raised, inflamed. Dried blood crusted his ear, matting his hair.

'Lydia?' His eyes were glazed, slightly unfocused. They slid towards me, lingering on my wet hair. He said my name, his voice slurred as if he were half-asleep.

'What happened to you?' Lydia pushed past me, dropping to her knees before him. She brought her hand up to his face but held off touching the oozing wound.

'Jakob was reprimanded earlier today.' Oskar's voice was hard. He had moved to stand beside the window. 'Along with three others.'

'Reprimanded for what?' Lydia pulled a handkerchief from the pocket of her skirt. 'And by whom?'

'For refusing to help them measure wood to build a platform outside the city to execute Jewish families.' Jakob eased out a shaky laugh. 'You know I never was good with numbers.'

Lydia made a strangled noise in her throat and lifted one hand to cover her mouth.

A finger of fear slid down my back.

Oskar looked at me, his eyes dark. 'There is more; they are setting up a holding place some streets away in an old gymnasium. It will house Jewish people until the execution area is ready.'

A heavy silence met his words.

At last Jakob spoke. 'You would have refused to help too, Kati. You know you would.'

'The Wehrmacht doesn't look kindly on anyone who disagrees with their *Ostplan*,' Oskar said. 'Not even partisans who helped clear out the Russians so they could march in waving victory flags.'

'At least if they kill me, you'll be able to take my rations,' Jakob said.

'This is not a game!' Lydia scrunched the bloodstained handkerchief in her hand.

Jakob sighed. 'I know. I'm sorry.'

Oskar's shoulders slumped. 'Jakob has put us all in danger.'

Jakob's eyes slitted. He brushed Lydia's hand away. 'What would you have me do, Oskar? Murder them? In cold blood?'

'Of course not.' Oskar swung around. 'But you could have waited! You could have held off for a little longer voicing your objections. At least until I found a way for us to extricate ourselves. There will be others who resist the Germans. We need to find them, join them. Now we are all under Wehrmacht surveillance. That will make it . . . difficult.' His eyes, when he turned to me, had that same haunted, hunted look I had seen back in my parents' farmhouse months ago. 'We've been given a day to review our actions. That's why it's so quiet. Everybody is too afraid to venture out now. I am only thankful that I did Koster a favour when he first arrived, giving up the names of some Russian spies that he was able to take to his commanding officer and claim as his own. He must think you're harmless or he would never have let you in.'

'What will happen to the ones who refuse?' I said, rubbing my cold hands together to try to warm the feeling into them. Somehow I already knew.

Oskar's mouth tightened. 'Those who don't comply with orders will be shot. Not everybody shares Jakob's opinions anyway. It seems the arrival of the Germans has not brought out the best in everyone. There are men here – Estonian men – who were happy to volunteer to round up Jews and help build the execution site.' He drew in a ragged breath. 'I wouldn't believe it if I'd not seen it with my own eyes. After everything we've been through. Everything that was done to us.'

I tried to swallow, to pull my eyes away from the wound that marred Jakob's face. 'We need to get Etti and Leelo away as quickly as possible,' I said. 'Technically they're not Jewish, but the Germans will still come for them. And Lydia—' I looked across at her, standing quietly beside my brother, the bloody cloth still clutched in her hand. Her skin was pallid. Raindrops shimmered in her dark hair like diamonds. 'It's not safe for her, either. If anyone discovers who she is, she will be arrested. If not worse.'

Fear flickered across my brother's face. 'We can't let that happen.' He reached up and gripped her hand, holding it tightly. The look of tenderness which passed between them was as intimate as a kiss.

Oskar said nothing. His hands along the windowsill were clenched. 'This isn't what I wanted,' he said, almost as if he was talking to himself. 'Swapping one enemy for another? This isn't what we planned.' His eyes blazed for a moment, but then his shoulders slumped. 'There may be a way to get them out. I have a contact in Narva with a speedboat. He has started running people back and forth to Finland, then a truck takes them on to Sweden. But it's slow going. And dangerous. Now that they're watching us . . . well. It will be difficult to pass a message along to him. It will take time. We will have to give them the impression we are compliant. That we agree with what they're doing.'

I looked away so that I would not have to see his face. 'How can we do that?'

'There are things we can do. Small acts of resistance that helped us fight the Russians. The underground press will have to start up again. We can find messengers to hand out fliers. Tell people about what is happening with the Jews. The Roma. The Estonian Russians. The *Ostplan* aims to eliminate all of them. We can put people into contact with smugglers, urge them to hide or escape while they can. But as for you and Etti . . .' His eyes flicked to Lydia. 'It will take time for me to secure passage. You will need to be stationed in Narva, ready to leave at any moment. I think it would be best if you went with them, Kati.' He looked across at me, and I understood his reluctance.

He was afraid. Afraid that if we stayed, something terrible would happen, but if we went, he could not be nearby to help. This knowledge made my temples pulse. If Oskar was afraid, scared enough to send us on to Sweden, then whatever the Nazis had planned for Estonia must be terrible indeed. In that moment, I could almost feel the invisible plates shifting below my feet. All I could do was cling to the hope that we would be reunited when the horror was over.

'What reason would we have to be in Narva?' I said.

'I can think of one.' Jakob lifted his head. 'The Germans are calling for volunteers to help at the textiles factory; Kreenholm. It's on a small island right next to the city of Narva. Operations have stalled since the Russians left, but the Germans need uniforms. They're asking women to travel there to help weave the cloth.'

'But what about Leelo?' Lydia asked. 'We can't leave her behind!'

'No,' replied Jakob. 'I was told there is a nanny to take care of children while women work.'

Oskar took my hand. I could feel his fingers but inside I was numb. 'It will be dangerous there. It's close to the border. The bombing will be worse. But that's why my contact chose it. The constant bombing means the river goes unguarded at night. It wouldn't be for long; we would get you out as soon as we could.'

'Narva.' I tested the word. I had never travelled there; indeed, I had never travelled anywhere apart from Tallinn a few hours away.

'It will be a limited operation until they can gather more women to help,' Oskar said. 'The Germans don't want to use forced labour yet. They will, though, if they don't get enough volunteers.' He grimaced. 'I don't like it. But Jakob is right. It would make a good cover and you will be ready to go when Jaan sends word. Etti and Leelo will need papers – that I can arrange.'

'What about you?'

A shower of rain suddenly hit the window, and lightning forked the sky, lighting up the dim room. Oskar's hand was still warm in mine.

'Don't worry about us. Jakob and I will stick together. And there is always the forest, if things get too heated here.'

'Desertion.' I hated myself for saying it. Oskar dropped my hand at once as if stung. I knew how keenly he would feel it, the betrayal of everything he had vowed to do when he joined the *Omikaitse*, the Estonian Home Guard.

'We are not like them,' Oskar said, echoing my own words. 'We are partisans, not Nazis.' He nodded, as if to reassure himself. 'Give me a day. I will speak to the *Reichcommandant* about your volunteering for the Kreenholm work. Perhaps we can undo the damage Jakob has done and restore his faith in us. If they suspect us, it will make it almost impossible for us to do anything to help others. Come – I'll escort you out.'

He nudged open the door.

Lydia did not move. She was staring at Jakob, her lips trembling. She looked so young, her damp hair clinging to her freckled skin. I knew she wanted to say goodbye.

I felt as if my insides had been emptied and I was nothing more than a hollow shell. Perhaps I was too afraid to let myself feel. If I hugged Jakob now, I would fall apart. And saying goodbye would be like asking fate to find us, when what we needed was to hide.

Without looking at my brother, I hastened outside.

Oskar followed me into the empty corridor, and after a few moments he frowned. 'What's taking her so long?'

'She . . . she likes Jakob.'

Like was too weak a word, but I did not trust myself to say *love*. It was too painful, too dangerous a word.

Oskar rubbed the back of his neck with his hand. 'If she likes him so much, she would be best to leave now. In case Koster comes searching.'

'You will keep him safe,' I said. 'You promise.'

Oskar sighed. 'Of course I will. He is my brother now, too. You've no reason to doubt me, Kati. I would not have any of your friends or family harmed. Not Etti, not Leelo. Not Lydia.'

'How bad do you think it will be here?'

At first, I thought Oskar had not heard me. 'The execution site and the holding site are just the start. The *Reichcommandant* was speaking about the construction of a bigger camp in Harju County. A place for unsavoury elements to be housed.'

'Like the gulags? A labour camp?'

Oskar frowned. 'Or worse. I fear . . .' He ran his hand over his cropped hair. 'If things are bad at Kreenholm, you must go into Narva and find my friend Heldur. He lives on Turu Street.' Suddenly, he leant down swiftly and kissed me, his lips crushed against my own. Desire pulled at my stomach, and I reached up a hand and cupped his cheek, feeling the scrape of his bristles beneath my palm. Oskar's arm slid around my back and I had a sudden flushing sense of shame that he would feel the thin spokes of my rib bones poking out. I tried to draw away but he held me fast. Slowly I relaxed, leaning into him, the most natural thing in the world.

A noise startled us and Oskar pulled back, releasing me so quickly I stumbled a little.

'I'm sorry.' Lydia's eyes were red, swollen with tears. She rubbed the heel of her palm across her nose. Unable to help myself, I looked back to see Jakob still sitting on the bed, holding the scrunched-up handkerchief in his fingers. He looked terrible again, all the colour had left his face. He was turning the handkerchief as if it held the answer to a riddle, trying to decipher the scrapes of rust-coloured blood dotting the fabric.

Oskar said nothing but turned away and led us back down the stairs. My face stung where his beard had scraped against the skin. Even when we stepped outside, and the rain washed down my cheeks like a river of tears, the feeling of heat did not abate. I held my palm to my cheek, wishing I could stop time. But the heat was already leaving my skin, replaced by the cold, misty air swirling up the street.

Crow Pattern

Lydia
September 1941

'TEN MORE HERE.'

The doors of the lorry opened with a grinding shudder. The women around us jumped. A German officer stood between the doors. Sunlight blazed around him, illuminating the corners of the truck and the women's faces.

Beside me, I felt Etti tense. Her foot jiggled against the metal floor. Leelo shifted in her arms and stretched, small hands balled into fists above her head. On Etti's other side, I saw Kati lean forward, tenting a hand to shield off the bright sun. The blaze of light made a halo of her yellow hair.

'It's all right.' She patted Etti's arm. 'Nothing to fear. Just picking up more workers.'

Etti's foot stilled, but her arms remained rigid. My own muscles hardened in response. I was waiting for the soldiers to grab me by the arm any second and throw me out. I could already hear their voices shouting in German and feel the nose of the gun pressed between my ribs.

Nausea churned my stomach. It burnt up my windpipe until I could taste it at the back of my throat like decaying flowers.

'It's all right,' Kati said again, her voice soothing. Her hand crept across Etti's lap to touch mine gently. A reminder that we were all together. I tried to smile at her and push away my fear. But I could sense it running in the background like a piece of music with no words. Somehow, I'd imagined that once we were in the truck, on our way to Kreenholm and, eventually, heading with Oskar and Jakob towards the safety of Sweden, I would be less anxious. Instead, I felt worse. I had spent long hours struggling with the idea of leaving Estonia. Had I come all this way, losing Joachim and my precious Olga into the bargain, only to now abandon Mamochka's birthplace? And what would we find in Sweden? It was a country I knew only a little about. When I tried to imagine it, all my mind could conjure up were the seventeenth century castles of Greta Garbo's movie, and the baroque houses crowded along the archipelago in Stockholm which had featured in our school textbooks. It was hard to imagine leaving Tartu behind when I had only just begun to find my feet and to build a small space of happiness around me. Even the apartment had become dear to me. The shawls hanging on the hallstand, the bed with its scratchy woollen coverlet. The screaming kettle. The apartment had become my sanctuary.

Leaving it made me feel utterly exposed to the world. But Kati was right. With the danger of arrest and execution so imminent, we had no choice but to go. Jakob agreed.

Jakob. I could not even think of him without tears welling in my eyes. The fact that we had not even had a chance to say goodbye properly hurt most of all.

The Germans had arrived at dawn, banging on the door of the apartment and shouting at us to hurry, the lorry was waiting. It was lucky our things were packed. Oskar had warned us there would be little time to prepare, that once the

Germans organised the minimum number of women needed to run the factory they would come for us. But somehow I had still imagined we would be given an hour or two, enough time to get to the barracks. When I saw Kati's haggard face, I realised she had hoped the same. Oskar and Jakob had come to our apartment every night they could get away during the fortnight before our departure, but every night had seemed as if it was our last. In the end, we had not been able to tell them we were leaving. It was agony to know that the barracks was only a few blocks away but it may as well have been America. And then the Germans were barking orders at us. There was no time.

In the pearly grey light, we had stumbled outside clutching our bags, Leelo snuggled in a blanket against Etti's chest, and helped each other up into the back of the truck where a middle-aged woman and her two daughters were seated. One of the girls, around seventeen, had offered Etti a half-smile while the German officer shouted at the driver. The girls' mother had frowned and the smile vanished, wiped clean like chalk from a slate.

The woman and her daughters had not spoken a word since. I understood their reticence as we made this second stop. Everything we said now could be misconstrued and twisted.

The officer disappeared, and moments later more women had clambered up beside us. They had to squash themselves into the cramped space. Kati's knee pressed against my thigh as she wriggled closer to make space.

The truck doors banged closed, leaving us in partial darkness again. The only light came from the small pockets where the green tent canvas covering was not fixed down. As well as light, the pockets let in drafts of fresh air; a

381

welcome respite from the prickly scent of sweat and the earthy tang of potatoes.

'Surely they can't fit many more of us in,' a woman in a green kerchief grumbled. She lifted a hand to wipe away the sweat that glittered on her lip. 'I feel as if we're off to a labour camp! Not heading off to do our bit for the war effort.'

'You had a choice, did you?' another woman said. In the sparse light, her face was craggy, lined with age. She gripped her carpet bag in her lap, lurching sideways into her neighbour as the truck began to roll forward again. A shawl was tied around her hair, hanging in a triangle down her back. She reminded me of Olga. I almost smiled until the memory of Olga – her arm lifted in farewell, her face set – punctured my heart and I dropped my gaze to my lap, my throat clogged with unshed tears. 'Of course I did.' The woman in the kerchief glowered. 'I couldn't stand to see the Soviets come back. Stinking Russians. They would stab you in the back as soon as speak to you. Any small thing we can do to help the Germans is worth doing.'

Her words cut me deeply but I heard the truth in them. How wrong I had been about my fathers, the real one and the one who had claimed me as his own. Perhaps I was no better than what this woman suggested: a betrayer. I could not hope to atone for the misery my family had caused. The best I could do was to keep my worst secret hidden, reducing the danger to Kati and Etti. Sometimes I wondered if I dared confide in Kati. She had accepted so much about me already. But then her words would swim up from memory to haunt me, bringing back with awful clarity that last day we had shared in the refugee camp before the Russians burnt it down.

Stalin is a monster. As is anyone associated with him.

It was enough to make the courage drain out of me.

'You could have stayed back in Tartu,' Etti suggested. Her tone was cool. I looked over at her in surprise. Etti was never confrontational. But since the decision had been made to leave Tartu, she had seemed stronger, more sure of herself. Perhaps it was because she felt some small measure of control over what was happening. Even her colour looked better, her eyes brighter. She'd tied on an apron and cleaned the whole apartment after we'd told her our plans, scrubbing it from top to bottom with lemon-scented cleaning fluid.

'If I am going to leave it behind,' she said, 'I want to make sure Mama would have been proud of it.'

She had cooked up the last of the grain into small cakes and then washed the clothes we could not take and hung them back in the wardrobe, hoping that Helle or one of the others from the knitting circle would find a use for them when we were gone. The other women would be glad of the extra layers as winter settled in.

'Helle will never forgive us when she finds out we are not coming back,' Etti had said as she clattered the last hanger into the wardrobe.

'One day we will send word to her,' Kati said. 'When it's safe.'

Etti had nodded, pushing the stray hairs off her face with the heel of her hand and marching off to check that she had packed enough warm clothes for Leelo for the months ahead. When the Germans had arrived this morning, Etti had not shown fear but been the first to tie on her coat and pick up her bag. She had not looked back as we climbed into the truck, too focused on her own survival and Leelo's to allow sentiment to endanger them.

Now she bounced the gurgling Leelo up and down vigorously on her lap. 'No need to travel all the way to Narva to do your duty, is there?'

Green Kerchief clicked her tongue but stayed silent. The woman with the carpet bag said nothing, but when our gazes connected I saw her give the slightest nod to me and a tiny smile pinched the corners of her mouth. White hair peeped out beneath her shawl like tufts of sheep's wool.

The truck's wheels rumbled over the road. And then suddenly it halted. Voices were heard from the front, asking questions in German. My skin prickled.

Green Kerchief sniffed. 'Another delay?' she said.

I exchanged looks with Kati. Together, we lifted the flap of the canvas behind us and peeped through.

Outside, the sun struggled to shine through a smattering of clouds. The truck had stopped on the side of the road near some grey paddocks. A few cars had also halted. German soldiers leant into the driver's side windows, speaking rapid German before waving them on. I heard Kati's sharp intake of breath, and when I followed her gaze my own heart began to flutter wildly. Next to the road beside us lay dozens of bodies. They were piled into an open ditch, their clothing stained with mud from the recent rain. Women and children, hands splayed at odd angles like the limbs of broken dolls. Yellow stars were still tacked to their chests.

As we watched, a German officer standing guard tumbled one of the smallest bodies into the ditch with his boot. Clods of earth scattered over the child's pale face. It was clear that the ditch the Soviets had desperately dug out before they left – to prevent tanks from reaching Tartu – provided a convenient place to dispose of Jewish bodies.

'What is it?' Etti asked. She was feeding Leelo cow's milk from a bottle. Leelo's wide blue eyes stared up at the truck's ceiling, her mouth slowly moving around the teat. She had grown so long in the legs that Etti had to lie her flat to drink her milk. She could lift her head now and look about and bring her tiny toes to her mouth.

I saw Kati give the slightest shake of her head.

'It's nothing,' I said quickly. 'An accident. They will sort it out.'

I turned back, trying to appear relaxed but inside I was sobbing.

What if Oskar and Jakob had been forced to take part in this terrible act? I prayed that Oskar had found a way for them to slip away and return to the forest where they would be safe until they could find us again.

As the truck began to move again, Kati shifted, climbing over Etti until we were side by side. In the rocking darkness, her damp fingers found mine. We held hands, not speaking, as the truck bounced and juddered over the road, racing towards Narva.

Hours passed; we lost track of the number. At some point in the darkness Kati told me what she knew of Narva.

'It's an old place, Narva. Older than Tartu. It belonged to the Danes once, then the Germans and the Russians. The Narva Fortress runs all the way along the river, connected by stone passageways carved out of the ground. I have never been, but Papa took my mother sightseeing there once. She said she didn't care for it. All those dark passageways made her feel as if she'd entered the underworld. She said she was glad to come back out into the light and find the world still waiting for her . . .'

She paused, looking ahead. I could see she was struggling to conceal her emotions. It was always the same for me when I had to speak of Olga, or if I was thinking about Jakob. The same stare which held all the things that it was unsafe to say. I knew Kati was thinking of her mother – and Oskar.

'What do you know about the factory?' I said, hoping to distract her.

Kati swallowed visibly. 'Not a lot,' she admitted. 'Everybody's heard of it, of course. Kreenholm. But Papa never told us any stories about it.'

'My cousin's wife worked there once,' the woman with white hair said. 'Before she moved south. There were ten thousand people employed there once.' She paused to let this settle. 'It's a huge place. Built on an island surrounded by a vast river. There are three buildings, she told me,' the woman went on. 'A textile mill, a spinning room and a weaving factory. Water turbines keep the machinery turning. There are probably more now than when she worked there. Those Russians knew how to industrialise.'

'Maybe,' said one girl with a constellation of freckles smattering her nose. 'But they knew nothing about clothes! When they arrived in Rakvere and occupied the houses left behind, some of the wives were heard to exclaim that they had never before seen so many varieties of clothing. All the Soviet clothes came from the one factory and they were all the same colour and the same shape. The Partorg in our area held a banquet at the Town Hall and invited all the Russian officials who'd just moved in; their wives showed up in nightgowns the Estonians had abandoned. They thought they were ball gowns!'

Some of the women snuffled with laughter.

'That's just a rumour.' The woman with the white hair smiled at me. 'I'm Jelena Ilves.'

'Lydia Androvna,' I told her, feeling only a slight twinge of guilt at the lie. Anyone who remembered the Partorg would surely connect us. All the same, Green Kerchief swivelled her gaze to me. 'This is my friend, Katarina Mägi, and her cousin, Etti. And the little dumpling you see there is Leelo.'

I grasped awkwardly for the hand Jelena extended. Her fingers were careworn and roughened. The truck rounded a bend and she laughed as our hands slipped apart.

'I imagine we will be seeing quite a bit of each other.' Jelena glanced around the truck. 'All of us. Best we know who our new companions are sooner than later.'

'I'm Agnese Rosenberg.' The woman in the green kerchief raised her chin. Her eyes glittered defiantly in the dim cavern beneath eyebrows plucked so thin they were almost invisible. Something tugged at me. A memory, a whisper. I almost spoke aloud in my head, asking Mama. But she'd been silent ever since the day after the deportations, the day of Etti's birth when I had sung her song and imagined her holding me for the first time. It was almost as if the pure intensity of that moment had severed our connection.

I tried to study Agnese. Had I seen her at the bakery? But the woman had already withdrawn into the darker shadows at the edge of the truck.

Other women called out from the semi-darkness, their voices mingling. Some sounded resigned, others hopeful.

I couldn't begin to know their motivations for coming to Kreenholm. They were all women like Etti and Kati. If it were not for their names and accents, which pinned them down to different geographic regions, I doubted that anyone would be able to tell them apart in the dark. It was only my accent which seemed unusual. All those years in Moscow made it impossible for me to speak Estonian with the ease of someone who had lived here all her life. I cautioned myself again to speak only when necessary. It was dangerous now to draw attention to anything which was at odds. A few weeks, that was all we needed to stay. A month at most. As long as it took Oskar to organise our passage and send word to us that it was time to run. We did not need to make friends.

Suddenly, Kati stiffened. 'Kreenholm,' she said, her head tilted to one side. 'Listen.' She gripped my arm. 'Can you hear it?'

The truck rumbled to a halt and the sound rose up beneath the throbbing engine. The roar of water. The churn of turbines. Lapping of waves against stone.

Twisting, I pulled back the flap of canvas again. The sunlight dazzled my eyes as I made out stacked chimneys, brick red. Huge buildings that rocketed skywards so I had to duck my head to fit them into view. A set of vast doors atop a flight of stone stairs.

And before it all, a pair of tall black iron gates loomed between two brick parapets.

German voices rang out as our driver spoke to the guard. Seconds later, the truck lurched forward as we crossed the threshold and mounted the small bridge that separated the township of Narva from the Kreenholm factory.

A small cry of relief rose up as the doors were unbarred and we tumbled out. Some women groaned as they unfolded themselves, rubbing joints made stiff with travel over the bumpy roads. Etti was smiling – the first genuine smile I had seen from her in weeks. Jelena chucked Leelo under the chin and Etti looked on indulgently. Kati, too, seemed pleased at first, although I saw her frown up at the buildings, so vast above us, almost as if they were built for giants from one of Olga's fairy tales.

I tried to look up, to see the place where the buildings met the sky but my neck resisted, cramping painfully. The German officer loudly instructed the women to move forward into the building and assemble. A noise broke the sound of feet shuffling towards the doors. It was the cawing of birds. I looked around and spied crows clustered on the bare branches of a tree in a flowerbed rampant with weeds. At least a dozen creatures, beaks tipped open, feathers ruffled by the breeze. Their black liquid eyes watched us impassively.

An arm slipped suddenly through mine. 'Pay them no attention.' Jelena's face was sour with dislike. 'I never cared for crows, either. But my mother always said if you leave them alone, they will find other people to bother. And my mother was a smart woman.' Applying slight pressure to my arm, she began to coax me towards the doors.

From the top of the steps, I could look back at the road that had brought us here. Rows of narrow houses lined the street beyond the gates. Flowerbeds heaped against their walls, late-blooming roses, bright as jewels, and brown spikes of seeding lavender. I could hear, but not see the water yet. I felt the ground shudder as the turbines spun.

It all looked so normal. Compared to Tartu's streets with their undercurrent of terror, it even seemed appealing, the rush of the water cleansing everything. A place of new hope, even if for just a few weeks until Oskar arranged our escape.

The crows were the only blight on the peaceful view.

Jelena squeezed my arm. 'You mustn't let them disturb you. This is their place, after all.'

'What do you mean?'

She gave a small shrug. 'Kreenholm. Roughly translated: crow island. Isle of Crows, my cousin's wife said.'

A prickle ran beneath my skin. Island of crows. Island of dead things and carrion flesh. I wondered what Olga would have made of that. I heard her voice. *A bird taps the window three times: death is coming.*

Before I could speak, Jelena had tugged me inside. The doors clanged shut behind us as the German officer from the truck shifted in behind us to stand guard.

Ahead, I could see Kati's plait swinging at her back. Etti stood beside her, soothing the grizzling Leelo with soft words. I made my way towards them, Jelena beside me. A long timber staircase wound up to the next level of the building. The other women were murmuring to each other, but their voices died when a man descended the stairs and paused a few steps from the bottom. He did not seem embarrassed to be half-dressed. A white starched shirt tucked into olive trousers and a silk brocade waistcoat cinched around his waist. A half-sewn jacket was slung casually over his clothes. One sleeve was missing, the other hung loosely, held together with pins. My heart caught when I saw the swastika symbol emblazoned on the armband as if a spider had found its way onto the fabric and been ironed in by mistake.

'Welcome ladies,' he said in Estonian. His German accent was thicker than my Russian one. He seemed to chew on the words before spitting them out. 'Thank you for leaving your homes and coming to where you are most needed. I am the manager here. My name is General Hans Burkhard.' He gestured with his hands at the two women standing a few steps below him. 'This is my wife, Frau Burkhard. And Hilda, the woman who will look after your children while you stay and work with us.' I dropped my gaze to study the two women standing near him. Frau Burkhard was at least a decade younger than the general. Her hair, so pale it was almost translucent, was knotted in an elegant bun at the top of her head. She stood so straight I thought her back must be aching, her face immovable as a statue's. Hilda, by contrast, was plump and wore a smile of welcome. A spotless apron was knotted about her waist.

'These are the two women who will be your greatest allies during your time with us at Kreenholm. If you have any needs, you may feel free to discuss them with Frau Burkhard, who is used to keeping everything at our factories running smoothly. I fear you will see little of me, as business generally keeps me confined to the offices upstairs. I must apologise that you've caught me in such a state of undress.' He paused to pluck at the sleeve of his half-made suit. 'It was remiss of me to arrange for my tailor to attend to my clothing this morning. But as you will soon learn, this is a great day for Germany and for all of those who fall under her protection. I simply had to come down to greet you and tell you the news personally.' His face contorted into a smile. 'We have just been informed German troops have reached the city of Leningrad.'

I felt my breath snatched away.

General Burkhard nodded as the women exclaimed openly. 'First Leningrad, then Moscow. Within a matter of weeks, we expect the Russian empire to fall completely into German hands. I trust you will join me in celebrating tonight in the cafeteria where we will indulge in the best quality foodstuffs that can be obtained during such hard times.' His eyes sparkled. 'I gather you all remember the sweet taste of vanilla pudding?'

Some women clapped their hands to their mouths.

I could not imagine the taste. All I could think about was the way Olga had described the Revolution to me; the sharp rattle of gunfire, the ashes from burning buildings that caught in her throat and stung her eyes. The people of Leningrad must be terrified. Tonight, the sky would be streaked with red. The city was besieged.

I blinked hard and stared up at the ceiling, trying not to show how the news disturbed me. When I looked down, it was to find Agnese staring hard at me. Outside of the truck, in the light of day, I could see she was not well. Cavernous shadows circled her eyes and her cheekbones strained against her white skin. The green kerchief tied over her hair was obviously meant to conceal the fact that much of it was falling out. There were patches where it was missing entirely.

Fear flared inside me.

I know this woman. But I could not place her. Did she know me? I turned to ask Kati if she remembered seeing Agnese in the street, but Kati and Etti were busy talking about pudding. When I looked back, Agnese had turned her back on me to discuss the siege with her neighbour and I wondered if I had imagined it all.

Money Pattern

Kati

'I ONLY HOPE THEY HAVE ENOUGH SENSE NOT TO HOUSE the Russians with the rest of us.' Agnese scrutinised the dormitory on the second floor of the factory into which we had all gathered. Over the past hour, another four lorries had arrived in the driveway, delivering their passengers before speeding off. Women and tired-looking children had been slowly shepherded up the winding staircase to the residential wing and deposited here, where we all waited for Frau Burkhard to return and assign us rooms. When Agnese's gaze fell on Lydia she paused. 'You can't trust them,' she went on. 'They'll betray us before long, you'll see. They will defect and run across the bridge to their friends and bring down a terrible hellfire to burn us all.'

Some of the women murmured uneasily. Lydia had looked down at her feet as if she wished she could melt into the floor. 'Nonsense.' Jelena Ilves pressed the back of her hand to her sweaty cheek. 'You're letting your imagination run away with you. Everyone who is here wants to be here. You're just cranky and tired. You would be better to conserve your strength for the long hours of work tomorrow. You know how the saying goes – a wolf will not break a wolf. We must work together. Agreed?'

The women around us nodded. I saw Lydia shoot Jelena a small grin. Of course. Lydia had already made a friend. Jelena had been charmed by the openness of her face and the charisma that always seemed to elude me. Still, I was glad that I did not need to defend Lydia alone.

Agnese opened her mouth to retort, but at that moment Frau Burkhard strode back in, Hilda bouncing along obediently in her wake. The women shifted to make way for her, breaking apart then forming a circle around the German woman. Etti scooped Leelo up from the bed on which she'd placed her.

'Your attention, ladies.' Producing a clipboard from beneath her thin arm, Frau Burkhard touched the bun on her head, sweeping invisible wisps of hair away from her face. 'You are to listen for me to call your name and follow Hilda outside to your dormitories. These are the rooms you will share with six of your companions for the duration of your stay.'

'Six?' Agnese glanced around in disbelief at the small space into which we had all somehow managed to squeeze. 'I hope we are not expected to share beds, too, with perfect strangers.'

Frau Burkhard's cool smile did not change. 'No. Of course not. But we simply don't have the staff to clean room after room, so resources have been combined. You will get to know each other soon enough.'

'What about the women who have infants?' Agnese shot a quick look at Etti. 'How can we be expected to catch enough sleep to perform our duties when we are disturbed by the wailing of children?'

Frau Burkhard waved a hand dismissively. 'Hilda will take care of them. In fact, it would be good for the children to get used to the nursery now, seeing as that is where they will be staying. Please bring your children forward.'

Nobody moved.

Frau Burkhard tapped her clipboard with sharp fingernails. 'Don't be shy, now. It's for their own safety. The machines in the factory are dangerous. They must be supervised.'

Slowly, the women moved to obey her. A young mother led her son and daughter to Hilda and kissed their cheeks before stepping away.

I saw Etti hesitate, her arms curved protectively around Leelo's body.

My throat tightened. Moving close to her, I placed my hand reassuringly on her back. 'It's all right,' I told her quietly, beneath the voices of the other women instructing their children to listen, to behave and do as Hilda asked. 'It's only temporary. Remember? Just until . . .'

I let my words trail off, but Etti understood my meaning anyway. As soon as Oskar sent word to us, Etti and Leelo could be together again.

Etti nodded. 'It's just temporary,' she murmured in the baby's ear. Kissing Leelo's pale hair, she passed her into Hilda's waiting arms. Leelo gave Hilda an appraising look with her clear blue eyes.

'She has a bottle every three hours,' Etti told the German girl. 'Please make sure she's not left alone. She rolls everywhere.'

Hilda smiled. 'Of course. Don't worry yourself.' With the other children following behind, she trotted out, disappearing upstairs towards the East wing, which we had been told housed the nursery and the schoolroom.

'I would now like to show you what it is you have been employed to do,' Frau Burkhard said crisply. 'But first you must find your correct dormitory and pack away your things. We will meet here again in twenty minutes' time. Please be prompt. There is much to show you and we do not have the energy or resources for time-wasters. As my husband said, it is imperative that what we produce here is sent as soon as possible to the factories where they will become uniforms for our brave men fighting at the front. Once I have explained your duties, we will venture outside to view the grounds. Your employment will start officially tomorrow. Please come and find your name.'

She held up the clipboard. The women surged forward, all talking eagerly.

I felt tired from the rattling truck journey. I tried to summon the energy that seemed to buzz through the throng of other volunteers but all I wanted to do was to find my bed and sleep.

'Etti has been placed with some other mothers,' Lydia said, returning to my side. 'But you and I are in a dorm together. With Agnese.' She looked troubled. 'I have the strangest feeling that I've seen her before. Do you know her? Do you remember her from Tartu?'

I shook my head. 'No. I don't think so.'

Lydia sighed and ran her hand across her hair. She looked as bone-weary as I felt. 'I'm probably imagining things. I've not slept well at all this past week. The strangest dreams. And I've had a griping feeling in my belly, as if somebody is walking a tightrope from one side of my body to the other.'

I looked at her with concern. 'Do you need the doctor?'

She blinked and shook her head. 'No. It comes and goes.

It's not worth troubling over. It's likely nerves. Let's put our things away quickly. I have a feeling Frau Burkhard would not forgive us for being late.'

The next day we woke to the grinding thump of machinery and the shrill summons of Frau Burkhard's whistle. Tying on our aprons, we marched downstairs. The sound of the machines was deafening as we entered the weaving room. It filled my ears like the thunder of waves.

Frau Burkhard was waiting for us in a starched suit dress.

'Remember what I told you,' she shouted as we filed past. 'You must keep a close eye on your machine. Even a slight over or under-correction could result in a jam. Each woman assigned to a loom will be responsible for keeping her machine running smoothly and ensuring empty yarn cylinders are replaced seamlessly!'

Etti supervised the machine on my right while Lydia took the left. I noticed Agnese step towards the machine on Lydia's other side. My skin prickled uncomfortably. The woman had followed us about the day before. It had not been so unusual when we were led around by Frau Burkhard, but once the tour of the factory was over she had followed us to the nursery where we visited Leelo and then hung about as we watched Leelo roll around on a blanket.

At supper the night before, Agnese had settled herself opposite Lydia, although there were many empty seats in the cafeteria. Lydia herself seemed nervous, picking at the food on her plate and then at last pushing it away before excusing herself to find the bathroom. At least Agnese had not gone after her, although I noticed she hadn't eaten much either and left her vanilla pudding untouched. Lydia had not returned but had gone up to the dormitory to rest.

I saw her glance quickly at me now as the looms spun back and forth, churning out the cloth. She made a small adjustment to the spindle with her hand as Frau Burkhard had shown us. As I looked out at the sea of machines whirring, the women scurrying about at their stations, I could not help thinking of how different it was to the comforting warmth of the knitting circle I had known. Instead of efficient machines, I imagined the squashy armchairs of Aunt Juudit's room and Helle and Leili chattering like birds. My grandmother carding wool the way her own mother had taught her – the way she had taught me – pressing the fibres between the paddles to get rid of clumps and impurities, making silver strands of yarn as thin as cobwebs. Instead of whirring machinery, the rooms would be full of voices. Conversation would float through the air, thickening it with laughter as tales of husbands and children passed from mouth to ear. There would be a little gossip – who'd fallen asleep in the Lutheran Church during service, whose daughter had danced with whose son at the local barn dance – but no malice. During a lull, when the words had dried up, someone might begin to sing, and the song would be taken up by myriad voices, each one blending until it was more like the bubbling of water than the expression of words.

A heaviness pressed on my chest as I thought of everything that would be forgotten once the women from the circle passed on. We were all scattered now. Who knew whether that knowledge would survive?

* * *

It took us a week to master the correct method of working with our looms. It wasn't too difficult once we got the hang of it, but the days were long and monotonous. Every morning we woke to the whistle and dragged ourselves downstairs to be greeted by the smell of oil from the machines and the rhythmic thump of the turbines. And each day, I expected Oskar's note to arrive, perhaps delivered by one of the few men who worked at the factory and whose job it was to distribute mail over our morning break or carry the heavy bolts of cloth into the lorries which arrived regularly to take the fabric back to Germany, where it would be sewn into uniforms. I could not imagine how else his contact would reach us.

When a month had slipped past, I began to grow nervous. At night, I lay awake, unable to sleep, replaying the moments of passion we had shared in the farmhouse. I soothed myself with these images, pushing away the little voice of doubt which whispered in the dark. Where were they? When would they come? I tried to talk to Lydia about it, but we were always interrupted. There was always someone nearby, either Frau Burkhard, yelling instructions, or Agnese.

She was like a burr we could not shake.

One night, weeks later, we were eating supper in the cafeteria. The fare was plain – a cup of milk, an overcooked egg – but I always tried to eat everything and encouraged Lydia and Etti to do the same. We would need all our strength when it came time to leave.

In between sips of milk, I tried to speak to Lydia about knitting. I had not forgotten how it felt to complete a shawl, how soothing to fall into the rhythm, but there'd been limited time for shawlmaking of late. We went to bed exhausted and woke up tired. If we did manage to summon up the strength to knit, we would only manage to do a few rows before our fingers gave up and we talked instead. To compensate, I'd begun to make up my own patterns, designing them with Lydia's help, thinking aloud of the way I would weave the shapes together. I found it calming, a way of distracting myself from the growing anxiety of Oskar's silence. I'd already constructed one for my parents; for Aunt Juudit. Every person I had lost would have their own stitch.

In this way, I had decided, I would honour them and their sacrifices.

Tonight, though, I could tell Lydia was tired. She answered my questions with single words. Her face was haggard, her hair unwashed and greasy, tendrils spilling from beneath the headscarf we were all forced to wear. She hunched over the plate where her egg remained uneaten.

'Etti?' I said, and my cousin turned from where she was sitting a few places away. 'Lydia's not feeling well,' I continued. 'I think she needs some air. Can you visit Leelo without us?'

Etti nodded. 'Of course.'

Lydia did not complain when I led her away from the cafeteria where the women were still talking and finishing their meals. When we reached the door, I looked back and caught the gleam of Agnese's eye. For a second, I imagined I saw stark hatred shining out. But it was gone in an instant.

Agnese dropped her eyes back to her plate. Beside me, I heard Lydia sigh.

'Let's take a walk to the lake,' I suggested. Lydia nodded, her mouth wilting. I squeezed her arm. She looked as if she might cry at any moment.

Taking her hand, I marched her along the corridor which led out into the grounds, praying Agnese would not follow.

'Why does she look at me like that? What does she want?'

Lydia's voice was shrill. The rush of the water and the crashing of the turbines ran beneath it, a discordant harmony. She hugged herself tightly. The wind whipped at her hair and the late afternoon sun intensified its dark red undertones so it shone like polished stone.

I shrugged helplessly, shivering. It was cold in the wind. I wished I'd thought to bring my coat. 'I don't know. She must be unhinged.'

'When will Oskar send for us?' she said. 'How long must we wait?'

I shook my head, too afraid to voice my own fears. Two months had passed now since we had arrived. Every night, I was shaken with terrible visions of Oskar being caught and Jakob shot. It had begun to feel as if we would have to stay here forever, if we were not discovered first and hauled before the police.

The great chimney stacks of the factory rose up behind us. Beyond them, the sun was setting, streaking the purple sky with fingers of pale rose.

Lydia groaned, bracing against the wind that rippled the surface of the lake. 'I'm afraid I will go mad here.' Her head was turned to the west, her gaze sweeping across the water to settle on the bridge that separated Kreenholm from the far shore.

I knew what she was thinking as clearly as if I heard Frau Burkhard's voice in my head, the echo of her words.

'On Kreenholm's side: Estonia or *Ostland*,' she had said. 'On the other: Russia.'

The enemy.

Lydia's forehead furrowed. She rubbed her palms against her arms.

Frau Burkhard had warned us not to cross the bridge or even to venture near the path of dappled light that led through to the walkway where the bridge began. The Russians were too occupied with Leningrad to bother yet with Narva, but the border patrol was active; a few men had been shot at, one wounded in the leg. The Russians had not forgotten what they had lost.

Handkerchief Weave

Lydia
November 1941

I DREAMT I WAS SITTING IN MY MOTHER'S BOUDOIR, staring at her bottles of perfumes and jars of cream. Pale light streamed through the curtains. I inhaled the air, jasmine-scented. Something stirred. I leant forward. Nestled among my mother's perfumes was a nest with an egg inside.

The egg's shell was smooth, speckled. A chink appeared in the surface, growing wider. I reached out my hand. Picked away the broken piece with my thumb. The fissure deepened. The egg trembled.

With a resounding crack, it split open. I gasped.

There was a baby inside.

Its eyes were closed. Brown hair swirled across its scalp, soft as feathers. Its tiny fingers flexed, its eyelids flickered as if it too was dreaming.

And then all of a sudden, the egg was gone. The nest was empty.

I opened my eyes.

The dormitory was dark. I heard the soft snoring of the other women. It must be midnight, or thereabouts. My hand fluttered over my stomach. I felt the tiny space the baby had made for itself, the presence of Jakob's child clinging to life like a bean on a vine. A sense of wonder and terror overwhelmed me as I relived the day's events.

I'd left the factory early, excusing myself on the pretence that I was unwell. I'd not even asked Kati or Etti to go with me. I had walked alone across the bridge to the City of Narva and asked a woman with kind eyes for directions to a good doctor. It had grown cold the past few days; the air filled with an icy chill which heralded winter.

The doctor had confirmed what I already suspected. In the frenzy of fleeing Tartu and the anxiety of waiting each day for Oskar and Jakob to arrive, I'd lost track of the days. It wasn't until my monthly courses had failed to appear for the second time that I began to wonder, and all the little clues – the waves of nausea, the heaviness in my breasts – seemed to conspire at last to reveal the truth. It had been two months now. Two months since we had left Tartu, and not a word from Oskar or Jakob. Where were they and why were they delayed? The constant worry tempered my joy. I wished I could find some way to tell Jakob. I wanted him to be the first to know.

As I'd trudged back alone towards the factory, I decided not to tell Kati or Etti. I would keep my surprise a secret until I could tell Jakob. I wanted to watch his face transformed by this good news among all the fear and anxiety.

I rolled over onto my side and closed my eyes, knowing I should rest. Something sounded a long way off, a distant hum. I stirred, aware of the heavy bedclothes, half-awake, half-asleep. Darkness. Then light. I heard a sound, a little like laughter and a shadow passed over me. I tossed my head, feeling its presence the same way I always knew when

Agnese was behind me or when she had followed me down to the lake. Her eyes always searching me out as we ate our food in the cafeteria, as if she was waiting to catch me out. It had frayed my nerves to breaking-point.

Someone ran to the window.

'They're here again.' It was Kati. She drew the curtain back, and something bright flared beyond the glass, turning the sky the colour of rubies. Black shapes danced against the light, swooping low before being jerked up, as if controlled by marionette strings. 'The Russians.'

The windows shook, rattling in their panes.

The other women were already moving, stumbling out the door. The corridor was filled with frightened voices. Kati seemed to shake herself. Her eyes were wide.

We rushed outside, almost colliding with Etti in the corridor. Leelo was clinging to her mother's chest, her voice raised in a high-pitched wail, her legs dangling against Etti's thighs.

Frau Burkhard appeared at the top of the stairs, her face lit by the glow of an oil lamp.

She looked tired, her usually immaculate hair escaping in pale wisps. Holding the lamp high above her head, she turned. The women followed the ribbon of her light weaving down the steps. The shuffle of bare feet reverberated in the stone stairwell. Everyone was quiet, but when another bomb exploded not far away some cried out and panicked, shoving forward, almost sending those at the frontline sprawling down the steps.

'Wait!' I whirled around. I had left my mother's shawl and her letter locked in the trunk. The bodies of the women pressed against me, a wall of flesh. I pushed forward, my eyes fixed on the door of our dormitory.

'What are you doing?' Kati grabbed my elbow, trying to steer me around. 'Are you crazy?'

'I have to go back.' I wrenched my arm free. Bodies jostled against me. A shoulder slammed into my arm. I reached the door of the dormitory and thrust my fingers into the pocket of my nightgown. I kept my key with me always, even when I slept. I could not risk anyone reading Mamochka's letter, discovering that I was her daughter.

Terror gripped my heart and squeezed. The key was gone. It must have fallen out as I ran or as I tossed and turned in bed, disturbed by dreams.

I stumbled into the room, Kati behind me. The room was dark. I fumbled to my knees, feeling about, tossing aside fallen bedclothes. Where was it? A shower of light exploded suddenly outside the window. I heard Kati cry out. I followed her gaze.

A figure was bent over my chest, rifling through the contents.

'Agnese!' The name burst from my lips.

She spun around, her mouth open. In her hand was my mother's letter. Kati ran across and snatched it from her. Agnese tried to grab it back, but Kati held it away from her.

'You're a liar!' Agnese pointed at me. Her voice was choked with emotion. She turned to fling her words at Kati. 'She's a spy! I know her. I know who she is!'

She was breathing hard. An explosion shook the building.

'Is that a message? A secret code?' She pointed at Mama's

letter. I stared at her, unable to speak, unable even to defend myself. Horror mingled with relief. She had not yet read the letter. She'd not had time.

I shook my head, terror muting my words.

'I was listening at the train station, the night of the deportations.' Agnese's voice shook. 'I followed him, that lieutenant of yours. I went to beg him for help. For my daughter, her husband. My grandson was sick. I heard what he called you.' She glared at Kati again. 'She's the Partorg's daughter. I know it. She could have stopped it. She could have stopped my daughter being sent away! My grandson might still be alive.'

My heart pounded so hard I thought it would burst. In an instant, I knew where I'd seen her. I was back at that station in Tartu, talking with Lieutenant Lubov before Juudit was killed. A woman stood near my elbow, trying to catch Lieutenant Lubov's attention. A green handkerchief was tied over her head. Her eyes were full of grief and despair.

A black space widened at my feet. My skin flared hot.

'You're mistaken.' Kati's voice carried over the noise of the planes. Her hands were trembling. 'Lydia was not at the station that night. She was at our apartment. I'm sorry for what happened to your family but . . . you're mistaken. Lydia is one of us. She's as Estonian as you and me.'

Agnese continued to stare at us with fierce eyes until suddenly her face deflated. Tears tracked down her withered cheeks. She knotted her hands about her face like claws and rocked as the Russian planes swooped outside. Her shoulders shook. She did not even seem to notice as

Kati seized her shoulder and dragged us both towards the corridor.

We stumbled from the room as a wave of fire seemed to set the night alight.

'Oh, thank God!' Etti surged to her feet and threw her arms around us as we staggered down into the cellar. Agnese, still sniffling, shrugged Kati's hand away and lurched past us, avoiding my eye.

Frau Burkhard's lamp cast its light across the weaving machines and the looms and the giant cylinders of cloth. 'Close the doors,' she said to her husband. General Burkhard was wrapped up in a thick dressing gown. He did not look afraid but wild and dishevelled, as if the air raid was an inconvenience of the highest order. But he did his wife's bidding, slamming the doors closed and bolting them.

Leaving the lamp on a shelf nearby, the Burkhards shuffled to the back of the cellar, as far as possible from the whimpering children and the women who had seated themselves on the cold floor. Above us, a muffled vibration shook the ground, sifting dirt down from the ceiling, scattering in the folds of my nightgown. I hugged Etti to me.

Perhaps we will die down here, I thought. Buried among the stone and plaster. I would never see Russia again, or Jakob. I would never see his face, or run my fingers across his skin. *I will never get to tell him that I am carrying his child.*

This thought pained me most of all.

Pulling us into a little alcove between two broken looms,

Etti made us sit beside her while she held Leelo, trying to soothe the little girl's cries. She listened gravely as we told her what had happened with Agnese upstairs. My body was still shaking. I hugged my knees to my chest and my breasts prickled at the sudden contact.

'I'm sorry. I don't think we can wait for Oskar and Jakob any longer,' Etti said. She was soothing the sobbing Leelo, who refused to lie down and instead flailed her arms and kicked her long legs, protesting the disruption of sleep. Leelo's pretty face was red, her eyes swollen. Half a tooth had broken through the skin at the bottom of her mouth. It was visible when she cried.

Etti tugged her against her body, trying to calm her. 'We've waited long enough.' Her eyes glimmered. 'We have Oskar's contact's name and his address. I think we should leave tomorrow. It's possible Agnese will believe you, Kati. But it is also possible she might report Lydia. Even without proof, they might listen to her claims and start an investigation.'

Kati opened her mouth as if she would argue. Then she closed it. Her shoulders sagged. She looked at me; a long look in which I read all the pain we shared and the question she could not bring herself to ask. Etti was right. We could not wait any longer.

I swallowed, thinking of Jakob's square jaw and his snub nose, as if someone had pressed their thumb against it as he slept. How could I leave him behind, as I had left Joachim to his fate? And then I remembered the dream, his child sleeping, curled in an eggshell. I had to protect us both.

'Tomorrow,' I agreed, turning away from the light of the

oil lamp to shield the misery in my face, the rush of helpless despair. A hand touched my arm.

'Lida?' Wiping my nose with my sleeve, I looked back to find Kati was holding something out to me. It was my mother's letter. I reached for it, just as Kati looked down. Her face changed. When I tried to take the letter from her, she held it fast.

'Whose letter is that?' she said.

I felt my cheeks colouring. I looked around, still wary of Agnese. But the woman was sitting at the far end of the cellar, legs drawn up, face in her hands.

'My mother's,' I whispered. 'She had a friend – they wrote to each other. I told you.'

'I recognise that writing.' Kati brought the letter up to her face, tilting it so that the light fell across the words. 'That is my grandmother's handwriting. Elina Rebane.'

We stared at each other, mystified.

'Your grandmother taught my mother to knit.' I felt the truth of this as if it was something I had always known, something which had lain hidden in plain sight. My connection to Kati, and to Jakob, too, had started years before we were born.

Kati and I had been lace sisters all along.

Lilac Pattern

Kati

IT WAS SNOWING AS WE PASSED THROUGH THE IRON GATES of Kreenholm and crossed over the bridge connecting the island to the Estonian mainland. The water flowed sluggishly between the river's banks, its currents blocked by a thin crust of ice encroaching steadily across the surface. There was only one road into town. Huddling together, we moved along it, passing bare trees and abandoned houses.

I tried to focus on the road, slippery with ice, but couldn't resist stealing curious glances at the old-fashioned terraces with their fine red bricks, dormer windows and gabled eaves dusted with snow. I remembered Frau Burkhard telling us that the houses had once belonged to the English managers placed in charge of Kreenholm during its glory days. They had all fled, of course, when the Russians arrived.

I felt my bones creak, complaining of the cold that bit and snarled in the air. The knapsack weighed down my back though it contained just one change of clothes and my knitting things. We had left everything we had been given – the trunks, the aprons and caps – behind. The factory had not been too badly damaged during the bombing raid as the planes had been targeting the supply depots on the outskirts of town. The Burkhards had not been happy to

411

see us go. Frau Burkhard had shouted and accused us of being ungrateful, but there was nothing they could do to keep us there. We had told them we planned to return to our family in Tartu. If they did bother to report us one day, we would be long gone, I hoped, already in Sweden . . . and waiting for Oskar and Jakob to join us there.

I slipped my hand into my pocket, fingering the address and the name Oskar had written down for me the last time I saw him. In the pocket on my other side, I kept his glove. The other I had pressed into his hands on one of our last nights together, when we had held each other close. One day, we would be reunited, just like the gloves.

We would need to ask someone for directions when we got into Narva. I hoped that Oskar's contact would help us, even though Oskar himself was not escorting us. My fingers tightened involuntarily around the slip of paper. *Oskar, where are you?*

Leelo gurgled and pointed over Etti's shoulder at the snow which circled down around us. Etti hoisted her higher up on her shoulder, teetering a little as she tried to balance her knapsack and the child, her boots surging against the mixture of slush and snow. Leelo's face peeped out between the layers of clothing and shawls we had swathed around her, her big eyes fixed on the street retreating behind us and the tall chimney stacks of the factory.

'I wish we had never come to Narva.' Lydia sounded broken. The altercation with Agnese had upset her. I looked over at her, trudging through the snow in Aunt Juudit's too-big boots. The wind streamed her hair back away from her gaunt face, her sharp cheekbones making her look all the more wolf-like.

Despite that, there was an elegance there, a spirit in the thickly fringed blue eyes that was not yet extinguished. No wonder Jakob had drawn close to her. She was everything I was not: warm and open, every emotion etched on her face as soon as it formed. I was a hard, brittle stick, unwilling to bend.

'We had no choice,' I said. I was so very weary, and suddenly I was afraid I could not go on. But Lydia beside me and Etti pushing through the sleet with Leelo wrapped around her chest meant I could not stop. I pressed the heel of my palm into my eye, as if I could massage the exhaustion out of the socket. 'No choice then, and no choice now.'

'I hope this Heldur has a warm fireplace.' Lydia shook herself, rubbing her shoulders with her hands.

'And a gramophone.' Etti's comment was so unexpected it made me look up.

She flashed me a smile. 'I would give anything to hear "*L'Internationale*" again,' she added, patting Leelo's back with her hand.

It seemed so ridiculous and so unlikely, and yet it broke the tension between us. As Etti began to babble, explaining Aunt Juudit's peculiar habits to Lydia, I let the cold air soak into my lungs, imagining the unimaginable at last: a home, a place we would all be safe until the war ended, whoever the victors might be.

I tried to conjure up an apartment filled with voices – Oskar's and Jakob's, Etti's and Leelo's. Lydia would sit beside the fireplace; there would indeed be a great one, a huge pyre of logs that burnt endlessly. Perhaps we would knit; I could show her at last how to piece together the sections of her mother's shawl just the way she had asked me to. First, the loop stitch. Then the hook. The lace edges would be sewn separately, dried on the timber frames before we attached them with care. I would let her choose the pattern she desired, though I would secretly hope for the wolf's paw.

When we were done, I would perform my final trick: I would pull the shawl through the gold ring I had removed from the fourth finger of my left hand. My ring. The one Oskar would give me to replace the small thread fastened there. A shining symbol of hope. The fine-spun lace would flutter, like magic. The test of quality and a knitter's skill. Lydia would smile.

Narva was teeming with German soldiers. We saw their panzer tanks rolling by and held our breath as they marched in formation through the square and up towards the huge castle overlooking the river, which must be where they trained and exercised.

We kept close to the shadows where we could, trying not to draw attention, Etti wedged between Lydia and myself. The first woman we met did not know where Turu Street was, but the next woman we approached pointed us towards a row of estate houses some little distance away. Heldur's house on Turu Street was no more than a narrow wedge of whitewashed plaster jammed between two bigger residences. The man who answered my knock was an older gentleman with close-cut hair and pale eyelashes.

'Are you Heldur?'

'Perhaps.' He folded his arms. 'Who are you?'

'I am Katarina. These are my cousin and my friend. Oskar Mägi sent us – we are hoping you can help us.'

Heldur did not uncross his arms, nor did his eyes leave my face, but he looked back over his shoulder and called, 'Kristiina!'

A harassed-looking young woman with a snub nose appeared abruptly at his side. Almost to himself, he said, 'Make up some beds, girl.'

The woman shot us a curious glance but moved away to do as she was bid.

As her footsteps retreated up the stairs, the man turned to look at her heels disappearing. 'She's a good daughter,' he said. 'Follow her up. She'll see to it you are clothed and fed and comfortable.'

He stood back to let us in, then turned away to clomp over to his desk. I felt the cold brush of his dismissal as if he had blown out a candle and left us standing in the dark.

'Aren't you going to ask us what we're doing here? Don't you want to see – see our papers?'

He shrugged without turning around. 'I see everything already just as it is. Oskar told you to come see me if you had trouble. You have trouble – or soon will have. You can stay here as long as you need.'

'Can you – can you pass on a message for us?' I swallowed. 'Can you tell Oskar we are here, that we need to leave as quickly as possible?'

The man paused. He straightened up and turned, and the look on his face felt like a slap to mine. 'I'm sorry to tell you this.' He drew in a breath. 'Oskar has . . . Nobody has heard from Oskar for a month.'

I stopped breathing. It could not be true. Questions burnt on my tongue. I tried to speak but only a croak came out.

'I'm sorry,' Heldur said again.

Heldur did not know what Oskar meant to me. He could not know we were married, or he would not be speaking in this cold, ruthless way. 'It's always possible he has gone back into hiding, into the forest,' he said. 'But it seems unlikely he would have disappeared without telling anyone.'

I found my voice. 'Did he take anyone with him?' My thoughts swirled with visions of Jakob. Jakob and Oskar, shot through with bullet holes.

'I can't say.' The old man pushed his glasses up on the bridge of his nose. 'I'm sorry. As I said, you can stay as long as you need to. Oskar told me you might need the services of Jaan's speedboat.' His mouth twitched. 'He comes once a month when the moon is dark. Looks to be the tenth today. So, tomorrow. Would you have me contact him? Will you be ready?'

My mouth was so dry I could not swallow.

'Yes.' Lydia took my arm. 'We will be ready.'

'So. You are all Jews?'

Heldur sniffed at the food Kristiina had put before him; a square of watery terrine mixed with leftover offal. Etti and I exchanged uneasy glances. Lydia was dangling Leelo while she batted at the orange cat who sat warming himself before the fire. I saw her glance over her shoulder at the front door, as if she expected it to burst open.

'Not exactly,' I said.

Heldur grunted. He speared a wobbling piece of terrine onto his fork. 'It makes no difference to me.' He chewed.

416

'We have had all sorts through here, haven't we girl? Jews. Gypsies. Once, a Jehovah's Witness. He had some interesting views, I can tell you.'

He paused to fork another mouthful in.

Kristiina, slicing the bread at the bench while the stew intended for us bubbled on the stove, threw a scrap of offal to the cat, who jumped to his feet to retrieve it.

'Aren't you afraid?' I said. 'To keep us here?'

'Afraid of what? The Germans?' Heldur shook his head. 'I'm not afraid for myself. I can't be, or I would never leave the house. I'm afraid for Kristiina, a little. For the people the Germans have targeted: certainly. We do not get many Jews coming now. Most of them tried to escape when the Germans came in. The ones who come now are escapees from the Klooga camp or people who have been in hiding until they could get a message out. They say bad things about that Klooga camp.' He paused, his fork halfway to his mouth. 'Bad things.'

'What kind of things?' Etti's face had blanched. She was not looking at Heldur, but at Leelo, now wriggling on the floor, inching on her stomach to where the cat sat cleaning its face and switching its tail.

Heldur chewed softly. He drummed his fingers against the tabletop. 'Klooga is a work camp. Prisoners have to work in the forest or in the quarry. Felling trees, breaking rocks, you know. Men and women. And children. When they get too sick or if they are too old to work they are . . . selected. *Selektion*.'

'Killed.' Lydia's eyes were shining.

'Just so.' Heldur picked up his plate and set it down

upon the floor. The cat fell on it. Pushing back his chair, he replaced the cap on his head. 'There is illness, too. Typhoid. It can wipe out whole families.'

'But you have had people come here. Escapees,' Etti said, her voice thin. 'People have escaped from Klooga.'

Heldur's mouth pinched. 'Just one,' he said, cupping his chin with his hand. 'The other we had to bury. You should ask the moon not to shine tomorrow. That would be best.'

Red Shawl

Lydia

'AIR RAID! HURRY! HURRY!'

A sliver of moonlight picked out Kristiina's pale hair. She half-turned, beckoning us out into the small garden as the air-raid siren continued to wail. I took a breath then plunged outside. The cold was immense, a great angry cloud pressing down around me, squeezing the warmth from my bones. My exhausted mind struggled to order it all: the wail of the air-raid siren; footsteps thudding up the attic stairs; the house vibrating as planes roared overhead.

Now this: the flight across the garden to where Kristiina hovered beneath the shadow of an oak tree. I heard Kati behind me, helping Etti with Leelo, the three of them struggling to see in the near-darkness. The wailing had begun a few minutes ago; we'd only just had time to throw on our coats before Kristiina was in the room, shouting at us to gather our things and meet her downstairs.

'This way.' Kristiina grasped my arm. 'Everyone who does not have a basement must gather at the Town Hall. It's less likely the bombers will target a large building with civilians inside.' Together, we hurried along the deserted streets, keeping to the shadows. Somewhere not far away an explosion rocked the earth, but Kristiina didn't pause. Scurrying around the square, she led us towards a tall building of whitewashed stone. People gathered at the entrance as German soldiers shouted orders.

'Just do what they tell you,' Kristiina said as she felt me hesitating. 'They will be too busy trying to protect the supply depots to worry about papers.'

She did not wait for me to reply, but pushed me into the throng along with Kati and Etti. The hall was packed. Lamps had been placed along the floor to light the way. Bodies lined the timber panelled walls; children with eyes aglow, tired-looking women slumped together. The lights threw up strange shadows in the concert hall, illuminating the faces of the gilded statues and the ornate Baroque scrollwork on the ceiling high above.

A German soldier directed us to an unfilled space between a few women who wriggled closer together to allow us to sit down.

I lowered myself carefully, thinking already of how I would look in six months' time, my belly swollen to the point where getting up and down would be difficult. Would Jakob be pleased when I told him, or afraid? Pleased, I decided.

I could not imagine him being afraid of anything.

Another shell shattered distantly. The women nearby whimpered.

Leelo began to cry, her breathless sobs echoing. This broken sleep was already too much for her. She would be cross tomorrow, refusing to take her bottle just as she always did when over-tired. Etti sang to her and patted her back but Leelo refused to be calmed. Kati sat beside her, watching helplessly, the bruised crescents that shadowed her eyes showing the toll the long days and nights at Kreenholm had taken on her. Something prodded my elbow, and I looked down to see a pair of knitting needles in Kati's hand.

'Take them,' she said. She handed me a ball of yarn. It looked dark in the dim glow from the lanterns. I realised it was not white but the crimson red of the light breaking over the Kremlin's walls in high summer.

'Kristiina gave it to me,' she said. 'She dyed it with blackcurrants. You can use it to start your own shawl. Here,' Kati said, teasing out the thread. 'I'll make the first stitch for you.' She made a small loop and slipped the needle through. Then she handed them to me. 'Try the pasque-flower,' she said. 'Just like we practised.'

As the sky continued to rumble, she drew out her own needles and a ragged length of yarn from an old shawl she had unpicked before we left Tartu. I saw some of the women stop sobbing and look up as her needles clicked steadily.

Kristiina had taken her hands away from her ears. Now she reached into her own bag. Her needles were short and chestnut-coloured. She shot me a smile as she hooked the loop stitch. She was making a fragile lace glove; I could see the shape of it already, half-formed, wavering like a silvery cobweb. Following Kristiina's example, other women, those who had brought their satchels with them, drew out their knitting. The children grew quieter as they listened to the familiar sound of the needles, the low murmurs of women exchanging stories about where they came from. Tales their mothers had taught them. Even the men in the hall were silent. One woman began to hum, and then the humming became words. Soon, others had taken up the song. I tried to tease out the melody but it was like trying to pin down the wind. The rhythm shifted and changed as the women sang, their voices lifting and falling, their words overlapping. I gave up and instead, let the melody wash over me.

When I looked over at Kati, I realised she was crying. 'It's runo song,' she said, swiping at the tears with the back of her hand. 'I never thought I'd hear it again.' Her fingers were shaking, and for the first time I saw her drop a few stitches. Wriggling closer, I leant my shoulder against hers. We listened together. It seemed fitting, almost, that we were sheltering in a concert hall that must once have contained the harmonic strains of an orchestra or a string quartet that sent their notes heavenward. Now, it was the strength of those women's voices that filled up the space, soft and defiant, tender and comforting. I felt the ghosts of many women crowding close, listening too; my mother beside me, and Kati's. An old woman; the grandmother she and Jakob always talked about. I laid my hand over the place on my belly where I knew my child was sleeping and wondered if it too could hear this miracle and if it stirred, awakened by the echo of voices from so long ago.

I woke in the grey dawn to find my face damp, as if I had been crying. In the hall around me, people were moving, raising their heads from the makeshift pillows they had fashioned from knapsacks, and staggering to their feet. Leelo grumbled as Etti lifted her from the small nest of blankets we had found to cover her. Kati stretched her arms over her head, arching her back like a cat.

'Are we still alive?' I said.

'I think so.' She twisted her spine one way and then the other. 'But I am stiffer than the second day of harvest.'

A German soldier at the doorway started to shout

that it was safe for people to return to their homes. As we collected our things and spilt out into the square, our breath clouded in front of us. The sky was grey, a cold mist hanging over everything. Away in the distance, a scribble of smoke etched itself above the remains of a blackened building. The reek of burnt timber drifted towards us, blown by the cold breeze.

Kati squinted. 'That must be the supply depot,' she said. 'At least the town seems mostly undamaged.'

Kristiina and Heldur caught up with us near the fountain at the centre of the square, and together we began to trudge back to their house. As we passed a small church, I chanced to look up at the sky, drawn by the church's steeple that glittered like a glass lancet piercing the sky. My eye snagged on the body of a bird mid-flight, its dark wings fanning the air. It circled the steeple, calling. Its tune was mournful, more like the piping of a flute than the cheery singsong of robins and sparrows.

I felt Kati stop beside me and follow my gaze.

'A stork,' she said. 'I think. I've never seen a black one before, though.'

Cold spread up my body. The stork continued to circle, its feathers like soot.

'It's so cold – I thought all the birds were gone by now,' I said.

'Perhaps he was injured,' Kati said. 'And he had to wait. He'd best hurry. If he gets caught in a snowstorm, he'll die.'

As we stood there watching the stork circling I heard my mother's voice. Her words were woven together with the stork's soft cries. I strained hard to listen, to distinguish the two. And then with a dreadful start I realised she was saying Jakob's name.

I saw Kati's eyes widen. 'What is it?'

'Jakob,' I croaked. I squeezed my hands tightly. 'There is something wrong with Jakob.'

Mamochka, I pleaded. *Help me!* I waited, listening to my own heartbeat drum and to my mother calling him. And then I was weeping.

In that moment I had grasped the truth. Jakob was dead.

I turned away from Kati and from Kristiina and Etti. I forced myself to look up, to search for the black stork that had soared above us, the stork who had waited until winter to leave behind his homeland.

But the sky was empty. Jakob's bird was gone.

The Wolf Shawl

Kati

LYDIA WAS STILL SOBBING WHEN WE REACHED TURU Street. It was almost deserted. There were only a few people about, returning to their homes, heads bowed against the cold.

The collar of Lydia's coat was spattered with tears. She could not catch her breath. Her boots kept slipping on the ice. I supported her on one side and Kristiina the other, both of us whispering encouragement as she said my brother's name again and again. Kristiina mouthed at me: '*What's wrong?*'

I could only shake my head, surmising that the stress of not knowing what had happened to my brother was taking its toll. Jakob could not be dead. Could he? A small voice of doubt whispered in my ear but I shut it out. I would know. I would know if my brother was gone. Just as I would know if Oskar had been arrested. When Jakob had first gone to live at the university dorms, I had missed his cheery face at breakfast and chores. I had even missed his teasing. His empty room seemed a sad reminder that he was gone. But in spite of the pain, I had known he was still out there. This was like one of those times. He must be hiding with Oskar in the forest. When it was safe, he would find Heldur and then join us. We would go on ahead, but eventually we would all be reunited.

rattle of each breath, long, laborious. It made the hairs rise on my arm. I looked up at him. Through the fog of happiness, I took note of his razor-sharp cheekbones, the shadows beneath his eyes. The eyes themselves were dull and sunken, the flesh around them tightly stretched. A little pinprick of fear niggled at my back.

'Kati. Is it really you?' Oskar's voice rasped. 'Or am I dreaming? I left the glove there, but I didn't want to stand in the doorway in case a patrol came past.'

He stroked my cheek with his thumb, and continued to look down at me, one arm still draped about my shoulder. His chest vibrated as he drew breath, the sound like buttons clattering in a jar.

'Yes. It's me.' I brought his hand up to my mouth and kissed it. It was shaking, the knuckles bruised. 'What happened to you?' I said. 'Why didn't you come sooner? Where is Jakob?' I looked around, expecting him to lope out and join us. Instead, I saw Heldur emerge from the house. He took Oskar's arm and gently pulled him inside. I followed behind, elation turning to worry.

Inside the house, Lydia was sitting in a chair. She was still crying, her mouth hanging open and her eyes glazed. Etti, with Leelo cradled in her arm, murmured softly about shock and tricks of the mind, but Lydia seemed unable to hear her.

The kitchen was cold, the fire burnt out to nothing more than a few embers. Kristiina hurried to relight it, fetching wood from the basket and fanning it with her breath, while Heldur barred the door and checked the window. Oskar was shivering, trying to warm himself beside what little heat remained in the grate. He was thinner than I had ever seen him. I went to him

I clung to this hope. I had to.

Etti and Heldur hurried on ahead to reach the house before us, and a German truck roared past, splattering mud across the snow.

Kristiina stiffened, but held firm to Lydia's arm until it had disappeared. The presence of the truck seemed to have startled Lydia back to reality. Shaking us off, she trudged towards Heldur's house. We stepped into the little front yard. Something caught my eye; a patch of scarlet glowing brightly against the snow near the front door. I blinked, uncertain if I was imagining what I was seeing.

Oskar's glove. The one I had given him back at the barracks. Its mate was still crushed in my pocket.

I bent down to touch it, just as Kristiina ushered Lydia inside. The wool glove was stiff in my fingers, the threads frozen. I picked it up, the cold biting into my palm and glanced up to scan the road. *Where?* My heart pounded painfully. Houses. Trees laden with snow. Telegraph poles. I waited, alert to any movement, any sound.

A figure lurched into view, staggering out onto the footpath from the shadows a few houses away. I recognised the set of his broad shoulders, his sharp nose. Oskar. I cried out, bringing my hands to my mouth to stifle the sound in the quiet street and ran towards him, so full of relief I thought my chest might burst. When I reached him, I flung my arms around his waist.

'You're alive!' I buried my face against his chest, unwilling to release him. *I will never let you go again.* His arms moved around me. The buttons on his coat dug into my cheek, but I ignored the pain. 'You're here!' I said again, my breath clouding. Oskar's chest rose and fell against my ear. I heard the and took his hands in mine, trying to rub the warmth back into them. He winced and I looked down. The skin on the backs of them was cracked and peeling. I kissed them tenderly. I bent my head to his, and despite the cold in his hands, his forehead was warm, flushed by fever or shock, I wasn't certain.

'Here, Oskar.'

Kristiina thrust a mug of liquid between us. Oskar took it and drained it in one gulp. Kristiina took it and refilled it and passed it silently back.

'He's dead,' Lydia said suddenly. 'Isn't he?'

Oskar's head jerked up. He stared at her.

'Jakob.' Lydia spoke calmly. 'He's dead. I know it.'

Oskar's hands began to tremble, and I wanted to reach out and hold them but I could not move. *Not true*, I thought. *Oskar will tell her it's not true.*

Oskar's tongue darted out to moisten his cracked lips. 'They caught us at Haapsalu,' he said. 'We were running messages back and forth to Stockholm. Using safe houses when we could. Barns. Sleeping under the stars sometimes. Putting people in contact with other runners. A man contacted us, asking for help. Said he needed to get out. He had two daughters. Could we help.' He shuddered. 'I didn't want to. I had . . . a feeling. But Jakob; you know how he is. How he – was.'

His voice broke and he looked at me. His eyes were heavy with pain and pity.

Trusting. Caring.

I remembered my brother cradling the scrap of puppy to his chest, nuzzling his ten-year-old face into its mangy coat. My mother's shriek of horror. The squeak of the door as she thrust it out into the yard.

But I'll clean him! I'll take care of him! Nobody wanted him; he would have died.

'Where did he fall?' I heard my own voice but didn't recognise it. It was the voice of someone hard and bitter, spoken through gritted teeth. It was the only way I could speak, though. If I allowed myself to process things properly, to feel, then I would come undone, entirely.

'They were waiting for us on the promenade. Cornered us beside the bathhouses.' Oskar stared down at his jerking hands. 'They shot Jakob in the chest. I saw him go down. Everyone started screaming. I ran.' His throat moved convulsively. 'I just kept running until I reached the safe house. I kept moving after that, never resting. I found a man who took me to Sillamäe. I walked here from there. I didn't stop, for anything.'

He ran his hand across his bloodshot eyes and then looked directly at me. 'I just wanted to tell you. It didn't matter if I was caught. I'm sorry, Kati. I promised you I would care for him and I . . . I failed. Jakob is gone but he . . . he died bravely.'

The room swam.

I felt as if I were sitting in a bubble that was shrinking, growing smaller with each inhalation of my breath. The air in my lungs would have to last. I felt my heart fluttering, beating against my ribs. The truth pressed in, circling, squeezing around me until at last I could not deny Oskar's words. Jakob was gone. The man who knew my childhood, who shared the last memories of my family. I was the only one left.

I groped blindly for Oskar. All I could think about was my brother's face, cheeks flushed warm by his blood, his beating heart. All gone now.

Arms snaked around my body and Oskar's bristled cheek pressed into my neck, and finally I felt myself break.

The air outside was as sharp as razors. Each breath I drew seemed an effort. Frost glittered on the trees and a thick pelt of fresh snow carpeted the ground.

I rubbed my arms against the cold. The street and everything beyond it was black, the curfew already in force. Etti's breath huffed in the air as she cuddled Leelo to her for warmth. The child's mouth hung open. The sleeping draught we had given her had worked quickly, softening her limbs. We could not afford to have her cry out and give us away, or wake up at a crucial checkpoint.

Only the scrap of moon left in the sky revealed the outline of the man before us.

'You are ready?'

Oskar drew us towards him, holding me awkwardly with his gloved hand. He was so thin, I could feel his bones beneath his coat. He looked at me. 'Kati?'

I nodded. 'I will fetch her.'

Lydia was standing in the kitchen near the warmth of the fire, clutching her bag. She had drawn her mother's shawl around her head and tied it beneath her chin. Her eyes were downcast, dark lashes spread against the mottled pink of her cheeks.

A pulse thudded in my throat. I felt sick, now that it was time to leave. The magnitude of our flight had not imposed itself upon me until this moment. Everything familiar would now be different. We had no choice but to turn away from the place where we had been born. We were the last living members of our families – Oskar and Etti. Lydia and me. Our dreams were buried here, along with those who had not survived. My heart ached bitterly for Jakob.

I went to Lydia and slipped my arm through hers. I squeezed gently. 'It's time.'

A tear rolled down Lydia's face. When she spoke, it was barely a whisper. 'I'm carrying his child.'

Shock rippled through me. I turned to stare at her. Before I could ask more, though, I heard Oskar's gentle cough. There was no time to talk now. I pulled Lydia out into the garden where the others were waiting.

Our guide led us through the banks of snow, his footsteps so light I was ashamed by my own clumsy ones.

I glanced back at the townhouse, searching for Kristiina or Heldur. But the house was dark and silent, receding as we marched away. All traces of us had been wiped clean. It was as if we had never been there at all.

The stars swirled overhead, polished clean and bright by the cold.

We walked until my legs ached, past blacked-out houses and down silent streets. It was strange and surreal, as if we were the only people still living.

'We should pray for no bombs tonight.' Jaan's voice was a thin thread. I searched to find it in the darkness; he was ahead, guiding us, Etti following close. I could hear Lydia's boots crunch behind me. Although my heart ached for her, I did not turn around. I was afraid she would disappear, like the girl in the story my grandmother used to tell who married a farmer and yet could not remember who she was or where she came from. When he told her, she vanished, leaving him to care for their children.

When we reached the river, Jaan left us beside a copse of trees. A small shoulder of black sand cupped the edge of the water. Jaan's boat was hidden beneath a pile of broken, twisted trees, their trunks ghostly in the dim light.

I felt Oskar shiver beside me, shifting from one foot to the other. I pressed against him, hoping that some of my warmth would leach into him, or at least that he would know he was not alone. In response, he wrapped his arm around my shoulder. I felt his lips bruise my forehead, the wind carrying away the sound of the kiss.

I wished Lydia would come to us, too. But she stayed rigid at the edge of the trees, her hands balled in her coat, staring down at the waves lapping against the shore.

The sound of heaving and grunting echoed up the shoreline, along with the whine of the cord being pulled uselessly as the engine failed to catch.

'Damn!' Jaan appeared before us. He smelt of saltwater and sweat. 'She won't start.'

Oskar's arm fell away. 'Let me try.'

He strode down towards the boat. A moment later, he'd returned, Jaan at his heels.

'It's no use,' he said.

'I have another hidden a little way upriver.' Jaan did not sound concerned. I wondered how many times he had done this, that he could sound so calm in the face of disaster. 'But it's a fair walk and the snow is beginning to fall.'

'We can't carry Leelo far in the snow.' I looked across at where Etti was standing, swaying back and forth with

432

the sleeping infant in her arms. 'We will have to go back to Heldur's . . . and try again.'

'I have a friend not far from here with a sled.' Jaan blew out a breath that hung in the air. 'If you can wait here, I will fetch it. It will make things quicker. Faster. Then we can be on our way.'

'Aren't you worried the Germans will hear us in a sled?' I said.

Jaan scoffed. 'The Germans don't know snow like we do. Don't worry.' But I heard the unspoken concern in his voice. Any patrol could spot us. A sled with panting dogs would be easy to see and hear.

I saw Oskar hesitate. The snow began to fall more heavily, clouding at our feet in banks of ice.

'Fetch it,' he said. 'Quickly.'

Jaan left at a run, and we watched in dismay as snow began to carpet the ground. But he returned only minutes later, sliding to a halt in front of us, the sled a dark shape against the pale snow. The dogs strained at their leashes, eager to be gone, excited by the prospect of exercise at this late hour. Their breath plumed white and the noise of their panting was deafening.

Oskar helped Lydia and Etti to climb in, then Lydia, and then he reached for me.

I slid into my seat, feeling the cold of the timber rising through my skirt. The sled was larger than the one my father had owned, with more seats. It was a transport sled, used to move people up and down between the parishes, not a commercial one like my father's with room for crates.

Jaan urged the dogs forward. The sled slid backwards, tipping a moment as the dogs tried to gain purchase. Then we rolled forward, bumping across the ground, the air filled with panting breath and the scrape of the sled on the ground below.

As a flurry of flakes blotted the sky, I watched the landscape move past, thinking of the many times Jakob and I had sledded as children, the squeals of joy, the wonder of moving seamlessly across the snow as if it were water. The memory dimmed.

Every memory would be like that now. I would have to live them all over, each one, remembering that Jakob was no longer here to share them with me.

'We're nearly there.' Jaan pointed to a small outcrop of trees and sand: the shoreline. The dogs surged forward, strings of saliva flying through the air behind them.

'Stop!' A voice rang out. Shots exploded from the dark.

Jaan jerked the reins. The dogs squealed and whined and the sled crashed to a halt, grounded in the snow. Bullets thwacked into the timber.

I heard Etti grunt beside me, saw her head topple forward, blood bubbling from two gaping holes in the back of her neck. I thrust out my hands as Leelo slid from her lifeless grasp. My throat seized.

'Run!' Oskar's hand yanked me fiercely into the snow. I heard his breath in my ears. I grasped Leelo to my chest, trying not to slip. My boots sank into the ground. I struggled, pulled them free.

A boat's engine roared to life. I tore towards it, a storm of sound swirling around me. Gunfire, shouts. A gasp tore from my throat as my legs hit the icy water. My skirts dragged me down, instantly waterlogged.

I saw Lydia's face above me, her hands reaching.

'Take Leelo!' I screamed.

The baby's weight was gone from my arms, and now there was only the tug at my feet, the press of water, sucking me in, pulling me down.

Give in.

I could. It wouldn't be hard. Snow scattered across my vision. My legs were frozen, all feeling lost. I felt the currents pull, one last tug, as gentle as a shawl unspooling. Pick one thread apart and the rest will come undone.

The water closed over my head. It filled my ears.

Then strong hands were grasping me under my arms. *Oskar. In the water with me.* He pulled me to the surface, and I kicked viciously against the current. The propeller buzzed, as angry as a wasp trapped inside a jar. Then I heard Oskar shout. His arms lifted me up and he pushed me into the boat.

My head slammed on the cold metal of the seat. I heard gunshots explode in the water nearby and I sat up. The world was spinning. I tried to see Oskar, feel him climbing in beside me, but the black waters were empty. All was darkness and ice. I screamed his name. Lydia's hands worked fast, stripping the waterlogged clothes from my body. I felt a blanket press around my legs. For a moment there was stillness. Just the buzzing of the boat. Then we were moving, shifting, flying through the dark.

I raised my head, my vision still spinning. The sky was a bowl of stars and arcing light. Gunfire crackled. In the blur of snow, I saw the shoreline recede.

I would later say that it was a trick of the light. Perhaps one of the dogs not slaughtered by bullets had limped to the shore, wanting to die in the water's cold embrace. But the shape I saw was not limping.

She stood proudly, her muzzle turned towards us, the long lines of her body glinting in the starlight. Her pelt was thick and full again, her eyes the same bright yellow they had been when we first met. My wolf. I tried to speak, to tell her to take care of Jakob and Etti, Mama and Papa. All the lost souls who would remain there together until we could one day find the courage to return. Until Estonia was free.

But my voice was frozen, trapped like icicles in my throat.

All I could do was call to her in the way I had used to, when words were not necessary, when knowing that she was there, that she understood, was all I had needed to force myself to go on.

Hüvastijätt. Farewell.

Epilogue

Kati
New York, 1953

'The Central Committee of the Communist Party, the Council of Ministers and the Presidium of the Supreme Soviet of the USSR announce with deep grief to the party and all workers that on 5 March at 9.50 p.m. Josef Vissarionovich Stalin, Secretary of the Central Committee of the Communist Party and Chairman of the Council of Ministers, died after a serious illness. The heart of the collaborator and follower of the genius of Lenin's work, the wise leader and teacher of the Communist party and of the Soviet people, stopped beating . . .'

'TURN IT OFF.'

Lydia's voice behind me makes me jump. My fingers spin the radio dial. The reporter's words disappear, swallowed by static. The ensuing silence enhances the bubbling of the *leivasupp* on the stove, the rippling of piano music from down the hall. Cars grind up and down Richmond Avenue, the sound of their motors swelling and receding as they nose closer to their destinations. Our little apartment always seems so quiet, but the everyday sounds offer comfort. They drown out the tidal roar of the past.

I lay down my ladle and turn to discover she is close behind me. Her shopping basket lies forgotten on the kitchen bench, a folded towel concealing the hidden contents. Her hair is short, slashed to just below her ears and dyed blonde. She wears a knitted jumper of crimson red in a boatneck style that reveals the delicate bones in her neck and throat and a long hand-sewn skirt that brushes the edges of her ankles. I have seen men turn to watch her as she passes by, their eyes drawn to the smooth arch of her neck. But she pays them no attention. If they ask, she holds up her hand to show them the band curled around her ring finger – the one we bought at a pawn shop the year we arrived – or points to the child always racing ahead, the boy with the mop of unruly brown curls.

A few silver bangles circle her wrist; presents from a well-off client she helped secure passage into America. With her language skills, it was easy for her to translate all the interviewer's questions and go back and forth between Russian and English. When she reaches out now towards the radio, the bangles strike against each other. The sound reminds me of bells. Her fingers pause on the dial, hesitant, unsure.

I wait, unwilling to push her. I can feel the past pulling at us, tugging. A force as powerful as the tide.

At last, she moves her hand away, curling her fingers up in her palm. 'He was never really my father,' she says. 'Not in the ways that matter.' She turns her back on the radio and goes back to her basket. Only the slightest tension in her shoulders gives her away.

As I watch her lay out the things – a carton of milk, a packet of biscuits, a loaf of dense bread to serve with the apple stew bubbling on the stove – I feel my own breath slow, my muscles ease.

Of course, she told me. It took almost a year; almost a year of nightmares and of waking at odd hours, stumbling about in the darkness, uncertain of who was still with us and who was gone. Aunt Juudit. Joachim. Olga. Etti. Jakob. Uncertain too of where we were. Tartu. Kreenholm. Helsinki, where Jaan's boat left us, speeding away while we stumbled towards the safehouse Oskar had organised, run by a volunteer group of women who spoke both Finnish and English and helped displaced persons claim refugee status. It was those women who encouraged us to travel to America. And now we are here: Manhattan.

The New World. As if the old one is so easily forgotten.

Wrapped up in a bedsheet to stave off the cold, the stories poured out of her. Extraordinary tales of a life spent beneath the shadow of the Kremlin. A world I could not imagine. A mother forced to abandon her heritage. A father who lied to protect himself. A nursemaid who had spun tales of brave girls who outsmarted witches and found their destiny in far-flung places. When she tried to speak of Jakob, how he had made her feel, at last a part of something greater, connected to the place where she belonged, she had found her voice choked by tears.

Those early times were the worst, for both of us. Grief was all around. Any small thing could bring it down over our heads. Our only shelter lay in each other, in the child growing daily in Lydia's womb and in the care of Leelo, a bright spark.

As if summoned, there is the thunder of feet in the room next door and a twelve-year-old girl with a heart-shaped face bursts into the room, braids swinging.

'You're back!' she trills, her hands already reaching for the biscuits. Lydia smacks gently at her fingers.

'Patience,' she says. Leelo purses her lips and I catch a glimpse of the adolescent she will become – challenging, questioning. A child who has forgotten the last years of the war and knows only freedom. At least we will always have the singing to tempt her with; the lessons she started a few years ago with Mrs Meelis down the hall have been a miracle for us, a way to reason with her and to bargain. When Leelo sings, it's as though a hundred women are singing with her, a chorus of voices reaching through time to be heard.

'Where is your shadow?' Lydia says.

Leelo sighs and pulls a face. 'Reading. I told him it's boring, but you know . . . he never listens.'

I catch a glimpse of Lydia's smile as she pulls the last item from the basket – a jar of strawberry jam – and places it on the pantry shelf. 'Leave him, then,' she says and I see him in her mind's eye: a serious child of eleven, cloistered in his room poring over the books of maps we have borrowed for him from the local library. He traces their borders with his fingers as if they are marks that will lead to treasure.

'Did you get anything else?' Leelo cranes forward. 'A present?' Her eyes gleam.

'Maybe.' Lydia taps her fingers on the countertop. 'But it's for your aunt.'

I can't hide my surprise. 'For me?'

In answer, Lydia brings out two soft balls of yarn, places them in my hands.

'For knitting circle,' she says, a smile teasing the edge of her mouth. 'Estonian wool.'

My breath catches. I finger the yarn softly, aware of Lydia watching me. Memories turn in my mind like Catherine wheels at the Fourth of July parade. Soft sheep's fleece between my hands. Crunch of apple. Mama's soft admonishing voice, Papa's pipe smoke. Jakob's smile. Oskar's blue eyes watching me.

I realise my hands are trembling. Murmuring my thanks, I leave the kitchen behind and step into the parlour where my knitting things are kept. It's a comfortable room; my favourite. Plenty of armchairs. A basket overflowing with wool – although none of it is Estonian. I can't imagine where Lydia found it. We don't hear much these days. Since the Germans lost the war and the Russians reclaimed it, Estonia has been hidden behind the Soviet wall again. When the women who come to sit with us and knit in the evenings ask me about what it is like there, I tell them about the way it was, before the Russians arrived, before the Nazis. The way I want to remember it.

My grandmother's Estonia.

The sound of the front door slamming makes me jump. The wool falls from my hand, unravelling on the floor. I bend and begin to wind it. Before I can straighten, arms slide around my waist. The smell of woodshavings prickles my nose. I close my eyes, inhale deeply. It is a good scent.

'*Tere*, Kati.' Strong hands turn me around, so that we are facing each other. And then Oskar kisses the tender place on my neck beneath my ear, his lips soft. 'Hello.'

His eyes are warm, like the ocean at sunset, when the sun spills across the waves, reluctant to cede the sky to the moon. There are marks on his body, small scars and burns.

All of them healed a long time ago. Only I see the invisible ones. Only I can help him when he wakes weeping, shivering in a cold sweat as he remembers the people he has killed and the things he has seen. For a long time, he claimed it was the reason we could not have children. That fate was punishing him. We saw doctors but nobody could find a reason. It seemed to confirm for him what he suspected to be true.

He glances at the wool in my hand and raises his blond eyebrows. 'Knitting? Again?'

I toss the wool in my hand, like a baseball player. 'Of course,' I say.

He shakes his head. 'You are always thinking of knitting.'

I run one hand through his hair, woodshavings coarse beneath my fingertips. There is no heavy darkness in moments like this. There is only pleasure, weightless like the wool in my other hand. 'Not always.'

His face breaks open in a grin. He thinks I am being coy. He doesn't know what I know; what I have been waiting all day to tell him.

I allow my hand to hover near my still-flat belly, wondering if our child will have blue eyes or green. Oskar's overalls are stained with oily varnish from his work at the furniture maker's shop a block away. When he presses me to him, though, I do not resist.

Long after we are gone, our souls remain.

They live in the trees we touched, the sigh of the wind we listened for. They exist not only to comfort our loved ones, but to comfort us, the parts of us that still watch and need strength. There is thread that binds us, all of the living things, to the past. It winds about us, sometimes playfully, sometimes twisting us in knots, tying us painfully to those memories that are heavy as stones. Sometimes it's an oak leaf in your hand. You pick it up. You remember. Sometimes it's a kringle pastry. You place it on your tongue. Those sweet times you shared.

Sometimes, it's a simple thing. An item you wear every day.

A shawl.

The folds of it brim with memories, good and bad. You wind it about your neck. It sits just so. It's so soft you can wrap it around the body of a newborn child; a baptism of wool, a protection of holy lace. You can pull it through your wedding band, a band of burnished gold as brilliant as your husband's hair. A simple trick that makes him smile, although the wounds are never far from the surface. They are the scars we all carry, those of us who left our hearts in another place.

One day we will go back.

Until then, we sing songs and tell stories to our children, to Leelo and to Anton. We knit together in the darkest hours before dawn, when the silence is too great to bear alone. *One stitch at a time*. That's what I tell myself. What I say to Lydia when she appears at my door, her hand balled around the yarn.

With every stitch, we heal ourselves.

Acknowledgements

THE LACE WEAVER IS A WORK OF FICTION, BUT MUCH OF it is inspired by real events. Although I've tried to be as historically accurate as possible, I have taken the liberty of referring to the Klooga concentration camp, which was not actually established until September, 1943. I could also only find one reference to Narva being attacked intermittently by Russian bomber planes between 1941 and 1943, although in 1944 it was completely decimated by Soviet forces. The town was rebuilt after the war.

There is scant information about the Forest Brothers which has been translated into English; much of it is hearsay, or gleaned from stories passed down from generation to generation. Some books suggest that there was no formal hierarchy in the organisation, at least not in the initial stages, but this may just be another 'fact' passed onto the Soviet authorities in order to deflect unwanted attention from the group. The last Forest Brother came out of hiding in 1995, four years after Estonia finally regained independence. Over the course of my research, I read many books but some of them truly stood out and I would encourage you to read them if you're interested in Eastern European history. They are: *Estonian Life Stories*, edited and translated by Tiina Kirss; *Everything is Wonderful* by Sigrid

Rausing; *Knitted Lace of Estonia: Techniques, Patterns and Traditions* by Nancy Bush; *Treasured Memories: Tales of Buried Belongings in Wartime Estonia* by Mats Burström; *Stalin's Daughter* by Rosemary Sullivan; *Moscow 1941: A City and its People at War* by Sir Rodric Braithwaite; *Forest Brothers: the account of an Anti-Soviet Lithuanian Freedom Fighter 1944–1948* by Juozas Luksa.

There were many people who helped get this book over the line. First, thank you to Fiona McIntosh for recognising something in me that I did not realise was there and for allowing me to come to your classes. You are Wonder Woman. Thank you also to Lisa Chaplin for guiding me through the process of writing during the early stages when I really needed feedback, for teaching me how to torture my characters and how to write a great action scene. I appreciate your generosity and advice. Thank you to early readers Helen Selvey, Donna Cattana, Dasha Maiorova, Sarah Mendham, Liang Lim, Emma Woods and Mel Sargent for your encouragement and feedback. Thank you to Kate Forsyth, Natasha Lester and Tess Woods for sharing your writing wisdom with me. Grateful thanks to Ave Põlenik-Schweiger for her invaluable advice.

Thank you to the wonderful team at Simon & Schuster Australia; first and foremost, my very special publisher and editor, Roberta Ivers. Thank you for believing in this story. Thank you to Larissa Edwards, Fiona Henderson and Dan Ruffino for your enthusiastic support of this project and your infectious positivity. Kim Swivel, Claire De Medici and Vanessa Lanaway – your edits taught me so much and improved the manuscript beyond measure. Kirsty Noffke, the marketing team and the sales reps – thank you for your stellar efforts.

When I was researching this book, many people offered their time and knowledge to help me understand Baltic culture and Russian history. Thank you to Helle-Mall Risti, for showing me your 'mystery shawl' and sharing your memories of Estonia, and Maie Barrow from the Estonian Archives for translating the lullaby for me. Thank you Imants Viesis for telling me about your father, a real Latvian Forest Brother, and Ahti Arak, my Estonian guide, for smiling so tactfully even though you thought I was crazy to want to visit a rundown old factory on the edge of the Russian border. Thank you to the kind ladies of the Haapsalu knitting circle for showing me the 'ring trick' and demonstrating how shawls are made.

It would not be possible for me to write without the generous help and support of my family. Although I thank them last, in my heart they are always first. To my husband Michael, thank you for encouraging me to follow my dreams and for not complaining about spending our seventh wedding anniversary eating smoked fish in an Estonian retirement village. Thanks also to my wise and brilliant mum for minding my children and providing moral and mental support and my wonderful dad for cultivating my love of books and for travelling to the other side of the world with me on a hope and a prayer. Thank you to my husband's parents for your constant encouragement. Lastly, thank you to my darling children, Lachlan and Lily, who were so disappointed to learn that I had not written *Harry Potter* or *Charlie and the Chocolate Factory*. I'm sorry. I'll do better next time. I love you both.

After working in the media sector for many years, LAUREN CHATER turned her passion for reading and research into a professional pursuit. *The Lace Weaver* was her debut, and her most recent novel is The *Winter Dress*. She is currently completing her Masters of Cultural Heritage through Deakin University in Victoria, Australia.

laurenchater.com